The Fa

A.J. Mackenzie is the pseudonym of Marilyn Livingstone and Morgen Witzel, an Anglo-Canadian husband-and-wife team of writers and historians. They write non-fiction history and management books under their own names, but 'become' A.J. MacKenzie when writing fiction. Morgen has an MA in renaissance diplomacy from the University of Victoria, but since the late 1990s has concentrated on writing books on leadership and management. Several of his books have been international best-sellers. Marilyn has a PhD in medieval economic history from the Queen's University, Belfast. She is a musician who writes music and also plays in a silver band and sings in an a capella trio. They have written two books of medieval history together, and also several novels, including the Hardcastle & Chaytor mysteries set on Romney Marsh during the French Revolution.

Also by A.J. MacKenzie

The War of 1812 Epics

The Ballad of John MacLea
The Hunt for the North Star
Invasion

The Hundred Years' War

A Flight of Arrows
A Clash of Lions
The Fallen Sword

A.J. MACKENZIE

The Fallen Sword

CANELO

First published in the United Kingdom in 2022 by

Canelo
Unit 9, 5th Floor
Cargo Works, 1–2 Hatfields
London, SE1 9PG
United Kingdom

A CIP catalogue record for this book is available from the British Library.

Print ISBN 978 1 80032 944 7
Ebook ISBN 978 1 80032 285 1

Look for more great books at www.canelo.co

Printed and bound in Great Britain by Clays Ltd, Elcograf S.p.A.

1

For Margot, a dear friend who is very much missed

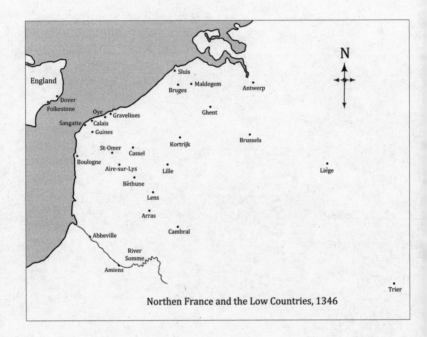

England

Dover
Folkestone

Sluis
Bruges • Maldegem
Antwerp

Oye
Gravelines
Sangatte • Calais
• Guines

Ghent

Kortrijk
Brussels

St-Omer
Cassel

Boulogne
Aire-sur-Lys
Lille

Liège

Béthune
Lens

Arras
Cambrai

Abbeville
River
Somme
Amiens

Trier

Northen France and the Low Countries, 1346

Dramatis personae

The herald and his companions

Simon Merrivale, formerly herald to the Prince of Wales and now in the king's service

Mauro, his servant

Warin, his groom

Tiphaine de Tesson, Norman noblewoman and daughter of an executed rebel

The English royal household

Edward III, King of England

Philippa of Hainault, Queen of England

Edward of Woodstock, Prince of Wales, their son

Princess Isabella, their daughter

Eustace, Lord Rowton, the king's friend and advisor

Thomas Hatfield, Bishop of Durham

Michael Northburgh, the king's secretary

Andrew Clarenceux, senior royal herald

Alice Bedingfield, the queen's lady-in-waiting

Elizabeth Chandos, one of the queen's damsels

Margaret Monceaux, one of the queen's damsels

Paon de Roet, man-at-arms in Queen Philippa's household

Brother Geoffrey of Maldon, Augustinian canon

Nicholas of Prague, court musician

Havel of Bohemia (Havel the Fiddler), court musician

Others besieging Calais

Thomas Beauchamp, Earl of Warwick and Marshal of England

Ralph Stafford, English man-at-arms

Maurice de Berkeley, English man-at-arms

Heinrich of Holstein-Rendsburg (Iron Henry), leader of German
mercenaries

Llewellyn ap Gruffyd of Conwy, captain of Welsh spearmen

John de Vere, Earl of Oxford

Henry of Grosmont, Earl of Derby and Lancaster

In Calais

Jean de Vienne, governor of Calais

Eustache de Saint-Pierre, mayor of Calais

Andrieu de Maninghem, merchant and alderman

Jehan Nortkerque, fishmonger and dealer in whale meat

Nicodemus, an English deserter

French and allies

Philippe VI de Valois, King of France

Odo IV, Duke of Burgundy

Guillaume de Machaut, composer and secretary to Charles, King
of the Romans

Guy de Dampierre, Count of Béthune

Yolande of Bohemia, Countess of Béthune and half-sister of the King of the Romans

Jean de Dampierre, her son

Louis of Male, Count of Flanders

Jeanne of Evreux, Queen of Navarre

Jean de Picquigny, acting seneschal of Picardy

Jean Marant, pirate

Estienne Massy, clerk in the Chambre des Comptes in Paris

Hugolin Bessancourt, clerk in the Chambre des Comptes in Paris

Flemish rebels, merchants and bankers

Gillis van Coudebrouc, burgemeester (mayor) of Bruges

Jan Metteneye, captain of the Bruges militia

Oppicius Adornes, banker

Maartin Adornes, his son

Willem (William) Blyth, Anglo-Flemish banker, formerly of Newcastle-upon-Tyne

Donato di Pacino de' Peruzzi, Italian banker

Sister Juliana, Beguine and one of the wise sisters of Liège

Fier Meike, a leader of the Pilgrims

Topaas, a Pilgrim

Garnier, Tomaset and Marcelis, musicians

Ecclesiastical figures

Étienne Aubert, Cardinal-Bishop of Ostia and papal ambassador

Raimon Vidal, his secretary

Roger Northburgh, bishop of Coventry and Lichfield

Balduin of Luxembourg, Archbishop of Trier

Knights of the Order of Saint John of Jerusalem

Loijis (Louis) DuSart, commander at Bruges

Brother Frido, one of the Knights at Bruges

Reynaud de Nanteuil, commander at Saint-Riquier

Philip de Thame, Grand Prior of England

Adela Seton, *consorore* (lay sister) of the Order

Others

Charles of Luxembourg, King of the Romans

Vilém Zajíc, Bohemia herald

Boček of Kunštát, Lord of Poděbrady, cup-bearer and chamberlain
to King Charles

A note about languages

Europe in the fourteenth century had a wide variety of languages and dialects, far more diverse than today. In real life, the characters in this book might have spoken any or all the following: several dialects of English including East Midlands, Kentish, Devon and Northern; North French, Norman French, Picard French and Mitan, a dialect of Walloon French; West Flemish and Brabantian Flemish; Middle Saxon, a form of Low German; several dialects of High German including Bavarian and Rhenish-Franconian; Czech; Occitan; the Tuscan dialect of Italian; Castilian Spanish; Cymraec Canawl (Middle Welsh); and for ecclesiastical figures and educated elites, Latin. Individual cities often also had their own dialects.

As a result, people tended to be quite polyglot, especially those who were better educated and well-travelled, and they could probably slip in and out of whatever language was required. Rather than attempt to replicate this rich linguistic complexity, we have rendered all their speech into modern English.

Place names have for the most part been given in the form most familiar to a modern English-speaker, hence Bruges, Ghent and Ypres rather than the more correct Brugge, Gent and Ieper. Calais was probably known to its inhabitants as Kales (West Flemish) or Calés (Picard); we have opted for the modern version.

Prologue

Rain swept across the fields of Flanders, battering the city walls and churning up the waters of the canals, blurring the silhouettes of windmills and church spires on the horizon. The night watch at the Gentpoort, volunteers from the fullers' guild, huddled in the gateway and wished they were home beside their warm fires. 'Of course the weavers get all the indoor jobs,' someone grumbled, 'guarding the town hall and the mint and the Steen, while the poor damned fullers have to stay out here in the rain.' The others agreed, muttering darkly that one day the weavers would get what was coming to them. The officer of the guard listened, but said nothing.

A column of men came down the muddy road towards the gate, thirty or so, all wrapped in cloaks with hoods pulled low across their faces. Some carried wooden staves. 'Who the hell are these?' the officer asked, rhetorically. 'Who comes to Bruges at this hour, and in this weather?'

'Guess someone had better find out,' said one of the men. He did not move.

The officer sighed. Gripping his halberd, he stepped out into the rain as the column approached. 'Who goes there?' he asked, trying to project authority. 'State your business.'

The column halted. Its leader threw back his hood, letting rain-water run down his face. He was a big man, with dark hair and a close-trimmed beard and a scar on one cheek. He looked the officer in the eye. 'I am a poor pilgrim, travelling in a perilous land,' he said. 'In God's name I am weary, and I seek shelter.'

The officer's blood froze. If he tried to turn these men away, would his own company support him? If he allowed them to enter, what would the burgemeester and the aldermen say? He swallowed hard, gripping his halberd, knowing that his career and possibly his life were at stake.

One of his own men came forward, raising a hand in salute. 'Welcome among us, brother,' he said. 'Rest now, and give praise to God.'

Silently, the leader pulled his hood down and walked through the open gate, followed by the others. Within a moment they were swallowed up by the rising darkness.

The officer looked at the man who had spoken. 'I hope you know what you're doing.'

The other man shrugged. 'It doesn't matter,' he said. 'What will happen, will happen. It's nothing to do with us now.'

I

Bruges, 14th of November, 1346

'How dare these people defy us?' demanded Philippa of Hainault, queen of England. Her face was flushed with anger. 'First they insult me by refusing my men entrance to the city, *now* they tell me I am not allowed to see the Count of Flanders. Not allowed! Who do these merchants think they are, telling me what I can and cannot do? By God, I'm minded to teach them a lesson!'

'That would be inadvisable, your Grace,' said Simon Merrivale. He stood before the queen, his herald's tabard brilliant yellow embroidered with three snarling red leopards. 'We need the support of the Flemish cities, and they know it. We shall have to bargain with them.'

'Bargain!' snapped the queen. Her hand tugged at the sleeve of her red velvet robe. 'Are you suggesting I play huckster with weavers and dyers? Blood of God, do these merchants not realise their position? With a stroke of a pen, we could cut off their trade and bankrupt their cities. That would wipe the smiles off their faces,' she added.

Standing beside Merrivale, Brother Geoffrey of Maldon cleared his throat. He was a lean, weather-beaten man in the black robes of an Augustinian canon. 'The herald is right, your Grace. The Flemings may be hucksters, but they have twenty thousand men at their backs, and they also control our supply lines. We need their ports to supply our army at Calais.'

Someone knocked at the door of the parlour. 'Tell them to go away,' the queen snapped. 'Bedingfield, see to it.'

Her lady-in-waiting, Alice Bedingfield, opened the door and spoke briefly to someone outside. 'The musicians are ready, your Grace,' she said, closing the door again. 'Our hosts are waiting for us.'

'They can wait a little longer.' The queen stared at Merrivale and Brother Geoffrey. 'Very well. What do you advise?'

'Patience, your Grace,' said Brother Geoffrey. 'I believe that when they refused your escort entrance to the city, they were actually thinking of your safety. Nothing is more likely to inflame the mob than the sight of foreign troops in the streets, even allied ones.'

Earlier today there had been a stand-off when the boats carrying the royal party arrived at the city gates. Her Grace and her attendants were of course welcome, said the captain of the watch, but her bodyguard was not. No foreigner was allowed to bear arms within the city walls. Eventually a compromise was reached; a dozen men could enter, two men-at-arms, six serjeants and four archers. The rest were forced to remain outside the walls, where they were presumably getting drenched in the pouring rain. It was a prudent measure, Merrivale thought, given the febrile atmosphere in the city, but one could see why the queen was offended.

'We can understand their position on the marriage too,' he said. 'They have fought hard to throw off the French yoke. In their eyes, they would be exchanging French tyranny for rule by England.'

'Body of Christ,' said the queen in exasperation. 'Who said anything about ruling them? *All* we are proposing is a marriage between the Count of Flanders and our own daughter. It will end the civil war in Flanders, guarantee an English alliance and allow the cities to prosper. We have neither the will nor the means to rule Flanders. Don't these *jokels* realise that?'

'They are suspicious, your Grace. We need to offer some guarantees that will protect their independence. And, as Brother Geoffrey said, we need to be patient. These things take time.'

'Do not lecture *me* on diplomacy, Merrivale. I was negotiating alliances and betrothals when you were still riding as a King's Messenger.'

'... Yes, your Grace.'

'And don't be so damned impertinent. I heard you sigh just now.'

'Yes, your Grace.'

The queen calmed a little. She looked into a silver mirror on the wall and adjusted the gold cap on her head. Her jewelled rings flashed rainbow fire in the lamplight. 'You gentlemen seem to think you know everything,' she said. 'Very well. You shall undertake the negotiations. Persuade the burgemeester to allow me to see the Count of Flanders, and consent to his marriage with my daughter. Make it so.'

Both men bowed. 'We will do our best, your Grace,' said Brother Geoffrey. 'If I may venture to say so, it would be discourteous to keep our hosts waiting much longer.'

It was the queen's turn to sigh. 'Yes, I suppose we must listen to these wretched musicians,' she said. 'Do you have a pin, Bedingfield? Good. Stab me if I start to fall asleep.'

The house of Gillis van Coudebrouc, burgemeester of Bruges, faced onto the canal known as the Groenerei. It was one of the richest houses Merrivale had seen, and his experience included the palazzos of Italy and Moorish *alcázars* in Spain. The great hall had a floor of black and white tiles polished to mirror smoothness, and gilded roofbeams that glowed in the light of candles and lamps. Every square inch of wall had been painted with pastoral scenes or geometric designs in dazzling reds and blues and yellows. A panel at one end of the room showed a scene purporting to be from the city's early history, a hunting party driving off a marauding white bear.

More than a hundred richly dressed people were crammed into the hall; guild representatives and their wives, envoys from the cities of Ghent and Ypres which, along with Bruges, made up the League of Three. Earlier they had dined lavishly. The queen had sat at the high table and listened while polite, smiling representatives of the League told her that under no circumstances would they consent to a marriage between her daughter and the Count of Flanders; nor would they allow her access to the count, a prisoner in their hands since his father was killed at Crécy.

Now the boards had been cleared and people wandered around the hall with goblets of wine in their hands, stretching their legs and chatting. They bowed when the queen swept back into the room, followed by her ladies, the herald, Brother Geoffrey and Paon de Roet, the captain of her pared-down bodyguard. Coudebrouc, their host, smiled his most emollient smile. He knew perfectly well that the queen was angry, and why. 'Does your Grace wish to be seated?'

Her Grace did. A gilded chair was brought, with a purple cushion to support the royal back. 'The musicians who will play tonight are among the best in Flanders,' said the burgemeester. 'And if I may be so bold, your Grace, that means they are among the best in Christendom.'

'I have no doubt of it, *meneer*,' the queen said smoothly. 'The minstrel school of Bruges is famous even in England. I look forward to a splendid entertainment.'

She took her seat, smoothing her skirts. Roet and her ladies stood behind her; the rest of her guards were outside the hall. Merrivale glanced at Bedingfield, who held up a small jewelled pin and winked at him. The three musicians entered, bowing and introducing themselves to the company; Garnier the singer, Tomaset who played the viol and Marcelis who alternated between psaltery and lute. They struck up a tune, a rondeau that Merrivale recognised at once.

Whiter than the lily, more red than vermilion,
Resplendent as a ruby from the Orient,
Nothing touches your unparalleled beauty.
Whiter than the lily, more red than vermilion,
The delight of my waking heart,
My desire is to serve you loyally
Whiter than the lily, more red than vermilion,
Resplendent as a ruby from the Orient.

A young woman in a green gown with shoulder-length red hair stood to one side of the hall, talking to a white-bearded man robed in rich black and leaning on an ebony stick. Quietly, Merrivale made his way through the crowd towards them. 'Sir herald,' the young woman said brightly. 'May I present Heer Oppicius Adornes, master of the bankers' guild of Bruges? *Meneer*, this is Simon Merrivale, herald in her Grace's household.'

The old man looked at Merrivale's tabard. His white eyebrows bristled a little. 'Welcome to Bruges, sir herald. Is this your first time in the city?'

'I have been here before,' said Merrivale. 'Though not as a herald.'

'But still in royal service, I assume.'

'Yes. Of a sort.'

Adornes nodded. 'I hope your stay in Bruges is a pleasant one. Now, if you will forgive me, I must pay my respects to her Grace.'

The old man turned and hobbled away. Others bowed respectfully as he passed. Merrivale looked at the young woman. 'He is willing to talk,' she said. 'Privately, at his house. The utmost discretion is necessary, he said. I have the name and location of the house, but you probably know it already.'

'As it happens, I don't.'

Tiphaine de Tesson looked up at him and smiled. 'You see? I can be useful after all.'

'I never doubted it.'

'Oh, yes, you did. You still think I need protecting.'

'On the contrary,' said Merrivale. 'After Scotland, I think the rest of the world needs protecting from you.'

Harder than diamonds
Harder than adamant
Is the hardness you show to me.
Lady, why have you no mercy for your lover
Whom you kill for desiring your love?

'Do I kill you for desiring my love?' asked Tiphaine, her voice full of irony.

'Not so far,' said Merrivale, scanning the crowded room.

'No? I saw Bedingfield wink at you.'

'It was a private joke.'

'Or perhaps a joke about privates? Don't scowl at me. I am no longer in a convent, I am allowed to be vulgar.'

'What do convents have to do with it? Many of the filthy stories I know were told to me by nuns. Have you noticed anything about the music? The repertory is interesting, don't you think?'

'No. After the convent, I spent two years in prison, remember. I saw only one minstrel during that time, and he was executed the next morning.'

'Every song they have sung so far is by the same composer. Guillaume de Machaut, the Frenchman.'

'Ah!' She paused, thinking. 'Someone has instructed the musicians. On the surface, they sing paeans to the beauty and power of the queen, but the music is French. The message is, the Flemings can abandon the object of their desire and go back to their French allegiance, if they choose.'

'So, treat us with courtesy and respect, or face the consequences,' Merrivale said. 'Do not kill us for desiring your love. The lute player is very good, isn't he? I feel I have heard him before.'

Marcelis sat on a low stool, head bent over the lute, hair falling forward over his face. Then he raised his head a little, and Tiphaine stiffened. 'Newcastle,' she said quietly.

'What?'

'Don't look at him, don't let him know he has been spotted. It is the man who played at Blyth's house. Remember?'

Merrivale let out his breath. 'I should have spotted him sooner.'

A few weeks earlier they had sat in the house of William Blyth, merchant and banker of Newcastle-upon-Tyne, and listened to a Flemish lutenist. Now Blyth was in hiding with charges of high treason hanging over his head. 'What is he doing here?' Tiphaine asked.

'Playing for hire, perhaps. Musicians are mercenaries, they go wherever someone will pay them.'

'Do you really believe that? We think Blyth escaped to Flanders. The queen is here, and so is Blyth's musician. I don't like the coincidence, Simon.'

'Neither do I,' Merrivale said. 'Wait here.'

Coudebrouc was standing beside the queen, still smiling as he watched the musicians. The negotiations during dinner might have been uncomfortable, but the entertainment was superb. Even her Grace appeared pleased.

He turned his head as Merrivale approached. 'A word, if you please, *meneer*,' the herald murmured.

The burgemeester frowned but he led the way into the parlour. Merrivale caught the eye of Paon de Roet and motioned with his head, and the captain followed them. 'What is it?' asked Coudebrouc, closing the door.

'In England, I received word of a plot to assassinate King Edward,' the herald said. 'But the king is in the midst of his army, and well-guarded. I think it entirely possible that the plot is instead against the queen, and that the enemy is planning to attack this house, tonight.'

He watched the burgemeester turn pale. 'How do you know this?'

'I do not know, not for certain. But we will take no chances with her Grace's safety.' He did not mention Marcelis; it was highly likely that Coudebrouc had hired the musicians, or a member of his household had. Anyone could be involved, including Coudebrouc himself.

'The house is well guarded,' said the burgemeester. 'The queen will be safe here.'

'She will not. You have only a handful of badly armed men, and your own servants. The enemy will have laid his plans carefully, and know exactly where and when to strike at her Grace. We are taking her away, now.'

'Of course.' Coudebrouc had begun to sweat. 'I will give orders to ready the boats.'

He raised his head. In the hall the music had ended abruptly. Voices murmured, some surprised, some outraged. 'That's it,' the herald said. 'They're coming. Sir Paon, alert your men and get the queen ready to move. Now.'

–

The musicians had halted their performance without warning and run from the painted hall. The guests stood staring in astonishment; no one could ever remember such a thing happening before. Not only was it discourteous to the queen and burgemeester, but they had not even waited to receive their pay. Everyone watched Roet bend and whisper in the queen's ear. She nodded and departed without a backward glance, followed by her surprised attendants. A whisper of alarm ran around the hall. Merrivale saw Adornes, standing at the foot of the hall and leaning on his stick.

The rest of the escort waited in the courtyard where flambeaux hissed and spluttered in the rain. 'Shall we get her Grace to the boats?' Roet asked.

'No. We'll use the boats as a deception. Send them out empty to draw the enemy away. We are going through the streets.'

'We will need lights.'

'Darkness is our friend,' Merrivale said curtly. 'I know the way. So does Brother Geoffrey.'

The narrow streets were indeed very dark, their gutters bubbling with water. 'I hope you know what you are doing, Merrivale,' the queen murmured. Her voice was quite calm.

'You may trust the herald, your Grace,' Tiphaine said quietly.

A distant sound in the night, a faint rasp of metal, then another; the clash of steel sword blades. The fighting died away as soon as it had started. 'They are here,' Merrivale said softly. 'Stay close together, everyone, and protect her Grace. Geoffrey, I need you with me.'

Bruges was a warren of narrow twisting streets, high walls and gate-ways, sudden arched bridges over canals, drains and gutters gurgling invisible in the shadows. Lamps outside the larger houses gave them occasional views down the street, but for the most part Merrivale and Brother Geoffrey felt their way in the dark, stopping occasionally to confer in whispers. That earlier clash of arms might have been an attack on the boats; if so, there was no telling how it had ended, or whether the deception had worked.

'Where do you think they will come?' Geoffrey murmured. 'In the streets, or outside the walls?'

'It could be either.' There were nineteen in the party; Roet and the escort, the queen and three of her ladies, Tiphaine, Brother Geoffrey and Merrivale. If they could win through to the gates, they would be safe; the rest of the escort would still be waiting outside. But it was a long way to the gates.

They reached the Hoogstraat, a long street running down to a bridge over the Sint-Anna canal. They passed a tavern shuttered against the rain; inside, someone was playing a symphonia, badly. Dogs barked in a nearby courtyard, throwing themselves at the gate as they passed. Merrivale strained his ears, listening for any sound in the shadows that might betray movement, but all he could hear was the falling rain. He murmured in Geoffrey's ear. 'How much further to the bridge?'

'We've just passed Meestraat. Up ahead the street turns to the right. The bridge is just beyond that.'

The bridge came into view moments later, a heavy stone span over the dark water. Another long street led away to the north-east, towards the Kruispoort and safety. They started across the bridge. Suddenly, Merrivale became aware of something bumping against the stone pillars of the bridge, and looked down. A long narrow boat drifted on the gentle current, another behind it. The dim reflected lamplight showed him the royal banner draped over the gunwales of the second boat and trailing in the water. It also showed him the bodies of two men lying slumped on the rowing benches.

Brother Geoffrey was beside him. 'Shot with crossbows,' he said. 'I can see the quarrels in the bodies.'

'Your eyes are better than mine. Where are the rest of the boatmen?'

'In the canal, probably.'

Merrivale turned. 'Your Grace, the boats were ambushed. I fear our attackers know we were not on board and are still looking for us. If they come for us, you and your ladies must back against the wall of the nearest house and crouch down. The rest of us will shield you.'

Paon de Roet looked at him. 'You have no weapon, sir herald, and no armour.'

'Heralds do not carry weapons,' Merrivale said. 'Protect the queen, Sir Paon. Nothing else matters.'

They advanced in a tight body now, the rain soft on their faces. The four archers were out on the flanks with arrows at the nock, the serjeants in a close ring around the queen and her ladies, Roet and the other man-at-arms, Basset, leading the way with Merrivale and Geoffrey behind them. Despite his orders, the three ladies-in-waiting were in front of the queen, shielding her. Bedingfield was her constant companion, Chandos's brother was in royal service, Monceaux had been wet nurse to one of her sons; they were ready to die for her. Tiphaine moved to join them.

They expected attack; they did not expect it from above. Crossbows clacked from the rooftops, iron quarrels struck sparks off the cobbles. Two of the archers were down before they could raise their bows. The queen's ladies were already pushing her into the shadows by the nearest wall, the escort following, the remaining archers shooting at shadowy shapes on the rooftops. A body tumbled down over the tiles and fell into the street. More crossbow bolts, and two of the serjeants went down, one shot through the body, the other hit in the leg and struggling to rise again.

The attackers came silently from every side, up the street, over the bridge, jumping down from first-floor windows. They had swords and staffs and they used them with vicious skill. The wounded serjeant dragged himself up to fight and was clubbed down at once. Basset was surrounded by hacking, stabbing men, two more serjeants trying to fight their way through to him. A dark figure came at Merrivale, jumping like a panther, wooden staff swinging towards the herald's ribs. The heavy tabard absorbed part of the blow and Merrivale seized the staff and ripped it out of the other man's hands, ramming the butt end into his stomach. The man doubled up and Merrivale hit him hard across the back of the neck, reversed his grip and hit the next man a double-handed blow on the side of the head and sent him reeling away. The rest hesitated, falling back to the far side of the street.

Roet was alongside him, breathing deeply, his sword blade covered in blood. 'We killed two more of them, but Basset is finished. They're regrouping.'

'Yes.' Merrivale could feel the swelling bruise over his ribs, but nothing seemed to be broken. Brother Geoffrey picked up the knife that Merrivale's second victim had dropped and stood beside the herald. Basset's sword was lying on the cobbles; Tiphaine dashed out and seized it, scrambling back as men advanced across the street towards her.

Silence in the street, apart from the rustle of footsteps and soft patter of rain.

They came fast, a dozen or more in a single hard wave. Merrivale hit the first man with his staff, driving him back onto his fellows, who shouldered him out of the way and came on. Brother Geoffrey stabbed someone with his knife, but a clubbing blow to the head sent him sprawling on the cobbles; Roet jumped over his body, lunging with his sword, and another heavy blow from a club hit the blade and broke it, leaving him with a three-inch stump standing out from the guards. Roet hurled the broken weapon into his attacker's face and drew his dagger. The man, who had a badly scarred cheek, lifted his club again, aiming at Roet's head. Merrivale hit him a hard, bone-shattering blow on the knee and he screamed and hobbled back, clutching at his leg. More screams behind and he turned to see Bedingfield and Chandos standing in front of the queen, faces full of terror as an attacker raised his sword; and then Tiphaine stabbed the man in the back, twisting her own sword as she drove it in. The man dropped his weapon and collapsed slowly at her feet. She stabbed him again for good measure and turned, raising the dripping weapon.

Over the clatter of metal and hoarse, rasping breath of struggling men came another sound, hard like the rattle of a drum; hoofbeats on cobbles. At once, without any signal or word of command, the attackers fled into the shadows. Down Hoogstraat and over the bridge came a column of mounted men, two of them carrying torches that fluttered and rippled with movement. Falling raindrops glinted like crystals in the sudden flare of light.

The leader reined in, looking at the bodies in the street. 'What is going on here?' he demanded sharply. 'Who are you?'

'We are the escort of her Grace the queen of England,' Merrivale said curtly. 'And who might you be?'

'The queen! My God!' The man slid out of the saddle and hurried towards them. 'I am Jan Metteneye, captain of the night watch. We heard the noise and came to investigate. What is her Grace doing here?'

'I am attempting to return to my lodgings,' the queen said, her voice firm. Bedingfield knelt beside her, clinging to her skirts and sobbing with relief; the queen rested a hand on her head, soothing her. 'I don't know what sort of watch you set in this city, Captain Metteneye, but five of my men are dead, as are the boatmen who conveyed us into Bruges. I think you have some explaining to do.'

'My God,' Metteneye said again, and he knelt on the wet cobbles. 'I beg your Grace's humble pardon. I had no idea you were in danger. Why did the burgemeester not send for me? I could have provided you with further escort.'

'Because there wasn't time,' said Tiphaine. Torchlight reflected off the blood on the front of her gown. 'Her Grace is right. You need to explain why this happened.'

There was a long pause. Torches spluttered in the rain. 'At the moment, I cannot,' Metteneye said.

'Then I suggest you escort us back to our lodgings at Maele without delay,' the queen said. 'In the morning, my herald will call on you and the burgemeester and demand a reckoning. That gives you plenty of time to think of an excuse, *meneer*. I suggest you make it a good one.'

2

Hesdin, 15th of November, 1346

Forty miles south of the war zone at Calais, two men walked past the deserted castle of Hesdin and into the park. Both wore long black cloaks to keep out the damp. The trees around them blazed with late colour, leaves golden and orange against the grey autumnal mist. Ahead lay a small lake, spanned by an ornate stone bridge. Monkeys wrapped in badger fur, with horns on their heads, perched on the balustrade of the bridge; as the two men drew closer, the monkeys swivelled their heads and waved their arms in the air. Raimon Vidal, secretary to the Cardinal-Bishop of Ostia, made the sign of the cross. 'This is the devil's work,' he said.

'Automatons,' said his companion. 'Mechanical devices made by the hand of man, not the devil. Surely you have heard of them.'

'I have seen automatons before,' said Vidal. 'That does not mean I like them.' He glared at the monkeys, who grimaced back. They crossed the bridge and walked on, passing fountains that squirted water in the air, mechanical knights tilting at each other, a brilliantly painted water clock resting on the backs of lions and shaggy-haired beast-men. 'What is this place?' Vidal demanded.

'It is called the Garden of Earthly Delights,' the other man said. 'The old Count of Artois hired craftsmen to come and build a pleasure park next to his castle. The count's granddaughter still pays for the machines to be kept in working order. She sometimes brings her friends here, for amusement.'

A whisper of wind rattled the dry leaves overhead. Vidal was not a superstitious man, but the sound reminded him of the clatter of bones. He crossed himself again.

At the end of the garden was a chapel with a smooth stone floor, its walls made almost entirely of stained glass; only the very thinnest of pillars supported the roof. It reminded Vidal of the Sainte-Chapelle in Paris, built by Saint Louis to house a relic of the True Cross. Instead of relics, this chapel contained more automata: gilded birds, a robed and crowned king who raised his arms in the air, a lion that pawed at the ground and lashed its tail.

'Why are we meeting here, I wonder?' asked the other man.

'You know how he likes to control things,' said Vidal. 'He hopes he can control us as easily as he directs these engines.'

'Actually, I am reliving old memories,' said a voice behind them.

Vidal turned. Three more men had entered the chapel, all similarly wrapped in dark cloaks to keep out the mist. The man who had spoken was in his late thirties, unremarkable in looks and bearing; you could pass him in the street, Vidal thought, and never notice him. He spoke excellent North French with barely a trace of accent, but Vidal knew he was English and a man of influence at the court of King Edward III of England. Beyond that, Vidal knew very little about him.

The other two were, or had been, well-known figures at the French court. One was John of Hainault, formerly one of King Philippe's closest advisors; despite being in his late fifties, he walked with the muscular ease of a champion jouster and fighting man. The other was younger, a little above thirty, with sleek dark hair; Guy de Dampierre, the Count of Béthune.

'I first visited this place when I was a boy,' the Englishman said. His voice echoed a little in the vaults of the chapel. 'The old man who maintained the machines showed me how they worked. I used to return sometimes, until the war intervened. Introduce your companion, Vidal.'

Vidal inclined his head. 'It is my pleasure to present Guillaume de Machaut, canon of Rheims, formerly secretary to the late King Jean of Bohemia.'

'My condolences on the death of your master,' said the Englishman. 'He was a great man. I understand you have now taken service with his son.'

Jean of Bohemia had been killed two months earlier, one of thousands shot down by English archers at the bloody battle of Crécy. Guy of Béthune's brother, the Count of Flanders, had been killed there too. 'Thank you, my lord,' said Machaut. 'King Charles has generously taken me into his service.'

The Englishman rubbed his chin. 'I was also expecting Zajíc, the Bohemia herald.'

'He is with the king in Trier at the moment, preparing for the coronation,' said Machaut.

'I see.' The Englishman rubbed his chin again. *You can see him thinking*, Vidal thought, *absorbing news, planning. His mind works like the wheels of these automatons. Perhaps he is one himself.*

'Thank you for inviting me to join you,' said Machaut. 'May I ask what your purpose is, my lord?'

'We intend to redraw the map of Europe,' said the Englishman.

Silence fell for a moment. The lion's tail swished, and one of the gilded birds spat water from its beak into a pool at its feet. *They must be hydraulic devices rather than clockwork*, Vidal thought. *Dear God, do not tell me I am becoming interested in these things...*

The Englishman was speaking again. 'England and France are both vulnerable. France is still reeling from the disaster at Crécy and King Philippe is chronically short of money and men. King Edward of England has settled down to besiege Calais, where sickness and desertion are thinning the ranks of his army. He too is desperately short of money.'

'When is he not?' asked John of Hainault.

'And now, King Charles of Bohemia has also been elected King of the Romans,' said the Englishman. 'A necessary step towards becoming Holy Roman Emperor. But of course, there is already an emperor, Louis of Bavaria, and he will not give up his position without a fight. There will be civil war in the German states.'

He does love the sound of his own voice, Vidal thought. But Machaut was intrigued; two decades in the service of Jean of Bohemia had taught him a great deal about empire-building. 'And you intend to profit from this, my lord?'

'Exactly. We are going to break kingdoms,' said the Englishman. 'Then we shall control the power and wealth of the West. Those loyal to us will have whatever reward they wish.' He looked at Vidal. 'Does your master desire to be pope?'

Vidal cleared his throat. 'Does a one-legged duck swim in circles?'

'Then pope he shall be. Machaut, does the King of the Romans truly wish to be crowned emperor?'

Machaut glanced at Vidal. 'Everyone knows he does.'

'Then we shall put Charles on Emperor Louis' throne. We shall have the power to do as we wish. We shall put our own candidate on the throne of France, too, and we shall bring together the squabbling states of the Low Countries and turn them into another kingdom for our friend here to rule.'

'And what of England?' Vidal asked. 'Have you some special plan for the land of your birth?'

'By the time we have finished, there will be no England, only smoking desolation,' the other man said. 'You will be welcome to scavenge among its ruins for whatever scraps remain.'

The silence this time was longer. The mechanical king raised his hands and let them fall, slowly. 'We have heard this before,' Vidal said. 'But your great scheme of last summer fell apart. Many of the plotters were killed at Crécy. Others walked away, vowing to have nothing more to do with you. And then, the disaster in Scotland. You made a bad mistake there.'

'My only mistake was in my choice of agent,' the Englishman said. 'He exceeded his orders, and has paid the price.'

'And Calais? Will the city fall to the English?'

'If useful to our purposes, yes,' the Englishman said calmly. 'Otherwise, Edward will sit outside its walls until his army rots away beneath him.'

'And the money,' Vidal demanded. 'Where will it come from, now that your bankers are dead?'

'I have acquired new bankers. Part of the money is in Bruges, the rest will come from the Knights of Saint John.'

Vidal's eyebrows rose. 'The Knights have agreed to rejoin us?'

'Enough have.' The Englishman regarded him with cold brown eyes. 'Do I detect doubt in your voice, Vidal?'

'Of course you do. My orders are clear. Cardinal Aubert and his allies will support you, but only if you keep your promises.'

'Then assure them my promises will be kept.' The Englishman looked at Machaut. 'What about you?'

'I need to consider my position,' said the secretary.

'Do you?' The Englishman smiled a little, mocking him. '*Fortune, whose will is never certain, has chosen to turn her wheel against me.*'

'That is a line from one of my songs, of course,' said Machaut.

'Yes. It shows you the reality of your position. At the moment, you are a Frenchman in a German court. If fortune's wheel should turn, even only a little; for example, if there should be a rupture between King Charles and King Philippe of France, you might be caught in the middle. I once saw a man executed by being ground between two millstones.'

'If I agree, what would be my reward?' asked Machaut.

The Englishman held up a hand. 'Let us see what service you perform first. If you are faithful, and successful, you can name your price. Gold, castles, lands, whatever you want. There will be more than enough spoils to go around.'

'What do you want me to do?'

'I want you to spy on King Charles. Keep us informed of his plans and movements.'

Machaut looked at Guy of Béthune. 'My lord, you are King Charles's brother-in-law. What could I possibly learn that you do not already know?'

'I am often away from court,' Béthune said. 'I need eyes and ears when I am absent. Secretaries see and hear things that other people miss.'

Vidal gathered his cloak more closely around himself. 'Do you wish me to spy on *my* master also?'

'Yes. The cardinal looks after his own interests first, as do we all. But if he should decide to make his own deal with the pope or the Knights of Saint John, I want to know about it.'

'Is that all?'

'No, there is one more thing. Tell the cardinal to open negotiations with the Queen of Navarre.' He turned to Hainault. 'I want you to meet her, as soon as possible. Find out whether she is willing to rejoin us.' Hainault nodded.

'Very well, gentlemen, that is all,' said the Englishman. 'Guy, escort them out, if you please. Make sure no one sees them depart.'

After the others had gone, the Englishman turned to John of Hainault. 'That was a good suggestion about Machaut. He will be useful.'

'Yes. Even so, making Charles of Bohemia into an emperor will not be easy. Guy will need the strength of Hercules to carry out the task you have set him.'

'Guy has two important qualities: greed, and ambition. They will serve him well.' The Englishman studied Hainault for a moment. 'You still look unhappy, my friend.'

'Vidal has a point. Many died at Crécy. We need new allies.'

The Englishman looked irritated. 'No, we don't. I have been too trusting, John. I thought we could rely on others to do our work, but it turns out we cannot. Rollond de Brus's betrayal in Scotland was the last straw. From now on we do this ourselves.'

'And the herald?'

'Zajíc?'

'You know who I mean. The Prince of Wales's herald, Merrivale. The man who wrecked last summer's scheme, and destroyed your hopes in Scotland. He remains a danger.'

'Perhaps.'

'We need to deal with him. Kill him, or buy him off. One way or another, get rid of him.'

The Englishman shook his head. 'I have a better idea. We set false trails for him and throw him off the scent. Even if he does learn the truth, it will be too late.'

'Risky,' Hainault warned.

'Not really. Merrivale is actually quite gullible, you know. He's just a rustic from Devon in a shiny tabard.'

'And if you are wrong? If he outfoxes you once more?'

'We have another weapon to use against him,' said the Englishman.

Hainault looked around, lowering his voice. 'Is Béthune aware of this?'

'He'll know when the time comes. Don't tell me you are squeamish, John.'

Hainault hesitated. 'No piece is too big to be played,' the Englishman said. 'Anyone can be sacrificed.'

'Even me?'

'Do you really want me to answer that question? I have been working on this plan for two decades, John, ever since we killed the old king. Nothing will stand in my way.'

Hainault nodded slowly. 'Very well. I shall take my leave. If you need me, you can find me with Burgundy. Philippe may blame me for Crécy, but Duke Odo has made me welcome.' He paused. 'If we fail, we will not get a second chance.'

'We will not fail.'

The Englishman listened to the sound of Hainault's footsteps receding. As silence fell he walked over to the mechanical king. Reaching up, he removed the painted wooden crown and set it carefully on his own head, turning it to find the best position.

'How easy it is to make a crown,' he said aloud to the statue. He spoke English now, with an accent that came from somewhere north of the river Trent; exactly where, only someone very familiar with the dialects of the region could have said for certain.

As if obedient to his command, the king raised his arms again. The Englishman smiled. Lifting the crown, he held it high above his head, and then hurled it down onto the flagstones. The crown smashed to pieces and the fragments skidded away across the floor, spinning and sliding to a stop.

'And how easy to break one,' he said.

3

'We are utterly appalled,' said Coudebrouc. Both he and Metteneye looked as if they had not slept. 'The thought that the queen might have come to harm... We can only beg for her Grace's forgiveness.'

Outside the rain had stopped. A watery light seeped through the lead-paned windows of the burgemeester's office. 'It remains to be seen whether she will grant it,' Merrivale said. 'She was fond of young Basset, the man-at-arms who was killed. Four others of her loyal servants died too.'

'Full compensation will be paid to their families,' said Coudebrouc.

'Of course. I would expect nothing else.'

Merrivale surveyed the two men for a moment. Tiphaine sat to one side, her hands resting in her lap. Brother Geoffrey had intended to come with the herald, but the blow on the head he had suffered last night had left him with a headache and blurred vision; the queen had ordered him back to bed. Tiphaine had volunteered to come instead.

'Have you recovered the bodies of the boatmen?' he asked.

'We found the last one this morning in the Groenerei,' Metteneye said. He frowned. 'There is a curious thing. Unlike the others, who were shot, this man had been strangled before being thrown into the water.'

'Strangled how? By hand?'

'There were no fingermarks. The killer used some sort of ligature, I think.'

'A wire?'

'The cuts on the skin were not deep, which I would expect with wire. It might have been something like catgut.'

Tiphaine stirred. 'The musicians,' she said.

Lutenists used catgut strings for their instruments; so did viol players. Merrivale looked at the burgemeester. 'Where were the players from?'

'It is difficult to say.' Coudebrouc looked helpless. 'Men like these drift around the country, looking for work wherever they can find it. Marcelis and his fellows are known for their music, but no one knows much about them.'

'I would like to speak to them. Can you track them down?'

'We can try,' Metteneye said, doubtfully.

Which means he can't, the herald thought. *Or won't.* 'And the men who attacked us? Did you catch them?'

The watch captain looked uncomfortable. 'No. We picked up three bodies and found some bloodstains, but that was all.'

Merrivale looked at him sharply. 'Are you still hunting for them?' And when Metteneye did not answer he said, 'You know who they are, don't you?'

'They call themselves the Pilgrims,' Coudebrouc said.

'And who might they be?'

'They are a secret society. They first emerged during the Peasants' War back in the '20s, and reappeared when the cities rebelled seven years ago.'

'They have allies among some of the bandit gangs in the countryside,' Metteneye said.

'So these Pilgrims are mercenaries for hire,' the herald said. 'Where do they come from?'

Coudebrouc raised his hands. 'We know very little about them. They might have come from anywhere, or everywhere.'

'Even from Bruges itself?'

Metteneye shook his head. 'The watch at the gates saw them enter the city yesterday, by the Ghent road.'

Merrivale stared at him. 'The watch *saw* them? And didn't try to stop them?'

'The officer in charge was too frightened. He thinks some of his own men might be in league with the Pilgrims.'

'Is he right?'

'Probably,' Metteneye said with reluctance. 'The watch was drawn from the fullers' guild.' He paused. 'According to rumour many of the Pilgrims are fullers, driven out of their cities after conflicts with the weavers.'

'Some of them might have come from Bruges after all.'

Metteneye looked down at his hands. 'It is possible.'

God, what a mess, Merrivale thought. *Factions within factions, and people as willing to fight each other as the French.*

'So, here we are,' he said. 'One of the queen's favourites has been killed, four more of her retainers have been slaughtered like cattle, and all you have to show for it is a few corpses. This failure will not sit well, *meneeren*. When the news gets out, people will draw their own conclusions.'

Coudebrouc and Metteneye looked at each other. 'We have already offered compensation,' the burgemeester said.

'You will need to do rather more than that. Their Graces will wonder how the Pilgrims were able to enter the city so easily, how they managed to penetrate your own household, and how they managed to escape without a trace. Unless, perhaps, they had assistance from people in high places?'

'Go on,' said Coudebrouc. His usual smile had gone; he looked faintly sick.

'England did you a great favour last summer, *meneer*. The old Count of Flanders was killed at Crécy, and many of his knights along with him. The count's son and heir is your prisoner. How long do you think you can keep him in custody?'

'As long as we wish,' said Metteneye.

'Or until some faction among your enemies – and God knows you have enough of them – manages to release him. If, or likely when, he is freed young Louis will call on French support, a French army will invade Flanders and you would have to fight for your lives.'

He paused to let this sink in. 'On the other hand, if the count can be brought over to the English cause through peaceful means, such as marriage to an English princess, your cities will be safe from attack.'

The others waited, watching him. 'But if the queen decides that elements within the League of Three have colluded in an attempt to assassinate her, the offer of marriage will be withdrawn and the English alliance along with it. And you, gentlemen, will be left to face France on your own.'

'We have already decided to oppose the marriage,' Metteneye said reluctantly.

Coudebrouc put his hands together, as if in prayer. 'Nothing is written in stone, *meneer*. We can reopen the discussion.'

'The guilds would have to give their consent. And the other cities, Ghent and Ypres.'

'I am certain you can persuade them to your new way of thinking,' said Merrivale. 'I shall inform the queen. That may appease her anger – for the moment.'

The canals were busy with boats and the streets teemed with people, weavers in dark coats, dyers in splattered aprons, country folk coming in to the markets with baskets on their backs, merchants wrapped in fur-trimmed cloaks, Beguines in dark robes with white wimples covering their hair. Earlier, the great marketplace next to the belfry had been so crowded they could barely force their way through. The stink of urine from the fullers' workshops mingled with the richer scents of spices. Every language in northern Europe could be heard in the streets; Merrivale heard several people speaking in Scots dialect, and once he heard something that might have been Russian.

The city was busy, he thought, but it was also febrile. War and revolution were part of the air they breathed; the tension was almost palpable. The faces around them were sombre, unsmiling.

'Do you think they told the truth?' Tiphaine asked.

'Not all of it. They know more about these Pilgrims than they are willing to say.'

'Perhaps they are a secret that everyone knows but no one talks about,' said Tiphaine. 'Who do you think was behind the attack? Could the burgemeester have paid the musicians, and the Pilgrims?'

'You were watching him. What do you think?'

'I don't think he hired the Pilgrims,' she said finally. 'He is not that stupid. He would not be mayor of Bruges if he was.'

'Don't count on that. But explain your reasoning.'

'All of these men are walking on the edge of a knife blade. To the French and their supporters, they are rebels and traitors. If France regains control, they will lose their offices, their estates and their lives, not necessarily in that order. They need the English alliance if they are to survive.'

'Which is why they will agree in the end,' said Merrivale.

'Unwillingly. I thought Coudebrouc looked like a man about to receive a singularly unpleasant suppository. You also did not tell the full truth, Simon.'

'Didn't I?'

'No. You did not reveal that there is another plot here in Bruges. Which is why you sent me out like a pig hunting for truffles last night, to find out which of those rich old men was Oppicius Adornes.'

'Yes, I concealed the truth,' said the herald. 'It is part of my trade. Just ask Geoffrey. I think this must be the house.'

—

Unlike the burgemeester's palatial residence, the house of the banker Oppicius Adornes was relatively modest, a low, plain range of buildings built of white-painted brick with red tile roofs. A porter opened the gate and ushered them inside. House servants conducted them across a courtyard whose silence contrasted with the bustle of the streets outside, and into a parlour where light from mullion windows reflected off a row of mirrors. The parlour's white walls were hung with enamelled brasses showing scenes from the life of Christ. One of these depicted the expulsion of the moneylenders from the temple. *Someone has a sense of humour*, Merrivale thought.

A coal fire burned on the hearth. A servant offered wine, another brought a dish of candied fruits. Merrivale's ribs ached from last night's blow. He thought about Brother Geoffrey, laid up in bed. Geoffrey had only just recovered from the summer, when he and the herald had been taken prisoner in Normandy. Merrivale had been rescued by the English army, but Geoffrey had been held prisoner for several weeks by the Bishop of Bayeux before being released. The bishop's hospitality had been enthusiastic, to say the least, and Geoffrey had been lucky to escape with only a broken collarbone and some spectacular bruises.

The door opened and Oppicius Adornes limped slowly in, leaning on his stick. A younger man followed him, plain-faced, with watchful hazel eyes. 'Welcome,' said Adornes, sitting down on a padded bench. 'This is my son Maarten. I thought it might be helpful to have him with us. My time is now largely taken up with guild business. Maarten manages the bank.'

Maarten Adornes bowed. 'I trust the servants have looked after you?'

'Your hospitality does you great credit, *meneer*,' Merrivale said.

'Let us get down to business,' said the older man. 'You wish to ask about Willem Blyth. William, as your people call him.'

The herald nodded. 'We know Blyth was born in Bruges, to an English father and a Flemish mother. His father was a trader. His mother's family was called Gistel, I believe. Were they bankers?'

There was a moment of silence. 'They were pawnbrokers,' said Maarten Adornes. 'Some would say there is no difference, of course.'

Silence again. 'Tell them the rest,' said his father.

'There was a scandal,' Maarten said. 'Several of the family were accused of counterfeiting and circulating false money.'

'Were the charges proven?'

'Yes. After the trial, three people were executed in the Burg. Katelijne Gistel, Blyth's mother, was one of them.'

That was unexpected, the herald thought. He glanced at Tiphaine. 'Blyth's father was imprisoned in the Steen but released,' Maarten continued. 'No evidence could be found against him. He returned to England, taking his young son with him. We heard no more of the father.'

'But you knew of Blyth,' Tiphaine said. 'You had business dealings with him.'

Oppicius Adornes sat silent, watching his son. 'Of course,' said the latter. 'He built up his business rapidly, through dealings in coal and iron and lead, and became a very wealthy man. When he diversified into banking, it was natural that he should come to us.'

'You had no qualms about dealing with him?'

'Of course not. The sins of the parent should not be visited on the child. And unlike his family, his money was always good.' Maarten paused. 'We only learned of his treasonous activities very recently.'

Merrivale nodded. 'Blyth fled from England last month before he could be arrested. Somehow, despite the laws against exporting currency, he managed to take his money with him. We don't know how much, but we estimate at least fifty thousand marks, probably more.'

Maarten Adornes glanced at his father, who nodded. 'That was not all of his wealth,' the younger man said. 'Blyth also has investments and partnerships in trading ventures all around the German Ocean. His bank had branches in Bergen and Hamburg, possibly elsewhere too. His fortune rivalled that of the Peruzzi; and indeed, our own. The value runs into the hundreds of thousands.'

'He also has control of the remaining assets of Sir Gilbert de Tracey, formerly your king's banker,' said Oppicius Adornes. 'That adds another hundred thousand marks at least.'

They are being very cooperative, Merrivale thought. 'Tracey told me he had entrusted his money to you.'

'He asked me to handle it, yes. When I learned of the circumstances of his brother's death, I temporised. No banker likes to be involved with traitors, it is bad for the reputation. How Blyth got his hands on the money, I do not know. And now that Gilbert is dead, like his brother, we may never know.'

'Do you know where Blyth is now?'

'He is not in Bruges,' Oppicius Adornes said. 'That is all I can tell you.'

'How can you be so certain, *meneer*?'

'He would not be welcome here. Bruges needs the friendship of England. If he were to be discovered, he would very quickly be arrested and handed over as proof of our goodwill.'

Ah, that explains it. They want us to know – or to think – that they don't know where Blyth is. No suspicion will attach to them. Business will carry on as usual. 'These investments of Blyth's. Has he begun to sell them?'

'Yes,' said the older man. He looked surprised by the question. 'According to my banking contacts in other cities and the Hanseatic League, he is selling his entire business. Ships, warehouses, cargoes, loan books, everything.'

Merrivale thought for a moment. 'Banks keep records of bills of exchange, when and where they are issued and redeemed. If Blyth is trading in bills, we can track him down.'

'Not necessarily,' said Maarten Adornes. 'There are dark exchanges, *donkere beurzen*, secret markets where bills are traded and redeemed without records and no questions asked. Blyth may be using these.'

'Blyth needs silver. Can bills be redeemed for specie in these markets?'

'Of course. The bills are heavily discounted because of the risk involved, but it is common practice.'

'Do you trade in these exchanges?' Tiphaine asked.

Maarten looked offended. 'No respectable bank would do so.'

'I am glad to hear that there are respectable banks,' she said. 'I thought bankers didn't care where their money comes from.'

'They don't,' said the older man. 'But they do care about their reputation, *demoiselle*. If they are discovered to be fishing in dark waters, officials begin to ask questions. That in turn makes customers uneasy and they withdraw their money. It is all too easy for a bank to collapse. Speaking personally, I have worked too long and too hard to risk everything by dealing with people like Tracey and Blyth.'

'I understand,' the herald said. 'But it is imperative that we find Blyth.'

'Why?' asked Oppicius Adornes. 'So your king can take his revenge?'

Merrivale looked at him steadily. 'The money Blyth is raising through these dark exchanges is funding attacks on the crown. Like the one last night.'

The older man nodded slowly. 'You said Blyth needs silver.'

'Of course. Assassins and rebels want payment in hard money, and Blyth and his masters need a great deal of it. You say he is not in Bruges. Do you have any idea where he might be?'

'No,' Maarten Adornes said finally.

'Someone is giving him shelter, protecting him. Might it be the Pilgrims?'

The younger man froze for a moment. A fleeting expression of fear crossed his face.

'It is possible,' Oppicius said finally. 'But if they are, we will never know. Not even we know their secrets. No one penetrates their wall of silence.'

'Have you tried?' asked Tiphaine.

Neither man said anything. Suddenly, Merrivale thought, they were no longer being so helpful. He rose to his feet. 'We need to stop Blyth from redeeming any more bills of exchange. Will you help us?'

Oppicius Adornes nodded. 'We will do what we can.'

'Thank you, *meneeren*,' said the herald. 'We will take up no more of your time.'

—

'What did you think?' Merrivale asked as they walked back towards the Groenerei and their waiting boat.

'I keep thinking about Katelijne Gistel. The penalties for counterfeiting are the same as for treason, aren't they? And for women, that means death by burning.'

Merrivale said nothing. 'Do you suppose they forced the boy to watch?' she asked. 'If so, it might explain a great deal.'

'The Flemish authorities executed her. Why would he bear a grudge against England?'

'He has had a long time to think, Simon. I also had a long time to think, while I was in prison. After a while, you start to bear a grudge against everyone. There was a time when I hated you, for rescuing me.'

It had begun to rain again. 'I can understand that,' Merrivale said finally. 'My mother and sisters died of hunger during the famine, and my father lost his lands soon after. There were days when I too hated the world.'

They passed a market, stalls selling eggs and turnips and red cabbages. 'You asked what I think about the Adornes,' she said. 'They know more about Blyth than they are saying.'

'I agree. They know where he is, and they also know how to communicate with the Pilgrims. The Pilgrims are dangerous, and bankers don't like danger. Wherever possible, they try to control it.'

'Bribes? They pay the Pilgrims to leave them alone?'

'Possibly, but it could be something more complex. What is more, Blyth will learn, very soon, that we called on the Adornes, and will know we are looking for him.'

'Do you think Blyth organised the attack last night? He knows Marcelis, after all.'

'He didn't organise it, but his money paid for it. Blyth is still the moneyman behind the conspiracy.'

'The man from the north,' she said.

'Yes. We still don't know who he is, or what his next move might be.'

'Sir herald,' said a voice. 'Will you please come with us? Our master wishes to see you.'

–

Two men stood before them. Both wore red cloaks pinned at the throat with clasps of a familiar design; the white eight-pointed cross of the Knights of Saint John. 'What is this about?' Merrivale asked.

'Our master wishes to see you,' one of the men repeated.

'Are you arresting us?'

'No, sir herald. This is a request, not an order.'

Brief memories flashed through Merrivale's mind; Knights of Saint John lying in the streets, riddled with arrows; another Knight riding downhill past the old Roman wall in Northumberland, pursued by Scottish horsemen. 'Very well,' he said.

The Hospital of Saint John was in the south of the city on the banks of another canal, the Dijver. Quietly and courteously, they were shown into a vaulted room with plain walls and a few pieces of simple wooden furniture. Two people rose as they entered, a tall man in a black tunic embroidered with the same white cross, and a woman in a simple black gown with a white wimple closely framing her face. At first Merrivale thought she was a Beguine, but then he noticed the little white eight-pointed brooch at the neck of her gown.

'Greetings, sir herald,' said the man. 'If I may introduce myself, I am Commander Loijis DuSart, the senior officer of our Order in Flanders. This is Sister Adela Seton, *consorore* of the Order.'

Merrivale looked at the woman. 'Seton,' he said. 'A familiar name.'

She nodded. She too was tall, nearly as tall as himself, and it was hard to guess her age. Her face was hollow with fatigue or recent sorrow; there were shadows under her clear blue eyes. 'Alexander Seton was my brother,' she said softly. 'I received news of his death ten days ago.'

Tiphaine bowed her head. 'I am sorry,' Merrivale said.

'Do you know what happened?'

'He was killed trying to protect the *demoiselle* and myself.'

Sister Adela watched his face. 'Please tell me the truth, sir herald. He was killed by his fellow Scots, was he not?'

Merrivale nodded slowly. 'The Demoiselle de Tesson and I discovered a plot to overthrow the crown of Scotland. Your brother helped us to escape from the Scottish army, and tried to draw off the pursuit so we could get away. We owe him our lives, and our eternal gratitude.'

'Then my brother is at peace with God,' she said quietly. 'He had been much troubled in recent years. He joined the Order to fight the Saracens, but lately, he said, he had begun to believe that the real enemy of Christendom was much closer to home.'

Commander DuSart cleared his throat. 'The plot against Scotland collapsed with the defeat of the Scottish army at Neville's Cross,' he said. 'What concerns us more is the rumour of a conspiracy against our Order. Brother Alexander spoke of this in his letters too. Did he mention it to you?'

'Yes,' said Merrivale.

'Thirty years ago, our brother order the Knights Templar was also the victim of a conspiracy,' said DuSart. 'Lies were spread, false accusations made, and the Templars were torn apart by men greedy for their lands and wealth. The Templars were martyred for their faith, their members exiled, imprisoned or burned. We have always known that one day, having devoured the carcass of the Templars, greedy, godless men would turn on us. We wonder if that day has now come.'

'Why do you think so?' Tiphaine asked. 'Because of Brother Alexander's letter?'

'Partly. But we have been receiving disturbing reports from the French priory of the Order for nearly a year now. If these reports are correct, the French priory is working against the rest of the Order and conspiring to destroy it from within.'

Merrivale watched him. 'Have you been spying on your fellow members of the Order?'

'We discovered that the Grand Prior of France was receiving very large payments from outside the Order,' said Sister Adela. 'We believe he was being bribed, but we do not know by whom. We were still investigating when the Grand Prior was killed at Crécy.'

'We?' said Merrivale.

'Yes,' she said. 'I was the spy.'

'Did anyone suspect you?' asked Tiphaine.

She smiled a little, and her face seemed suddenly lighter. 'I am a woman. They barely noticed my existence.'

'Here in Flanders we have a long tradition of nursing sisters and *consorores* playing a part in the governance of the Order,' said Commander DuSart. 'Elsewhere, some of our brethren have not yet seen the light.'

'Was it only the Grand Prior who received payments?'

'No, there were several others,' said Sister Adela. 'One was his cousin, Reynaud de Nanteuil. He holds the commandery of Saint-Riquier, and is very influential in the Order.'

'Were other priories involved?'

'I am afraid so. Payments were made to the priors of Bohemia and High Germany.' She paused for a moment. 'And England,' she said.

Merrivale glanced at Tiphaine, seeing the expression on her face. Philip de Thame, Grand Prior of England, had been under suspicion for some time, but this was the first firm evidence. *This conspiracy is like the hydra*, he thought. *Every time we cut off one of its heads, it grows two more.*

'Thank you for telling us,' he said. 'What do you want in return?'

'Anything that might help us,' said DuSart. 'The future of our Order is at stake. How can we defend it?'

Merrivale rubbed his chin, wondering how much to tell them. Alexander Seton had died for him and Tiphaine, and with his last words he had enjoined Merrivale to pass on what he knew to the rest of the Order. And Seton's sister was owed the truth.

Or some of it, at least.

'There is indeed a conspiracy,' he said. 'Not just against the Knights, but against England, Scotland, France and the papacy, perhaps the Empire as well. The man at the centre of the conspiracy is English. We know him only as the man from the north, because he is said to speak with a northern accent. The only other thing we know, or suspect, is that he is close to King Edward.'

'A man with a grudge against the king?' asked Sister Adela.

'Possibly.' He remembered what Tiphaine had said. 'But I think this man has a grudge against the world. And, of course, he seeks to profit from the downfall of others. Chaos always brings opportunities for those ruthless enough to take advantage of them.'

'And we saw how people profited from the fall of the Templars,' DuSart said grimly. 'Including our own Order, of course. We took over the Templar lands and commanderies here in Flanders without a qualm.'

'You also gave refuge to Templars fleeing persecution, and protected them,' Merrivale said. 'No blame attaches to you.'

'But we sowed the wind nonetheless. And now we are about to reap the whirlwind.'

'Not if we stop them.' The herald looked at Sister Adela. 'Can you learn more about Reynaud de Nanteuil?'

'I can try,' she said.

4

Calais, 25th of November, 1346

Report on the affray at Bruges on the XIVth day of November, in the nineteenth year of the reign of King Edward III.

Item, the men who attacked her Grace the queen have not been found. It is likely that they fled the city soon after the attack.

Item, it seems probable that the musicians, who left the burgemeester's house without hindrance, warned the men known as the Pilgrims that her Grace was about to depart. Thus the Pilgrims were able to ambush the queen's party en route rather than attack the house as originally planned. The musicians too have disappeared without trace.

Item, the League of Three have now agreed to support the marriage of the Count of Flanders to Princess Isabella. The betrothal arrangements can proceed as planned. There is a risk that the conspirators will see this marriage as a threat to their own plans. I recommend that both the count and the princess be closely guarded at all times.

Item, the whereabouts of the fugitive William Blyth are unknown, but he is probably in or near Bruges. It is possible that he too is receiving protection from the Pilgrims. The banker Oppicius Adornes has promised to try to locate Blyth, and also to use his influence in the exchanges to make it more difficult for Blyth to raise money.

Item, information received from the Knights of Saint John strongly suggests that the Grand Prior of England, Brother Philip de Thame, is also implicated in the conspiracy. I recommend that he be watched and, if necessary, put to the question.

Item, my conclusion is that the conspiracy, whose existence we first discovered in the summer, is as strong as ever. All possible efforts must be made to eradicate it.

Simon Merrivale, heraldus

–

'Phew!' said Alice Bedingfield. 'The stench out there is worse than London.'

The air in Merrivale's chambers smelled of candle wax and newly sawn wood and, wafting in from outside, salt water and sewage. A small town was springing up along a low ridge outside the walls of Calais, complete with houses for the nobles and knights, shops, taverns and a marketplace. Some wit had christened the settlement Villeneuve-la-Hardie, the brave new town. The archers and Welsh spearmen lived in huts on the lower slopes of the ridge where they mostly stayed dry, except for days when the spring tides came in across the marshes and flooded their huts, and also the latrines. Days like today.

Tiphaine had gone to the market, taking the herald's manservant Mauro with her. Merrivale looked up. 'How may I be of service, Alice?'

'Her Grace wishes to see you,' the lady-in-waiting said, smiling. 'I'll take you to her now, if you like.'

The herald frowned. 'I have just been summoned to the king.'

'She knows. She wants to see you first.'

Merrivale rose to his feet, reaching for his tabard. 'Don't look so put out,' said the lady-in-waiting. 'After all, this gives you a chance to spend a few minutes in my company, doesn't it?'

'And no man could refuse such a pleasure,' said Merrivale. 'How are you, Alice? Recovered, I hope?'

She smiled again. 'I am my old self, for better or worse.' The smile faded a little. 'It was the shock of it all. When the crossbows began to shoot, I thought my heart would stop. How did you remain so calm?'

'You get used to it,' said Merrivale.

'Do you? I'm not sure that is a good thing.'

'Neither am I.'

'You could give it all up, Simon. You are owed far more than you receive for your services, you know that. The king would give you a fine manor somewhere, if you asked him. You could marry, settle down, raise a family to carry on your name. Have you never thought of that?'

Merrivale shook his head. 'To be honest, Alice, the idea of settling down is completely foreign to me.'

Her smile faded a little. 'What a pity,' she said. 'Come. We must not keep the queen waiting.'

--

The queen was in her painted chamber in the King's House, sitting in a high-backed chair and propped up with cushions. Unsurprisingly for a woman who had given birth to ten children, she suffered from back pains, and the journey to and from Bruges had made these worse.

'I have not thanked you properly for your services,' she said as Merrivale entered the room. 'Without your perception and prompt action in Bruges, we would have been trapped in the burgemeester's house with little chance of escape.'

Merrivale bowed. 'The Demoiselle de Tesson is the one to thank, your Grace. It was she who spotted the musician.'

'Yes. I like your little *demoiselle*. I have a fondness for waifs and strays.'

'Your pardon, your Grace, but she is not my *demoiselle*.'

'Isn't she? Do you deny that she is sharing your bed?'

Ever since the death of her former lover, burned to death slowly in a fire she had deliberately started, Tiphaine suffered from nightmares. Time and time again she watched Rollond de Brus die; sometimes, she was sucked down into the burning pit of coal along with him. When she awoke, sweating and shaking and physically sick, she needed someone to cling to. Merrivale never told her how badly he himself slept, knowing what was happening in her dreams.

'No,' he said. 'I do not deny it.'

Alice Bedingfield stuck out her lower lip. 'Then you have a responsibility for her,' the queen said briskly. 'What do you intend to do?'

'With the greatest of respect, your Grace, I don't think the decision is mine to make.'

'What a thoroughly unsatisfactory answer. Why did the Pilgrims want to kill me? To stop the betrothal?'

37

'Probably, but I suspect there is more to it. Your death would also have robbed the king of his most trusted councillor.'

There was a long pause. 'This conspirator,' she said. 'The one you call the man from the north. You think he is a member of the royal household.'

'I would go further, your Grace,' he said quietly. 'I believe it is someone very close to the king, someone he knows well and trusts.'

'Have you told him so?'

'No, your Grace.'

'Then don't, not until you have gathered your proofs and are certain beyond doubt. Any personal betrayal touches the king deeply. He is loyal to a fault and expects it in return. I still remember his grief when my uncle John of Hainault crossed over to France. He trusted John, and that wound took a long time to heal. I want to be absolutely certain we have the right man. Is that clear?'

Her loyalty to the king was matched only by her fierce protectiveness of him. Merrivale bowed again. 'I understand, your Grace.'

'Good. Now, it is time you attended on the king. Show him the way, Bedingfield, if you please.'

-

'Let's go over this again,' said King Edward III of England. 'Just to make certain everyone understands the plan, Thomas.'

Thomas Beauchamp, Earl of Warwick and marshal of England, pointed to a map of the city, sketched out on a piece of parchment. 'The main effort will be against the Saint-Omer gate, sire. Ralph Stafford and Maurice de Berkeley will lead the storming parties, with German mercenaries in support. If they can gain a foothold on the walls, the rest of the vanguard will go in. The remainder of the army will cover the perimeter, to pin down the defenders and guard against any possible sortie.'

'Who is guarding the left flank?'

'Llewellyn ap Gruffyd's company, from Conway. They are deployed in the dunes above the beach, in case the French try to break out to the south.'

'Good. And the Saint-Omer gate is the weakest point on the walls?'

'So my spy tells me,' said Lord Rowton. He was stocky man, richly dressed in a blue coat and hose. It had been his suggestion to besiege

Calais in the first place, and the king had been persuaded by him. 'They've had a couple of hard winters, and frost has weakened the ramparts. Money was sent for repairs, but it vanished into someone's purse. The gatehouse itself has a strong garrison, but the walls each side are weakly defended.'

Brother Geoffrey of Maldon, in his usual severe black robes with a neat white bandage around his head, looked surprised. 'I was unaware we had an agent in Calais.'

Rowton nodded. 'The agent is mine. My family lived here in Artois before they came to England. Maninghem, the family holding, is not far away. When the king decided to lay siege to Calais, I offered to contact a cousin who lives in the town. He agreed to help.'

'Out of family loyalty?' Geoffrey wondered.

'Sadly, that is not a quality my family are famous for. Money, and certain concessions once we take the city.'

Brother Geoffrey smiled. 'That does sound more in keeping with human nature.'

'When do we attack?' asked the king.

'At nones, sire. We'll give the siege engines an hour to soften them up before we go in.'

'Good. Make it so.' Dismissing the subject of the assault, the king turned to Merrivale. 'This information from the Knights of Saint John. Is it reliable?'

'I believe so, sire,' said the herald. 'The Knights in Flanders have supported the League for years, and fought against France. They have no reason to give us false information.'

'I can't arrest Philip de Thame just yet. But I will order an inquisition.'

Lord Rowton intervened. 'Sire, you have instructed Thame to raise troops from the Order's lands in England and bring them to join the army. If Thame is conspiring against us and he comes to Calais, there is a risk he might defect to the enemy. Better keep him safe in England, I would suggest.'

The king nodded. 'A very good idea, Eustace. Northburgh,' he said to his secretary, seated at a desk to one side of the room, 'see to it. Make certain the order reaches the prior as soon as possible. Thame is to remain in London until he receives further instructions.'

Thomas Hatfield, the Bishop of Durham, wagged one finger in the air. 'I agree, sire, a wise precaution. And also, we should discover whether Thame is conspiring with others.'

'What do you mean?' asked Rowton.

'On their own, the Knights are not strong enough to threaten the stability of the kingdom. But suppose they are in league with some of our high officials in London, the chancellor, or Archbishop Stratford, president of the council. They could wreak havoc in the king's absence.'

Rowton stared at Hatfield in astonishment. The king frowned.

'With respect, my lords, there has been no hint that either the chancellor or the president of the council is involved,' Merrivale said.

Hatfield looked sceptical. 'Then let them prove their innocence. Furthermore, if someone is bribing Thame, we need to discover where the money is coming from.'

Michael Northburgh looked up from his desk. 'Presumably it comes from Blyth.'

'But how does the money get from Blyth to Thame?' demanded the bishop. 'Are couriers bringing purses of gold and silver? Or are the conspirators using dark exchanges? If we can find out who these middlemen are, we can trace them back to Blyth.'

'You clearly have expertise in these matters,' said Rowton.

Hatfield looked supercilious. 'I have some knowledge of how money markets function, yes.'

Rowton turned to the king. 'Then perhaps the investigation of Philip de Thame should be left to Bishop Hatfield, sire. His officials in England can undertake the work at his direction, and report to us here at Calais.'

'You are full of good ideas, Eustace,' the king said humorously. 'That's your second today, by my counting. Very well, Hatfield, I leave this to you. Find out if Thame is indeed receiving bribes, and if so where the money comes from. Report as soon as you learn anything useful.'

Hatfield bowed. 'What are your orders for myself and the herald, sire?' Brother Geoffrey asked.

'For you, Geoffrey, I have something very much suited to your talents. The knights and barons of eastern Artois are planning to rebel against their overlords, and have asked for assistance. I want you to go out and stoke the fires. Northburgh will give you money to recruit men if needed. Do what you did so well back in Savoy, Geoffrey, and I will be very well pleased.'

'I shall do my utmost, sire.'

'Merrivale, you are needed here,' the king continued. 'We have also received word that the King of the Romans is sending an embassy. Some rubbish about mediating the quarrel between us and France. I need you to deal with them.'

Merrivale tried to conceal his irritation. *Did the king not read my report?* he wondered. *The search for the man from the north must surely take precedence over everything else.* Aloud he said, 'Andrew Clarenceux is the royal herald, sire. Would I not be interfering in his duties?'

'Andrew will of course receive the envoys formally and conduct the ceremonies. I want you to find out what the Germans *really* want. That's what you're good at.'

Merrivale persisted. 'And the conspiracy, sire?'

'Bishop Hatfield will deal with the Knights of Saint John, and we'll leave the Pilgrims to the burgemeester of Bruges. They're in his province, not ours. You did very well, Merrivale, and for that, you have our gratitude. But other problems also demand our attention, and your services are needed here. Is that clear?'

'Yes, sire.' Merrivale caught Brother Geoffrey's eye and saw the latter's fractional nod.

'Good.' In the distance they heard the bark of a cannon firing, followed by another. 'Very well, gentlemen, you have your orders,' the king said. 'Now, let's see if that Saint-Omer gate is as weak as Lord Rowton thinks it is.'

–

A wet wind blew in off the sea and whipped across the marshes. To the south the skeletons of burned out windmills stood on the heights above Sangatte, blurry through a veil of sea spray. Closer to hand the siege engines were at work, and the thump of trebuchets and the hard impacts of stone shot on the walls of Calais reverberated in the air. Michael Northburgh laid a hand on Merrivale's arm. 'You seem a little short-tempered, old friend. Is your *demoiselle* giving you trouble?'

'She is not—' Merrivale stopped. 'You know the danger we are in,' he said. 'And yet the king pulls me hither and yon. First I am packed off to Bruges with the queen, now I have to sit idly by and wait for some German embassy to arrive. And now Hatfield is interfering, and that is the last thing I need.'

'Hatfield is a highly intelligent man without a grain of common sense,' the secretary agreed. 'If anyone can botch this, he can. It could be worse, you know. You could be back in the Prince of Wales's household.'

'God grant me strength.' Since covering himself in glory at Crécy, the young Prince of Wales and his companions had thrown themselves boisterously into what they imagined to be adult pursuits, namely drinking games, all-night gambling sessions and telling boastful stories about the women they wished they had slept with.

Merrivale drew breath. 'I have had word that my father's condition is growing worse. There is a friend in England who can look after him, but I need to write to her.'

'Bring the letter to me, and I will put it in the courier's pouch along with the royal letters. That way you may be sure it will reach its destination.' Northburgh looked at him in concern. 'You look tired, my friend. Are you sleeping well?'

'No,' said Merrivale. He realised he had spoken more sharply than he intended. 'But I thank you for your concern. I will be well. I just need to see this through.'

–

Tiphaine was waiting at their lodgings. Merrivale's two servants, Mauro and Warin, were there too. Warin, the groom, had been in his service since he became a King's Messenger, and like himself was a native of Dartmoor in Devon. The son of a tin miner, he was plain-spoken, blunt and utterly reliable. Mauro was a Moorish man of uncertain antecedents who had joined the herald's household in Spain two years ago. Soft-voiced and gentle in manner, he had killed for Merrivale, and would die for him.

'I have asked Brother Geoffrey to join us,' the herald said. 'Apart from the three of you, he is the man I trust most in the world. I want to hear his views.'

Geoffrey arrived a few moments later. 'How is your head?' Tiphaine asked.

'You are kind to ask, *demoiselle*. I still have headaches from time to time, but the physician says that is to be expected.' He sat down on a wooden stool and looked inquiringly at Merrivale. 'What is on your mind, Simon?'

Another gun boomed in the distance. 'We have known each other for a long time, you and I,' Merrivale said. 'We have fought many a dirty, bloody, lonely war together. In Savoy, we nearly bought a kingdom.' He paused for a moment. 'But nothing we have done so far compares to the task that faces us now.'

The others waited. 'The man we seek is hiding in plain sight,' Merrivale said. 'He is close to the king, who trusts and reposes great faith in him. We know the king is loyal to his friends, sometimes loyal to a fault. Exposing him could incur the king's anger. And the queen has instructed me not to proceed against this man unless I have unimpeachable evidence.'

'That is understandable,' Brother Geoffrey said thoughtfully. 'Whom do you suspect, Simon?'

'I can think of only three people in the king's inner circle who have northern origins. All three were in the room with the king just now.'

He paused for a moment. 'One is Lord Rowton, whose lands are in Lancashire and Cheshire. The second is the Bishop of Durham, who hails from Yorkshire. The third is Michael Northburgh, the king's secretary, who also comes from Lancashire.'

He looked around at the others. 'I would swear on my soul it is not Northburgh. I have known Michael for years, even longer than you, Geoffrey. In my experience, the crown has no more dedicated servant.'

'But you yourself said it could be someone with a grudge,' said Tiphaine. 'Has Master Northburgh failed to secure a post he desired? Does he feel he has not been fairly rewarded for his services?'

'I don't know.' Merrivale paused. 'We can try to find out... As the king's secretary, Michael has a great deal of power. He sees every letter that goes to and from the king, and knows everything the king knows; more, probably... But is that enough for a conspiracy of this size and scale?'

'He could have allies,' Tiphaine pointed out. 'We know the man from the north has friends and supporters. Guy of Béthune, John of Hainault, Blyth. Can we connect Northburgh to any of them?'

'Possibly with Hainault,' the herald said slowly. 'Northburgh's uncle, the Bishop of Coventry, is an ambitious man; he once campaigned to be made a cardinal. He was also a strong supporter of the old king, but he defected to Mortimer's cause as soon as the rebels landed in England, and then abandoned Mortimer when our present king arrested him. Much as Hainault did.'

There was silence for a moment. John of Hainault had led the troops that overthrew Edward II of England and handed power to Queen Isabella and her lover Roger Mortimer, the Earl of March. Hainault had been present at Berkeley castle that night in 1327 when the old king was murdered; the man from the north, Merrivale believed, had been there also. Could that have been Bishop Northburgh? Or his nephew, Michael?

If so, and if this plot had its origins in the events of that night, the situation was doubly complex. The king was determined to put his father's death behind him, and did not want old wounds to be reopened; as his Grace himself had said many times, what mattered now was the future, not the past. Back in the summer he had forbidden Merrivale from investigating any links between the present conspiracy and his father's death.

'We can't rule him out, of course,' Merrivale said abruptly. 'What about the other two?'

'I am similarly inclined to discount Lord Rowton,' said Brother Geoffrey. 'He has been at the king's side for more than twenty years. He helped the king to arrest Mortimer. No one has been more loyal than Eustace Rowton.'

Rowton's father had also been caught up in the political turmoil of the late 1320s; initially a supporter of Mortimer, he had broken with the would-be usurper and later been reconciled to Edward III. 'Then why is he still plain Lord Rowton?' asked Warin. 'Why have titles and lands not been showered on him? That is usually what kings do, is it not?'

Geoffrey rubbed his chin. 'It is a fair question. Montacute became Earl of Salisbury and William Bohun is Earl of Northampton and constable of the kingdom. Rowton, so far as I know, has received nothing.'

'Perhaps he does not seek titles or offices, señor,' suggested Mauro. 'Perhaps he serves the king only for friendship.'

There was a short silence. Tiphaine sniffed. 'That would make him unique among men.'

The herald pondered. 'He may not have received material rewards, but he remains one of the king's closest friends.'

'The king likes him, but does not trust him?' asked Warin.

Brother Geoffrey shook his head. 'The king does trust him. He is present at all the king's counsels, and he is also providing information from inside Calais.'

Tiphaine looked surprised. Merrivale explained about Rowton's spy in the town. 'How does he communicate with this man?' she asked.

'He did not say,' said Brother Geoffrey. 'Are we agreed that Lord Rowton is an unlikely suspect?'

'Yes,' said Merrivale. 'That leads us to the bishop, Thomas Hatfield. Of the three, he is the only one not connected in some way to the death of the old king.'

'What do we know about him?'

'Not a great deal, as it happens. We know nothing of his family; supposedly he comes from a humble background, but he attended Merton College and entered the royal household in his mid-twenties. After that he rose very quickly, Receiver of the Chamber, Lord Privy Seal, and last year he was chosen as Bishop of Durham at the king's request. He is still only thirty-six, two years older than the king.'

'The king trusts Hatfield too,' Geoffrey pointed out. 'Enough to give him command of a division of the army last summer.'

'Yes… Hatfield was very quick to point the finger at others today. The chancellor and president of the council, also men whom the king trusts. I wondered if he was trying to discredit them, and put himself in line for either or both positions. That would make him the second most powerful man in the land, after the king himself.'

'Is there anything to these allegations?' Geoffrey asked.

'I know someone who can find out. The same friend might help us learn more about Hatfield's background, too. Are we agreed that Hatfield seems more likely than the other two?'

They nodded. 'But we do not neglect Northburgh and Rowton,' Tiphaine said. 'My father was betrayed to his death by a man he had considered a friend. The prospect of power drives men mad, and they will make any sacrifice to reach it.'

'Agreed.' The herald looked at the two servants. 'Mauro, Warin, I want you to watch all three of them. Talk to their servants, keep an eye on comings and goings in their households. Tell me anything you learn.'

Outside a trumpet sounded a ragged fanfare, notes splitting in the damp air. 'The assault is beginning, *señor*,' Mauro said.

'Shall we watch?' asked Brother Geoffrey, rising to his feet. 'It has been years since I last saw a good escalade.' He smiled at Merrivale. 'I missed all the excitement back in the summer.'

'I have had enough of sieges,' Tiphaine said with feeling. 'Go and watch, by all means. If Calais falls, you may come back and tell me all about it.'

-

The air was full of thunder. More guns had been brought over from England; there were ten of them now, newer and larger than the ones used on the field at Crécy, emplaced to concentrate their fire on the walls around the Saint-Omer gate. Stone shot hurtled from the mouths of the guns and splintered against the walls. Beside the guns, trebuchets wheeled their long wooden arms and more stone shot arched into the air; closer to the walls the archers prowled across the muddy flats, shooting at the enemy on the ramparts. Storming parties were forming up under the red chevron banner of Stafford and the white chevron and crosslets of Berkeley, men carrying boats and scaling ladders with close escorts of dismounted men-at-arms and flanked by more wedges of archers. Holstein's German mercenaries were moving into position behind them.

The king and his officers stood at the edge of the camp, watching the scene. Lord Rowton turned as Merrivale and Brother Geoffrey approached. 'By God, I'm starting to have doubts about my spy. Those walls do not look particularly weak to me.'

The walls around the gatehouse were scarred by shot, but showed no signs of crumbling. 'Calais is proving a rather tough nut to crack,' Brother Geoffrey said thoughtfully.

'Tougher than we first thought, certainly. There's a double moat, so we can't undermine the walls, and we can't starve them out because we don't have enough ships to blockade the harbour. An escalade is our only chance.'

Sickness and desertion had thinned the army that had fought at Crécy; there might be seven thousand men in the lines outside the city, if that. Most of the fleet had been paid off at the end of the summer when their contracts ended. Money, as ever, was tight and getting tighter.

The trumpet sounded again. 'Right,' said Rowton. 'Let's see what Stafford and Berkeley can do.'

The tide had receded a little, and the storming parties ran forward through shallow water, carrying their ladders and dragging the boats behind them. The guns roared again. In response, two French cannon emplaced on the gatehouse spat smoke and tongues of flame, and stone shot tore through the English columns, knocking men and down and smashing one of the boats. Stafford's men faltered for a moment, but Berkeley's company pressed on, archers fanning out with their bows raised, seeking targets. Crossbowmen leaned over the ramparts of the town to shoot back at them, and the archers picked them off one by one, their bodies collapsing backwards or falling heavily into the inner moat.

The storming parties reached the outer moat. Boats splashed into the water and men crowded into them, carrying the precious ladders. Swiftly they crossed the moat, climbed onto the dike on the far side, dragged the boats out of the water and launched them again in the inner moat. The defenders threw stones down on them, followed by jars of burning oil; two boats were shattered and sank in the moat, leaving their cargoes of men struggling in the water. The other boats bumped against the walls, ladders were raised and men-at-arms began climbing towards the ramparts.

None reached the top. The English archers smothered the ramparts with clouds of arrows but more stones fell, smashing ladders and pitching men into the water below. More incendiaries came down too, leaving black scorch marks on the walls, and even at a distance the watchers could hear the screams of burning men. Five minutes after the first ladders were raised the trumpets sounded the recall, and what was left of the storming parties paddled back across the moats, abandoned their boats and ran towards the safety of the English lines. The archers fell back more slowly, covering their retreat.

'Well, that's that,' the king said. 'We've tested their defences, I suppose. We'll do better next time.' He did not say what all of them were thinking, that they could hardly have done worse.

'I am sorry, sire,' said Lord Rowton.

'These things happen. We'll carry on, of course. We must. You are right, Eustace, laying siege to Calais is the best course of action. We need a harbour on this side of the Narrow Sea, and Calais is the best one on this coast.'

The rest of the army began to pull back towards the camp, splashing across the marshes. The mood was silent and glum. Stafford and Berkeley had lost several dozen men, and barely scratched the defences of Calais; the German mercenaries had not even engaged the enemy. Rowton turned to Merrivale. 'I'd like a word, herald, if you please.'

'Of course, my lord.'

Brother Geoffrey walked away. 'The king has been deeply affected by the attack on the queen,' Rowton said. 'More than he lets on.'

'I understand, my lord.'

'This conspiracy you uncovered back in the summer has shaken him too. The news of John of Hainault's involvement was particularly galling. Hainault is the queen's uncle, and there was a time when both their Graces counted him as a good friend.'

The queen had made the same point, Merrivale remembered. His lordship paused for a moment. 'What I am trying to say is, don't think the king is trying to prevent you from breaking up the conspiracy. You must carry on, of course.'

'To do that, I need to find the man at the centre of the conspiracy,' the herald said. 'I need the man from the north.'

'Then find him. Do whatever you have to do. I ask just one thing of you.'

'Name it, my lord.'

'When you do find this bastard, let me know. He has betrayed the king's trust, and for me, that is unforgivable. I want to be there when he dies.'

5

'I have laid out your writing materials, *señor*,' Mauro said, bowing. 'Is there anything else you require?'

Merrivale looked at the writing table, where parchment, pen, inkwell, sandbox and candle had all been arranged with neat precision. Mauro took pride in his work. 'Have you mixed a fresh batch of ink?'

'Yes, *señor*.'

'Is there any oak gall left?'

Mauro looked surprised. 'A little, *señor*.'

'Bring it to me, please.'

Looking even more surprised, the servant departed. Merrivale sat down at his desk, dipped the wooden pen in the inkwell and began to write.

> *To my trusted friend Lady Mary Percy, I send greeting. I trust you and your family are in good health. The demoiselle de Tesson also sends greetings. I write to ask a favour, which I hope you will find it in your power to grant. My father, as you know, suffers from a disorder of the mind in which he no longer remembers recent events or recognises those around him, and lately he has begun to suffer from a soreness of the skin that galls him terribly. An apothecary has recommended a remedy, the application of a solution of green copperas whose healing power will remove the sores and restore the condition of his skin; also, it is said, the copperas will in time heal his mind and restore to him a full memory of things past. I therefore beg you to procure some copperas from wherever you may find it, and deliver it to him without delay. I will of course defray any expenses you may incur. I remain your most obedient and humble servant, Simon Merrivale, heraldus.*

'The oak gall, *señor*,' Mauro said, setting a bowl of cloudy liquid on the table.

'Thank you.' Looking down at the lines of clean black script flowing across the page, Merrivale wiped his pen carefully on a piece of cloth. Dipping it into the pure oak gall, he began to write carefully between the lines. The pen left no mark on the parchment; the words he wrote now were invisible.

> The Grand Prior of England, Philip de Thame, may be conspiring against the kingdom. He may also have support from others such as John de Ufford, the lord chancellor, and the Archbishop of Canterbury. You have friends at court, and your father is close to the archbishop. I beg you to learn as much as you can and write to me secretly in the same manner as this letter. I also desire information on three other men, Michael Northburgh, Bishop Thomas Hatfield, and Eustace, Lord Rowton. Anything you can learn about their past histories, particularly any connection they might have with the events around the late king's death, will be important.

Holding the parchment up to the candlelight, Merrivale examined it from various angles. No trace of the second message could be seen. Oak gall dried clear on parchment; copperas gave the ink its black tint. Now all he had to do was hope that Lady Mary was familiar with the ancient discovery by Pliny, that words written invisibly in gall could be made visible by rubbing the parchment with copperas. Somehow, he felt sure that she did; she was an avid reader, and it would be surprising if there was not a copy of the *Medicina Plinii* somewhere in her house.

Sealing the letter, he rose, pulled on his tabard and stepped out into another cold, bitter afternoon. Dark rain clouds drifted above the towers of Calais. Geoffrey of Maldon rode down the muddy street, reining in his horse as he reached Merrivale. 'On your way to join the rebels?' the herald asked.

'I am, carrying with me a saddlebag full of silver and a long list of promises. The former, I imagine, will be more persuasive.'

'I am surprised the king is taking this revolt in Artois so seriously. The rebels can do a great deal of damage, especially under your guidance, but they can hardly hope to bring down France.'

'Not France, but Burgundy. Artois is a fief of the duke of Burgundy, remember, and the king hopes to drive a wedge between the duke and

France. Put enough pressure on the duke, and Burgundy might even come over to our side. And that really would be a blow to France, especially if other high nobles can be tempted to follow him.'

One forgot, sometimes, how far-sighted Edward III could be. 'The Flemings have already reduced half of Artois to a desert,' Geoffrey said. 'My task now is to desolate the other half.'

'May God watch over you, old friend.'

Geoffrey smiled a little. 'Let us hope He does so rather more effectively than He did at Caen.'

The canon nudged his horse with his heels and rode away. Merrivale walked through the rain to the King's House where he found Northburgh in his little office, working through a small mountain of parchment. 'Are you busy?' the herald asked.

'Busy? Try victualling and paying for an army on the wrong side of the ocean, and then ask me again. I'm clerk to the Exchequer, the Chancery and the king's purveyors all rolled into one. Is that your letter? Put it on the desk and I'll see to it. There is a ship leaving Gravelines with the tide this afternoon, bound for London.'

'Thank you, Michael. I really am sorry to intrude at a time like this, but... Do you have a moment?'

Northburgh laid down his pen. 'You are looking very serious, my friend. What concerns you?'

'Your uncle, the bishop of Coventry. He was high up in government back in the 1320s and '30s, wasn't he?'

'Indeed he was. Keeper of the Wardrobe and Treasurer on several occasions. He likes to joke that he has served three kings, the two Edwards and Roger Mortimer. He managed to move from each administration to the next quite smoothly. Rather too smoothly, some might say.'

'How well did he know John of Hainault?'

It was Northburgh's turn to grow serious. 'That's what this is about, is it? To be honest, I don't know because I never asked him. But I imagine they worked closely together, especially during the Mortimer regime.'

'Out of curiosity, why have you never asked him?'

'I don't really see that much of him. Uncle Roger helped me in the early part of my career, but... I don't really like the old rascal, if I'm honest.'

'Why not?'

'You mentioned John of Hainault. He has one of those cold, calculating minds that is always looking for an opportunity, always trying to create a chance for himself, and be damned to the rest of humanity. Uncle Roger is another. He overreached himself in the end, as his kind always do.'

A disappointed and bitter man with a grudge against the king and links to John of Hainault. *Are we looking at the wrong Northburgh?* the herald wondered. He decided to chance his arm. 'Did he have any connection with Thomas Hatfield?'

It took a moment for the implication to sink in. Northburgh's eyes widened a little. 'Hatfield is much younger, of course. He didn't really rise to prominence until after Uncle Roger departed. Are you thinking what I think you are thinking?'

'At the moment I am not really thinking anything,' Merrivale said, not entirely truthfully. 'I have a handful of tesserae, and I am trying to see where they fit in the larger mosaic.'

Northburgh pondered for a moment. 'Have you talked to Maurice de Berkeley? He and his brother both know Uncle Roger well, and they were very much involved in… events. Particularly in 1327. He will know more than I do.'

–

Maurice de Berkeley was in his late forties, but had an air of elegance that made him seem younger. His left hand was heavily bandaged, covering burns received during the failed assault. Despite his and his family's troubled past, he was one of the king's favourite captains. *Berkeley is an example*, Merrivale thought, *of what the king does so well; he convinces people to forget the past and put their trust in him, while showing that he trusts them as well.* It was a skill that his adversary, Philip of France, had never learned.

'Why are you trying to rake up the past?' Berkeley asked. His voice was calm, but the herald could see tension in his face.

'Because someone else won't let us forget it,' Merrivale said. 'Are you aware that there is a plot against the king?'

'I hear rumours, but pay no attention to them. People are always plotting against kings. It is one life's inevitable evils, like taxation and mouldy bread.'

'Sometimes the plotters succeed,' the herald reminded him.

Berkeley flushed a little. 'So, you *are* raking up the past. Look, you know the facts. The old king was imprisoned at Berkeley castle, and my brother was one of his keepers. But my brother was absent from Berkeley the night he was murdered, and was not to blame. He was tried as an accessory by a court of his peers, and was fully exonerated.'

'I know. I also know that your father starved to death in a royal prison a year earlier. If anyone had a right to a grudge against the old king, it was the Berkeleys.'

'What are you insinuating, herald?' Berkeley was on his guard now, his eyes watchful.

'Your brother was not to blame for the king's death, and neither are you. But I am willing to bet that both of you knew Mortimer was planning to murder him. Who was the presiding judge at your brother's trial?'

Berkeley was startled by the question. 'The Bishop of Coventry. Roger Northburgh.'

'Who was on the jury?'

'Twelve men, knights and barons. I don't remember all the names.'

'Was Lord Rowton one of them?'

Berkeley looked even more surprised. 'Eustace?' He paused. 'No, but his father was, old Gerard. He had just come back into favour at the time.'

'Was Thomas Hatfield involved with the trial in any way?'

'Hatfield hadn't even come to court yet. Why does this matter, herald?'

Merrivale ignored the question. 'How long have you known Rowton?'

'We met not long before the old queen went over to France. Rowton had joined her service a few months before.'

'Was that where he met the king? The Prince of Wales, as he was then?'

'Yes. They're almost exactly the same age. I wasn't particularly close to either of them, but I heard they got along well from the beginning. By the time the queen and Mortimer returned and overthrew the old king, Rowton was one of Edward's closest confidantes. He was one of the party that helped the king arrest Mortimer and seize power in 1330.'

'So he was in the old queen's service originally, but exchanged that for joining the king's household. In the end, he turned against the queen.'

'In the end, we all did,' Berkeley said bleakly.

'Between the old king's death and the coup in 1330, was Rowton in his Grace's service the entire time?'

'So far as I know. Why all these questions? To repeat what I said earlier, why does it matter?'

'Because Rowton is close to the king,' the herald said, 'and it is my responsibility to know everything I can about the men around him. Including you, Sir Maurice.'

They looked at each other, Berkeley's face a mixture of disbelief and puzzlement. 'Just one more thing, if I may,' said the herald. 'Three people came to the castle the night the king died, bearing orders from Mortimer to kill him. One was Sir John Holland, now deceased. The second was John of Hainault. Who was the third?'

'The night the old king died, I was at my own manor of Stoke Gifford, twenty miles away. I didn't hear what happened until the following day. You have my word of honour on that.'

The herald regarded him for a moment. 'You asked why this matters, Sir Maurice. The plot against the king is already in motion. Whoever wants to kill him also had a hand in the murder of his father. I know everything that happened that night. I know how the king died, and who killed him. The only thing I do not know is the name of the third man.'

Berkeley nodded. He was calm now, his face thoughtful. 'I understand. I appreciate what you are trying to do, herald, and why. But sometimes we are not meant to know everything. Some things should remain undiscovered and in the shadows. Are you familiar with the story of Pandora's jar?'

'I am.'

'Once a secret is made public, it cannot be made secret again. Beware the consequences of what you are doing. Or you too may end up destroying the people you love.'

Paris, 28th of November, 1346

When it rained, as it had done ceaselessly for the past week, the waters of the Seine rose and the big chamber in the Palais de la Cité became even more damp and cold than usual. Candlewicks spluttered and parchment sheets were covered in a layer of greasy slime that had to be wiped away before they could be written on. There was plenty of room in the castle and it would have been easy to move the offices of the Chambre des Comptes somewhere higher, dryer and warmer, but the authorities never got around to doing anything about it. This was, the clerks agreed, typical of the king's government these days and explained why the country was in such a dire state.

Dire, and getting worse. After the defeat at Crécy the king appeared to have gone mad, accusing the men around him of treason and dismissing many high officials from their posts. The latest victim was Pierre des Essarts, the president of the Chambre des Comptes, who had been arrested and thrown into prison. 'It stands to reason,' murmured Estienne Massy, one of the clerks of the Chambre. 'The king is desperate for money. So of course it is perfectly sensible that he should imprison the only man in the kingdom who actually understands government finances.'

Another clerk, Hugolin Bessancourt, nodded towards the two red-cloaked Knights of Saint John who stood at the back of the chamber, hands on their sword hilts and staring aggressively around the room. 'And now they've put the soldier-monks in charge instead. What do you make of them?'

'Idiots,' Massy said behind his hand. 'I'm told the Knights have been brought in to "reform" the Chambre, whatever that means. That lot couldn't reform their own arses. Do you know they can't even read an account book? I asked one of them if he understood what a balance carried forward meant, and he looked at me like I had two heads.'

Bessancourt shook his head. 'I know. And look at them strutting around now, pretending to be in charge. Stupid pricks.'

The two clerks sniggered behind their hands. Both were young, and not naturally inclined towards respect for authority. The Knights glared at them, and they bent their heads and dipped their pens in their inkwells. Around them the other clerks laboured, checking accounts and writing reports. A tall woman in a long black habit and white wimple entered the room and made a courtesy to the two Knights, who ignored her. Quietly she walked around the room, collecting the finished reports the clerks left on the edges of their desks.

Bessancourt concentrated on the parchments in front of him, checking the sums on his abacus. The documents made dismal reading. One of the functions of the Chambre des Comptes was to check the records submitted by tax collectors. The crucial thing was to ensure that the money the tax collectors claimed they had sent to the treasury had actually been received. Much of the time, it had not.

In Paris and out in the provinces, royal officials were stripping the country bare. New taxes were being levied and loans were demanded from merchants and guilds, loans that everyone knew would never be paid back. The assets of the Italian bankers had been seized, including their loan books. Churches and monasteries were being forced to hand over their sacred vessels; even reliquaries containing bones of the saints had been melted down. And yet, the royal treasury remained mysteriously empty.

He leaned towards Massy. 'Seriously. Did you say the Knights of Saint John have been brought in to reform the Chambre?'

'That's what I was told. Some fellow called Reynaud de Nanteuil, the Commander of Saint-Riquier, has been appointed to take over from old Essarts. He has a great reputation as an administrator, known for his drive and enthusiasm.' It is not easy to whisper sarcastically, but Massy was making a fair job of it. 'He's going to stamp out corruption and make us more efficient.'

'I've never heard such bollocks in all my life. I can't believe these reports, Estienne. A fortune should be flowing into the treasury, but where is the money? These receipts from Picardy; we're getting a tithe of what the *procureurs* claim to have taken. Are the bastards eating the money?'

Massy rolled up the parchment he had been reading and slid it under the table. 'Read this,' he murmured.

Bessancourt looked around. The two Knights were talking to each other, ignoring the clerks; the woman – who was she, anyway? – was on the far side of the room. He unrolled the parchment and began to read.

Almost at once the hair rose on the back of his neck. This was no ordinary report from a minor official; it was from the French seneschal of Picardy, addressed to the president of the Parlement in Paris. The seneschal was complaining about a sudden increase in the circulation of counterfeit money, so much so that *of the coin collected by tax farmers since Michaelmas barely one-third is genuine with the rest being false*. In the markets and the streets people were losing confidence in the money, the seneschal wrote, adding *it is whispered that this is a treasonous plot by the king's corrupt officers to defraud the people and hoard the money for themselves*. The seneschal demanded that the Parlement conduct an urgent inquiry and punish the purveyors of false money without delay.

'We were not supposed to see this letter,' murmured Bessancourt.

'No. Some idiot of a courier must have put it in his mailbag along with the other reports and forgot to deliver it.' Massy nodded towards the two Knights. 'Shall we tell the pricks?'

One of the Knights had broken off his conversation and was looking at the two clerks. Even at a distance his face was full of suspicion. Bessancourt bent his head. 'No,' he said out of the corner of his mouth. 'They'll accuse us of stealing the letter. We don't want anything to do with counterfeiting, brother. We stay well away from this.'

'All we did is read a fucking letter.'

'A letter we weren't meant to read.' Bessancourt waited until the Knight looked away and passed the parchment quickly back to Massy. 'Put it along with the completed reports,' he said. 'Hopefully the sister will take it away.'

They returned to their work. The cold miserable day drew to an end. Across the city the bells began to toll vespers, and the Knights grudgingly agreed that the clerks could finish for the day. Bessancourt reached into his purse as he walked towards the door, counting the coins he had left and calculating how much wine he could buy. Had he turned his head, he would have seen the woman move quietly towards their desk and begin sorting through their reports.

6

'Here they come,' said the king, shading his eyes with his hand. The royal household was up on the heights above Sangatte not far from the ruined windmills, waiting for the embassy from the King of the Romans; Calais and the camp were distant behind them. It was, for once, a bright sunny day, and the wind coming in off the Narrow Sea rippled the standards and banners overhead.

'A red cross on white, and a red eagle,' said the king. 'Do you know the devices, herald?'

'The banner with the cross belongs to Archbishop Balduin of Trier, sire,' said Andrew of Clarenceux. 'The eagle is Boček of Kunštát, Lord of Poděbrady and chamberlain to the King of the Romans.'

Seated on horseback beside his father, the Prince of Wales reverted briefly from being a battle-hardened captain of men to a querulous sixteen-year-old boy. 'Why is he called the King of the *Romans*? He's not Roman at all, he's German. His subjects are all Germans too.'

'It is a courtesy, Highness,' Clarenceux said dutifully. 'The man chosen by the electors to rule the Holy Roman Empire receives the title King of the Romans. He cannot call himself emperor until he has been formally crowned by the pope.'

'So he is not really king of anything, is he? *And* my archers shot him last month. Honestly, I don't see why we're bothering with him.'

'Nevertheless, we will hear what his envoys have to say,' the king said, a little curtly. The prince subsided into moody silence, probably thinking of the dice and half-finished wine cups he had left behind at the camp. Clarenceux watched the oncoming column of horsemen. 'There is a herald with them, as well, in Bohemia's colours,' he said. He looked across at Merrivale. 'That will be Zajíc, I think.'

'Yes.' Merrivale's scalp tingled a little. He knew Vilém Zajíc, the former herald of King Jean of Bohemia. Zajíc's presence with this embassy was not a matter of chance. He had been sent to seek out Merrivale.

Find out what they really want, the king had said. And it was a fair guess that Zajíc's orders were similar.

The embassy was not a large one; the two envoys and the herald, a dozen secretaries and attendants, an escorting file of twenty men-at-arms in brightly burnished armour and embroidered surcoats. They reined in a hundred paces away and dismounted. The king, the prince and their own attendants stepped down from the saddle and walked forward to meet them. Archbishop Balduin was in his early sixties, a sour-looking man with deep-set eyes and downturned mouth; Poděbrady looked like everyone's idea of a Bohemian warrior, red-faced with a bristling black beard. The red eagle on his surcoat had garnets for eyes, which were probably supposed to be impressive but instead made the bird look like it was recovering from a drinking binge.

The two parties came together. A trumpet sounded a brief fanfare. The archbishop made a speech: *The King of the Romans is grieved at the strife between England and France... he regards both kings as his brothers... he is willing to mediate their quarrel and help them become reconciled... we bring new proposals for a full and lasting peace.*

King Edward made a somewhat shorter speech: *fraternal greetings to his Grace the king... delighted to hear any new proposals for peace... however, unless these proposals are genuinely new and different to the rubbish we have heard before, this will be a damned short meeting.*

A pavilion had been erected overlooking the sea. The king, the prince, the envoys and their secretaries went into the pavilion and sat down, leaving their respective escorts to stare at each other. Two of the younger English men-at-arms began miming the draw and release of a longbow until Merrivale told them to stop. 'We are the hosts of this meeting. We do not show discourtesy to our guests.'

Muttering, they stopped. Merrivale turned to Zajíc, who wore a tabard with the unusual device of the kingdom of Bohemia, a white lion rampant with two tails on a field of red. 'Walk with me, Vilém.'

-

They stood on the heights, looking out over the vivid blue sea and watching sunlight dance on the waves. The cliffs of England were visible on the horizon. 'Why are we meeting here?' Zajíc asked. 'Why not at your camp?'

'The camp is surrounded by marshland, and the low-lying ground is full of miasma. For the sake of your envoys' health, we felt it would be better to meet up here, where the air is cleaner.'

Zajíc glanced at him. 'So, there is sickness in your camp. Your numbers are thinning out. The siege is not going well, and you do not want us to see the condition of your army.'

'Things aren't as bad as all that.' *Not yet, at least.* 'Are you with the King of the Romans now?'

The Bohemian herald nodded. He was a humourless, gloomy man. Royal heralds knew each other and often got on well, but Merrivale had never been fond of Zajíc. There were, he acknowledged, personal reasons for this.

'He offered me a post after his father was killed,' Zajíc said. 'Some of the others, too. Machaut is serving as his secretary now.'

'I heard someone play his music the other day. Give him my regards, when next you see him.' Merrivale's relations with Guillaume de Machaut had been even more complex than those with Zajíc. 'Are you enjoying the new position?'

Zajíc shrugged. 'It is less interesting. Life was never dull with King Jean.'

'No,' Merrivale said dryly. 'My own encounters with your late master seldom lacked excitement.'

Zajíc watched him. 'You should not have bedded his daughter. I warned you. So did Vidal.'

Involuntarily, Merrivale's fists clenched. He forced himself to relax. 'What terms have the envoys brought?'

'A truce to last for ten years, and a return to the borders as they existed before the war.'

'Then this will indeed be a short meeting. We have heard these terms before, and rejected them every time. Your envoys must have known this, so why are you here?'

Zajíc said nothing. Merrivale clicked his tongue. 'Come along, Vilém. Two months ago Charles was an ally of France, riding into battle against us. Now he is offering to mediate in peace talks; except he offers terms he knows we will not accept. What game is he playing?'

'King Charles was reluctant to join the conflict,' Zajíc said finally. 'King Jean, his father, commanded it. Now that his father is dead, he is free to pursue his own course. His eye is on the bigger prize.'

'He wants the imperial crown,' Merrivale said. 'Only someone is already wearing it. Louis of Bavaria is the crowned emperor, and he has the support of the Free Cities and the Hanseatic League. Your man has the backing of most of the German clergy, and the pope, for what that is worth. But it will take a great deal more to shift Louis off his throne.'

He watched Zajíc's face. 'Does Charles still cleave to his father's alliance with John of Hainault and his friends? Is he counting on them to put him in power?'

There was a long silence. Behind them, banners rippled and snapped in the wind. 'My king does not know if Hainault can be trusted,' Zajíc said finally. 'Or the others, Guy of Béthune or the Englishman.'

'Béthune is his brother-in-law.'

'Charles is fond of his sister. He is not so enamoured of her husband. He would have married her off to someone else.'

'Why does he distrust Hainault and the others?'

'He is not sure if they will keep their promises. And after what happened in Scotland, he wonders if they are as clever or as competent as they claim to be.'

'So, King Charles is considering his options. Is an alliance with England one of them?'

They stared at each other. 'Anything is possible,' Zajíc said.

'I admire your king's pragmatism. Two months ago the surgeons pulled two arrows out of his leg, and now he is contemplating an alliance with the men who shot him. There is a problem, however. Empress Margaret and Queen Philippa of England are sisters. Could you prevail upon King Edward to turn against his sister-in-law?'

'No,' said Zajíc. 'But you could, Simon.'

'You overestimate my influence.'

'No, I don't. And they're all related to each other, aren't they? King Charles is married to King Philippe's sister, and his daughter is married to King Philippe's son. God knows how many heads *their* children will have. But that won't stop King Charles from putting his own interests first.'

'You are quite right, Vilém, of course. You do wonder why they bother with these dynastic marriages, don't you?'

'It makes work for the lawyers,' Zajíc said. 'And brings in money for the papacy. Dispensations are not cheap.'

61

'Very well, suppose we support your man's claims to the imperial throne. What do we get in exchange? An alliance against France?'

Zajíc shook his head. 'I cannot promise that. But we would be prepared to support the Flemish marriage.'

'Do we need your support? We have the Count of Flanders in custody. We can sign the contracts whenever we like.'

'Hainault and the conspirators are determined to prevent the marriage, Simon. They do not wish to see Flanders bound to England. But perhaps we can help you.'

'How?'

'The leader of the conspiracy is an Englishman. I believe you call him the man from the north. Suppose I tell you his name. Would that be enough to sway your king?'

Merrivale stared him. 'Do you know who this man is?'

Zajíc shook his head. 'The Count of Rožmberk dealt with him, but he too died at Crécy. But I can discover his name.'

'How?'

The Bohemian shook his head. 'I need your answer. Will England support King Charles?'

'Two things,' Merrivale said. 'First, I think you are pretending to know more than you do. You have no idea who this man is, or where to start looking. King Jean may have known, Rožmberk certainly knew, but they did not confide in you and now both are dead. Second, your new master is desperate. France is too enfeebled to give him the support he needs, and he knows full well that the conspirators will only back him so long as it suits them. These men don't make kingdoms and empires, they break them. He believes that England is the last hope.'

He paused for a moment. 'But why should England help you? We don't need you. We already know the shape of the conspiracy and what its object is. We only lack the name of the man behind it. Once we have him, we can pull the rest down.'

'Now who is pretending?' Zajíc demanded. 'If you know so much already, why haven't you discovered the rest? You know nothing, Simon. What you think you know is only what you see on the surface. The rest is hidden, buried deep. And you will not find it alone.'

There was a long silence. *Are you familiar with the story of Pandora's jar?* Maurice de Berkeley had asked. 'I have no reason to trust you,

Vilém,' Merrivale said finally. 'None at all. Bring me the name of the man from the north, and then we will talk. Not before.'

'Then it seems we are done,' the Bohemian said. 'The offer is genuine, but we will not help you unless you also commit to supporting us. You need us.'

'Forgive me if I disagree with you.'

Zajíc shrugged and pointed to the pavilion. The king and archbishop were already walking out into the sunlight. 'You were right. It was a short meeting.'

'I am sorry you had such a long journey for nothing,' Merrivale said shortly.

'Yes,' said the Bohemian. 'So am I.'

-

'I hope I did the right thing, sire,' Merrivale said. The king had sent for him as soon as they reached camp; they were in the King's House now, the queen sitting beside her husband, their principal advisors Warwick, Hatfield and Rowton standing to one side.

'The possibility of King Charles changing sides is interesting, but Zajíc wanted a firm commitment. I refused.'

The king nodded. 'Archbishop Balduin indicated that they want to keep the negotiations open. I told him to come back when he had something new to say, but I did not shut the door in his face. So, let's see what they do next.'

'Balduin knew what Zajíc was going to say,' said Warwick.

'Yes. Presumably the archbishop is worried about spies in his own entourage, so the mission was entrusted to Zajíc.' The king stroked his chin with one hand. 'Well, well. This makes things interesting, does it not?'

Rowton stirred a little. 'Our policy has always been to support Emperor Louis.'

'Nonsense,' the queen said briskly. 'Our policy has always been to support whomever could help us gain the victory. As I recall, we have paid tens of thousands of marks to Louis, nearly bankrupting ourselves in the process, and received nothing in exchange. If Charles is willing to talk, we should listen.'

'But can we trust him?' demanded Hatfield. 'If he is sincere in his intentions, why not say so openly, rather than sending his herald to deliver a message in secret? This sounds like a distraction.'

'That is entirely possible, my lord,' Merrivale agreed. 'But the choice of envoys is interesting too. Archbishop Balduin is Charles's uncle and close advisor, and the lord of Poděbrady is one of the new men, whose first loyalty was to Charles and not his father. The one I distrust is Zajíc. Charles and Balduin must know about our past entanglements. So why would they send Zajíc to talk to me?'

'Only you can answer that, herald,' said Lord Rowton.

Merrivale said nothing. The king rubbed his hands together. 'Then we are agreed. We continue to try to separate the adversary from his allies. The Count of Flanders is in our hands, Geoffrey of Maldon's rebels will press Burgundy hard, and we shall encourage the King of the Romans to keep talking. Well done, gentlemen. I am pleased with this day's work.'

-

Tiphaine was waiting. 'How did the negotiations go?'

'About as well as expected.' Merrivale told her briefly what had happened. 'The king says he is pleased. I am… unsettled.'

'Why? Because this too is raking up the past? This is taking you too close to Yolande?'

'Partly that, yes… Zajíc seemed sincere at the end. Perhaps I misjudged him.'

'Perhaps that is what he wants you to think,' Tiphaine said. 'This arrived while you were away.'

She handed Merrivale a small roll of parchment. He glanced at the broken seal, a simple blob of wax with no device or mark.

> *To the demoiselle de Tesson, greeting. I wish to speak to you privately. Come to the castle of Ecou on the day before Advent.*

There was no signature. The writing was plain, anonymous; any educated person could have written it. 'How did this arrive?'

'One of the Welsh archers handed it to Warin while he was feeding the horses. Someone else had given it to him to deliver. The archer didn't know the other man's name, only that he paid in good coin.'

'Good coin?'

'Warin says that counterfeit coins are turning up in the archers' pay. Halfpenny bits and farthings, mostly. The men are starting to grumble.'

'I'm not surprised. Have you any idea who this might be from?'

'Hardly anyone in Flanders knows me, and if anyone in the army wanted a secret rendezvous they would not go so far as Ecou. At a guess, it is someone I once knew in Normandy. Perhaps my past is catching up with me also,' she added.

'Where is Ecou?'

'Lord Warwick says it is not far from Saint-Omer. There is also a French garrison at Saint-Omer,' she added. 'This could be a trap, of course.'

'Of course.' The herald put the letter down. 'Will you go?'

'I must,' she said.

Ecou, 2nd of December, 1346

In the aftermath of the French disaster at Crécy the Flemish militias had ripped through northern Artois, plundering and burning at will. A few of the stronger towns such as Saint-Omer and Béthune had held out, but elsewhere the Flemings had destroyed everything in their path. Merrivale and Tiphaine rode through a landscape of ruins, villages reduced to blackened cob walls and charred timbers, roofless churches, a plundered abbey with its doors smashed in. In the cloister, pages torn from books fluttered in the cold wind.

Merrivale had insisted on accompanying her, and bringing Mauro and Warin with them. Bands of foragers and plunderers still wandered through these desolate lands. According to the laws of war, heralds and those who accompanied them were sacrosanct and could not be impeded or harmed. That worked, so long as people remembered the laws, or knew them in the first place... But no one molested them. The open fields were empty of people; the loudest sound was the hissing of the wind. Merrivale's tabard was a solitary splash of colour against the dreary lands around them.

Ecou was, or had been, a small village on the edge of the marshes along the river Aa. The stone stump of a windmill stood at one end of the village, surrounded by blackened timbers. Beyond was a small castle with a water moat. Merrivale halted beside the windmill. 'Warin and I will wait here. Mauro, you will go with the *demoiselle*.'

'Yes, *señor*.'

Tiphaine opened her mouth to say she did not need an escort, but realised she would be glad of company in this haunted landscape.

Slowly the two of them rode towards the castle. The drawbridge was down and the gates had been battered open with a ram; inside, the hall was burned out and roofless and there were unburied bodies in the courtyard, reduced to heaps of rags and bones after several months of exposure.

'This place smells of death,' Mauro murmured. He was not referring to the bodies.

Hoofbeats thumped on the drawbridge. Tiphaine's heart skipped a beat and she looked for a place to hide, but there was no time. A file of men-at-arms rode into the courtyard and stopped with a jingle of harness. They carried lances and wore armour over mail coats; their surcoats were plain with no device. Behind came another figure in a dark cloak. Halting, the rider pulled back the hood of the cloak to reveal a woman's face with high cheekbones, a broad nose and intense dark eyes. Tiphaine's breath hissed in shock.

'Your Grace!' she said. 'Was it you who sent the letter?'

'Yes,' said Jeanne of Evreux, Queen of Navarre. 'Forgive me, *demoiselle*, for summoning you to this wild place, but it is important that we not be seen together. I hope the presence of my men has not alarmed you.'

'Not at all,' Tiphaine said, untruthfully. 'How may I serve you?'

'I wish you to convey an offer in secret to my cousin, King Edward of England,' said Jeanne. 'I intend to declare myself neutral in the war between France and England. In return, my lands in Normandy and Navarre must be left in peace. He must promise that his troops will not molest them.'

Tiphaine took her time about replying. Jeanne of Evreux was one of the most powerful landowners in eastern Normandy, and was also sovereign of the mountain kingdom of Navarre far away in the south; her loss would be a blow to France.

'Why choose me as your messenger?' she asked.

'Because I know you and respect you, *demoiselle*, as I knew and respected your father. I trust you.'

'I am flattered,' said Tiphaine. 'But I think the king would be better pleased if you openly joined his cause. Declare for him, and persuade the other Norman lords to do likewise.'

Jeanne laughed. 'How English you have become in a few short months. I will not lead a Norman rebellion against France, *demoiselle*. That hour has come and gone. Your father rebelled, and was executed.

66

Harcourt rebelled last summer, and came crawling back to France with his tail between his legs, begging King Philippe's forgiveness. I am too proud to beg, and too young to see my head on a spike. Neutrality is the best Cousin Edward will get from me, and I advise him to accept it. He will need all the assurance he can get, when the storm breaks.'

Tiphaine stared at her. 'Storm? What storm?'

'An attempt will be made to kill the King of France and his son in Paris, today. If it succeeds, the throne of France will be vacant.'

Tiphaine felt a chill that was nothing to do with the wind. 'The king has other heirs. So does his son.'

'All are children, and they lack followers. If they do try to take the throne, they will be overthrown and killed within days, children or no.'

'I beg your pardon, your Grace, but how do you know this?'

Jeanne drew a deep breath. 'Three days ago, I met some of the conspirators. Cardinal Aubert, Guy of Béthune and John of Hainault. They offered me the throne, when Philippe and his son are dead.'

Tiphaine said nothing. 'It is not the first time they have approached me, of course,' said Jeanne. 'Like your king, they wanted me to join their rebellion last summer. I turned them down then, and I turned them down now. I will not be their puppet. For one thing, I have a feeling that I too would not sit long upon the throne.'

'If your Grace refused them directly, you may be in danger,' Tiphaine said. 'These men do not like being thwarted.'

'Do not fear for me. I have five thousand men-at-arms at my back, and I am guarded night and day. But Cousin Edward needs to take care. There are spies in his court, listening and watching. They told me they control what happens in Calais, too.'

Tiphaine frowned. 'How?'

'They did not say. But it goes much further. They are already taking steps to control the papacy and the Knights of Saint John, and they will soon have the empire in their hands as well. Guy of Béthune boasted about this, to show me how powerful they are.'

Tiphaine thought about the herald waiting by the ruined windmill. 'Guy of Béthune is a provincial nobleman. How can he possibly threaten the empire?'

'He is also the brother-in-law of King Charles. He sits on the high council in Trier, and advises the king on policy. He is also the uncle of the young Count of Flanders.' Jeanne raised one finger. 'Warn Cousin Edward. And tell him to consider my offer carefully.'

She turned her horse and rode through the gate. Her escort wheeled and followed her. Within a few moments the drumming of their hooves had died away.

Back at the windmill Tiphaine let out a long breath, dispelling some of the tension she felt. 'We must return to the camp,' she said. 'I have an urgent message for the king.'

'What happened?'

Tiphaine told him. She watched his face change at the mention of Guy of Béthune. 'Did she say where Béthune is now?'

'In Trier, with the king.'

Merrivale nodded. 'We need to know more about this plot against the empire. There is someone near to hand who might be willing to help.'

'Yolande,' she said quietly.

'Yolande,' the herald repeated.

'Are you going to see her?'

'I have no choice. If there is a chance, any chance at all that she knows the name of the man we are looking for, then I must find her.'

'Shall I come with you?'

'No, the message for the king is urgent. Mauro will accompany you back to the camp. I will take Warin with me. God speed you, Tiphaine.'

'You too,' she said. She watched with troubled eyes as he mounted his horse and rode away towards the east, followed by Warin. The red and gold of his tabard glinted briefly in the dull landscape, and then he was gone.

7

Paris, 2nd of December, 1346

First came the outriders with torches, lighting the way for the rest; then a solid corps of men-at-arms pounding through the streets, iron-shod hooves striking sparks from the cobbles. After the bodyguard came the royal standard-bearer, the lilies of France rippling overhead in the torchlight, and finally King Philippe and his companions. Even though he was only riding from the Louvre to Notre-Dame the king wore full armour, as did the men around him.

The king was angry, as he often was these days; since Crécy there were few days when he was not in a rage. 'What in God's name are you playing at, Odo? Your men have done nothing to stop the English from investing Calais, nothing! And now the rest of Artois is rising in revolt. The entire northern march is in flames, and you're not doing a damned thing to stop it!'

'The revolts are being fomented by English agents,' said Duke Odo of Burgundy. 'You know that as well as I do. And no, I can't stop them, because I don't have enough money or enough men. If your Grace was willing to fund a proper defence—'

'Money, money! Body of Christ, do you think I am made of money? I can barely afford to pay my own garrisons. If you don't put these rebels down and bring Artois back under control, Odo, I will confiscate the entire county, do you hear me? I will take Artois into the royal domain. Now stop these damned revolts!'

'Yes, sire,' said Burgundy in a voice dark with anger.

'And there's another thing. You've given shelter to that damned rogue John of Hainault. Turn him out of your court, at once, and send him to me. In irons, if necessary.'

'Sire, he is part of my wife's family—'

'I don't care! Do it! God's blood, Odo, are you defying me?'

'Are you questioning my loyalty, sire?'

'Yes, God damn you, I am!'

The cavalcade was turning down Rue Sainte-Catherine towards the dark bulk of the Châtelet, the sound of hooves hammering off the walls. The king's son, Jean of Normandy, intervened. 'Sire, remember that the duke's son was killed in our service this past summer. He has given plenty of proof of his devotion to our cause.'

'Not by giving aid to Hainault, he hasn't. I want him back, Odo. I hold him responsible for our defeat at Crécy, and I intend to make him pay.'

Burgundy was still sulking. 'As I understand it, sire, your defeat at Crécy was caused by the rashness of your brother and the incompetence of your marshals.'

'Damn your soul! Do not besmirch my brother's name now that he is dead!'

'For God's sake, Philippe! He was plotting against you!'

'And you, Odo? Are you plotting against me? Just like all the others?'

The outriders were swinging left now, passing between the Châtelet and the silent halls of the Boucherie. Just as the king's party turned their horses, a shower of crossbow bolts flew from the upper windows and rooftops of the Boucherie, black streaks in the air. Two horses went down dead; another screamed and reared up, throwing its rider. The standard bearer fell from his saddle, a bolt transfixing his shoulder. A second volley of bolts tore through the air; two clashed off the king's breastplate, leaving fist-sized dents in the metal. He reeled in the saddle and hunched over, gasping for breath.

More bolts flew, more horses and men went down. The reek of hot blood was strong in the air. The captain of the guard was screaming at his men. 'Back, back! Get the king away! Back to the Louvre!' Hands grasped the king's bridle, turning his horse, and the cavalcade retreated back through the streets. One last volley of crossbow bolts clashed off the cobbles behind them. 'Are you hurt, sire?' Odo asked.

'Damn you, as if you care. Captain! Find the traitors! Hunt them down!'

'Yes, sire. Surround the Boucherie! Seal it off, search every hall and chamber. Quickly, quickly!'

Men jumped down from their horses and ran, holding up their shields to ward off more bolts. Philippe managed to sit upright in the saddle, still gasping and holding his side. 'Traitors,' he repeated.

'Working in league with the damned English,' said Jean of Normandy darkly.

'Not just the English. There are enemies on every side. By God,' said the king, 'I will have blood for this.'

'Yes, sire,' the Duke of Burgundy said grimly.

Amiens, 4th of December, 1346

'Word has just come from Paris,' said Vilém Zajíc the herald. 'There has been an attempt on the life of the king.'

Archbishop Balduin and Boček of Poděbrady were in the guest quarters at the bishop's palace overlooking the river Somme, finishing a breakfast of bread and wine. They looked at each other. 'Is the king unhurt?' asked the archbishop.

'Yes, apart from his pride. The attackers struck in the heart of his capital, and escaped unscathed. No trace of them has been found.'

'Who was behind the attack?' asked Poděbrady.

'Take your pick from the rumours,' said Zajíc. 'Parisian malcontents, Italian bankers, English agents and Flemish rebels have all been blamed. Hundreds have been arrested on suspicion of aiding the assassins, and mobs have attacked the houses of foreign merchants.'

Poděbrady stroked his beard. 'When in doubt, attack the foreigners,' he said.

'Yes,' said the archbishop. He looked more sour than ever. 'And the mobs seldom distinguish between friendly foreigners and the enemy.'

'Which are we?' asked Zajíc.

Silence fell. 'If word gets out that we were secretly negotiating with the English, rather than just trying to arrange a truce, they will come for us,' the herald warned.

'How would anyone find out?'

'People talk. Servants' gossip, men-at-arms exchanging news. Nothing stays secret for long.'

Poděbrady looked out the window, as if he expected to find a mob with torches and pitchforks already massing in the courtyard. 'I don't like running away from danger,' he said, stroking his beard. 'But we only have twenty men. I think we should leave as soon as possible.'

'I agree,' said the archbishop. 'The nearest imperial fief is Cambrai. The bishop there supports the French, but the people do not. We will be safe there.'

'It may not be as easy as that,' Zajíc said. 'The direct road to Cambrai leads us through eastern Artois, and rebellion is spreading like wildfire.'

'See if the garrison will lend us a few more men. Lord Poděbrady, make ready to depart.'

—

Climbing up out of the valley of the Somme the cavalcade rode swiftly across the undulating plain to the north-east. At first all was peaceful, but around midday they spotted the first destroyed farms and as the afternoon wore on they passed increasing numbers of burned-out villages and ruined castles. In some cases the burning was fresh, smoke still drifting in the air. 'Press on,' said the archbishop. 'We must reach Cambrai tonight.'

But by the time they came to Bapaume an early winter dusk was falling, and Cambrai was still fifteen miles away. They rode on, a north wind whistling around them. Ahead lay another village, this one unburned. Zajíc turned to the archbishop. 'Your Grace, perhaps we should halt here for the night—'

A flicker of movement caught the corner of his eye. He turned sharply to see a line of crossbowmen rising out of a sunken road, weapons levelled. A body of men with spears and axes stood formed up beside them, led by several men-at-arms.

'There's more behind us,' said Poděbrady. 'Shall we try to break out?'

'Don't be ridiculous,' the archbishop said. 'There's at least a hundred of them. Tell the escort to keep their hands away from their weapons.'

The men were coming closer, surrounding the envoys and their escort and hemming them in. The archbishop rode forward, throwing back his cloak so everyone could see his ecclesiastical robes. 'How dare you interfere with us?' he shouted, raising his pectoral cross in the air. 'Can you not see that I am a man of God?'

'As am I, your Grace,' said a cheerful voice. The ranks of the crossbowmen parted and a black-robed man walked through, leaning on a wooden staff. 'Permit me to introduce myself. I am Brother Geoffrey of Maldon, canon of the Augustinian Order.'

'You are English? But this is the embassy to the King of England! You cannot interfere with us!'

'*I* am English, yes. These gentlemen are in rebellion against the Duke of Burgundy, so their allegiance is really only to themselves. If

I may make a suggestion, your Grace, the high road can be rather dangerous at night. If you and Lord Poděbrady would kindly ask your men to lay down your arms, we will take you somewhere safe.'

'Are you taking me as well?' demanded Zajíc.

Brother Geoffrey glanced at his tabard and the lion with two tails. 'You are a herald, and therefore free to go where you please. You might want to come along, though. We could use your help arranging the ransoms.'

Calais, 4th of December, 1346

Tiphaine did not go directly to the king, because to do so would first mean approaching Michael Northburgh. Very well, Simon trusted Northburgh; that did not mean she should also. Changing into a clean gown, she went to the King's House and asked instead to speak to the queen.

Alice Bedingfield was not on duty, and she was glad of this. She knew Bedingfield had a fancy for Simon, and resented this for reasons which were not entirely clear in her mind. Instead, it was Elizabeth Chandos who came out to see her. Tiphaine liked Chandos; she was tall with a rather serious face and beautiful grey eyes. '*Demoiselle?* Her Grace will see you now.'

The queen was sitting with her feet up, a small book with painted wooden covers lying face down in her lap. She pointed to a stool by the fire. 'Be seated, *demoiselle*. What is your news?'

Tiphaine told her about the meeting with Jeanne of Evreux. The queen listened intently, Chandos standing immobile by the door. 'You have done well,' Philippa said at the end. 'Do you think Jeanne will keep her word?'

'She is an unusual woman,' Tiphaine said. 'She has all the power and wealth she desires, and wants no more. She can be trusted, I think.'

'This business about the empire. Tell me again exactly what she said.'

'They will soon have the empire in their hands. The Count of Béthune sits on the imperial council and advises the King of the Romans.'

'And while he does so, our own chances of reaching an accommodation with Charles will be slim indeed. We know how bitterly Béthune hates England.'

'And yet, King Charles still made the approach,' Elizabeth Chandos said thoughtfully. 'Perhaps Béthune does not control everything, not yet.'

The queen nodded. 'We shall have to chart our course carefully. Thank you, *demoiselle*. You have done good service.'

—

The queen was interested in matters of state, because she was a queen. Tiphaine was interested in the little things, the things left unsaid or partly spoken, because she was a survivor, and survivors know that God is in the details.

They told me they control what happens inside Calais too, Jeanne of Navarre had said. All the way back from Ecou to the English camp Tiphaine had pondered those words, wondering how the man from the north and his friends were 'controlling' the town.

Standing at the edge of the camp, she studied the scene before her. The siege engines were at work again, long arms swinging in the air and launching stone shot at the walls, and every so often a cannon boomed, belching yellow smoke. She smelled sulphur and salt water.

The army was preparing for another assault. Behind the barricades men were piling up more materials, boats and ladders and ropes with grapnels. There were barrels of pitch and tar, too; that meant incendiaries, which in turn probably meant a night assault. The engines were battering at the Dunkirk bastion, at the north-east corner of the walls, so presumably this was where the escalade would take place. She wondered what Lord Rowton's spy had said about the bastion.

How would one get a message in or out of the town? she wondered. By land would be difficult; a messenger would have to escape from the town without being noticed, cross the two moats and the marshland beyond, and get into the English camp without being shot by either French crossbowmen on the walls or the ever-watchful archers patrolling in front of the English lines. Of course, if one or both sides knew the messenger was coming and had orders to hold their fire, it would all be much easier...

Beyond the town was the harbour, enclosed by a narrow spit of land called the Rysbank. South from the Rysbank was a long line of dunes tufted with grass, running all the way to Sangatte in the distance. Cross the harbour and you could work your way down the dunes, but then you would run into another hazard, Llewellyn ap Gruffyd of Conway and his tough Welsh spearmen who were posted out on that flank. She knew Llewellyn and his men. They liked killing people, and they were very good at it.

She looked out towards the rolling grey sea. A strong west wind was blowing and surf was piling up on the Rysbank and the dunes, throwing white spray in the air. She could see the red sails of a few ships in the distance, but could not tell if they were French or English. Closer inshore small boats moved towards the harbour, fishermen coming home with their catch.

Or were they all fishermen?.

She returned to the King's House and asked to speak to Elizabeth Chandos. The lady-in-waiting looked surprised. 'Do you wish to speak to the queen again, *demoiselle*?'

'No, it was you I wanted to see. I have a question, but I am not sure who to ask. I thought I would come and see you first, because you are clever and you know things.'

Chandos gave one of her rare smiles. 'I never thought of you as a flatterer, Tiphaine.'

'I also don't want anyone else to know I have been asking questions.'

The smile vanished. 'You may rely on my discretion. What is it?'

'The French are running supplies into Calais by sea. Do you know where the boats come from?'

Chandos blinked; whatever question she had been expecting, this was not it. 'According to Lord Warwick, they come from various ports along the coast. Boulogne is the chief one, I think. It is only about twenty miles from here, so their ships usually have an easy passage.'

Tiphaine thought for a moment. She knew the name of one captain from Boulogne; everyone along the coast did, all the way down to Normandy. In peacetime he had preyed on the commerce of every nation; since the war began, he had stuck loyally to burning and sinking only English ships. 'Is Jean Marant one of the captains who brings in supplies?'

Chandos looked even more surprised. 'Yes. I have heard Lord Warwick mention his name several times, usually accompanied by a fair amount of blasphemy. From this, I gather that Marant is a very good captain.'

'He is one of the best,' said Tiphaine. 'Thank you, Elizabeth.'

'Really, that is all you wanted to know? Am I allowed to ask why?'

'Idle curiosity,' said Tiphaine. 'I once met Marant, that's all.'

—

'I want to go into Calais,' she said to Mauro a few minutes later. 'And I want you to come with me.'

Mauro considered this. 'What happens if I refuse, *señorita*?'

'I will go anyway, of course. But I am much more likely to come back again if I have you to help me.'

Mauro gazed at her, considering where his duty lay. He had joined the herald's service in Spain two years ago, putting a life of hardship and slavery behind him, and he was devoted to Merrivale. He knew the herald trusted him, and because of that he was determined to do the right thing.

The problem was, what was the right thing? Which would make the *señor* more angry; going with Tiphaine de Tesson into an enemy town under siege, or letting her go alone? *Roll the dice and take your chances*, he thought.

'I think we will need some disguises,' he said.

Béthune, 5ᵗʰ of December, 1346

It was only thirty miles from Ecou to Béthune, but getting there took Merrivale and Warin three days, circling around to the north past the Flemish fortress at Cassel to avoid the worst of the devastation caused by the earlier raids. Even so, the final day's journey down to Béthune was a bleak one. They saw more burned villages and desolated towns and rode past old battlefields with bones protruding from the earth, hearing the howl of wolves in the distance.

In the afternoon they came to a causeway crossing a broad expanse of silent, deserted marsh. The church spires of Béthune were visible on the horizon. Merrivale reined in for a moment, looking around. Off to the right, a little huddle of fisherman's huts stood on a rise in ground. There were no boats, and no sign of life around them.

The herald pointed to the huts. 'Wait for me there, and stay out of sight,' he said. 'There is a French garrison in Béthune, and they may send out patrols.'

'Yes, sir. If I may ask, what happens if you don't return?'

'I will return,' Merrivale said. 'The French have no authority to detain me, and the lady has no reason to.' Or so he hoped.

Warin dismounted, leading his horse towards the huts. Merrivale rode on, reaching the end of the causeway and crossing fields blackened with fire where the Flemings and English had camped during their unsuccessful siege of Béthune back in August. As he drew closer he saw the faubourgs outside the walls had been reduced to heaps of rubble and ash, and the walls themselves were scarred and pockmarked by bombardment. Broken stone shot lay scattered on the ground.

The guards at the gate were suspicious. 'What is your business here, herald?'

'I have an urgent message for the countess.' Merrivale touched his embroidered tabard. 'This is my passport.'

The gates were opened and he rode slowly through the cobbled streets. People turned and stared at him, but their gazes were not hostile. More Flemish than French, the population of Béthune had no particular animus against the English; most of them just hoped to keep their heads down and let the storms of war blow past them.

He passed the new wooden belfry in the market square and reached the castle on the southern side of town, enclosed by high walls of its own. This time the guards held him up and demanded he wait until her ladyship should consent to admit him. He waited, tense, his heart beating hard in his chest. Until two months ago, he had not seen Yolande for many years, but she still had a grip on his soul.

The household steward came to the gate, bowing his head stiffly. 'Sir herald? My lady will see you now.'

-

The great hall was cool and dark, with no candles or torches. A fire gleamed on the hearth, lighting high plastered walls with clerestory windows and a cavernous ceiling. She stood in the middle of the hall, hands clasped in front of her; she was dressed all in white, for she was still in mourning for her father. Her fair hair was coiled at the sides of her head, covered with a light veil. Her face was still and cold, like an angel on a rood screen.

'I must apologise for my poor welcome,' said Yolande of Bohemia, Countess of Béthune. Her voice echoed a little in the hall. 'We seldom receive guests, not in these troubled times.'

The barrier she had built around herself was almost visible. His tabard was his armour; the cold chill in her voice was hers. The only way to deal with her coldness was to match it.

'I have arrived without warning,' he said, bowing. 'The discourtesy is entirely mine.'

They faced each other. Under the white gown her body was rigid as iron. When he had met her in Scotland in September, she had been tender and soft, full of tears and sorrow for the past they had once had, and lost. Now she was brittle as glass. *If I touch her she will break.*

She was the fire and the flame. She was the lily, and the rose. But that was in the past. He must remember that.

'I am glad to see you came safely away from Scotland,' she said finally.

'As did your husband. Guy's escape from the slaughterhouse at Neville's Cross was a remarkable achievement. But then, Guy always looked after himself first.'

The words were brutal and intentional; he needed to shatter that icy detachment and make her speak freely. He almost succeeded. Her hands tightened, her knuckles clenched white. 'What do you want, Simon? Why are you here?'

Merrivale glanced around the hall. 'Is the boy here?'

'No. Guy says it is time to make a man of him. He has sent him to be a page at the house of Vaudricourt, one his knights.'

'Make a man of him. How old is he? Seven, eight?'

'Don't you know?' she challenged.

'Until last month I was unaware of his existence. You concealed all evidence of his birth from me. Do you see him often?'

Yolande was silent. 'That means no,' Merrivale said. 'Guy is taking him away from you, as you took him away from me. Did Guy know you were pregnant when he married you?'

She took a half step forward and stopped, with an effort. 'What do you want, Simon?' she repeated.

'An answer to my question.'

'Yes. He knew.'

'And still he agreed to marry you.' It was a statement, not a question.

'Why not? I am a bastard, but a royal bastard, and I was my father's favourite. Marrying me pulled Guy up the ladder. And if you think

78

he worries about rearing your son as his own, think again. He enjoys possession of the boy. It is a sign of his triumph over you.'

'I never believed I was in competition with Guy. I loved you for your own sake.'

'Guy sees things differently. You still haven't answered *my* question. You did not ride all the way from Calais to question me about my marriage.'

He had meant to unsettle her, but it was he who was losing his detachment. He stood unmoving for a moment, controlling his emotions. When he spoke again his voice was level and calm. 'Your husband is conspiring with John of Hainault and others to overthrow the thrones of England and France. This much we know. What are their intentions towards the empire?'

'Guy does not discuss his affairs with me.'

'I find that a little hard to believe. The Count of Béthune is a middling nobleman from the western marches of the Empire. Like his late brother, his sympathies are more French than imperial. How did he suddenly rise to high places and become a councillor of the King of the Romans? I doubt if his intelligence brought him to those heights, and it certainly wasn't his charm and sparkling wit.'

Her fists clenched again. 'I used my influence on his behalf, of course. Charles is my brother. Even though I am a bastard, he has always been fond of me.'

'Who asked you to do this? Hainault?'

'Guy asked me. I did it for him.'

'And King Charles gave Guy a position in his household as a favour to you?'

'Yes.'

Now he could feel the force radiating from her, like she was physically repelling an attack. *She wants rid of me.*

'I find that hard to believe,' Merrivale repeated. 'Charles doesn't trust Guy, and he certainly doesn't like him. Did you know your brother wanted you to marry someone else? Who was it, I wonder?'

She flinched as if he had slapped her, but said nothing. Merrivale closed his eyes for a moment, then opened them again. 'In Scotland, you told me that your husband and John of Hainault were close,' he said. 'Are you certain Hainault didn't ask you to intercede for your brother? Or did he discuss it with Guy?'

'I have no idea what he and Guy talked about. I told you, I don't like Hainault.'

'Did an Englishman ever join them? Someone from King Edward's court?'

'I have no idea who you mean.'

'You are not telling the truth,' he said. 'You know who this Englishman is. Tell me his name.'

They stared at each other. 'I am so sorry, Simon,' she said quietly. 'Sorry for everything that has happened between us.'

'Are you? Do you wish we had never met?'

'Yes,' she said. 'I do wish that.'

He felt the pulse of danger in the air, and his nerves began to tingle. It was too late now. Whatever was about to happen would happen. 'Why did you come to see me in Scotland? Did Guy send you?'

Her eyes were dark and blank. 'Do you doubt me, Simon?'

'I don't know. You said in Scotland that you would run away with me. Will you run with me now? The way is clear; we could be safe in Flanders in a few hours.'

'No,' she said abruptly. 'Things have changed since we last met. Now, I know where my place is.'

'Yes,' said Guy of Béthune. 'She does.'

–

Concentrating on Yolande, he had missed the sound of footsteps behind him. He turned to see Béthune facing him, armoured and covered in dust from hard riding. More men-at-arms entered the hall, fanning out to surround Merrivale.

'She knows her place,' Béthune said, walking forward. 'And now, you upstart peasant, I shall teach your yours.'

Merrivale held up a hand. 'A moment, my lord. I am a herald on a mission from King Edward. You may not impede me.'

'You lying bastard. I know exactly why you are here.' Béthune motioned to his men. 'Take that ridiculous garment away from him.'

Twelve men with swords surrounded him. Unarmed and alone, Merrivale made no resistance. Two men gripped his arms and a third hauled the heavy tabard over his head and threw it on the floor. Béthune stopped in front of Merrivale. 'You know what happens now,' he said.

'Killing me will not change the past.'

'No. But it will make the present much more enjoyable.' Béthune's fist did not travel far, but it hit Merrivale in the midriff like an iron bar. He had tensed his muscles, expecting the blow, but he still doubled up, unable to think or see or do anything except gag and gasp for breath.

The next blow hit him in the groin, sending sheets of agony flooding through his body. The men holding his arms let go and he sank to his knees. Béthune let him recover a little and then kicked him hard, twice, knocking him onto his back. Through a mist of pain Merrivale saw Béthune's face looking down at him, gloating. 'Splendid,' the count said. 'Come closer, my lady. Come and look. Does my beating him excite you? Does it inflame your passions? By God, I tell you it inflames mine.'

Béthune's boot slammed into the side of Merrivale's head. Stunned and unable to move, he lay listening to Yolande's voice cold with indifference. 'Do as you wish with him. He means nothing to me. He never did.'

'Really?' said Béthune. 'Well, in that case he is no damned use to anyone,' and he motioned with his hand.

The other men closed in. Merrivale covered his head with his hands as best he could and lay prone while their boots hammered into his body. After a while he could no longer feel the individual blows, just a red sheet of pain which continued even after they stopped. Dimly, he heard Béthune's voice again.

'Take him to the oubliette, and manacle him. See that he gets water, a little, but nothing else. Let us see how long he lasts.'

–

They dragged him out into the courtyard and down the steps into the oubliette. Rough hands hauled him upright and clamped manacles around his wrists and ankles, fixing him to the stone wall. Then they left him; he heard boots rasping on the stairs, and the slamming of a door overhead.

At first he could think of nothing but the pain. Eventually he managed to raise his head and look up to see a small high window. Outside, daylight was fading. He wondered how long Warin would wait, and whether the groom would make it back to Calais. He wondered what Tiphaine would think when Warin returned alone.

A fresh wave of pain washed over him and he lapsed into semi-consciousness.

Some time later he heard the door at the top of the stairs open. The light was going fast now, and at first he could barely see the figure coming down the stairs. The figure came closer, and he saw it was Yolande.

She stopped in front of him, so close that even through the pain he could smell the scent of her body. He ran his tongue along his lips, moistening them so he could speak.

'Was it a trap all along?'

In reply, she slid the neck of her gown down over one shoulder and withdrew her arm. In the dim light he could see the bruises dark on her skin. 'There are more like these, elsewhere,' she said. 'Do you want to see them?'

Merrivale said nothing. 'If I betrayed you, this is my fee,' she said, pulling up her gown again.

'Is that what you came to tell me?'

'I can try to get word to your camp at Calais. Maybe your men can rescue you. Or at least register a protest at the arrest of a herald.'

'By the time anyone arrives from Calais, I shall be dead.' He regarded her, wondering why she was here. The bruises were genuine, at least.

She stood in front of him, swaying a little, and he realised she too must be in pain. 'Is there nothing I can do?'

'Tell me the Englishman's name,' he said. 'I must know.'

'No,' she said sharply. 'I don't care if they hurt me, but I do care if they hurt our son.'

She turned to go. 'Yolande,' he said quietly.

It was the first time he had spoken her name. Shocked, she turned and looked at him. 'What is it?'

'Did Guy beat you in Scotland, after you came to see me?'

She stared at him for a moment, then turned and walked away towards the stair. A moment later he heard the door open and close. Night fell, and utter darkness descended in the cell.

8

'Jean Marant is a pirate captain,' Tiphaine said. 'One of the very best. When people talk of pirates in the Narrow Sea, his is the first name they mention.'

'When you say pirate captain, don't you just mean captain?' Mauro asked. 'In my experience, any mariner will turn pirate, given the chance.'

He and Tiphaine were both dressed in rough cloaks over brown tunics and hose with scuffed boots. Cloaked and hooded, she could easily pass for a boy; no one in the street gave her a second glance.

'Yes, but Marant is a true fighting sailor,' Tiphaine said. 'He was one of the few to escape the destruction of the French fleet at Sluys. If anyone can get us into Calais, he can.'

Rain swept in off the sea, hanging in pale sheets around the castle on its hill. Cobbled streets lined with stone houses ran down to a harbour crammed with ships, North Sea cogs with clinker hulls, roundships with huge red sails furled along their yardarms, long lean galleys with high-beaked prows, whalers with racks of harpoons and ballistas mounted in the bows. The air around the harbour stank of fish and blubber. Some of the houses had whalebones framing their doors like ceremonial arches.

Near the waterfront they found a tavern, its façade covered in carved whalebone plates all bleached and cracked by the weather. Tiphaine pointed. 'This must be the place.'

A beggar, a man with no legs huddled in a doorway trying to keep out of the rain, had told them Marant could usually found at the *tavern of the dead whales*. Mauro had given him some coins and the man had pocketed them and lapsed back into his misery, paying them no further attention.

Mauro pushed open the door and entered the tavern, Tiphaine following him. The room was nearly empty apart from a man sitting in a high-backed chair near the fire, wine cup in hand. Tiphaine glanced at him for a moment, then looked away. Two more men were perched on wooden stools behind him; they had been dozing, but they came alert when strangers entered the room. Both had knives at their belts.

A fourth man stood leaning on the counter, staring at the newcomers. 'What do you want?'

'A warm, friendly welcome would be nice,' Tiphaine said. She threw her hood back and stood in the middle of the room, hands planted on her hips. 'And when you are done with that, you can tell me where to find Jean Marant.'

The two men on the stools stood up. 'Who is looking for him?' asked one.

'The daughter of the seigneur de la Roche Tesson,' Tiphaine said. 'He will remember my father, if not me.'

After a long pause, the man sitting by the fire slowly turned his head. 'Come here,' he said.

Tiphaine walked over and stood in front of him. She saw a strong mouth and vivid pale green eyes, sharp and keen under bushy eyebrows. The history of his long years at sea was etched in tiny lines into his face. One cheek bore a deep hollow scar, the relic of an old arrow wound. 'Jean de la Roche Tesson,' the man said. 'Yes, I remember him well. He talked me into joining his rebellion. He nearly got me killed.'

'He got a lot of people killed,' Tiphaine said. 'Himself included. You were lucky. I did not think it would be so easy to find you, captain.'

Marant gestured around the tavern. 'This is my home, when I am not at sea.' He studied Tiphaine's face, frowning. 'I think I do remember you. We met at your father's house.'

'Christmas of '42,' Tiphaine said. 'I was home from the convent, and you had just returned from Brittany where you fought at the River Penfeld. You met my father and his confederates and agreed to raise ships to support their rebellion.'

'Yes. Afterwards, I had to pay a lot of money for a pardon. Joining your father was not my worst mistake, but it was a mistake nonetheless.'

'Really? What was your worst mistake?'

His green eyes flickered a little. 'I haven't made it yet. Why are you here, dressed in this fashion, and who is this fellow with you?'

'He is my servant,' Tiphaine said. 'We need to get into Calais. Will you take us?'

Marant looked at Mauro standing silent in the firelight. 'Can you pay?'

'Of course. But I imagine you charge more to bring people out of Calais than you do to take them in.'

A smile flitted around the captain's lips. 'Oh, yes. I remember you were a pert child.'

'I wasn't a child,' Tiphaine said.

'No, I don't suppose you were. What is your business in Calais?'

'I am looking for someone. A man called Maninghem.'

'Andrieu Maninghem? The merchant? What do you want with him?'

'My father's business,' said Tiphaine.

'You still desire to raise rebellion? You don't have a hope. Normandy is under King Philippe's thumb now.'

'In July I buried my father's skull,' Tiphaine said. 'It was all I could find of him. I want revenge, captain. Surely you must understand that.'

'I served your father as a mercenary, for pay.' Marant drained his wine cup and held it out. One of his men took it to the counter, refilled it and brought it back again. 'But, yes,' the captain said. 'I understand revenge.'

He took another drink of wine. 'I liked your father. He was a man of principle, with all the good and bad that entails. We sail tomorrow with the tide. Be at the harbour just after lauds. My ship is called *La Charyté*.'

'And for your charity, I am grateful,' Tiphaine said. 'Thank you, captain.'

Marant smiled again. 'Don't thank me yet. This venture might turn out to be my worst mistake.'

Paris, 5th of December, 1346

The bells rang vespers, and the clerks in the Chambre des Comptes rose from their desks. The two Knights of Saint John, talking at the far end of the room, ignored them as usual. The tall woman moved around the room, collecting finished reports.

Bessancourt and Massy walked out past the jewelled glass windows of Sainte-Chapelle, crossed Rue Saint-Bartélemi and went into a wineshop. They were regular customers here; the landlord nodded in greeting as they entered and poured two cups of wine, and the two clerks carried them over to a table in the corner and sat down. Massy looked at his friend. 'Who do you think is doing it?' he asked.

'Doing what?' asked Bessancourt.

'The counterfeiting. Is it the English?'

'You're still thinking about that?'

'I can't stop thinking about it. It's bad news, Hugo. That seneschal was right. When people stop trusting their money, that usually means trouble. And on top of the attempt to kill the king...' Massy shook his head. 'Have you heard the latest?'

'You're the one who listens to gossip, Estienne, not me.'

'This isn't gossip, brother, this is truth. The king's ministers are going to debase the coinage again.'

Bessancourt stared at him. 'Oh, Christ, not again! The coins are already so clipped and filed and full of base metal they're practically worthless. What in God's name are they going to do now? How do you debase shit?'

'Trust our officials, Hugo. They will find a way.'

They drained their wine cups, paid the reckoning and walked out into the street. Stars peeped through the broken clouds overhead; it was going to be a cold night. They started across the Pont Saint-Michel heading for their lodgings on the left bank. A beggar crouched against the wall of one of the houses that lined the bridge, a bandage covering his eyes and a weeping sore on his cheek. He held out his hand in supplication as they approached. 'I am a poor pilgrim, travelling in a perilous land,' he said. 'In God's name I am weary, and I seek shelter.'

Bessancourt looked at the man. He did not look much like a pilgrim; there were no badges from pilgrimage shrines on his coat or hat. Massy reached into his purse and pulled out a half-obol, dropping it into the beggar's hand, and a dagger flew out of the shadows along the bridge and hit Massy in the chest, burying itself up to the cross guards. He took a step back, looking down as the blood began to flow, and sagged to his knees. Bessancourt started towards him, and then saw the dark shapes coming towards him like wraiths. One raised his arm, and there was a dim flash of lamplight on steel.

Bessancourt ducked just in time and the knife flew over his head. Massy fell forward onto his face, blood pouring from his mouth. A voice in Bessancourt's head screamed at him *run, you fool!* and he fled across the bridge, hearing his pursuers behind him. Something flew through the air, just missing his shoulder. He reached the far end of the bridge and ran on into a maze of narrow streets and ruelles, twisting and turning, trying to throw off his attackers. Once he thought he had done so, and he sank to his knees gasping for air. The watch should be patrolling these streets, but of course the fucking watch were never there when you needed them. And there was the pounding of boots again, echoing in the street behind; he staggered up and ran on.

A church loomed up ahead, high walls beyond it; the convent of the Carmelites. It was possible to climb the wall; he remembered this from his student days, when breaking into the convent and stealing wine from the nuns' cellar had seemed like an innocent pastime. Legs aching, lungs burning, he jumped and managed to catch the upper edge of the wall with his fingertips. His boots scrabbled for purchase, and then he heaved himself up and over, tumbling down into the convent garden just as his pursuers ran past. Bessancourt lay still, listening until the sound of their footsteps disappeared.

It was a few minutes before he could move. He lay still, chest heaving as he sucked in cold air, seeing again the dagger in Massy's chest and the blood running from his mouth as he fell. Shocked and horrified, he still could not understand what had happened. Massy's death was not just a random killing in the street. This was a deliberate ambush, set by men who wanted them both dead. But why would anyone want to kill Massy, or himself? They were two junior accounts clerks in an obscure office of government, men of absolutely no importance.

He couldn't stay here; sooner or later his pursuers would realise they had lost him and begin searching the district. He stood up, still feeling shaky. His arms and legs were weak and he had to jump several times to reach the top of the wall and drag himself over. Letting go, he fell heavily into the street, wrenching his knee. He dragged himself upright, and then fought back a scream. A tall dark figure was standing in the street, only a few feet away.

Bessancourt backed against the wall, wishing desperately he had some way of defending himself. The dark figure advanced deliberately towards him. 'Please don't kill me,' he said. 'I have done nothing wrong.'

'I'm afraid you have.' Through a daze of fear he realised it was a woman's voice speaking. 'You probably don't realise it, but you have, you and your friend.'

'What have we done?'

'Seen something you shouldn't have seen.' She was speaking in French, but he could detect an accent, sibilant but with hard consonants. 'Come with me.'

'Where… Where are you taking me?'

'Somewhere safe. You cannot go back to your lodgings, they will be waiting for you. Come, quickly, before they return.'

There was a tone of authority in her voice that could not be denied. He followed her, noticing through his daze how she moved almost silently through the cobbled streets and trying to do the same. A dog barked and she held up her hand and stopped, listening to the night, but all was silent around them. She motioned again and they moved on.

Up ahead was another bridge, the Petit-Pont, and he heard the creak and splash of mill wheels on the riverbank. Quietly she walked to one of the mills, opened a door and led the way inside, closing the door behind them. He heard the rasp of flint on steel; sparks flashed and a spill began to glow. She lit a small rushlight and he saw her face for the first time, thin with a long nose and wrinkles at the corners of her eyes. 'There,' she said. 'We are safe here, at least for a little while.'

'Who are you?'

'All in good time. Tell me what happened this evening.'

'We stopped to give money to a beggar. Except I don't think he was a beggar. He claimed to be some sort of pilgrim.'

Her face was very still. 'What did he say?'

Bessancourt tried to remember. 'Something about being weary and needing shelter, I think.'

'I am a poor pilgrim, travelling in a perilous land,' she said softly. 'In God's name I am weary, and I seek shelter.'

'Yes. That was it.'

'My young friend, you are in grave danger, more than you can possibly realise. Tell me about the letter you read.'

'Is this why…?'

'Yes. Tell me what you know.'

Bessancourt swallowed. 'The seneschal of Picardy reports that much of the money in circulation is false coin. I remember thinking it was odd that this was happening, especially at the same time as reports from tax gatherers don't match the returns coming into the Treasury. And the government plans to debase the coinage again. On their own, none of these things is unusual, fraud happens all the time. But all three happening at once...' His voice trailed off.

'All three happening at once is a plot,' she said. 'You are right, of course.'

Bessancourt thought about the two Knights of Saint John in the Chambre. 'Do you think the Knights found out about the letter?'

'Yes. It took them a while, or you and your friend would have been dead even sooner. They will still be hunting for you. You must get out of Paris, as quickly as possible.'

He swallowed again. 'Where will I go?'

'You have two choices,' she said. 'You can go home, back to your own village, and hide there. The Knights and the Pilgrims *might* not look for you there, although you can never be sure. Or you can come with me, and perhaps avenge the death of your friend.'

'Where are you going?'

'Picardy,' she said. 'I am going to find the seneschal and try to discover who the counterfeiters are.'

There was a long silence. 'Who *are* you?' he asked again.

'My name is Sister Adela Seton, and I am a *consorore* of the Order of Saint John.' She saw the sudden fear in his eyes and held up a hand. 'My commandery is not part of the conspiracy. We are fighting against it.'

'Conspiracy?'

'I will explain on the way to Picardy. If you are coming with me?'

Bessancourt looked for a moment at the candle flame. 'I keep thinking about my friend,' he said. 'I keep seeing the blood on his face.'

'I am sorry, but your friend is dead. Nothing will bring him back.' She paused for a few moments. 'How long have you known him?'

'Not long. We've been working together for a few months. We used to go drinking together... But I still can't believe he is gone.'

'You must put him out of your mind, if you can. Your task now is to stay alive. You cannot return here and you should not go home. Will you come with me?'

'Why not?' he said finally. 'As you say, I have nowhere else to go. And who knows? Perhaps I might be able to do something useful.'

Adela smiled a little. 'I am counting on it,' she said.

The master will go too far one day, Mauro often grumbled, and this time it looked like he had. Waiting as twilight fell over the fields and marshes, Warin wished fervently he had Mauro with him. And the *demoiselle*, too. She was only a young woman, but she had a good head on her shoulders and was handy when things got warm. But they were not here, and he had to do this on his own.

He considered the options. He could go to Béthune himself, try and talk his way into the town and attempt to find his master, but he had never been to Béthune and had no idea where to start looking. The nearest Flemish garrison was at Cassel, twenty miles away; he could ride there and try to persuade the captain to send a rescue party. But he did not know how many men were at Cassel, or whether they would believe his story. Similarly he could return to Calais and report what had happened; the king would probably send a large force to demand his herald's return, but Calais was several days away and by the time the army arrived it might well be too late.

There was another possibility. The herald's old friend Brother Geoffrey was in eastern Artois, stirring up revolt. Warin had a fair idea of the geography of the region and knew the county of Béthune adjoined that of Artois. The county seat of Artois was the town of Arras, which should be somewhere to the south-east, not too far away.

Full night had fallen. A light twinkled like a star just above the horizon, the lantern on the belfry in Béthune. In the distance a wolf howled, long and lonely in the night. Warin's horse stirred uneasily, and he patted the mare's neck. He was a Dartmoor man, born and raised in a remote mining village; he knew the habits of wolves. Mostly they kept away from people, except when they were hungry. The problem was, you never knew when they were hungry; at least, not until it was too late.

Mounting his horse, he looked up at the sky. A dim moonlight, diffused through the clouds, showed him the ground close to hand. He had found his way across Dartmoor in nights darker than this, and he had the lantern in the belfry for a point of reference. Slowly he picked his way along the edge of the marsh, steadying the mare when her hooves sank hock-deep into the mud, steering a fine line between getting too far into the bogs and too close to the walls of Béthune, listening for the clink of harness or thud of hoof that might indicate a French patrol was nearby.

He heard nothing. Gradually the light on the belfry passed away to his right. Once it was behind him, Warin turned his horse southeast onto higher, dryer ground. This was champion country, open fields without walls or hedgerows, and the only obstacles were occasional groves of trees that loomed up out of the darkness. A wolf howled again, nearer now. Another joined in, eerie cries echoing and harmonising in the night. The mare whinnied, and again Warin stilled her with his hand.

The air grew bitterly cold. Even wrapped in his cloak, he could not stop his teeth from chattering. The clouds began to break and he saw stars now, hard and bright, and the full moon dipping into the west. He passed a small hamlet, a huddle of dark huts and byres, and heard the restless shift of cattle and smelled the smoke of dead fires. The wolves howled, again and again, but he was no longer worried about the wolves. The greatest danger now was his fellow men.

An icy breeze ruffled the dead leaves on the ground. The horse stumbled, and he could feel it was growing tired. Sliding out of the saddle, he took the reins and walked forward across fields coarse with last year's stubble and crisp with frost. Ahead lay another grove of trees. A wolf howled, startlingly close, and the mare reared up, whinnying with fright. Warin dragged on the reins, pulling her down again, and he was still trying to steady the horse when dark figures swarmed out of the trees and knocked him unconscious.

Boulogne, 6th of December, 1346

In the dim morning a coracle took them out to *La Charyté*, a sleek cog moored in the river estuary. Her crew were loading the last of her cargo, barrels of flour and salt beef, from a barge moored alongside. There seemed to be a lot of men on board for a provision ship, and Tiphaine saw harpoons and crossbows hanging on hooks and further forward a big ballista mounted on the deck with a rack of iron bolts beside it. The ship smelled heavily of whale oil and there were bloodstains on the deck.

'Welcome aboard,' said Marant. 'My apologies for the smell. When there are no English ships to plunder, we go whaling. To be honest, whaling pays better than piracy these days.'

'Then why be a pirate?' Tiphaine asked.

Marant's eyebrows raised. 'Why be a rebel? If you go to the forward deck, you will be out of the way.'

'How long will it take us to get to Calais?'

'If the wind holds fair, about four hours. It'll veer to the north later, though, and if it does before we make port we could be out here most of the day.'

'What about the English?' asked Mauro.

'If they spot us we'll fight.' Marant gestured to the men around him. 'Or if the numbers are against us, we'll run. *La Charyté* is faster than any English ship.'

Tiphaine stood beside Mauro, wondering if this was madness and she was taking Mauro and herself to their deaths. *Too late now*, she thought philosophically. The anchor was raised and the ship began to move with the tide, drifting towards the harbour mouth. The big rectangular sail was unfurled and sheeted home; two men leaned on the tiller, turning the ship as it passed the bar. The wind filled the sail and *La Charyté* began to pick up speed, rolling heavily as she met the waves coming in from the beam. Tiphaine staggered a little and gripped the rail for support.

North from Boulogne the cliffs rose steeply from the water's edge, running out to the great promontory of Gris-Nez. She watched waves crashing against the foot of the cliffs, exploding in sheets of spray. The sailors were talking as they worked the ship, and she found she could understand them without difficulty; their Picard dialect was not unlike her own Norman French, even if some of the words were unfamiliar. They were talking about Calais and the progress of the siege, and the vulnerability of the English supply ships coming into Gravelines. Marant had already captured several of these, she heard, and they were looking forward to taking more. The crews of the ships they captured had been thrown overboard, and watching the English drown had apparently been a source of much entertainment. Tiphaine glanced at Mauro, and looked away again.

The wind was blowing harder, the waves increasing in force. Sheets of spray flew across the deck. Gris-Nez was on the beam now and the sailors hauled on the tiller again, turning the ship north-east to parallel the coast. Someone shouted, pointing out to sea. For a moment Tiphaine could see nothing, and then the ship lifted on a wave and she saw two red sails emerging out of the mist a mile away.

'English?' asked Mauro.

'Yes,' said the captain. 'And they have the wind advantage. We'll have to fight.' He turned to his men. 'Break out the weapons, and man the ballista.'

Men ran across the slippery, sloping deck handing out crossbows and bundles of quarrels. Others wound back the arm of the ballista and nocked a heavy iron bolt. Tiphaine could see the other ships clearly now, big cogs with fighting castles on the bow and stern, ships fitted out for war. *La Charyté* was moving fast through the water; Gris-Nez was already falling behind and there were more cliffs ahead, which she realised must be the heights above Sangatte. Calais was only a few miles away. But the English ships would intercept them before they reached port.

One of the English cogs was closing in quickly, coming in at an angle from the left; the other vessel was perhaps a quarter of a mile behind. She saw the pale faces of men on the first ship's deck and in the fighting castles, and the sudden ripple of motion as they raised their longbows. 'Get down!' shouted Marant, and they crouched behind the railing as the first arrows thumped into the deck and hull. The wind and the rolling of the two ships meant that most of the arrows flew wide, but one of the men at the ballista went down with a shaft in his leg. Another jumped to take his place. The ballista went off with a heavy thump and the iron bolt streaked through the air, embedding itself in the forward fighting castle of the English ship. Men lay on the deck with crossbows, aiming at the English archers as the horizon rose and fell. More arrows flew back, embedding themselves in the deck like a hedgehog's spines.

Marant was beside the ballista, aiming it himself, stepping back and nodding to its crew to shoot. The second bolt splashed into the sea. 'Wait for the upward roll, you fools!' Marant snapped. 'You're not shooting whales now.'

The crew wound the arm back and fitted another bolt. More arrows hissed in the air around them. Ignoring them, Marant aimed the ballista and crouched, hand on the trigger himself this time. The ship rolled with the waves and he shot, the bolt flying high. At first it seemed he had missed entirely, but then the yardarm of the English ship twisted around and fell, dragging the great sail with it. *La Charyté*'s crew roared with delight as the other ship slewed around broadside to the waves, out of control.

The English crew were desperately trying to hoist the sail again, while wind and waves pushed them towards the cliffs. No more arrows came from her deck. The enemy ship passed within a hundred yards of *La Charyté*'s stern, the French crew watching in silence.

'Is there anything we can do to help them?' Tiphaine asked.

One of the ballista crew looked at her. 'Why would we help them?'

Spinning helplessly on the waves, the English ship entered the white surf. They saw her capsize as she struck the rocks, and another wave lifted the hull and smashed it against the cliffs. When the surf receded there was nothing to be seen but a jumble of broken timbers and cordage, and the remnants of one of the fighting castles still drifting in the white foam. 'God rest their souls,' someone said.

'They're English,' the first sailor said, and he spat over the rail into the sea. 'They don't have souls.'

The second cog, slower than the first, was falling away astern. In silence *La Charyté* continued on her way. Up ahead, the towers of Calais began to emerge out of the sea mist.

9

'Your Grace raises an excellent point,' Brother Geoffrey of Maldon said thoughtfully. 'Is virtue a single thing, a unified concept that permeates the entire cosmos? Do we reach out to take hold of virtue when we need it, rather like going to draw water from a well? Or, do we each have our own virtue, unique to ourselves, separate and distinct from the virtue of any other person? Is virtue one thing, or many?'

'It is many things, of course,' said Archbishop Balduin. His down-turned mouth looked more sour than ever. 'Each of us has our own virtue, and the virtue of each is subtly different. Which is probably why there are so many quarrels in the world,' he added.

'But surely we all know what virtue is,' objected Zajíc. 'A thing, or an action, is either virtuous or it is not. Everyone knows the difference between right and wrong.'

'Really?' said the archbishop. 'Do you actually believe that, herald?'

Zajíc thought for a moment. 'No, perhaps not,' he admitted.

'Look.' The archbishop pointed to a rabbit roasting on a spit over a little charcoal fire. 'Is that rabbit an individual rabbit in its own right, or is it part of some greater entity called Rabbit, infinitely divisible into a multiplicity of other rabbits?'

'Once we have eaten it, it will be neither,' Poděbrady pointed out.

Balduin waved a hand in irritation. 'You're all missing the point. Philosophical realism is a waste of time. Why do we have to postulate these ridiculous universal concepts? It's completely unnecessary. A rabbit is a rabbit is a rabbit, and there's an end to it.'

They were in a roofless house in the centre of Lens, surrounded by a wilderness of ruins. Once a prosperous weaving town, Lens had been devastated in another Flemish revolt forty years ago, its population killed or driven out. No one had the time or money to rebuild it, and now the remains of the town were subsiding back into the ground. Thickets of brambles swarmed over the ruined walls of buildings; wild boar roamed in the overgrown marketplace and young oak trees grew in the nave of the church. Brother Geoffrey and the leaders of the Artois rebels had made their headquarters here, fanning out to raise revolt across the rest of the county.

'But the herald has a point,' Brother Geoffrey said. 'There is a common view of virtue. Most of us, most of the time, do share a view of what virtue is. Society would be impossible if we did not.'

The archbishop nodded. 'That is exactly my point. Virtue is not a universal concept; it is something we create in our own minds. We choose to live together in communities, united by the love of God, and we agree on a common definition of virtue so as to enable us to live in peace and harmony.'

The rabbit sizzled a little. 'What about God?' asked Poděbrady. 'I thought He created virtue.'

Balduin looked even more impatient. 'God created the law, which is not the same thing at all. Having created the law, He then gave us the desire to love Him and obey. It is because of this love that we choose to live virtuous lives. We derive our understanding of virtue in part from our own minds and hearts, and in part from the wise teachings of others, and thus we learn to live in accordance with the will of God. Virtue is a desire, an understanding in our minds, nothing more. It has no real existence.'

Geoffrey smiled. 'Aristotle would not agree with you.'

'Well, Aristotle wasn't right about everything, was he?' Archbishop Balduin crossed his arms over his chest with the satisfied air of a man who has won an argument. 'Where did you study, Geoffrey?'

'At Paris. It seems like a very long time ago.'

'Paris, eh? Not so long ago as me, I'll be bound.'

'Who were your masters?'

'Godfrey of Fontaines, mostly. I listened to some of Meister Eckhart's lectures, too, about the nature of transcendental being, and the one, the true and the good. Didn't understand a damned word. What about you?'

'Peter Auriol, among others. Buridan was just coming to prominence, too. I was fortunate to study with him for a while.'

'Buridan? You *were* fortunate. I'd love to hear him speak. Is it true he once threw a shoe at the pope?'

'I was there when he did it.' Geoffrey cleared his throat. 'I fear it may have been me who put the idea into his head.'

Zajíc looked shocked, but the archbishop barked with sudden laughter. 'Serves the pope right. Pompous French prick. Damn it, Geoffrey; I bitterly resent you for kidnapping me, but otherwise I quite like you.'

Geoffrey smiled again. 'I believe this is not the first time your Grace has found yourself in this position.'

Poděbrady looked blank. 'It was about twenty years ago,' Geoffrey explained. 'Countess Loretta of Sponheim ambushed his Grace's ship and took him prisoner. It was an amicable captivity, I believe. You gave her every concession she demanded, and even guaranteed a loan for her, so she could build a new castle.'

'I had been wrong about her,' Balduin acknowledged. 'She had a fair complaint, and had been badly treated. She deserved recompense. After a while, I came around to her point of view.'

There was a little pause. 'This is where you ask if I have come around to *your* point of view,' said the archbishop.

'We have only held you for a day and a half,' Geoffrey said. 'It would be rather sudden.' He looked at Zajíc, who was watching the archbishop closely. 'What is Your Grace suggesting?'

'You are, obviously, an agent of England. Do you know the English herald, Merrivale?'

'I know him very well.'

Balduin glanced at Poděbrady. 'Are you aware of the purpose of our embassy?'

'According to public report, to mediate the conflict between England and France and bring about a lasting peace.'

'That is not the real reason,' said Balduin.

'I did not for a moment think it was,' said Geoffrey. 'May I know the real reason?'

Balduin hesitated.

'The king's orders were to tell no one except Merrivale,' Zajíc said.

'I know. My nephew is not always as clever as he thinks he is. Tell the brother what you told Merrivale.'

There was a long silence. Zajíc studied Brother Geoffrey. 'I remember you from Savoy,' he said.

'And I recollect you also. You were an honourable opponent. More so than your late master, God rest his soul.'

'King Jean believed in victory by any means,' Zajíc said. 'Your discussion about virtue would not have meant much to him. A couple of years ago, after he returned from Prussia, the king became involved in a conspiracy that he hoped would enrich him, and give him an empire.'

'I am aware,' Geoffrey said quietly.

'Now the conspirators are pressing King Charles to follow in his father's footsteps and join them. With their support, they say, he can take control of the Holy Roman Empire. But Charles does not trust them.'

'How wise of him. Go on.'

'On King Charles's instructions, I went to see Merrivale in hopes of opening negotiations with Edward of England. If the English will back him, Charles no longer needs the conspirators and can turn his back on them. But Merrivale was suspicious of me.'

'You can't really blame him for that,' Geoffrey pointed out. 'Not after what happened in Savoy.'

'No,' Zajíc said bleakly. 'I wish things had turned out differently there.'

'So do I, but perhaps not for the same reasons. What do you want from me? To intercede with Merrivale?'

'Bluntly, yes,' said Archbishop Balduin. 'This conspiracy is like a demon clinging to my nephew's back. We need to free him of it.'

'That could be dangerous,' Geoffrey said. 'These men do not take kindly to being thwarted.'

'We will deal with the danger. Can you persuade Merrivale to meet with our herald again?'

'I can try.' In the distance someone whistled. Geoffrey held up a hand for silence, and they heard the sound of men coming nearer. 'Brother?' said a man's voice. 'We found a stranger last night. He says he wants a word with you.'

Geoffrey stepped out of the hut, followed by the archbishop, Zajíc and Poděbrady. Two men were coming down the path through the dead weeds that choked the street, holding another man between them. This man had blood on one side of his face. 'Dear God!' Geoffrey said sharply. 'Warin! What are you doing here?'

'Hoping to find you, sir. Praise God I have at last.'

'Release him,' Brother Geoffrey said, and the men obeyed. Warin stood, swaying a little. 'Where is Simon?' Geoffrey asked.

'In Béthune, sir. He went yesterday to meet the countess. He didn't come back.'

'Are they holding him prisoner?'

'I don't know, sir. All I know is that he didn't return, or send any message. So I came to find you, hoping you could help.'

Zajíc was indignant. 'For Christ's sake, Merrivale is a herald! They can't kill him, or detain him! It is against the rules of war!'

'Someone forgot to tell them in Béthune,' Geoffrey said. He nodded to his men. 'See this man's wounds are tended and give him food and a place to rest. Treat him kindly, like he was your own brother.'

'Thank you, sir,' said Warin. 'But with respect, I think we need to be riding to Béthune. We may be too late already.'

Geoffrey hesitated. 'Our men are scattered all over Artois,' he said. 'And even if we bring them together, I don't think it will be enough. The entire Flemish army was repulsed at Béthune back in August. I doubt if we can succeed where they failed.'

Poděbrady's beard bristled. 'I never thought I would hear myself say this, but there is no need for fighting. We shall simply ride to Béthune and demand Merrivale be released. If he is alive, they will hand him over. If he is dead, they will give us the body.'

'Just like that?' asked Zajíc.

Brother Geoffrey nodded. 'Just like that,' he said. 'Guy of Béthune is one of King Charles's councillors, but his Grace is also on the council and my lord of Poděbrady is the king's chamberlain. Béthune's officers can hardly disobey them both.'

'And I for one will enjoy wiping the smile off Béthune's face,' said Poděbrady. 'Arrogant bastard.'

Geoffrey looked at Zajíc. 'You should come with us. By helping set Merrivale free, you may restore some of his trust in you. If he is still alive, that is.'

'If we go to Béthune,' Zajíc said, 'there will be no more talk of ransoms. His Grace and our entire party will be free to go.'

'Of course,' said Brother Geoffrey. He smiled a little. 'I have my own understanding of virtue. Rouse your men, Lord Poděbrady, and I shall send for the horses.'

'Maninghem lives in Rue Saint-Nicolas, the street next to the castle gate,' Marant said. 'I have not asked your business with him.'

'I told you,' Tiphaine said. 'This concerns my father.' She paused for a moment. 'Were those English ships waiting to intercept you?'

'Of course. They have a spy in Calais, who knew I was coming.'

La Charyté was anchored in the harbour behind the shelter of the Rysbank, and Marant was eager to offload his cargo as quickly as possible and get underway again. Tiphaine suspected he intended to go looking for the other English ship. 'A word of warning, *demoiselle*,' he said. 'You are playing with fire. Andrieu Maninghem is one of the leading men of Calais, wealthy and powerful. If you ask him to support your intended rebellion, he is likely to hand you over to the authorities, or order his men to take you outside and cut your throat. His fortune is tied to France.'

Not if Calais falls, it isn't, Tiphaine thought. A small boat took them ashore. She had half expected to be stopped and questioned when they landed, but no one paid them any attention; the men on the waterfront were more interested in the salt beef and flour Marant's crew were unloading. Those who did glance at them saw only a Moor and a boy in a ragged tunic. *La Charyté* was clearly well known in this port, Tiphaine thought.

Away from the waterfront, the red-brick houses of the town were quiet and eerily silent. Outside the walls the siege engines were at work again and the thump of stone shot could be felt as well as heard, a faint vibration in the cobbles under their feet. A cannon boomed, echoing in the empty streets. 'What do you intend to do?' Mauro asked quietly.

'Talk to Maninghem, and discover whether he really is Lord Rowton's spy.'

'What makes you think he might be?'

'According to Simon, Lord Rowton is in secret correspondence with a cousin who lives in the town. And Rowton's family name is Maninghem. I want to find out whether his lordship is telling the truth.'

Some of the houses they passed had holes punched in their roofs, and the streets were littered with broken bricks and tiles. Just as they

reached Rue Saint-Nicolas two more stones from the English trebuchets whirred through the air and smashed one after another against
the wall of a house opposite. Stone fragments cascaded around them.

At the end of the street was the gateway to the castle, a separate
moated fortification at the southern end of the town. Banners flew
over the gateway, bright red and yellow diagonal stripes; Simon, she
thought, would have known whose colours they were. A large brick
house, apparently still undamaged, stood next to the gateway. Tiphaine
took a deep breath and knocked at the gate. A few moments passed
and then a small shutter opened, revealing a window covered by a
metal grille.

'Who is there?' a harsh voice demanded.

She had revealed herself to Marant in order to get his cooperation,
knowing he had no motive to betray her. But if word of her presence in
Calais ever reached the English camp, she would very soon be dead.
She kept her voice low and her hood over her face. 'I wish to see
Andrieu de Maninghem,' she said.

'Do you have a name?'

'I am called Le Normand. My friend and I were in the service of
the Lord Harcourt. We come from the English camp.'

'Wait.' The shutter banged shut again. They waited, listening to the
slow repeated boom of the cannon. Gulls wheeled in the air over the
harbour, long mournful cries grating on their nerves.

Eventually they heard the sound of keys in the lock and the gate
opened. Two men in mail coats stood in the gateway, swords in their
hands. 'Are you armed?' demanded the one with the harsh voice.

Tiphaine and Mauro opened their damp cloaks to show they had
no weapons. The other man motioned with his sword and they walked
into the courtyard, hearing the gate close behind them. In Tiphaine's
imagination, it sounded like the closing of a prison door. She had
hoped never to hear that sound again.

In the hall a large fire burned on the hearth, roaring in the chimney
and drowning out the noise of the bombardment. Two men stood by
the fire, both dressed in black. One was in his forties, with fiery red
hair parted in the centre and falling down to his shoulders, and a gold
chain of office around his neck. He was speaking quickly, in a mixture
of North French and West Flemish, shaking his finger in the air for
emphasis.

'An entire warehouse full of provisions, ruined,' he said. 'The fish stinks and is full of maggots, the flour is wet and rotting. Yet the casks were sound when they arrived.'

'We can find more food,' the other man said calmly. He was perhaps ten years older than the red-haired man, nearly bald with a fringe of dark hair at the back of his head. Neither bore even a passing resemblance to Lord Rowton. 'The English do not control the sea. Marant can run in victuals as often as we like.'

'Yes; and how long until these too are spoiled? And there is the water. Half the wells in the town are contaminated with salt water and unusable. If food supplies are cut off we can eat our own boots, if we have to, but we cannot live without water.'

'Set up barrels to catch rainwater,' suggested the bald man. 'There are plenty of empty casks in the warehouses now. God knows there is no shortage of rain this winter.' He turned towards Mauro and Tiphaine. 'Are these the ones?'

'Yes, sir,' said the man with the harsh voice.

The bald man stared at them. His thin, wrinkled neck and prominent nose made him look like a crow. 'Who are you and what do you want?' he demanded.

'My name is Le Normand,' Tiphaine said again. She kept her voice in the low register. They would see a boy standing before them, she knew, because it would never occur to them that she might be a woman. 'My friend and I were both in Harcourt's service before he left the English army.'

'And why did you not follow Harcourt?'

'Because he ordered us to stay,' Tiphaine said, and waited.

'So, Harcourt set you to spy on the English,' the red-haired man said. His voice was full of irony. 'One moment he is England's best friend, the next he is their sworn enemy. So much for loyalty.'

'My lord of Harcourt is loyal to Normandy,' Tiphaine said. 'As I imagine you are to Calais, sir.'

'You are very forward,' the bald man said sharply. 'How do we know if any of this is true?'

'Do you think my friend and I would risk our lives getting into Calais merely for sport? If you do not wish to listen to us, we will go. There are others who will listen, I am sure.'

She turned to go. 'Wait,' the bald man said. 'How did you get here? Why are you seeking me in particular?'

So the bald one is Maninghem, Tiphaine thought. *I wonder who the one with the chain is...* 'We came by sea, from Boulogne. As for you, I heard Lord Rowton mention your name,' she said, untruthfully. 'I know his family comes from nearby. I thought you might be a kinsman.'

Maninghem stared at her for a long time, his eyes dark in the firelight. 'Lord Rowton? His family left to seek their fortune fifty years ago. They have cast their lot with England now, and they are no kin of mine. Mention his name in my presence again, and I will cut out your tongue.'

'Easy,' said the red-haired man, holding up a hand. 'You have still not told us why you are here, boy.'

Tiphaine took a step forward. Her face was still shadowed by her hood, but there was no mistaking her anger. 'I may be young and a mere page, but I am of high birth, and *you*, sir, are a merchant. Call me *boy* again at your peril.'

The red-haired man looked down for a moment, and Tiphaine thought he was stifling a smile. 'Very well,' he said, straight-faced. 'Why are you here, master page?'

'Lord Harcourt told me to make myself useful to the French cause,' Tiphaine said. 'So here I am. I have information about the English that will be useful to you. If you care to hear it, of course.'

The two men glanced at each other. 'Very well,' said Maninghem. 'Tell us what you know.'

'I overheard several men conversing with Michael Northburgh, the king's secretary. England is very short of money. There is no silver to hire ships to come and enforce a blockade of Calais, and the king's attempts to impress ships have failed. They have barely enough vessels to bring supplies over to Gravelines.'

'This is not news,' the red-haired man said dismissively. 'Is that all you have?'

'No. There will be another assault on the town, very soon, tomorrow, perhaps even tonight. They will attack the Dunkirk bastion under cover of darkness, using incendiaries.'

She had their attention now. 'How do you know this?' asked the bald man.

'I heard this from Northburgh also.' In fact she had observed the preparations in the camp herself, but she wanted to test them with some names. 'He was talking to Thomas Hatfield, the Bishop of Durham,' she added.

'This tallies with what we already know,' said the red-haired man.

'Yes, but this information is hardly worth paying for,' said Maninghem.

Tiphaine spread her hands. 'Did I say anything about payment? My lord Harcourt pays me, and I carry out his orders.'

'How very altruistic of the lord Harcourt,' Maninghem said sarcastically.

'He desires to do a service for the king of France. He wants to win back the king's favour.'

'Until he starts his next rebellion. Thank you, but no. I want no involvement with Harcourt and his schemes. You would be wise to stay clear as well, Saint-Pierre. If the governor hears we have even met this boy, we are all in trouble.'

'The governor has his own problems,' said the red-haired man, Saint-Pierre. 'But I agree, there is nothing here that our spies in the English camp are not already telling us. Very well, master page. You and your companion may go.'

Maninghem was silent. 'That's it?' Tiphaine said angrily. 'We risk our necks coming here, and all you do is turn us away? My lord Harcourt shall hear of this.'

'Tell him whatever you please,' the red-haired man said indifferently. 'And be thankful you are leaving with a whole skin. Noble blood or no, if I hear any more of your impertinence, I shall beat it out of you.'

–

Tiphaine turned on her heel and strode out of the hall, Mauro following her. Silently, the guards opened the gate and let them out. The cannon had stopped firing but there was smoke in the air and the street stank of brimstone. Tiphaine threw back her hood and let out a long breath. Mauro was puzzled. 'Did we learn anything?'

'Yes, and no,' Tiphaine said. 'They reacted when I mentioned Bishop Hatfield, but I have no idea why.'

'But not Northburgh. And Maninghem was angry when you mentioned Lord Rowton's name.'

'Yes.'

Footsteps sounded behind them and Tiphaine hastily pulled her hood forward again. 'Forgive my words earlier,' Saint-Pierre said. 'It was necessary to disguise my intentions. May I ask where you are going?'

'Back to the English camp,' Tiphaine said.

'How will you get there?'

'We will find a boat. After dark, we can row down the coast and land behind the English lines.'

'I will find you a boatman,' Saint-Pierre said. 'Be at the harbour at vespers. He will be waiting for you.'

'Thank you,' said Tiphaine. 'But why should you want to help us? We do not even know who you are.'

'My name is Eustache de Saint-Pierre, and I am the mayor of Calais. I want you to carry a message for me. To Thomas Hatfield, the Bishop of Durham.'

A tingle ran down Tiphaine's spine. 'What is the message?'

'Tell Bishop Hatfield that I want to negotiate the surrender of the town. Ask him what terms the king will give.'

'Why the bishop? Why not send word to the king himself?'

'Because I know Hatfield and I trust him,' said the mayor of Calais. 'Take this message to him, and bring me his reply. You claim to serve without thought of reward, but if you perform this service you will be rewarded, richly. You and the Moor both.'

Mauro's face was still. 'I shall carry your message,' said Tiphaine, and she bowed a little. 'It may be some time before I return.'

'Do not be too long,' said Saint-Pierre. 'Time is running out for all of us, faster than we think.'

10

The wind had veered around to the north as Marant had said it would, and the air was wet and icy cold. 'What do we do now?' Mauro asked.

'Wait until nightfall and see what happens,' Tiphaine said. The days were growing short now, and vespers would come early; they had only a couple of hours to wait. 'But first, find some food.'

The bombardment had paused for a moment, and a few people were out in the streets. A public kitchen on the corner of Rue Saint-Croix had opened; they stopped and bought a couple of meat pies and stood in the street eating them, wiping the sauce from their chins. 'They were very ready to believe you,' Mauro said.

'They wanted to believe me,' said Tiphaine. 'In fact, it felt like they were waiting for someone like me. People see what they want to see.'

Mauro looked dubious. 'What if they have second thoughts?'

Tiphaine pointed towards the harbour. 'Can you swim?'

Someone else came up to the kitchen and asked for a pie, laying a coin on the counter. He was a tall lean man wrapped in a cloak, indistinguishable from the people around them, but something about his voice caught Tiphaine's attention.

'Here you go,' said the man behind the counter, wiping his hands on his apron. 'Eat it while it's hot, brother.'

A cannon boomed in the distance. 'Sounds like everything is about to get hot again,' the cloaked man said. He raised a hand in salute, picked up his pie and walked away down the street. Tiphaine stood rigid with shock. She had not seen the other man's face, but she recognised the voice now; she had last heard it on a dark night outside Abbeville, just over three months ago. *Don't be so fastidious, King's Messenger. You've done dirty deeds yourself in your day.*

'It's Nicodemus,' she whispered to Mauro.

Mauro stared at her. 'That evil bastard? What is *he* doing here?'

'I don't know,' said Tiphaine. 'But I don't like this, Mauro. He is a vicious murdering bastard who will kill you as soon as look at you. If he finds out we are here, we're butcher's meat.'

'But what is he doing in Calais?' Mauro persisted.

'The devil only knows. We need to follow him and find out.' She threw the crust of her pie to a hungry dog crouched sorrowfully in a doorway. 'But for God's sake, be careful.'

Nicodemus was wary. He twisted and turned through the narrow streets of Calais, often looking back to see if he was being followed, seemingly unmoved by the stones whistling through the air overhead. Mauro and Tiphaine trailed him at a discreet distance, changing the lead from time to time, never looking directly at him but watching him from the corners of their eyes. Finally, just when Tiphaine had begun to think they would play this game forever, Nicodemus stopped and knocked at the door of a modest-looking house. Tiphaine strolled casually past him, not looking around, apparently absorbed in picking her teeth with one fingernail.

'Who is it?' demanded a voice behind the door.

'I am a poor pilgrim, travelling in a perilous land,' Nicodemus said. 'In God's name I am weary, and I seek shelter.'

The door opened at once. 'Welcome among us, brother,' said the man inside. 'Rest now, and give thanks to God.'

Nicodemus walked through the door, which closed behind him. Tiphaine nodded to Mauro and they found shelter in doorways at opposite ends of the street, sitting slumped like beggars and listening to the hard thump of stones against the walls and towers of the town. Perhaps half an hour elapsed before the door opened again and Nicodemus came out. He glanced once down the street and hurried away towards the harbour. They waited until he turned the corner, and rose and followed him.

This time Nicodemus did not seem concerned about any pursuit. He walked straight to the harbour without looking back. A wooden shallop was moored along the waterfront, two oars already shipped. Nicodemus climbed into the boat and cast off. As Tiphaine and Mauro watched he rowed straight across the harbour, passing *La Charyté* whose crew were raising anchor and making sail, and out towards the open sea. They saw the shallop rise and fall on the incoming waves, and then it turned past the harbour mouth and was lost to view.

'He will land somewhere behind the English lines, between here and Gravelines, and then report to the man from the north,' said Mauro.

'Yes,' said Tiphaine. 'We need to find out who lives at that house.'

Discreet inquiry at a tavern, accompanied by a couple of coins, told them the house was owned by Jehan de Nortkerque, who in peaceful times was a dealer in fish, primarily *walfisch*, or whale meat. Tiphaine considered this. Jeanne of Navarre had said that the man from the north and his friends controlled what happened in Calais, but a fishmonger was unlikely to be their chosen instrument. Nortkerque must be another link in the chain, like Nicodemus. But what about Marant, who said whaling paid better than piracy? Suddenly she longed to be back in the camp, telling Simon what she had found. He would help her make sense of it.

She sat for a while, staring into space. So many things were going on at once. Nicodemus, she had no doubt, was running messages into Calais on behalf of the man from the north. At the same time, someone was sending messages *out* of the town to Lord Rowton, and despite his protestations she had no doubt that this was Maninghem. And finally, Saint-Pierre had asked her to carry messages between himself and Hatfield, in effect helping him to betray the town. *I know Hatfield*, the mayor had said. But how?

She thought again about Nicodemus. Eight years earlier, French pirates had raided the port of Southampton and held it for several days, looting and killing. Some of the townspeople were ransomed, but the pirates had sold dozens of captured English children into slavery. Nicodemus, himself an Englishman, had acted as agent and helped arrange the sale. He was more than just an assassin. A defrocked priest, he was clever and educated. And if he was back in the game, the danger they all faced had just increased.

Mauro touched her arm. 'The bells,' he said. 'It is vespers.'

The north wind whipped the echo of church bells through the streets, distorting them into a disharmonious clangour. Another shot from a trebuchet, flying high, hissed overhead and punched through the roof of a house opposite, sending broken tiles sliding into the street. She saw flashes of light, the incendiaries the English were launching at the walls, partly to drive the enemy back and partly to give themselves light to see. She heard shouting, men yelling loud and urgent, hoarse with tension and fear. The assault had begun.

They hurried to the harbour. A stone shot landed in the water, throwing up a fountain of spray. A man stepped out of the falling shadows, pointing to another small wooden shallop moored nearby. 'That is your boat. Be careful when you reach the open sea, the waves will be steep.'

Tiphaine stared at him. 'You're the boatman. Aren't you coming with us?'

'I was told only to hire the boat.' The man turned and walked away.

'I can row,' Mauro said. He jumped down into the boat and cast off the mooring rope. Tiphaine followed him. Taking up the oars, Mauro turned the boat and began to row steadily towards the harbour mouth. Beyond the town wall the incendiaries flickered like lightning. Another stone splashed into the water, showering them with spray. Tiphaine wiped water from her face and stared at the waterfront. In the reflected glow she could see another boat casting off, and another. They were bigger, with more men at the oars.

'Change of plan,' Tiphaine said. 'Mauro, run us ashore on the Rysbank. As soon as the bottom touches ground, get over the side and run like hell.'

'Who is following us?'

'I don't know.' Maybe Nicodemus had spotted them. Perhaps Maninghem was playing them false. Perhaps Saint-Pierre was. 'But they're overtaking us. We need to get to the dunes. There is a Welsh post just beyond them.'

Orange light flared like hellfire over the roofs and spires of the town. Drums rolled like thunder, punctuated by cannon fire. The shallop passed a couple of moored fishing boats and Tiphaine felt its bow slide on mud. The other two boats were a hundred yards away and closing. They vaulted over the side and began to run. The tide was nearly full again and the Rysbank was virtually an island, a bank of sand and mud with the spit connecting it to the mainland covered in shallow water. Tiphaine and Mauro ran along the spit, gasping and splashing. Behind them, they heard the pursuing boats hit the shore.

A crossbow bolt whistled through the darkness, missing Mauro by a few inches. Looking over her shoulder, Tiphaine saw a dozen men, perhaps more, running after them with knives in their hands.

'Faster!' she screamed at Mauro, and they ran for their lives, heads down and arms pumping as they raced through the shallow water. Another crossbow bolt splashed into the mud almost at her feet.

The ground rose. They were in among the dunes now, sandbanks covered with clumps of grass. They scrambled through the night lit by flashes of fire from the town, floundering in the soft sand. Suddenly, dark shapes loomed up out of the dunes, surrounding them. One grabbed her from behind, clamping a hand over her mouth before she could scream. She bit his hand; he cursed, but held on. From behind came a sudden clatter of arms, screams and cries of pain, a short savage fight over almost before it had begun, and then men were all around her, talking quickly and excitedly in a language she could not understand. Desperate, she tore the man's hand from her mouth and screamed at them. '*Who are you?*'

Flint scraped on steel and a torch fluttered into life. 'Well, Christ strike me blind,' said a big man, clutching a bloody spear in one hand and staring at her. 'Will you look who it is, now? Do you remember me? It is Llewellyn ap Gruffyd of Conwy! We helped break you out of La Roche Guyon, remember?'

Once they knew who she and Mauro were, Llewellyn and his men were kindness itself. The man she had bitten even apologised for seizing her. 'We were trying to stay quiet,' said Llewellyn. 'One of our scouts saw men running up from the Rysbank and we thought we would set a little ambush for them. We didn't see you coming, though. Why were those fellows chasing you?'

'I don't know,' Tiphaine said. She needed, more than ever, to find Simon. 'Thank you, very much, for rescuing us.'

'Think nothing of it, *demoiselle*. It's a fine habit to be falling into.' Llewellyn looked at her, obviously wanting to ask what she and the herald's servant were doing, but not quite daring to. 'If I were you I'd be getting back to camp, *demoiselle*. Our lads are falling back from the walls now, and if the French were to try a sortie it could get a little bit exciting out here. Best you get away to safety while you can.'

The guards were reluctant, but the combination of the archbishop's episcopal robes and Zajíc's tabard eventually swayed them. The battered gates were opened and the little column of men, the archbishop's escort and some of Brother Geoffrey's rebels, rode into the town. People turned to stare at the unfamiliar coats of arms and banners. In the market square a jongleur stood before the wooden bell tower, playing a lute. Brother Geoffrey looked at him sharply. He recognised the tune, of course; Machaut's *Riches d'amour*, a popular song, but even more he recognised the precise, accurate fingering of the lute. Even though the man did not raise his head, he was recognisable as Marcelis, the lutenist who had played at the burgemeester's house in Bruges.

There was nothing to be done; the French held sway in Béthune. He rode on, wondering.

At the castle gates the men-at-arms on watch were adamant; no one was allowed to enter. 'Béthune is expecting a rescue party,' Geoffrey said quietly. 'He is afraid of a *coup de main*.'

Poděbrady was still arguing with the captain of the guards. Archbishop Balduin raised his voice. 'Summon your master!' he ordered. 'Bring him here, or I swear by the blood of Christ I will place this castle and everyone in it under a ban of excommunication! That includes you, captain! Do it now!'

Several minutes passed before a postern gate opened and Guy of Béthune stepped through. He was fully armoured with a sword at his belt. 'Your Grace,' he said, making no effort to disguise the anger in his voice. 'To what do I owe the honour?'

'You have wrongly imprisoned the herald Simon Merrivale. I command you to release him immediately.'

'*You* command? What business is this of yours?'

'You have disobeyed the wishes of King Charles. Release Merrivale now, and I will say nothing. The king need never know.'

Béthune took a step forward. 'What happens in my house is none of King Charles's business!'

'I shall be sure to tell him as much, when next I see him,' Balduin said. 'I wonder if he will agree?'

'Damn you! Béthune is my county, my lordship! The only laws that matter here are mine!'

'Wrong,' said Balduin. 'There is also God's law. Hear me, Béthune. Release Merrivale, or I will excommunicate you and your entire household. You will be outlaws in the eyes of the church, and your souls will be sent to damnation.'

Béthune rested his hands on his hips. 'Go on, then, your Grace. Do it. And I will send word to my friend Cardinal Aubert, who will intercede with the pope and the ban will be lifted. I give it a month at most.'

'Will Aubert intercede?' asked Zajíc. 'Would either the cardinal or King Charles approve of your imprisoning the herald? I believe you have acted beyond your authority, my lord.'

Béthune's face turned red, and his hand went down to his sword hilt. 'Do not draw that blade, my lord,' Poděbrady warned. 'If you do, I will kill you where you stand.'

'Rot in hell!' snapped Béthune, and he turned and strode back through the postern into the castle.

–

The pain of Merrivale's cuts and bruises had merged with the ache in his legs and arms from the manacles, and his mouth was burning with thirst. *Give him a little water*, Béthune had said, and they had; enough to moisten his lips and no more, to remind him of the taste of water and how soothing it could be. This made the torments of thirst still worse, which was of course their intention.

The room was bitterly cold, so cold he could see his own breath in the pale light. His body shivered uncontrollably, rattling his manacles. He could have coped better with the cold, and the thirst, if he was not in so much pain. Twice in the night they had woken him from his agonised sleep, hanging in chains, to beat him again; the last time, Béthune had used a whip. He had no idea how badly he was hurt, or how much blood he had lost. He heard the door open at the top of the stairs and footsteps running down, and he closed his eyes, bracing his wounded body as best he could for another onslaught.

'Sir! Wake up!'

The voice was familiar, but it took him a moment to place it. Merrivale opened his eyes to see Warin standing in front of him, a bandage around his head. Another familiar face swam into view; Zajíc, the Bohemian herald.

He ran his swollen tongue around his mouth and spoke, voice rasping. 'What is happening?'

'We are releasing you,' Zajíc said. He looked angry; the steam of his exhaled breath was like smoke. 'This should never have happened.'

Two men were already unfastening his manacles. Merrivale staggered as they came away, and Warin and Zajíc stepped forward and caught him before he fell. 'He cannot walk,' said Zajíc. 'Send for a litter.'

'No,' said Merrivale. 'I can walk.'

Using the walls for support, with Warin close behind to catch him if he fell, he hobbled slowly up the stairs. With each step, bolts of pain shot through his left leg. The courtyard was empty apart from a couple of frightened servants. 'Bring water,' Zajíc ordered. 'And find the herald's tabard.'

The servants ran to obey. Slowly, wincing in the pale light of the winter sun, Merrivale walked across the courtyard to the gate and outside. At the sight of him, face crusted with dried blood, shirt hanging in rags over his bruised and bleeding ribs, Brother Geoffrey stepped down from his saddle and hurried towards him. 'Mother of God, Simon. What did they do to you?'

'Béthune has been wanting to do this for years,' Merrivale said. 'He was trying to make up for lost time.'

They brought him water and he drank, carefully. He raised his arms and Warin lowered his tabard over his head and arranged it over his bloody shirt. Poděbrady unfastened his own cloak and draped it around his shoulders. Merrivale began slowly to realise that he was not about to die. 'What happens now?' he asked.

'We are going to Lens,' Geoffrey said. 'We'll feed you up and let you recover, and then get you back to Calais.'

Merrivale bowed to the archbishop. 'Thank you for coming to rescue me, your Grace,' he said. 'And if you are ever short of money, I would be delighted to help you secure a loan.'

Poděbrady guffawed. 'Does everyone know that damned story?' the archbishop demanded. 'Come on, everyone, get moving. Daylight won't last forever.'

The archbishop, Poděbrady and their escort turned and rode away past the belfry towards the town gates. The lutenist had gone, Geoffrey noticed. Zajíc lingered for a moment. 'This should not have happened,' he said again.

'No,' said Merrivale. 'I do not congratulate you on your choice of friends, Vilém.'

'The choice was not mine.' Zajíc was silent for a moment. 'King Jean was a good master,' he said. 'But you are right, he did not always choose his friends wisely. You asked me for a name, Simon. I can give you one.'

'The man from the north?'

'No, but his newest ally. Guillaume Machaut.'

Pain forgotten, Merrivale stared at him. '*Machaut?*'

'You know him, of course.'

'Of course. He was Jean of Bohemia's secretary, back in Savoy.'

'He was one of the men who tried to have you killed,' Brother Geoffrey said. 'And you, Vilém, were another of them.'

'That was a long time ago,' Zajíc said.

'In some ways it feels like yesterday,' Merrivale said. 'Has Machaut met the man from the north?'

'He has, although I doubt he knows his name. Machaut is spying on King Charles and his household.'

'And you aren't?'

Zajíc said nothing. 'I see,' said Merrivale. 'You think Machaut is also spying on you, and are reluctant to give me too much in case it gives the game away. But you were part of the embassy, Vilém. They must suspect you already.'

'They suspect everyone,' said Zajíc. 'Even each other.'

'And perhaps that will be their downfall.' He still did not find Zajíc likeable and he was still not sure he trusted him, but the Bohemian herald had helped to save his life. 'Go carefully, Vilém. Watch your back.'

'You too, Simon.' Abruptly, Zajíc pulled his horse around and rode away down the street, following Archbishop Balduin and his escort.

II

11

Oye, 7th of January, 1347

The waters of the marsh had frozen, a thin translucent layer of ice over the mud beneath. The church of Saint-Médard stood on a low island, surrounded by trees white with frost. Under the trees were long mounds of piled earth, the mass graves of English and Welsh soldiers who had died during the siege of Calais; sometimes by violence during the assaults on the town, mostly of cold and flux. Men brought the bodies here to Saint-Médard in the deserted hamlet of Oye, far enough from the English camp to prevent corruption spreading into the water, and dug long trenches and laid the corpses in them; when each trench was full, they covered it with earth and dug another.

A line of frozen reeds marked the line of the river Aa crawling its way through the marshes to the sea. Other islands could be seen in the distance; the burned-out castle of Saint-Folquin, the monastery of Saint-Marie, and beyond them the walls of the Flemish citadel at Bourbourg, protecting the vital port of Gravelines. Oye and its church lay in the debatable land between armies, and no one ever came here except to bury the dead.

'Which makes it an excellent place to meet,' said the man from the north. He looked at the others, four men cloaked and muffled in the cold dawn light. 'I assume you all took precautions to make sure you were not followed.'

The others nodded. 'No one in their right mind would follow anyone into this wasteland,' said Raimon Vidal. 'I preferred Hesdin.'

'You know the rule,' said John of Hainault. 'Never meet in the same place twice.'

The Englishman nodded. 'Yes. Every time we do meet, we take a chance. You are only here now to receive instructions.' He turned to another member of the group. 'Allow me to present our banker, Master William Blyth.'

Protected against the wind by a fur-trimmed cloak, Blyth bowed. If he had suffered during his rapid flight from England, or missed the wife and children he had abandoned there, he did not show it. 'It is a pleasure to meet you, gentlemen. You must tell me how I can serve you.'

'Where is the money?' demanded Guy of Béthune.

'The coin and bullion are safely in my strongroom. The bills of exchange I brought from England are proving difficult to negotiate.'

The man from the north looked at him. 'Why?'

'Someone told Oppicius Adornes about my dealings in the dark exchanges. As head of the bankers' guild of Bruges, he has taken steps to suppress the exchanges. All bills must now be negotiated through the official bourse, with records kept.'

'What can we do about this?' asked the Englishman.

'I will need to use intermediaries. I also need to shift them slowly, one at a time, so Adornes and his informers don't notice any large transactions. I won't have the money before Easter, that is certain.'

The man from the north nodded. 'Take no risks,' he said. 'Move only when it is safe to do so. We have time in hand now, and money too. We'll be ready by Easter.'

'Money?' said Béthune. 'From where?'

'The Knights of Saint John have moved more quickly than anticipated. The attempt to assassinate Philippe of France played into their hands.'

Crows cawed in the distance. 'But the attempt on the king did not succeed,' said John of Hainault. 'Nor did the attack on Philippa. At Hesdin, you said you would not fail.'

'Nor have I. Be patient, John. If one of those crossbowmen had managed to kill Philippe, well and good, but the attacks alone have added fuel to the fire. Edward of England is more suspicious than ever now, and convinced one of his inner circle is about to betray him; which, of course, they are.'

Hainault said nothing. The man from the north looked around the group again. 'Our task is simple. We keep Edward pinned at Calais, and let dysentery and low morale tear his army to pieces. We bankrupt Philippe and paralyse him, unable to raise troops, unable to move. When we are ready, we kill them both.'

Guillaume Machaut, the last member of the group, stirred a little. 'Ready for what, exactly?'

'Ready to seize power,' said the man from the north.

'In England and in France, I understand. What about the Empire? You must have some plan for it. You would not have recruited me otherwise.'

'Of course. The collapse of France will rob the pope of his only important supporter. It will be easy to replace him.' He nodded at Vidal. 'We have already suggested that Cardinal Aubert would make an excellent pope, and the cardinal agrees. That will give us a hold over the King of the Romans, whose support depends on the German clergy. He will comply with our wishes, or we will turn his supporters against him.'

He looked at Machaut, his face challenging. 'Do you agree?'

Machaut shrugged. 'You are paying me well. You can put the devil on the papal throne, for all I care.'

'Be careful what you wish for,' warned Vidal. 'You said you had instructions for us.'

'Yes. Béthune, I want you to take soundings among the German bishops. Find out which ones can be bought. For those loyal to Charles, find out who might be prepared to rebel against them. Meanwhile, make sure you wife is at Charles' court. Make sure she is seen, and noticed. Tell her to use her charms on those with power.'

Béthune stiffened but said nothing. The man from the north looked at him for a moment, and then turned to Hainault. 'Write to your niece, the Empress Margaret and tell her France is having doubts about Charles. Suggest she and her husband the emperor approach France and open negotiations.'

Hainault looked dubious. 'Do you think either side will agree?'

'They might. And even if not, it will add to the uncertainty. No one will be certain where anyone's loyalties lie. Except us. Blyth, you will receive the money from the Knights of Saint John. Be prepared to make disbursements when I send word.'

The man from the north turned to Machaut. 'I will introduce you to some musicians I know. They already admire your music, and you will enjoy their playing. You will get along well.'

'Why send them to me?'

'They are also messengers. When the time comes, they will give you my orders.'

Machaut's eyes narrowed a little. 'You asked me to be a spy, nothing more.'

'And as you pointed out, we are paying you a princely sum.' His eyes bored into the secretary's face. 'Too late to back out now,' he said.

Machaut was silent. The man from the north looked at Vidal, his eyes still hard. 'When this is over, France will need a new monarch.'

'You had one,' Vidal pointed out. 'Jeanne of Navarre. You let her slip through your fingers.'

'I wanted to find out where her loyalties lay. Now she has declared herself neutral, which is perfect for our purposes. We can destroy her at our leisure. When Cardinal Aubert becomes Pope... What regnal name will he choose, do you think?'

'He has already chosen it,' said Vidal. 'He will take the name of Innocent.'

'Pope Innocent. Well, at least we know he has a sense of humour. We need someone on the throne of France who can work with him.'

'And with King Charles,' said Machaut. 'When he becomes emperor.'

'Of course. Vidal, tell your master to start thinking of names.'

'I can give you one already,' said Vidal. 'Duke Odo of Burgundy. The king has accused him openly of disloyalty and exiled him from court. And he has taken Artois into his own hands and replaced Burgundian officials with French ones. Philippe is determined to stamp out the revolt.'

'Good. He may as well squander his remaining treasure on that cause as on anything else. Odo is a useful prospect, but tell the cardinal to keep thinking.'

'There is another possibility,' said Machaut. 'Why not offer the throne to King Charles? He could bring France and the Holy Roman Empire together, one and indivisible. With France, Germany and Italy behind him, he could unite the whole of Christian Europe, and you, my lords and gentlemen, would be the power behind his throne. He could be a new Charlemagne and bring you all unlimited power.'

The man from the north started to say something, then checked. Relaxing visibly, he put a hand on Machaut's shoulder. 'Good idea,' he said. 'I shall give it some thought.'

A gust of cold wind whipped around them. 'It is time we departed,' said the man from the north. 'Contact me in the usual way when you have news. Guy, a word before you go.'

The others mounted their horses and rode away down the causeway towards the river. Béthune turned to the Englishman. 'What is it?'

'What the hell were you thinking? We're supposed to be sending Merrivale haring around the countryside chasing false leads. Instead you beat him half to death and then lock him up.'

'I saw a chance to get rid of him, and I took it.'

'Damn you for a liar. You found out he was coming to Béthune and you couldn't stand the thought of him being with your wife. Control your emotions, Guy. Don't let jealousy get the better of you.'

Béthune glared at him. 'It will not happen again.'

'No. It won't. And Charles? The Germans are ready to play their part. Are you?'

'Of course. But we need to watch Zajíc. He may be colluding with Merrivale.'

'Let me worry about that. Do not let me down again, Guy.'

'Again? When have I failed you before?'

With surprising power, the man from the north grabbed Béthune's cloak at the throat and dragged him forward until their faces were only an inch apart. 'You failed me in Scotland,' he said, low-voiced. 'You let Brus run wild, and very nearly jeopardised our entire venture. Are you worth the prize I am about to give you?'

'Yes,' said Béthune, with an effort.

'Good. Because if I have even so much as a whisper of doubt about you, Guy, I will kill you. Remember that.'

12

It was a raw winter day, the air full of sea damp, and freezing fog filled the valley of the Somme. Even at midday it was necessary to light lamps and candles to give enough light to read by. Squinting over a parchment roll, Jean de Picquigny, the acting seneschal of Picardy, looked up in irritation as his secretary knocked and entered the office. 'What is it now?'

'There is a man to see you, my lord. He says he has been sent by the Parlement in Paris. You recall the letter you wrote about false coinage?'

'For God's sake! That was nearly two months ago.' He paused. 'Why have they taken an interest now?'

The secretary shrugged. 'Who knows? Perhaps the letter got lost, and they have only just found it. Shall I show him in?'

'Oh, very well.' Picquigny sat back in his wooden chair, running a hand through his thinning hair. The arrow wound he had taken at Crécy last summer still ached in the cold. 'Maybe we can finally get some answers.'

He had expected a grey-bearded lawyer from the Parlement in a fur-trimmed robe. Instead, his visitor was young, dressed soberly in plain dark clothing and rather nervous. *A clerk*, the seneschal thought bitterly. *God damn them, they've fobbed me off with some underling.*

The young man bowed. 'Messire de Picquigny? My name is Hugolin Bessancourt, and I am in the employ of the Chambre des Comptes. I am here at the instruction of the Parlement of Paris.'

'So I understand. What do you want?'

'You wrote a letter complaining about false money, my lord. I have been sent to investigate.'

'About damned time, too.'

'I apologise for the delay, my lord, but be assured that the Parlement takes this matter very seriously indeed. Yours is not the only complaint to have reached their ears.'

'I am sure it is not. Well?'

'My instructions are to trace the source of the false coins. Do you... Perhaps you have some examples that I could examine?'

Rising, Picquigny took out a key and opened a cupboard set into the stone wall and removed a soft leather pouch that clinked a little. Upending it, he poured out a handful of small silver coins. The young man picked up a half-obol and held it up to the light, turning it over in his hand. 'This is remarkably crude,' he said slowly. 'I had expected to see silver adulterated with some base metal, a billon coin of some sort, but this is not even that.'

'What is it then?' demanded Picquigny.

'It looks to be lead, sealed with a thin layer of silver foil and stamped. See here, the foil has already split to reveal the base metal beneath.' Bessancourt picked up several more coins and then stopped in surprise. 'This is English money.'

'Yes. A number of English pennies and half-pennies have come to light. The forgers seem to be coining our money and theirs indiscriminately.'

Bessancourt frowned. 'I don't recognise the mint mark on the French coins,' he said. 'V. DIF; it means nothing to me. Where is the nearest official mint? Rouen?'

Picquigny shook his head. 'The Knights of Saint John have received permission to establish a mint at Abbeville, just downriver from here. It has been going for several months now. The Knights have substantial reserves of silver at their commandery of Saint-Riquier, and are coining it to replenish the royal reserves.'

'That is very loyal of them,' said Bessancourt. He seemed nervous again, the seneschal thought.

'The Knights have always been good friends to us. Many of them died at Crécy,' Picquigny said sombrely.

'Yes... My lord, I think I can track down those who are making the false coin. But I may need armed assistance. Can you supply me with men?'

First the German envoys, now this upstart from Paris. 'No, I can't. Half of my men have already deserted because I have no money to pay them. I can barely defend this castle, let alone the town.'

Bessancourt frowned again. 'As seneschal, you have the power to command the men of this province to serve.'

'What men? Most Picard men-at-arms were killed at Crécy, including my predecessor in this office.' In his dreams, Picquigny still heard the deadly rattle of arrowheads striking metal armour, saw his friends and neighbours falling around him. 'And even if I did call up the survivors, how in hell would I pay them? With false coinage?'

'No, but—'

'We're hanging on by our fingernails, Bessancourt. I'm sorry, but coinage is a national concern, not a provincial one. Parlement should have provided you with whatever force you need.'

'I suspect they are in the same predicament,' Bessancourt said. He bowed. 'Thank you, my lord. You have been most helpful.'

-

A quarter of an hour later he stood in a deserted alley not far from the city's marketplace, bending over with his hands on his knees. 'God, I feel sick. If they had discovered who I really am...'

'Well, they didn't,' said Sister Adela Seton, her voice devoid of sympathy. 'What did you learn?'

Still shaking, Bessancourt told her. 'You say the forgeries are very crude,' Adela said slowly at the end. 'As if the forgers don't care that people know the coins are bad.'

Bessancourt wiped sweat from his forehead with the back of his hand. 'If you pump out enough bad coinage, people are forced to use it because they have no alternative. Bad money turns into good. One of the university doctors, Master Oresme, told me that.'

'Meanwhile, what happens to the good money? The real silver?'

'I don't know, but there must be a lot of it. These bastards, whoever they are, are gathering a fortune.'

Adela glanced along the street, making sure they were alone. 'Explain.'

'The mints are owned by their masters, but they have a contract with the crown. For each consignment of coins they are entitled to take a small percentage, known as *brassage*. Another percentage goes to the crown as a fee, called *seigniorage*. The rest goes into circulation as coin. When false moneyers reduce the amount of silver, usually through debasing, they keep the difference as an undeclared portion of their *brassage*. You can only go so far, though, before people realise the coins are debased and report you. Then the king's men come and chop your balls off.'

'But in this case there is hardly any silver in this coinage at all,' Sister Adela said. 'I see what you mean.' Her voice had hardened. 'They want people to know the coinage is false. They want people to lose confidence in the money, and by extension, in the crown itself.'

'Not just in France,' said Bessancourt. 'England too. But who would do this? Who would *want* to do it?'

'Can't you guess?' asked Adela. Her face framed by the white wimple was a grim as her voice. Bessancourt gaped at her.

'My God! But *why*?'

'That is what we need to discover,' said Adela.

'We? For God's sake, I'm in enough trouble already. Don't drag me in any deeper.'

Adela gazed at the clerk. 'I rescued you in Paris. I helped you lie low when the Knights sent men to hunt you.' Her long finger stabbed Bessancourt in the chest. 'I kept you fed and safe and alive for weeks. You owe me something, young man.'

Bessancourt felt sick again. He swallowed. 'What do you want me to do?'

'I'll tell you when we get to Abbeville,' said Sister Adela.

Abbeville, 18th of January, 1347

The Knights of Saint John had chosen the location of their new mint well. Abbeville's walls were very strong, and the town was one of the few places to have repelled the marauding English army the previous summer. The church of Saint-Sépulcre in the centre of the town had its own walled precinct; the Order's powerful commandery of Saint-Riquier was not far away.

The mint was located in several brick buildings within the Saint-Sépulcre's precinct, with heavily armed Knights of Saint Jean standing guard. They looked scornfully at the slender white-robed *consorore* as she approached. Women were allowed to join the Order, but that did not mean anyone had to respect them.

Snowflakes curled through the air. Sister Adela stopped in front of the captain, who was wrapped in a red cloak with the white cross of the Order. Her breath curled steam in the cold. 'I am a poor pilgrim, travelling in a perilous land,' she said softly. 'In God's name I am weary, and I seek shelter.'

The demeanour of the men around her changed at once. They stiffened with sudden tension, one resting his hand on the hilt of his sword. The captain stared at her for a long time. 'You are meant to answer,' Adela said quietly.

'Welcome among us, sister,' the Knight said, grudgingly. 'Rest now, and give thanks to God.'

'Praise to God I shall certainly give. I come with a message for the commander. Is he here?'

'He is within.' The Knight motioned with his hand. 'Come.'

Reynaud de Nanteuil was a tall man with curling dark hair falling down over the neck of his red tunic. He turned sharply as Adela approached. 'Who is this?'

In the distance Adela could hear the boom of furnace heat echoing in a chimney. Charcoal smoke rose in thin curls among the snowflakes.

'She didn't give a name,' said the other Knight. 'But she knows the password.'

Nanteuil looked her up and down. 'I recognise you.'

'Of course. My name is Sister Adela. I was present at the meeting of the Grand Priors in Paris last spring. You were there, supporting your late cousin the Grand Prior of France.'

Nanteuil waved a hand, dismissing the other Knight. 'You were spying on us.' It was a statement, not a question.

'On behalf of the Pilgrims, yes. I am their agent inside the Flemish commanderies. We know Commander DuSart and his brothers have turned against us. We need to know where your own loyalties lie, commander.'

Nanteuil continued to stare at her for a long time. His hand toyed with the hilt of the dagger at his belt. 'DuSart is a traitor,' he said finally. 'We will deal with him when the final reckoning comes.'

'Treason is often a matter of opinion,' Sister Adela said coolly. 'Some would say he is loyal to his Order. However, we are not interested in DuSart. We are interested in you, who has taken over at Saint-Riquier and looks to succeed his cousin as Grand Prior of France. Are you still loyal to our cause?'

'Who sent you?' Nanteuil demanded.

'I am not at liberty to say.'

Nanteuil folded his arms. 'Come on, sister. You will need to do better than that if you want me to trust you.'

Adela looked at him, challenging. 'Did I say I desired your trust, or needed it? Do not answer back to me, brother. My orders come from Liège. That is all you need to know.'

There was a long pause. 'What do you want here?' Nanteuil asked.

'The distribution of false money is having the desired effect. The French coinage is no longer trusted by the people, and the English are also growing restless. How long can you continue production?'

This time the pause was even longer. 'How do you know about that?' Nanteuil asked.

Adela planted her hands on her hips. 'For God's sake, brother. Who do you think planned the entire venture? Who gave you your orders? Why do you think you were given the password, if not to recognise our agents?'

'The Pilgrims are part of the conspiracy,' Nanteuil said slowly.

'The Pilgrims *are* the conspiracy. Answer my question. How long can you continue?'

'As long as necessary,' Nanteuil said, still reluctantly. 'We have plentiful supplies of lead, and silver is still flowing in. So long as we control the royal taxes, we can milk the towns and merchants for as much money as we like.'

'And this location? It is secure?' Adela pointed to the church. 'I am surprised the canons allowed you to establish here. Do they know what you are doing?'

'They know nothing. We seized the buildings by force, and threatened to burn the church if they protested. They are quiet as mice.'

'That won't last,' Adela said.

'Perhaps not. But by the time they complain to the king, it will be too late. Our work will be done.'

'And the men who work here? Can they be trusted?'

'All of them were carefully chosen,' said Nanteuil. 'They are loyal to us.'

'What about the royal officials, the contra guard and the assayer? Do they know what is going on?'

Nanteuil smiled for the first time. 'Of course,' he said. 'Every man has his price, and theirs is a percentage of the *brassage*. The assayer writes false reports to Paris, and he and the contra guard keep their counsel and fill their pockets.'

'Ask the assayer to bring me a copy of one of his reports,' Adela said.

'Is that necessary?'

'If I say it is, yes.'

Nanteuil turned towards the mint buildings and shouted an order. 'Cahon! Fetch a copy of your latest report to the Cour des Monnaies.'

A man came out of the mint a few moments later, fairly ordinary looking with greying hair and a bald patch like a tonsure at the back of his head. He looked sharply at Adela. 'Who is this?'

'You don't need to know. Give her the report.'

Cahon handed it over. Adela handed over the parchment and read it swiftly. 'You have specified the purity of the coinage produced by the mint. Do you send a sample of coins with each report?'

'Of good coins, yes. We produce a few of these for that purpose. The Cour des Monnaies asks for ten livres tournois with each report.'

'Good,' said Adela, handing back the report. 'Thank you, Monsieur Cahon, that will be all.'

The assayer turned and went back inside the mint. 'Are you satisfied?' Nanteuil asked. 'Or do you wish to see the mint itself?'

'There is no need. I am prepared to accept your assurances. I need to report to my superiors, and wait for their reply. I shall remain in Abbeville until I receive fresh instructions.' She smiled a little, unbending at last. 'But I shall report that you have carried out your orders faithfully. Well done, brother.'

—

Snow was falling more heavily now, white flakes like ghosts in a blue dusk. Paul Cahon, the assayer, stepped out of the mint, pulling his cloak around his shoulders to ward off the freezing north wind. He said good night to the red-cloaked guards and walked down past the marketplace towards the western end of town. Small canals ran through this part of town, embanked streams running down from the marshes to the north and into the Somme; in summer, boats came up these canals to bring fish to the market, but in the dead of winter they were covered by a thin sheet of ice. Crossing a bridge over one of the canals, Cahon came face to face with a young man, muffled and hooded against the cold, who held up a hand to stop him.

'Your pardon, sir. I have just arrived in Abbeville and I am seeking lodging for the night. Can you tell me if there is an inn nearby?'

Cahon opened his mouth to give directions just as a knife slammed into his back. The point pierced his heart; he staggered, coughing up blood, and then fell forward on his face where he lay twitching for a moment. Hugolin Bessancourt stared in horror at the hilt of the knife protruding from his shoulder blades. 'Jesus Christ! You killed him!'

'Of course I killed him,' said Sister Adela impatiently. 'What did you think I was going to do? Help me get the body out of sight.'

Bessancourt felt rather dizzy, as he often did in Sister Adela's company. Quickly they dragged the body out of the road, and Adela pulled the knife from the wound, deftly avoiding the gush of blood that followed it. Rummaging in the corpse's pocket she pulled out a cluster of silver strips, pierced and bound by an iron ring. 'Take these,' she said.

Bessancourt looked at them. 'These are assayers' needles.'

'I know what they are, you idiot. Take them. Now, let's dump him in the canal.'

Together, they carried the body to the edge of the canal and dropped it in. There was a splintering sound as the ice broke and the body slid under water. A gentle current carried it along under the water. Cahon's body might not be found until spring. Or if the current and tides carried it down to the Somme and thence out to sea, it might never be found at all.

'Does it not bother you?' he asked. 'Killing someone in cold blood?'

'These men murdered your friend, remember? Consider this to be justice.' She patted him on the shoulder. 'Now come along. We have work to do.'

Abbeville, 27th of January, 1347

Bessancourt was anxious and afraid, but knew what he had to do. He and Adela had remained in hiding just outside Abbeville for the last nine days. During this cold, uncomfortable time, Adela had given him more details about how part of the Knights of Saint John were plotting against France, and he knew just how high the stakes were. The killing of the assayer had revolted him; he was not a violent man and he hated the sight of blood, although he had got used to skinning and gutting the rabbits Adela trapped in the snares she made. He wondered, sometimes, if she felt remorse for the death of Cahon. He suspected it was not her first killing.

'Do you really think this will work?' he asked. 'What if Nanteuil suspects me?'

'He has no reason to. Enough time has elapsed since Cahon's disappearance that he shouldn't suspect any connection. Also, he didn't seem that bright to me. I think his cousin got the lion's share of the intellect in that family. You can pull the wool over his eyes, I am sure.'

'God moves in mysterious ways,' Bessancourt said sarcastically.

Wind whipped around the spire of Saint-Sépulcre, tugging at the red cloaks of the Knights standing watch. Bessancourt approached them, clearing his throat. 'Any chance I could have a word with the mint master?'

'No,' said one of them. 'Piss off.'

'I'm looking for work,' Bessancourt persisted. 'I used to work in the mint at Rouen, but they threw me out. Come on, just a quick word. I can be useful.'

The Knight stared down at him. 'Listen carefully while I say this one more time. Piss. Off.'

Bessancourt swallowed hard and stiffened his resolve. He leaned a little closer. 'I can make you rich,' he said. 'All of you.'

There was a pause. One of the other Knights looked at the first. 'I'm listening,' he said.

'I've worked at lots of mints, Rouen, Paris, Lyon. I know all the tricks. I can make silver vanish, and reappear elsewhere. In your pockets, for example.'

The Knights said nothing. 'I need work,' Bessancourt said. 'Let me talk to the mint master. Once I am employed here, I'll see you gentlemen are well rewarded.'

The first Knight looked around. 'Well, boys? What do you think?'

The second man nodded. 'I'll take him up to the commander,' he said. He looked at Bessancourt. 'If you do get taken on, rest assured we will be waiting for our share.'

'I won't forget,' said Bessancourt.

'No. You won't.'

Inside the building they were met with a wall of hot air. Bessancourt heard the roar of a furnace, and smelled the tang of hot metal. Men stood bare-armed over workbenches, dies and hammers in hand; from somewhere in the building came a relentless clattering sound, like someone was beating out sheet metal. Upstairs was a row of smaller offices. In one of these a red-robed commander of the Knights of Saint John sat with his booted feet up on a table, reading a parchment roll. The guard shoved Bessancourt through the door and followed him, closing the door behind them. The commander looked up. 'Who is this?'

Swallowing hard again, Bessancourt repeated the story Sister Adela had drummed into him; he was a mint worker who had fallen on hard times, had gambling debts and maybe drank a little too much wine, and had begun dipping his fingers into the silver. He was clever enough not to get caught, and by the time people did suspect he had always moved on to another mint in another part of the country. 'I made sure my friends were looked after. The mint masters, too. The *brassage* was twice what it was before I came, and the masters took a good share.'

'And what makes you think we are here to enrich ourselves?' the commander asked.

'All mint masters want to enrich themselves. Otherwise they wouldn't be mint masters. No one becomes a coiner as an act of charity.'

This last was said in a challenging tone, and for a moment Bessancourt wondered if he had gone too far, but after a moment the commander nodded a little. 'Which jobs can you do?' he asked.

'I can turn my hand to anything, engraving dies, trimming coins. It's all the same to me. I even worked as an assayer once.'

He saw Nanteuil's eyes flicker. 'What is your name?'

'Pierre Tremblay. I've, um… used other names in the past.'

'And you said your last job was at Rouen. What happened there?'

'It turned out the contra guard was a little more honest than I expected. I had to depart rather quickly, at an inconvenient hour.'

'We'll check this story, of course.'

'Of course.' Adela had anticipated this. It would take two days to get a message to Rouen and two more to return; more than enough time for their purposes. 'Give me a job,' Bessancourt said. 'I need money, I need wine and a roof over my head. You'll be surprised at how useful I can be.'

Nanteuil swung his feet down to the floor and stood up. 'Hmm. You said you have worked as an assayer. Do you have a set of keys?'

'In my baggage. What happened to your assayer?'

'None of your business. Do you want the job or not?'

Bessancourt stood silent, listening to the steady drumbeat of his heart. 'You are a thief and a fraud, and I would be within my rights to hang you here and now,' the commander said. 'But… you would appear to be man of talent. I can make use of you.'

Bessancourt bowed. 'I am at your service, my lord. What do you wish me to do?'

'Take over the assayer's post. You will write regular reports to Paris. I will tell you what information to send, and I will provide you with samples of coin which you will declare you have assayed and found to be consistent in quality. You will obey every other order you receive from me without question. If you do so, I won't inform the Cour des Monnaies or the mint master at Rouen of your activities and you will receive a regular share of the *brassage*. Is that clear?'

Bessancourt nodded. 'Very clear, my lord.'

'The contra guard will give you your instructions. Follow them, and we will reward you. I am sure you can guess what will happen if you fail.'

—

Unlike the Knights, the contra guard turned out to be surprisingly friendly. Like the assayer, he was a royal official, posted by Paris to ensure that the mint operated in an honest fashion and the mint master did not cheat the government. In practice, as Bessancourt knew, many mint masters nominated their own officials or even appointed them directly and informed Paris afterwards. A discreet bribe to the Cour des Monnaies ensured no questions were asked.

'This isn't a mint like any other,' the contra guard said as they walked downstairs.

Bessancourt contrived to look surprised. 'What does that mean?'

'It means we produce false coin.'

'Jesus! What did you say?'

The contra guard grinned. 'You heard me. It's a highly secret operation, all organised by the Knights. They are trying to undermine the currency of England and Flanders with forgeries. We make small denomination coins and release them into circulation where the enemy are likely to acquire them. It's very clever.'

'Yes,' Bessancourt said slowly. 'I suppose it is. What happened to the previous assayer?'

'I don't know. I don't ask questions, son, and I don't advise you to either. Come on. I'll show you around.'

The forge boomed and roared with pale flame. Men moved quickly around it, some feeding in charcoal, others working a vast bellows. More men, protected by heavy leather aprons, pulled small cauldrons of molten metal from the fire and poured the liquid into moulds. Cooled, the moulds were opened to reveal cylinders of shining lead, which were cut carefully with saws to produce round thin round planchets, blank coins.

In the next room they were beating silver into thin sheets of foil and wrapping the planchets before sending them off to be coined. The stamping rooms were full of more men bent over their workbenches, the sound of hammering a constant din in the air. As Bessancourt watched, the man nearest him took a foil-wrapped blank planchet and carefully placed it on the head of a die fixed to his bench. Picking up the other die, he placed it on the planchet, adjusting it to ensure both dies were lined up. Satisfied, he hit the upper die a hard blow with a hammer and then removed the die. Bessancourt picked up the coin and looked at it. He saw what to all intents and purposes was a French denier, stamped on both sides. The legend around the outside was the same as the ones he had seen in Amiens: PHILIPPUS REX FRANC – V. DIF.

'They're doing a few genuine coins too,' the contra guard said. 'You'll send some of those to Paris as samples for the Cour des Monnaies. The rest we keep as *brassage*.'

'This is a French coin. This isn't just an attempt to undermine the enemy, is it?'

'Like I told you,' the contra guard said. His voice was still friendly. 'Don't ask questions.'

The die room was full of the tap-tap-tap of chisels. He counted four men making dies, which meant they must be producing a great quantity of coin; a set of dies normally lasted two or three days, until the heads began to wear with impact and the impressions on the coin were too blurred to be usable. These men were working steadily, engraving impressions and inscriptions onto the heads of the iron dies and he saw baskets full of these waiting to go into the stamping rooms. Looking through the dies in the baskets, Bessancourt found French deniers, obols and half-obols, English halfpennies and farthings. The French dies all had the same mark as the ones he had seen earlier; the English ones of course had a different inscription, EDWARDUS REX Ā – VIL Ā DIFELIN. He was tempted to take some of the dies, but knew this might draw attention to himself.

His workplace was a closet next to the die room. He spent the rest of the day here, reading through the records of the dead assayer and memorising as much detail as he could. It seemed that the contra guard thought the mint, if not exactly above board, was at least serving the national interest in some way. But that did not explain the false French coins, and this was the same organisation that had killed Massy and hunted Bessancourt himself. Whatever their purpose was, it was not benign.

He picked up another parchment, a small scrap without any kind of mark or seal, and read it. In an instant he felt the hair stand up on the back of his neck. There were only a handful of words, abbreviated in the way clerks often wrote when they were in a hurry: *ultimas vig quat mil marc hic ad usum Br factae*. The latest shipment: twenty-four thousand marks for use in *Br*, wherever *Br* was. That explained where most of the silver was going. The Knights were not just making false coin. They were also shipping silver somewhere, which meant they were defrauding the French treasury, and on a huge scale.

Somehow, he managed to get through the afternoon without collapsing in a heap of nerves. At the end of the day the contra guard came to find him. 'Do you have somewhere to stay, son?'

'Yes, I have a room. But thanks for asking.'

'If you ever need anything, come and ask me. Do you fancy a cup of wine? There's a good tavern over beyond Saint-Sépulcre.'

Bessancourt hesitated. 'I have a woman waiting,' he said finally. It was true, in a way.

The contra guard grinned. 'You young dog. Well, you don't want to keep her waiting too long.' He hesitated. 'By the way, the commander sent a courier to Rouen today. It seems he wants to check on your antecedents.'

'Yes. He told me he intended to do so.'

'It'll be a few days before the reply comes back.' The contra guard studied Bessancourt for a moment. 'So if there's anything you want to tell me, now is the time. If there's something you would rather the commander didn't know, maybe I can help you.'

'I have nothing to hide,' Bessancourt said.

'Everyone has something to hide, son. Especially a man who carries a set of assayers' needles at his belt almost exactly like the ones Paul Cahon used to have. Poor fellow. A fisherman found his body in a canal an hour ago, stabbed in the back.'

Bessancourt moved towards the door, but the contra guard barred his way. The genial, smiling face was gone now. 'Care to tell me about it?' the other man asked.

In the die room the engravers were still hard at work, chisels tapping and pinging. The clerk thought quickly. The contra guard could have gone straight to the commander, in which case red-cloaked Knights would now be dragging him out by his hair. Instead, he had come quietly to find Bessancourt, which meant one of two things: he wanted to extract a confession he could take to the commander in exchange for a reward, or more likely, he had seen an opportunity for blackmail. 'What do you want?' Bessancourt asked.

'That depends,' said the contra guard. 'What is my silence worth to you?'

The words were barely out of his mouth before Bessancourt hit him in the groin. The contra guard doubled over and Bessancourt brought his knee up hard into the other man's chin. There was a satisfactory crunch of bone and the contra guard fell unconscious. No one in the die room seemed to have heard anything. Bessancourt dragged the other man into a corner of the office and closed the door behind him. Picking up his cloak he called good night to the engravers and walked casually towards the door.

Outside, the watch had changed; a new batch of Knights stood sentry now, and they paid him no attention. Concealing his nerves, Bessancourt hummed a little tune under his breath as he walked out through the gates and strolled casually across the little square in front of Saint-Sépulcre, expecting all the time to hear booted footsteps coming after him. Only when he was out of sight beyond the houses on the far side of the square did he begin to run.

–

'I'm not going back there,' he said to Sister Adela.

'You certainly are not.' She was already pulling on her cloak. 'Did you kill the contra guard?'

'I have no idea. I didn't check.'

'Careless.' She clicked her tongue. 'When he wakes up, they will realise the truth, and Nanteuil's vengeance on us both will be swift and severe. We need to leave Abbeville now, to get ahead of the pursuit.'

'I still don't understand what it all means. Dif, or Difelin, must be a place; *villa Difelin*. Maybe they stole dies from a mint there and are using them as models to make their own. And what or where is *Br*?'

'*Br* is Bruges,' she said. 'Where Difelin is, I don't know, but I know a man who might. Come.'

'Where are we going?'

'To hide from Nanteuil's red cloaks,' said Adela. 'After that, we are going to Calais.'

13

'Good to see you up and about, Simon,' Michael Northburgh said. He glanced at the stick in Merrivale's hand. 'Are your wounds still paining you?'

Merrivale smiled a little. 'Only in bad weather.'

'Which must mean most of the time. This winter is worse than any I can remember. I'll take you through to his Grace.'

King Edward was seated behind a wooden table in a small chamber in the King's House, his back to a glowing coal fire. Lord Rowton and Hatfield, the Bishop of Durham, stood to one side, the latter with arms folded over his chest. *They have been quarrelling*, Merrivale thought.

He bowed to the king. 'Glad to see you're on the mend,' Edward said. 'Are you fit to return to duty?'

'Yes, sire.'

'Good. We have need of you.' The king rose and stood by the fire for a moment, warming his hands. They could hear the wind whistling around the building, blowing rain and salt spray across the marshes.

'I won't mince words,' the king said. 'We've lost more than a thousand men since we arrived at Calais, most of them to the flux. Several hundred more have deserted. Most of those that remain are sick, miserable and in no condition to fight. Berkeley's retinue and Lord Rowton's men are still reliable, as are Llewellyn's Welsh and the German mercenaries. The rest just want to go home. I can't say I blame them.'

Merrivale said nothing. 'All is not yet lost, sire,' Lord Rowton said.

'I did not say it was,' said the king. 'I have already given orders for more men to be raised, and I am expecting Lancaster with seven thousand archers by Easter. We're impressing more ships, and this time the shipowners know I won't take no for an answer. And this time too we'll have the money to pay them. Northburgh?'

'The Upper Chamber have agreed a forced loan of twenty thousand sacks of wool,' said the secretary, 'and the vintner's syndicate have financed a mortgage on the Great Crown. The money has already been deposited with the exchequer. The coin has all been tested and found true.'

'Thank God for that,' Hatfield said dryly. 'There is so much false money in circulation at the moment that one can hardly tell bad coin from good.'

The king looked irritated. 'That matter is being dealt with,' he said shortly. 'We also need funds to buy the Count of Flanders. That is where you come in, Merrivale.'

Merrivale raised his eyebrows. 'I thought the marriage had been agreed, sire.'

'So did we all. The boy gave a solemn oath on holy relics that he would marry my daughter. But since then, someone has been putting pressure on him to change his mind.'

'The League of Three? They agreed to support the marriage. Have they gone back on their bargain?'

'Possibly,' said Hatfield. 'But we suspect France may also have a hand in the matter. Our adversary still regards Flanders as his own fief.'

One never spoke Philip of France's name aloud in front of the king; he was always referred to as the *adversary*. 'It seems likely,' Merrivale said. 'How may I serve, sire?'

'I want you to return to Bruges. Find out if the League *are* interfering, and if so, put a stop to it. Talk to the count and offer him money to get his agreement, whatever he asks for. Bishop Hatfield is drawing up the betrothal contract, and he will accompany the queen to Bruges at Easter. I want to make damned certain the boy will sign that contract.'

The king paused for a moment. 'We need this marriage, gentlemen. Once the contracts are signed, Flanders will be in our pocket and the French may as well give up and go home. Calais will fall into our hands like ripe fruit. But if we fail to secure Flanders, both the siege and this war could drag on forever. It seems there are no weaknesses in Calais' defences, and the defenders appear to be numerous and well fed.'

'The town will fall, sire,' Rowton said. 'I have a plan for blocking the harbour mouth to stop French supply ships from getting in. Even if we can't breach the defences, we can starve them out.'

'They won't run out of food any time soon,' Hatfield objected. 'They have already had plenty of chances to fill their magazines. That captain from Boulogne, Marant, has made runs into the town every month, and we hear of fresh convoys assembling at Dieppe and Saint-Valery.'

Rowton shook his head. 'I had a message from the town yesterday. The garrison are still having problems with spoilage, and are short of fresh water too. Once we cut their supply lines, they won't last long.'

'But it will take too long for a blockade to work,' Hatfield replied. 'I think we should negotiate with the citizens, sire. Bribe them to open the gates and hand over the town to us. Once Calais is in our hands, we won't need the Flemings. It will be them who are beholden to us, not the other way around.'

Rowton started to speak, but the king raised one finger and both men fell silent. 'I encourage my captains to speak their minds at all times,' Edward said. 'I do not encourage them to indulge in senseless bickering. We will wait for reinforcements to arrive, then invest the town as closely as possible and compel its surrender on our terms. Meanwhile, every effort will be made to secure the Flemish marriage. Am I clear?'

Both men bowed. A bell rang in the hall next door. 'The feast is ready, sire,' Northburgh said.

'Good. Let us go and join her Grace. After dinner, some of Holstein's men are going to dance for us. That should be amusing.' The king smiled and clapped Lord Rowton on the shoulder. 'Don't look so glum, Eustace. You're too impatient, that's always been your problem. Wait, and victory will be delivered to us.'

'Yes, sire,' Rowton said. 'So you keep telling us.'

—

The king departed, followed by Hatfield and Northburgh. Merrivale turned to go, but saw Rowton still standing and staring into the fire. 'My lord? What is it?'

'Nothing,' Rowton said after a moment. He looked up and forced a smile. 'Good to see you back on your feet, herald. You looked like you were at death's door when they brought you in.'

'I very nearly was,' said Merrivale. Loss of blood, thirst and cold had hit him hard. By the time they reached Brother Geoffrey's stronghold amid the ruins of Lens he was burning with fever. Geoffrey had studied medicine, and Warin was a patient nurse who never left his bedside, but it had taken him weeks to pull through. Not until after Christmas did Geoffrey deem it safe to transport him back to the camp outside Calais, and the rigours of winter travel meant that more convalescence was required when he arrived.

'The king was furious when he heard what happened,' Rowton said. 'He wrote a formal protest to France, and another to the papacy. At one point I thought he was going to order the whole army to march to Béthune and lay waste to the place.'

'I am flattered,' said Merrivale. 'But that would have achieved very little.'

'But it shows how highly he values you. He reposes a great deal of trust in you, herald.'

'As he does in you, my lord. And, increasingly, in Bishop Hatfield.'

'Yes.' Rowton studied him for a moment. 'And do you think that is entirely wise?'

Merrivale chose his words carefully. 'I know nothing to his discredit. Do you, my lord?'

'Nothing at all. He is diligent in his duties and he works extremely hard. But he is ambitious.'

'The same could be said of many people.'

'Not everyone. I am not, and from my observation, neither are you. We do not actively seek honours and rewards. The service we give is enough.' Rowton paused, choosing his words. 'But Hatfield is… different. Take this business about negotiating with the townspeople, now.'

Merrivale waited.

'As you know, I have a cousin in the town and am buying information from him,' Rowton said. 'He has been valuable to us, providing us with details about the defences. Now, Hatfield is insinuating that *he* has some sort of contact in Calais as well. He won't say who it is, but claims he wants to negotiate the surrender of the town. He wants to take sole charge of the negotiations, reporting only to the king. It is a matter of secrecy, he says. I find that rather insulting, and so do some of the other commanders.'

'Understandably so,' said Merrivale. 'Has the king agreed?'

'He hasn't given his formal approval, but he hasn't said no. My concern is that Hatfield will open negotiations anyway, the French will get wind of it and all will be lost. My cousin could be exposed or killed, and we would lose a valuable agent. But I don't know how to stop Hatfield.'

'Only the king can do that,' Merrivale said. 'On the other hand, it sounds like his Grace also wants Hatfield to join the queen and negotiate the betrothal contracts. That may keep him too busy for anything else.'

'Yes. Perhaps so.' Rowton sighed. 'And, I have to be honest with myself. Perhaps I am just jealous. I have been at the king's side for many years. Maybe deep down, I resent another having so much influence.' He smiled a little. 'Not a very attractive trait, jealousy.'

A thought struck Merrivale. 'Do you know anything about Hatfield's career before he joined the royal household, my lord?'

Rowton was surprised by the question. 'Not a great deal, no. When I first met him he was in Henry of Lancaster's service. Not the present earl, but his father. Why do you ask?'

'Like you, I am always curious when a man rises suddenly to prominence and influence,' Merrivale said. The bell rang again, and he bowed. 'I think, my lord, that we should go in to dinner.'

–

In the great hall, at least, they were snug against the weather. A stone fireplace had been added since Merrivale was last here – the stone, it was rumoured, had come from a church demolished by the Prince of Wales's archers during a raid last month – and a fire roared on the hearth. As it was Friday, Coloyne, the yeoman of the kitchen, and his staff had used their imagination to present the company with a variety of fantastic dishes, some in the shapes of sea creatures. Elaborately decorated eel pies were surrounded by sculpted fish made of pastry dancing across the platters, accompanied by whitefish mousse moulded into shapes of whales, dried salmon cleverly formed into shapes of seahorses, salmon sausages with beer sauce, plaice, codling, pike, bream and carp all served with variety of brightly coloured sauces flavoured with garlic, parsley and spices, apple fritters and tarts, more apples baked in pastry coffins dyed red, and baskets of fresh apples on every table.

The central attraction of the feast was an automaton in the form of a richly dressed young woman, holding a wine goblet in one hand

and a towel in the other. Wine flowed from a hidden reservoir inside the automaton into the glass, and as the glass filled the figure glided forward, raising her arm to offer a drink to each guest; when the glass was returned the other arm raised, holding out the towel so the drinker could wipe their lips. Once the towel was replaced, the statue glided away again. 'That is astonishing!' said Iron Henry. 'How does it work, do you think?'

'I commend to you a book entitled *The Knowledge of Ingenious Mechanical Devices*,' said Brother Geoffrey, who had finally returned to camp the previous day. 'Written by a Syrian scholar named al-Jazari. I suspect a design for this device can be found there.'

Iron Henry roared with laughter. Formally known as Heinrich of Holstein-Rendsburg, he was an endlessly cheerful man with a black beard even more wild than Poděbrady's and a fund of vulgar stories; observing him, Merrivale thought, you would never guess that he was one of the most battle-hardened mercenary captains in Europe. His own men called him *der eiserner Heinrich*; the English archers, who admired him immensely, translated this as Iron Henry. The name pleased him greatly.

'A Saracen designed this marvel?' he said. 'No wonder the crusades are going to shit. We'll never beat people as clever as this.'

'What a pity we did not realise this two hundred years ago,' said Tiphaine. 'Think of all the dreary crusader music we could have avoided. *Lady, the fates command and I must go*, and all the other sanctimonious rubbish.'

'You would prefer something modern, *demoiselle*?' asked Maurice de Berkeley, smiling. 'Something by Machaut, perhaps?'

'I would, actually. Machaut is romantic to the point of vulgarity, but at least there is happiness in his songs. Some of them, anyway.'

Brother Geoffrey glanced at Merrivale. 'More in his songs than in his life, I think.'

'Oh, yes, I forgot,' Tiphaine said. 'You and Simon know him. But then, you are both so much older than I.'

Tiphaine was in a curious mood, the herald thought. After his return to camp she had taken over from Warin as his nurse, and cared for him with a tender concern that he found both touching, a little surprising and occasionally alarming. As he recovered, she returned to something like her former self, but the previous day she had been summoned for a long talk with the queen. *She wanted to discuss my future*, Tiphaine had said, and she would say nothing else, but she had been behaving oddly ever since.

Her place in the herald's own household was now taken for granted. She sat between Merrivale and Brother Geoffrey, with Berkeley and Iron Henry opposite them. Around them the hall resounded with noise. All four royal households were there, those of the king, queen, Prince of Wales and his younger sister Princess Isabella, the intended bride of the Count of Flanders. The king doted on his daughter; her relationship with the queen was that of any fourteen-year-old girl and her mother, while the prince made no secret of his contempt for his little sister. He and the young knights of his own household had taken control of the automaton and were attempting to drink its hidden reservoir dry. The prince, Merrivale was sorry to see, had also lifted the figure's skirts and was peering underneath while the others shrieked with laughter. The queen glared at him. Merrivale glanced at Alice Bedingfield, who rolled her eyes.

The king's players were struggling to make themselves heard over the noise. 'Do I understand that some of your men are dancing for us later?' asked Berkeley.

'Yes,' said Iron Henry. 'They will dance the Tiggerens Tanz; in English, you would call it the Beggar's Dance. Very popular among our people. Very lively too. I hope your players can keep up with the music.'

Brother Geoffrey of Maldon pulled the sweetmeat tray closer and selected a piece of candied apple. 'I see a couple of new faces among our band of musicians.'

Berkeley nodded. 'They were engaged just before Christmas. The citole player is Nikolas of Prague, and the viol player beside him is Havel of Bohemia. The others call him Havel the Fiddler.'

Tiphaine studied the players. 'Why would they come to play during a siege in the middle of winter? They could have gone to any city or castle and played for Christmas feasts in nice warm halls, with comfortable beds to fall into afterwards.'

'Money,' said Berkeley. 'In peacetime or back at court they would get fourpence a day, but on campaign they get twelvepence. My archers still only get fourpence, and they have to live down the hill in a mess of salt water and their own shit. Don't think they don't resent the favour shown to the musicians.'

'It would appear there is more money to be made in music than in fighting,' Brother Geoffrey observed.

'Then why don't we all give up fighting, and turn to music instead?' Tiphaine asked. She had, she recalled, asked Jean Marant much the same question about whaling.

Iron Henry had a more ready answer than Marant. He chuckled. 'Fighting is a natural state of affairs, *demoiselle*. We learn how to dance and make music, but we are born with the ability to fight. That is why there are more soldiers than musicians.'

'Even though they are less well paid,' said Geoffrey. 'Perhaps some things are more important than money.'

'Especially the money we have now,' said Berkeley. 'Half the coin in the army seems to be false these days.'

'Ah, you are right, my friend,' said Iron Henry, nodding. 'Some of my men went to the market last Friday to buy beer and herrings, and every farthing they had was bad money. I have complained to the king and he will make restitution, but no one likes being paid in false coin. It is not good for the spirits.'

'No,' agreed Berkeley. He glanced at the canon. 'Good to see you back among us, Brother Geoffrey. How does your venture progress?'

'God's work has been done,' said Geoffrey, his voice dry. 'Most of eastern Artois is a smouldering wasteland and the rebels have captured several important towns. Hence, I have been ordered to return for fresh instructions.'

'Any idea what the king intends?' asked Merrivale.

'I believe I shall be sent to the German court, fairly soon. As soon, that is, as the king makes up his mind what he wants.'

'You could be waiting some time,' said Berkeley.

Geoffrey smiled. 'And yourselves? The siege of Calais continues?'

'Say rather that the siege endures,' Berkeley said.

'Have the French made no move to dislodge you?'

'Apart from the garrisons at Boulogne and Saint-Omer and Béthune, the nearest French troops are at Amiens, several days' march from here. We have been unmolested, but in turn we make no impact on the walls of Calais. We could be here until doomsday.'

'Reinforcements are on the way,' Merrivale said.

'Of course they are. Every month we are told they will arrive next month. The next month arrives and we are told it will be the following month, and so on and on it goes, unstoppable as that pretty automaton... Oh, dear. I think the young men have pulled her arm off.'

'Boys don't really change,' said Tiphaine. 'Do they?'

'Some do,' Merrivale said quietly.

'Of course they do.' She squeezed his hand in sudden sympathy. 'I am sorry.'

He had been thinking, she knew, of Peter de Lisle, his young apprentice who had been killed on the Scottish borders in October. Clever, brave and good, Peter had been loved by all of them, and his loss was still painful. Merrivale smiled at her. 'Don't be,' he said quietly. 'As soon as the king and queen retire and we can escape, I want to talk to you and Geoffrey.'

'I know,' she said. 'It's time we returned to our own war.'

–

In Merrivale's hut, Brother Geoffrey sat down on a bench and smoothed his black robe over his knees. 'I take it you are returning to duty, Simon?'

'I must. The king has commanded me to Bruges again, to bully Count Louis into agreeing to the royal marriage.'

Geoffrey looked pensive. 'I have never believed this marriage project will end well. Has anyone asked Princess Isabella for her views?'

'She is all in favour,' said Tiphaine. 'She is young and romantic, and in love with the idea of being married. And she wants to get away from her mother, whom she professes to hate.'

'Who told you this?'

'The queen,' said Tiphaine. 'She likes me, it seems.'

'Then she has exquisite taste in friends,' Geoffrey said smoothly.

Tiphaine stuck out her tongue at him. 'Has anything more been seen of Nicodemus?' Merrivale asked. 'The fact that he is alive and free, and has some connection with the Pilgrims, worries me deeply. I wish he had been killed last summer.'

'I have asked Llewellyn to help us,' Tiphaine said. 'His Welshmen have been watching out for Nicodemus. He has been spotted a few times in the camp, but always disappears before he can be arrested.'

'Was anyone with him?'

'Once he was seen talking to some of Berkeley's men. Another time was outside the stables near Bishop Hatfield's house. He was alone that time.'

'Let's hope they lay hands on him soon.' Merrivale gazed at the fire for a moment. 'He is more than just an assassin, of course. His crimes include the selling of enslaved children. The world will be a better place when he is dead.'

'And it is not just Nicodemus,' Tiphaine said. 'One of those three musicians is also likely to be a killer. And then, as you say, there are the Pilgrims, and who knows what their strength is.'

'The forces ranged against us are powerful,' Brother Geoffrey observed. 'Even more powerful than before, it seems.'

'Yes,' said the herald. 'Sometimes I wonder why we bother. Actually, more than sometimes.'

Tiphaine and Geoffrey glanced at each other. 'You are tired,' Tiphaine said.

'I cannot remember not being tired. This conspiracy is like a weight pressing me into the ground.'

He shook himself a little, and looked at Tiphaine and the two servants. 'Shall we discuss our suspects, so that Geoffrey is up to date?'

'Have you received a reply from Lady Mary?' Tiphaine asked.

'Not yet. The weather has been bad, of course, and not many ships have crossed the Narrow Sea in recent weeks. Let's look at what we have to hand. Shall we start with Michael Northburgh?'

Tiphaine nodded. 'I mentioned Northburgh's name when I was in Calais, but it brought no reaction. I am not certain if Maninghem or Saint-Pierre even knew who he was.'

Merrivale looked at Mauro and Warin standing by the door. 'Come and sit down, both of you. Anything to report on Northburgh?'

'Much the same as before, sir,' said Warin. 'He spends long hours in his office, as you might expect. Once a week he goes to the tavern out on the Saint-Omer road and drinks beer with old Wetwang, the king's treasurer. Other than that, he rarely goes out.'

'The picture of a hard-working civil servant,' Merrivale said.

'Appearances can be deceiving,' said Tiphaine. 'I know you want to believe your friend is innocent, Simon, but we must continue to watch him.'

'I know.' His face was pale in the firelight, Tiphaine thought, and he looked older than when he went away to Béthune. *He still does not know whether Yolande deliberately betrayed him.*

'What about Lord Rowton?' Merrivale asked.

'He is still receiving messages from his cousin in Calais. Maninghem denied he was sending messages, but he was lying.'

'How do the messages come?'

'The same way Nicodemus came out of Calais, señor,' said Mauro. 'The messengers take a boat out of the harbour and along the coast, where they land behind our lines and make their way into the camp. One arrived only yesterday.'

Merrivale rubbed his chin. 'Rowton makes no secret of this,' he said. 'He has never concealed the existence of his spy, at least not from the king. He also wants to prosecute the siege more actively, and is willing to court the king's displeasure to advance his views.'

'He trusts in the king's friendship,' Geoffrey said.

'Yes... Is there anything else to report?'

Warin shook his head. 'He rides out of camp every so often, to exercise his horses, according to the grooms. Many of those with horses do the same.'

'Does he ride alone?'

'Usually, sir. Although of late, he has taken to riding with Sir Maurice de Berkeley. The two have become friendly, it seems.'

Merrivale pondered this briefly. 'What about Hatfield? Does he go riding as well?'

'Yes, señor,' said Mauro. 'But not as often, or for as long.'

'He usually sends his groom instead,' Warin said. 'I tried talking to the groom, but he's a surly brute. I couldn't get anything out of him.'

'Hatfield stays close to court,' said Tiphaine. 'He is becoming even more influential with the king. The queen does not like him, I think.'

'She will have to work with him,' Merrivale said. 'The king has ordered him to draw up the betrothal contract for Count Louis and Princess Isabella. He has a finger in many pies, it seems. Now he has his thumb in that one as well.'

'In his defence, he is a very fine canon lawyer,' Brother Geoffrey said. 'No one is better suited to writing a contract for a royal betrothal.'

'We still haven't answered the question of how he knows the mayor of Calais,' said Tiphaine.

'No. Nor does anyone seem to know anything about his background, except that he was in the service of the old Earl of Lancaster. And he is dead, so I can hardly ask him for details.'

'You were herald to Lancaster's son before you joined the royal household,' Tiphaine pointed out. 'He might know something.'

'He might.' Henry of Grosmont, now Earl of Lancaster in his father's place, was in England, raising troops at the king's command to reinforce the siege of Calais. Merrivale looked at Brother Geoffrey. 'You are frowning, my friend. What troubles you?'

'A memory,' said Geoffrey, 'of something I had half forgotten… After the death of the king's father, the old earl led the council of regency. Roger Mortimer and Queen Isabella had the real power, but Lancaster was scheming for ways to wrest control away from them.'

'Unsuccessfully.'

'Yes. But one move in the game was to send an envoy to France. It was fairly obvious that Charles the Fair would die without male heirs, leaving the throne of France vacant. Lancaster wanted to test the water and see whether the French nobles would be amenable to accepting our own king's claim to the throne.'

'They weren't,' said Tiphaine.

'No, of course not. They chose Philip of Valois instead, and thus we have our present war. But this was not certain at the time. Lancaster arranged a meeting with representatives of the French court at Calais, but by this point his eyesight was already failing. He sent one of his household to represent him.'

'Hatfield,' said Tiphaine.

'Possibly. I was never told the envoy's name. But if it was Hatfield, that might explain a few things.'

Merrivale looked sceptical. 'That is far too subtle a scheme for Lancaster to have dreamed up on his own. I wonder who put the idea into his head?'

Geoffrey gazed at him sombrely. 'It was John of Hainault,' he said. 'And if you are curious about how I know this, I was originally chosen to be the secret envoy. Hainault insisted on someone else, I was not told who. But if it was Hatfield, and that is an *if*, we have a link between him and the conspiracy and Calais.'

'A potential link,' said Merrivale after a while. 'This does not amount to proof.'

'No. The *demoiselle* is right, the present earl might know something more. But there is also another man who can help us.'

Tiphaine nodded. 'The mayor of Calais,' she said. She turned to Merrivale. 'Is this where you forbid me once again to do anything risky?'

'It would be rather hypocritical, wouldn't it, after my little jaunt to Béthune.'

'It would,' Tiphaine agreed. 'Especially as I always manage to come back in one piece.'

Merrivale bowed to her. 'How will you get into Calais? You can't use Marant again, he will grow suspicious.'

'I know how to get us both into the town,' said Brother Geoffrey.

'How?'

The canon smiled. 'We will knock at the door,' he said.

14

After the events at Béthune, the king no longer trusted that the herald's tabard would keep Merrivale safe. His message, relayed by Northburgh, was specific and blunt; Merrivale was instructed to wait until safe-conducts and an escort had been sent from Bruges, and was not to set foot outside camp until then. 'I know you still believe in the laws of war,' Northburgh said. 'But you seem to be about the only person who does.'

Zajíc does, Merrivale thought. He remembered the Bohemia herald's anger at the way Béthune had treated him. His leg throbbed briefly with memories. What had happened in the oubliette had left its scars on him, in more ways than one.

The weather was fine, unusually so for the time of year. The sky was full of high white clouds and the wind had lost its raw edge, making it possible to believe in the eventual arrival of spring. Down in the siege lines the trebuchets were in action again, their long arms rising and falling, stone shot arching through the air to smash on the walls or disappear inside the town. This was activity for its own sake, Merrivale knew, to keep the men busy and give them something to think about besides the cold and the flux. The last attempt to storm the walls had been more than a month ago; now, all attention seemed to be concentrated on Lord Rowton's plan to block the harbour entrance. The siege, as Maurice de Berkeley had said, endured.

A few people wandered through the muddy streets of Villeneuve-la-Hardie, enjoying the watery sunshine. A man stood against a wall playing the viol and singing. Merrivale, leaning on his stick and watching, recognised one of the new musicians, Havel the Fiddler. He was singing one of the crusader *ballades* that Tiphaine despised.

When the nightingale in the thicket

Seeks for love, and bestows it
By pouring out its faithful song of joy
And gazing with eyes of love at its mate,
And all the streams are clear, and the meadows fair
Then a great delight reigns over me
And joy rests in my heart.

A thought crossed the herald's mind. Limping back to his house, he summoned Mauro and Warin and gave them fresh instructions. They looked surprised, but obeyed.

The long-awaited message from Lady Mary had arrived from England; the outer packet was stained with salt water but the letter inside was intact. Merrivale broke the wax seal and unrolled the letter, written in a neat, precise hand. As expected, the letter informed him that an apothecary had been consulted and the desired solution of green copperas had been delivered to his father, whose health was now somewhat improved. A few minor items of gossip followed before the writer signed off.

Opening his writing box, Merrivale took out a vial of copperas and poured it into a small bowl. Dipping a brush into the liquid he began carefully to paint the empty spaces of parchment between the lines. As if by magic, the words of the real letter sprang to life.

Philip de Thame holds fast to his priory of Clerkenwell, and does not go out or receive visitors save for members of his own Order. He waits for something, but no one knows what. I have spoken to my father about Lord Ufford and the archbishop, for he knows them well. His verdict is that they would never commit treason, nor give consent to any such act, but their ultimate loyalty is to England.

Michael Northburgh is well respected by all who know him, and no one has an ill word to say against him. His uncle and patron, Roger Northburgh the Bishop of Coventry, is very close to Archbishop Stratford and Lord Ufford, and may well be of the same mind as his friends. Eustace Rowton is admired for his unwavering fealty and friendship with the king. He always tells His Grace the truth, no matter what the situation. Bishop Hatfield has climbed high but aims higher. He has designs on Canterbury, and some say he desires a red hat, or even perhaps

a set of keys. Like many men of great ambition, he comes from a
poor family; his education at Cambridge was paid for by Queen
Isabella. This is all I have been able to discover.

Tiphaine came in just as he finished. He handed her the letter and waited in silence while she read it. 'This is enigmatic,' she said.

'She had to choose her words carefully. Other people know the secret of invisible writing. Philip de Thame and Ufford and the archbishop know something is in the wind. They are waiting and will make up their minds when they know more.'

'Their loyalty is to England, she says. Not to the king. Meaning they will not act against the king, but they may not necessarily move to save him. And Lord Rowton? He is admired only for telling the truth?'

'Telling truth to kings can be risky,' Merrivale said.

Tiphaine looked sceptical. 'Not this king. He likes men who do exactly that. Look at yourself, for example. You and Rowton are similar in some ways, you know.'

'Yes,' Merrivale said, thinking about the scene before the Candlemas feast. 'His lordship has taken to confiding in me. I don't know why.'

'Perhaps he likes you. And Hatfield desires to become an archbishop and a cardinal, and perhaps even pope one day.'

Merrivale nodded. 'Last year, Vidal as good as admitted to me that the conspirators plan to replace our current pope with Cardinal Aubert. But he is thirty years older than Hatfield and will not live forever. Our bishop has plenty of time.' He paused. 'Much of this we already know. What is new, and what worries me, is this connection with Queen Isabella. She is not noted for dipping into her own purse to pay for anything, let alone the education of promising young clerics.'

Tiphaine handed back the letter. 'Why does this worry you?'

'Isabella was a bitter and vengeful enemy to her husband, the old king. Some believe it was she, not her lover Roger Mortimer, who gave the orders for the king's murder. We know three men rode to Berkeley castle the night the king died, and we know who two of them are.'

He paused again. 'I wonder if the third was Thomas Hatfield,' he said.

There was no way to be sure, of course. The only three living people who might know were Queen Isabella, now living in luxurious exile in Norfolk, John of Hainault and Hatfield himself, and none were likely to tell the truth.

Merrivale waited for the promised escort from Bruges, while the weather closed in once more and a cold rain began to fall. The army squatted in the mud outside Calais, and the dreary days passed.

'You were right, sir,' said Warin. 'Havel and the other musician, the one from Prague, met with someone last night out on the Saint-Omer road. I was close enough to hear them talking, but I couldn't understand the language. It wasn't French or Flemish, I don't think.' He hesitated for a moment. 'I wondered if the man they were meeting might be Nicodemus.'

'I doubt it. And I'll give you odds the language they spoke was Czech,' the herald said. He rose to his feet, picking up his stick. 'Come with me. I may need you if things get rough.'

In fact there was no need. The two musicians, Nikolas of Prague and Havel of Bohemia, were in a tavern on the edge of the camp, looking out over the half-flooded marshes towards the coastal dunes. They rose to their feet and stood respectfully as Merrivale approached. 'Come outside,' the herald said. 'I wish to speak to both of you.'

They followed him out into the cold wind. Fine rain misted their faces. 'Who sent you here?' Merrivale asked.

The two men looked at each other. 'The truth,' Merrivale said. 'Or I will extract it from you by force.'

'The lord of Poděbrady sent us,' said Nikolas. He was the taller of the two, and fairer; Havel was broad-shouldered and dark.

'You are spies.'

Alarm shot through both their faces. 'No, sir,' said Havel. 'We are observers.'

'It is a distinction without a difference. You are agents of an enemy power.'

Nikolas held up a hand. 'His lordship doesn't see it that way, sir. He wants to make peace between the Empire and England.'

'Then why doesn't he simply ask for terms?'

'It's not that easy, sir, as I am sure you know,' Nikolas said. 'Many of the nobles wish to continue with the French alliance.'

'Go on.'

'We were sent to make contact with the court, to observe and to deliver messages. Believe me, sir, what we do is in England's interest as well as our own.'

'You met someone on the Saint-Omer road last night. Who was it?'

'It was Zajíc, sir,' said Havel. 'The Bohemia herald.'

'*Zajíc?* What was he doing here?'

'He carried a letter, sir. He passed it to us, and instructed us to deliver it to the court. He did not want his presence known.'

'Why not?'

'We only obey orders, sir,' Nikolas said quietly.

'To whom did you give the letter? Northburgh, the king's secretary?'

'No, sir.' Havel hesitated. 'We were instructed to deliver it to one of the king's councillors. Thomas Hatfield, the Bishop of Durham.'

A long silence followed, while the wind whipped around them. If Hatfield was involved in the conspiracy, and if Zajíc was carrying letters to him, then that meant Zajíc was still involved too. *If, if. Damn it, why are there so many questions, and so few answers?*

He looked at the two men in front of him. Both looked worried, and with good reason.

'You may go, on two conditions,' said Merrivale. 'You tell no one about this conversation, especially not Hatfield or Zajíc. And in future, if I have need of you, you will obey my orders.'

They looked at each other again, relief plain their faces. 'The Bohemia herald did say that we should assist you if necessary, sir,' said Havel. 'He said we could trust you.'

Which is a damned sight more than I can say about him. He nearly said it aloud, but bit back the words in time. He felt tired, and his leg was paining him once more. 'Get out of my sight,' he said curtly.

'May I ask a question, sir?' asked Warin when the two men had gone. 'Why didn't you arrest them?'

'That would solve nothing. They are intermediaries, nothing more, and almost certainly they are not the only Bohemian or imperial agents in our camp. Also, it is possible that they are telling the truth.'

'Yes, sir,' said Warin. He sounded as dubious as Merrivale felt.

'Also, they both play beautifully. Hanging them would upset the king. I may need his goodwill before long.'

'Yes, sir. I had another thought. Next time a message comes, you could have ordered them to bring it to you.'

'I had the same thought. But the moment I break the seal on the parchments, Zajíc and his friends will know I am reading them. Even more so if they are also using invisible ink. And anyway, I can probably guess at the contents.'

–

It *was* possible that the two Bohemians were telling the truth. Equally it was possible that while the ostensible letters contained proposals for peace, written invisibly between the lines were messages for Hatfield. He thought about going straight to the king and asking him to force Hatfield to hand over the letters, but he still had no proof; if Hatfield was innocent, the king would not react well and neither would the queen.

He thought also about sending men to ambush Zajíc on his next visit and steal copies of the messages, but he had no idea where or when to send them. The Bohemia herald knew his craft well, and would never use the same meeting place or the same route twice.

He wanted to talk to Tiphaine, but she had gone out early that morning without saying where. Instead, two people were waiting for him at the house, their cloaks and boots splashed with mud. One was a young man in dark coat and hose, the other a tall woman in travel-stained white robes. It took him a moment to recognise Sister Adela Seton.

'My God! Where have you come from?'

'That is hard to say exactly,' said Sister Adela. The planes of her face had sunken a little, which made her nose more prominent; in the pale light, she reminded him strongly of her dead brother. 'We have been pursued across half of northern France, sometimes by horsemen, sometimes by men with dogs. I am still not quite sure how we escaped capture.' The young man was shaking with exhaustion. 'Sit down' Merrivale said. 'Both of you. Mauro, bring them wine and find them some food. Sister, will you introduce your companion?'

'This is Master Hugolin Bessancourt, a clerk in the Chambre des Comptes in Paris.'

Merrivale blinked. 'Paris?'

'Indeed so. I will let him tell you his story.'

The wine arrived. Bessancourt gulped down half his cup, which brought a little colour to his cheeks. Hesitantly at first, he recounted his story, the letter Massy had discovered, Massy's murder and his own rescue by Adela, and what he had discovered in the mint at Abbeville. 'It's not just the false money, it's the silver. The Knights are stealing it, vast quantities from taxation revenues. Twenty-four thousand marks in just one shipment, and God knows how many others have been dispatched.'

'Where are they sending it?'

'Bruges,' said Adela. She smiled, a little ruefully. 'I have travelled across half of France only to find the secret was on my own doorstep.'

'Are the Knights receiving the silver also?'

She shook her head. 'DuSart is honest. But Bruges has plenty of banks, and not all of them trade legally.'

'No,' said Merrivale, thinking of his conversation with the Adornes. He looked at Bessancourt. 'You said you were puzzled by the stamps on the coins.'

'They weren't marked as being minted at Abbeville, obviously. The French coins had a simple mint mark, V. DIF. The mark on the English ones was more full, VIL Ā DIFELIN. *Vil* means town. The rest I do not understand.'

'*Difelin* is another word for Dublin,' Merrivale said.

Silence fell. 'Is there a mint in Dublin?' Bessancourt asked eventually.

'Not that I am aware of, nor has there ever been.' England had always tried to control the coinage of Ireland, just as it tried to control everything else there.

Adela's face was blank with incomprehension. 'Why would Nanteuil forge coins with an Irish mint mark?'

'Two possibilities,' said Merrivale. 'Either this is a false trail designed to lead us off the scent, or the conspiracy has also expanded to include Ireland. The possibility of an anti-English uprising should not be discounted. Do the Knights have many properties in Ireland?'

'Yes,' she said. 'There is a commandery at Wexford, and another at Kilmainham.' Realisation dawned. 'Which is just outside Dublin,' she said quietly.

'To whom do the Irish commanders report?'

'The Grand Prior of England. Philip de Thame.'

The pieces were starting to fall into place. 'I need your help,' he said. 'Both of you.'

Bessancourt looked surprised. 'I'm just a French clerk. How on earth can I help you? We are at war with the English.'

'We are,' said Merrivale, 'but I need your help in a different war. In the conflict I am talking about, we are on the same side. Do you want to avenge your dead friend? Do you want to get your old life back and live in peace?'

'Yes.' It was not clear which question Bessancourt was answering.

'Good.' Merrivale turned to Sister Adela. 'Will you return to Bruges? Take your friend with you, if you will; he knows more about money than we do, and should be useful. I am going to the city myself, on a diplomatic mission. Contact me through Adornes if you find anything.'

'Of course.' Adela paused for a moment. 'You know the closer we get to uncovering the conspiracy, the greater the danger will be.'

'Of course,' Merrivale repeated. 'That is always the way.'

Mauro and Warin gave them a hasty meal and accompanied them as far as Oye, out of the range of English patrols. Tiphaine returned a little later, and he told her about the two musicians and the mint at Abbeville. Her mouth twisted a little. 'Ireland,' she said. 'The rot is spreading.'

'This Dublin mint mark perplexes me. I cannot think what it means.'

'Why don't you write to Sir Nicholas Courcy? It will take time to receive an answer, but if anyone knows, it will be him.'

Courcy was an Irish man-at-arms who at various times had also been an engineer, an apothecary and a maker of gunpowder. He and his wife had served with the English army the previous summer, but had returned to their home in Kingsale. 'That is a good idea.'

'I have them occasionally,' Tiphaine said. 'What is happening to the silver, the real silver they are taking from the mint?'

'My guess is that some of it, at least, is being used to bribe the Count of Flanders to break off the English marriage. The king has ordered me to make sure the marriage goes through. I am hoping Adela and the Frenchman can trace the money.'

'The money is going to Blyth,' Tiphaine said.

'I am sure you are right. While they follow the trail, I shall put more pressure on the Bruges authorities to find Blyth. One way or another, we might be able to interrupt the flow of money and force some of them out into the open. Are you remaining here?'

'Yes. Brother Geoffrey and I are going into Calais, remember.'

'Why not let Geoffrey go on his own?'

'Because he doesn't know Saint-Pierre. I do.'

'Of course.' Merrivale eyed her for a moment. 'I know it is none of my business, but where were you this morning?'

'The queen summoned me again,' Tiphaine said. 'For one of her little chats.' Her mouth twisted again. 'She wanted to talk about *my future*, she said.'

'And what does she see in your future?'

'That really is none of your business,' Tiphaine said. 'Now take off that stupid tabard and come to bed.'

Calais, 7th of February, 1347

The following morning Merrivale sought out Brother Geoffrey and told him about the musicians and also about Adela and Bessancourt. Brother Geoffrey approved of Adela. 'She sounds highly capable. We could have used her in the old days, back in Savoy.'

'She does seem rather handy with a knife,' Merrivale agreed. 'I think the young man is frightened of her. I wonder if there is any way of disrupting the activities of this mint at Abbeville.'

'Inform the French authorities,' Geoffrey said.

'If the information comes from our side, it won't be believed.'

'There might be another way. What about Hatfield, and this link with our friend Zajíc?'

'I don't know whether to believe that story or not. Do you?'

'There is a way to find out,' Geoffrey said. 'The king has finally made up his mind, and is sending me to Trier at the end of the month. If the two musicians were telling the truth, Charles will talk to me, which will also cut Hatfield out of the loop. It will be interesting to see how he reacts, won't it?'

'Yes,' said Merrivale. 'On the other hand, if they weren't telling the truth, Charles may send your head back in a box.'

'There's little fear of that. He sent Zajíc to negotiate with you, remember?'

'That was three months ago. Kings change their minds, you know.'

Geoffrey smiled. 'So we're betting on Hatfield, are we? He is the man from the north?'

'I don't know,' said Merrivale. 'But increasingly, the evidence is pointing that way.'

'Be careful, Simon. That may be exactly what the enemy wants us to think.'

'Believe me, I have not forgotten the other two. But either way, if our suspicions turn out to be correct, Thomas Hatfield has some very serious questions to answer.'

Geoffrey smiled again. 'True enough.' The smile faded. 'Watch your back, old friend.'

Merrivale picked up his stick and rose to his feet. 'You too,' he said.

15

'Welcome back to Bruges, sir herald,' said Gillis van Coudebrouc, the burgemeester. 'What news from Calais?'

'The king has sent for reinforcements from England. Sooner or later, Calais will fall.'

'The sooner the better,' said Jan Metteneye, the commander of the town watch. 'The French have begun to muster their own army, at Amiens. Philippe is said to be on his way there now.'

It was bitterly cold in Bruges; the winter had been a hard one, and the waters of the Gronerei outside the window were still frozen hard. Men passed by on skates, some carrying enormous loads on their backs. The faint promise of spring in the air at Calais had receded.

'In which case, his Grace will be glad of the continued support of the Flemish cities,' the herald said.

'Please assure his Grace that we stand ready to aid him. We too are raising men, and reinforcing our positions along the frontier.'

'That is good to hear,' said the herald. 'Of course, above all else, the king desires the marriage of his daughter to the Count of Flanders. As we discussed, this will bring Flanders permanently into the English alliance, and England's army will help defend Flemish cities from attack. I take it you are still of this view?'

Coudebrouc smiled and nodded, but Metteneye was frowning. 'Forgive me, sir herald, but what makes you think we might have changed our minds?'

'Well, there is the behaviour of the count himself,' Merrivale said. 'We hear he is reluctant to undertake the marriage. He has refused to take part in negotiations over the betrothal contract. Have you any idea why?'

Coudebrouc had stopped smiling. 'What are you suggesting?' demanded Metteneye.

'I am suggesting that someone is working secretly against us. If that person is part of the League of Three, there will be grave consequences. I hope I make myself clear, gentlemen.'

'The League is true to its word,' Coudebrouc said. For the first time since Merrivale had met him, he sounded almost angry. 'Yes, we were hesitant about committing ourselves fully to this alliance, but that is in the past. We have given you no cause to doubt our fidelity, none whatever.'

'Then why is the count dragging his heels?' the herald asked.

There was a pause. 'We do not know,' Coudebrouc said finally. 'I spoke with him a week ago, and urged him to resume the negotiations. He refused.'

'How closely is he guarded?'

'He is held at the castle of ten Berghe, north of the city,' Metteneye said. 'A detachment of militiamen keep watch over him, commanded by our most reliable officers.'

'Could any of these men also be Pilgrims?'

'They are reliable,' Metteneye repeated, but Merrivale thought his voice lacked conviction.

'How often are men rotated in and out of the guard detachment?'

'Never. The same men are guarding him now as when we first captured him.'

'Then at the very least you must change the officers, and preferably the entire guard, once a week. Have the Pilgrims been active recently?'

'No,' said Coudebrouc, glad of the chance to give positive news. 'The city has been remarkably quiet. Tranquil, even.'

'Were you able to trace the three musicians? Marcelis and the other two?'

'They left the city,' said Metteneye. 'We heard they went to Ghent and thence to Liège. They are genuine musicians,' he added. 'We have spoken to other travelling players who have met them. It is possible they were not involved.'

'They were involved,' Merrivale said. 'Can you find out any more about their movements?'

'There is a music school in Bruges during Lent,' Coudebrouc said. 'Musicians come from all over Europe. Perhaps we can learn more then.'

Lent began tomorrow. 'We are also still searching for William Blyth, the English banker. Any word on him?'

'Heer Adornes informed us of your interest. The city has been thoroughly searched and there is no sign of him.'

'And the countryside? The towns?'

'We have limited authority outside the city,' Metteneye said. 'But we continue to make inquiries.'

Neither their words or manner filled Merrivale with confidence. 'Blyth had family here. His mother's name was Gistels. Has he tried to contact any of her kin?'

'The Gistels family were exiled from the city after the execution of Blyth's mother. We think some of them went to Sluis, but... it was a long time ago.'

They are not looking for Blyth, Merrivale thought. *They are not even trying. And they have made no attempt to prevent someone from influencing the Count of Flanders?*

Aloud, he said, 'I want to see the count, as soon as possible.'

'Of course,' said Coudebrouc. 'I will conduct you to him myself.'

'No,' said the herald. 'I want to see him alone.'

Kasteel ten Berghe, 14th of February, 1347

The castle was about two miles north of the city. Riding with his escort over the frozen fields under an icy blue sky, Merrivale could see it on the horizon, a massive fortress of red brick gleaming in the pale sunlight. As they drew closer he saw high walls overlooking a frozen moat and the figures of armed men at the gates and up on the battlements. The place looked secure enough. But money, he knew, could penetrate even the strongest fortification.

'Welcome, *meneer*. I am the count's steward. He waits for you in the hall.'

'He is expecting me?'

'Yes, *meneer*. Word came from the city yesterday.'

That damned burgemeester, Merrivale thought. *Never mind. I have bullied noblemen into submission before, and I can do it again*. He followed the steward up the steps into the high-ceilinged hall where tall windows let in shafts of sunlight. Fires burned in hearths at either end of the room, and the floor was warmed by encaustic heating. Heavy woollen wall hangings, decorated with hunting scenes, help seal in the warmth.

A young man stood at the far end of the hall, hands behind his back. He was richly dressed in an embroidered blue coat and white hose; his shoes were of red leather, and his hair had been recently curled. Merrivale walked slowly towards him, red and gold tabard glittering in the sunlight. The ferrule of his stick tapped softly on the floor.

'Have I the honour of addressing the Count of Flanders?' he asked.

'Yes,' the young man said shortly.

'Good.' The herald pointed to a bench beside the fire. 'Sit down.'

'I prefer to stand,' said the count.

'I said, sit down.'

The young man's fist clenched. 'Who are you? How dare you speak to me this way?'

Merrivale rapped his stick hard on the floor. 'I don't think you understand the situation. I give the orders here, boy, and if I give the order to have you taken out and drowned in the moat, that order will be obeyed. Now, *sit down.*'

Resistance went out of the young man like air from a deflating bladder. He sat down, staring up at the herald in a mixture of fear and resentment. 'What do you want?'

'I want to know what game you think you are playing.' He waited.

'Game?' the count said eventually.

'You swore an oath before God and man that you would wed Princess Isabella. Now you are refusing to discuss the betrothal contracts. Have you taken leave of your senses? You have no bargaining space, boy, none whatever. Fulfil your oath, marry the princess and have done.'

The fear was growing now. 'I'm not certain I can.'

'Why not? For the love of God, you're a sixteen-year-old boy who has been offered a royal virgin to play with. Think about her. She is comely, she has soft skin and golden hair and the scent she uses smells like violets. Any other man your age would be slavering at the chance. Why in hell's name are you delaying?'

The count said nothing. Merrivale reached under his tabard and brought out a small roll of parchment bound with a red ribbon, and handed it to him. 'This is a bill of exchange for ten thousand marks of silver, drawn on a bank in Bruges. It is yours. Your attendants will help you negotiate it, and will bring you the money. At Easter, the queen and the Bishop of Durham will arrive with the betrothal contract. Once it is signed, another ten thousand marks will be paid to you.

At the same time, the estates you inherited from your father will be handed over. Croesus and Midas will envy your wealth.'

The young man stared up at him, holding the unopened roll in his hand.

'Someone is offering you more,' said Merrivale. Still the count said nothing. 'I doubt if you will ever see the money they are promising you. It is far more likely you will end up dead.'

'I cannot stop them. Neither can you.'

'You are frightened of them.'

'Everyone is frightened of the Pilgrims. Even the guards. That is why they let them in.'

'The Pilgrims come to see you?'

'Yes. There are three of them, musicians. One is called Marcelis. I can't remember the names of the others.'

'Tomaset and Garnier,' Merrivale said.

'Yes. Tomaset and Garnier, that's right.'

God damn it, the herald thought in sudden anger, *they are working right under our noses. I would like to break that smiling bastard Coudebrouc, and Metteneye too. But we cannot offend Bruges, not yet.*

'When you are Count of Flanders in your own right, with an English army at your back, then *you* will hold the whip hand,' he said. 'You can destroy the Pilgrims then. We will help you.'

The count did not respond. 'It is the only way,' Merrivale said quietly, looking down at him. 'The marriage and the English alliance offers safety and security, for you and your people. The road you travel with the Pilgrims and their masters will lead to a quick and early death. Make your choice, my lord.'

After a long moment the young man stood up. 'I will sign the contracts. Tell me what to do.'

'Give me a letter telling me you accept the terms the king proposes. At Easter the contracts will be signed, and the marriage will take place as soon as possible thereafter. She is a bright and beautiful girl, who longs to be married. You will not regret your choice.'

'If the Pilgrims learn of this meeting, they will kill me.'

'You will be protected. You have my word on that.' He would tell Metteneye to strengthen the guard at ten Berghe, and to rotate the watch and ban the musicians from the castle. As soon as possible, English troops needed to reinforce the guard. At all costs, this young man must survive.

'Thank you,' said the count.

Merrivale looked surprised. 'For what?'

'For helping me to make up my mind, and giving me the courage to defy them. For that, I shall be forever grateful.'

Returning to the city, Merrivale found a Knight of Saint John waiting for him at the gate, cloaked and muffled against the cold. 'Sir herald? Commander DuSart begs you to attend on him as soon as you may.'

DuSart received him in the same vaulted white room as before. Sister Adela and Bessancourt were with him. The latter looked a little less nervous, which was faintly surprising. With them too, wrapped in a black fur robe and leaning on his ebony stick, was Oppicius Adornes.

'We have found the trail of the French silver,' said DuSart. 'It was not easy. They ship the money by water, along the rivers and canals. The convoys move only by night, and the guards are alert and wear no identifying devices.'

'How do they bring the silver into the city?' Merrivale asked.

'They don't. They take it to Maldegem, about twelve miles from here. Maldegem is also a commandery of the Knights of Saint John.'

Merrivale digested this. 'You told me last year that the Flemish knights are loyal to the League of Three.'

'They are. The Flemish commanderies were part of the Priory of France, but they broke away nearly fifty years ago. But Maldegem is part of the bailiwick of Utrecht, which in turn is part of the priory of Germany. Thus outside our control.'

'And we know some of the German knights have been approached,' said the herald. 'Including the Grand Prior.' He remembered Tiphaine's words. *The rot is spreading.* 'Once the money reaches Maldegem, what happens next?'

'We don't yet know,' said Sister Adela. 'We have no eyes or ears inside that commandery. Relations between our own houses and the German priory have been strained since we broke away.'

'Nothing at all? You said Maldegem is only a dozen miles away.'

Adela smiled. 'This is Flanders. You can find a great deal of history in a dozen miles.'

'They must have selected Maldegem for a reason. Its proximity to Bruges, perhaps. *Meneer* Bessancourt, you saw a letter that referred to Bruges.'

'Yes,' said the Frenchman. 'The money is to be used in Bruges.' Perhaps he was getting used to being afraid all the time, Merrivale mused. 'We have discovered one thing about the Knights at Maldegem,' Bessancourt continued. 'They are converting silver into gold, and have been doing so for some time. It makes sense, of course. The French silver coins they stole are heavily debased, and gold is more portable. A single gold ducat is worth two hundred and forty silver pennies. You can transport a lot more wealth at one time.'

'How is it that you have only just discovered this?' Merrivale looked at Adornes. 'When people trade silver for gold on the money markets, men like you quickly come to know about it.'

'They did not use the ordinary bourses,' Adornes said, speaking for the first time. 'The Knights have their own dark exchange.'

'How does it work?'

'We mint our own ducats.' DuSart reached into the pocket of his robe and pulled out a gold coin, which he laid on the desk in front of him. Merrivale examined it. The obverse showed a Knight of Saint John kneeling before the figure of John the Baptist, while the reverse held the image of an angel. The inscription read MAGISTER D. GOZON – RHODE; coined in the name of Grand Master Dieud-onné de Gozon, minted in the town of Rhodes.

'I have never seen one of these,' Merrivale said.

'Few people have,' said DuSart. 'The coins are new, we only started minting them last year. They are used primarily for business dealings between houses of the Order. We also use bills of exchange, of course, but for smaller transactions payment in coin is sometimes simpler. But these ducats rarely enter circulation outside the Order.'

'Several months ago, the commander at Maldegem wrote to some of the other commanders and offered to buy their ducats at a good discount,' Sister Adela said. 'He did not write to us, of course; as rebels, we are cut off from the rest of the Order, and so the news came late. A Scottish compatriot of mine serving in another commandery heard of this and, knowing of my interest, passed the news to me.'

'And this is only one channel by which they are acquiring gold,' said Adornes. 'You are right, sir herald. Gold is scarce, and when men trade it in quantities, we hear about it. We think William Blyth is also buying gold.'

Merrivale looked at him. 'Did you not close down the dark exchanges?'

'All that we could find. We think Blyth continued to trade a few bills at a time, using intermediaries, but we could not track these. A few weeks ago, word began to circulate that someone is offering to discount bills for anything up to a third of their value. But the redeemer must make payment in gold.'

'Are people taking up the offer?'

'Our own bankers and merchants know better. But some of the outland merchants, who don't know Blyth or his history, are rushing to make bargains.'

'The conspirators are preparing their next move,' the herald said.

'It would seem so,' said Adornes.

'Where is Blyth?'

No one answered. Merrivale gazed steadily at Adornes. 'A storm is coming, *meneer*. In a little while, it will break. When it does, you will not be able to sit by and watch it pass. Coudebrouc and Metteneye think they can, but they are wrong. This cataclysm will consume all of us, unless we stop it.'

Adornes said nothing. 'Someone is aiding Blyth,' the herald said. 'One does not conduct banking operations of this scale on one's own. Such a thing needs clerks, messengers, agents in the bourse. Blyth has people around him. You must know who some of them are.' He paused. 'All you have to do is tell us what you know. We will do the rest.'

Slowly, gripping his stick, Adornes rose to his feet. 'When the family of Katelijne Gistels fled Bruges they went first to the town of Sluis,' he said quietly. 'Later they settled in the village of Sint Anna, near the town. The rumour on the bourse is, if you wish to buy cheap bills of exchange, take your gold to Sint Anna. The people you refer to may be members of the Gistels family. That is all I know.'

Or all you will tell me, Merrivale thought. He looked at DuSart. 'Shall we go to Coudebrouc and Metteneye and ask for men?'

The commander shook his head. 'I trust my own Knights more than the Bruges militia. It will take a day to assemble them. Tomorrow, we shall go.'

Sluis, 15th of February, 1347

You can find a great deal of history in a dozen miles.

Thirty Knights answered DuSart's call; less than Merrivale had been expecting but more than enough, DuSart assured him, to deal with any opposition they might encounter. Professional to their fingertips, they arrived fully armed and armoured with heavy black cloaks over their red robes. DuSart handled them with a quiet confidence that Merrivale admired. *I have underestimated him*, the herald thought. *He is a good man, and a useful ally. I must remember to work more closely with him.*

Adela and Bessancourt remained in Bruges. The Knights rode to Sluis in the afternoon, arriving at dusk while the colours of sunset were still brilliant in the sky, red and gold in the west, pink and deep lavender in the east with the first stars shivering into life overhead. Sluis was a collection of brick houses and a big church with a high tower that doubled as a lighthouse, huddled at the mouth of a muddy river emptying into a shallow bay. The tide was out, and the rotting planks and sternposts of sunken ships could be seen protruding from the ooze; French ships of war destroyed by the English seven years earlier. On the far side of the bay, the burned-out churches and houses on the island of Damme were black silhouettes against the flaming sky.

DuSart had sent scouts ahead, and now these came riding back. 'Sint Anna is two miles west of here. There are a dozen houses in the village, along with a church and a manor house. No lights are showing.'

'Is the place deserted?' DuSart asked.

'No. We heard horses moving in one of the barns.'

The commander nodded. 'So, they are waiting for us,' he said. 'It makes no odds. If Blyth is in Sint Anna, we'll have him. What is the ground like around the village?'

'Between here and Sint Anna is a salt marsh, pretty much impassable. But there's dry ground on the far side.'

'Then we'll circle around and wait for the fall of night. Once it is fully dark, we go in. I'll take the manor house; Joren, you and your men make for the church, and Lutgart and his file will search the village. Frido, your lot are the reserve; if we run into opposition, come in hard and fast.'

Brother Frido was a big man, bearded and bear-like in his black cloak. He nodded. Quietly the Knights went about their preparations, checking weapons, muffling the harness of their horses with rags, pulling hoods over their bascinets so there would be no betraying gleam of metal in the starlight. 'You should wait here,' DuSart said to Merrivale.

The herald shook his head. 'I want to be there when Blyth is taken.'

'Do you want a sword? We can lend you one.'

'Heralds are forbidden to carry weapons, commander. You know that.'

Beneath the raised visor of his bascinet, DuSart grinned. 'You're not exactly an ordinary herald.'

As the sky darkened they forded the sluggish river and splashed through the marshes beyond, coming quickly to the dryer ground. Frost crunched on the grass. Steam spouted from the nostrils of their horses. In the silver glow of starlight they could see the huddled cottages of Sint Anna, the church tower and larger bulk of the moated manor house. Nothing moved there; all was dark.

Slowly the Knights turned towards the village and fanned out, breaking up into separate parties each making for its objective. Brother Frido's reserves followed them. Merrivale rode behind DuSart, watching the shadows.

They were fifty yards from the village when the church bell clanged once, a single note echoing in the cold air, and then fell silent.

DuSart held up his hand. His men stopped. 'Who goes there?' the commander shouted. 'Come out and show yourselves!'

In answer came a man's voice, quiet but carrying, and the hair stood up on Merrivale's neck.

'*I am a poor pilgrim, travelling in a perilous land,*' said Nicodemus the assassin. '*In God's name I am weary, and I seek shelter.*'

'It's a trap,' Merrivale said sharply, but he was too late. An arrow hissed out of the night and struck DuSart at the base of the throat, just above his breastplate. The commander clutched at the shaft embedded in his body and rolled out of the saddle, falling heavily to the ground. Another arrow followed, killing the horse of the man beside him. Roaring, the rest spurred their horses towards the village, Brother Frido's men thundering after them. Merrivale jumped down and knelt beside the commander's body. He was already unconscious, blood pouring from his throat; he would be dead within minutes.

Fighting erupted in the village, shouting and screaming and the clatter of weapons on armour. Rising and grasping his stick, Merrivale hurried towards the village. Bodies already lay in the street. Up ahead the Knights fought with a cold, disciplined fury, carving their way through the dark figures that swarmed out of the houses to attack them. A solid phalanx led by the big figure of Brother Frido reached the door of the church and smashed it open, rushing inside. Breath steaming, his wounded leg aching, Merrivale hurried after them. He spotted a single dark figure leading a horse away from the gate of the manor house. '*Blyth!*' he screamed, and ran towards the other man.

It was not Blyth. The man turned as Merrivale approached, and the herald saw he was tall and lean. He had a longbow in his hands, an arrow at the nock. It would take him only a second to raise the bow and shoot. Merrivale halted, holding out his hands to show he was unarmed, but he knew this would make no difference.

'Nicodemus,' he said.

'Ah, you remember me,' the other man said mockingly.

'I would hardly forget a hell-spawn like you. Where is Blyth?'

'Where you'll never find him, herald. The Pilgrims are protecting him.'

Merrivale pointed towards the village where the Knights were hunting down and killing the defenders. 'The Pilgrims are dying.'

'They don't mind. They'll get their reward in heaven, or they think they will, just like your crusaders. But there's thousands more Pilgrims, herald. They're everywhere, all around you, just waiting for their moment.'

'Are you going to kill me?' Merrivale asked.

'Nothing would give me more satisfaction, but it's not your time to die. When that time comes, he wants the pleasure for himself. Those are his orders.'

'Whose orders? The man from the north?'

'Yes. He knows you call him that, by the way. It amuses him. That's what the old queen used to call him, he says. Her man from the north.' Nicodemus raised his bow. 'Walk away now, herald.'

'You said you had orders not to kill me.'

'I could cripple you, though. You're already lame in one leg. If I put a shaft through the knee of the other, you'll never walk again. Now, turn around and go.'

Merrivale said nothing. An arrow hissed and thudded into ground between Merrivale's feet. Nicodemus already had another arrow at the nock. 'Go,' he repeated. 'While you still can.'

The herald turned away. Behind him, he heard Nicodemus mount the horse. Suddenly furious, heedless of the danger, he wheeled around and began to run, but Nicodemus was already spurring the horse. Pain shot through Merrivale's bad leg and he halted, leaning on his stick and gasping, unable to do anything but watch as Nicodemus rode away.

Bruges, 16th of February, 1347

They sat silently in the white room at the hospital in Bruges; Merrivale, Adela, Bessancourt and Brother Frido, who had been elected by his fellow Knights to take charge of the commandery. They had brought DuSart's body back that morning, and two other men whose wounds required treatment. The Knights had been badly outnumbered, but their training and discipline had won out; DuSart had been the only fatality. The Pilgrims had fought to the end, refusing all offers of surrender; the last of them had been hacked down before the altar of the church, still fighting. The sanctity of the church was of no avail to them.

Bessancourt was the first to break the silence. 'We could go the burgemeester and ask him to take action against the Pilgrims.'

Adela shook her head. 'Coudebrouc is afraid,' she said. 'Afraid he will be next.' Her voice was dull with fatigue and emotion. She had been fond of DuSart; everyone had. His Knights had been in tears as they gathered up his body at Sint Anna. *I should have known this was an ambush*, Merrivale thought. *I could have saved him.*

'The Pilgrims are everywhere,' Brother Frido said. 'Their power and reach seem to have no limits.'

'What do they want?' Merrivale asked. 'Are they intending to overthrow the governments of the League of Three?'

'They have never made any public statement of their aims,' said Brother Frido. He paused. 'Although, I did hear they were behind the revolution in Liège two years ago.'

'What happened in Liège?'

'The commune overthrew the bishop, and defeated the army he led against them. Many Pilgrims supported the commune, and still do.'

'The Pilgrims also defend Poperinge against the militia of Ypres,' said Adela.

'And they are in league with the man from the north,' Merrivale said tiredly. 'His power, and theirs, seems to grow with every passing day, and it seems there is not a damned thing we can do about it. Nor are we any closer to establishing his identity.'

He looked at Adela and Bessancourt. 'Our only hope is to trace the money. Will you remain here and continue your work? Get Adornes to help you.'

'Adornes is the one who sent you to Sint Anna,' Bessancourt said sharply.

'I very much doubt if he knew what was going to happen. Someone fed him false information. Nevertheless, he is now in a difficult position. Blackmail him if you need to, but get him to help you find the right trail.'

Adela nodded. 'What will you do, sir herald?'

'I leave for Calais in the morning. I must report to the king.'

16

'Bishop Hatfield wants to open negotiations with the burghers of Calais,' Queen Philippa said. 'He thinks they will persuade the garrison to surrender.'

Having spent half an hour manoeuvring the conversation around to this point, Tiphaine remained silent. The queen shifted a little on her cushioned seat. She was pregnant again, for the eleventh time in seventeen years, and her back pains were worsening. She looked sharply at her ladies in waiting. 'Well? Is he right?'

'I think it unlikely,' said Alice Bedingfield. 'What would they have to gain? So far, at least, the defences have held. And they must be hopeful that the French army will come to their rescue.'

Elizabeth Chandos considered the matter. 'The defences won't hold forever,' she said. 'Lord Rowton's intelligencer speaks of food shortages already, even though we have not blockaded the port. If we do close the port, the townspeople will soon begin to starve. The burghers may want to avoid that fate.'

'Perhaps we need to find out,' Tiphaine suggested.

The queen looked at her. 'What do you have in mind, *demoiselle*?'

'The king could send his own ambassador into Calais to discover the situation. I know Simon Merrivale is away in Bruges, but Brother Geoffrey is still in the camp.' She paused for a moment. 'After all, if anyone is going to open negotiations with the enemy, surely it should be the king and not the bishop.'

'I agree,' the queen said. She did not like Hatfield, as Tiphaine already knew. 'An excellent suggestion, *demoiselle*. I shall speak to his Grace this evening.'

Gripping the arms of her chair, she began to rise. The others rose too, and Bedingfield hurried forward to give her an arm. The queen looked at Tiphaine. 'Have you thought further about my offer?'

'Yes. Your grace is most generous.'

'You need to find a place, *demoiselle*. You cannot carry on as the herald's dependant forever. You need to make a decision.'

'I will do so, your Grace. I just need a little more time.'

'I should like your answer by Easter, *demoiselle*.'

'You shall have it, your Grace.'

Outside, she hurried to find Brother Geoffrey. 'She has agreed. She will tell the king tonight, and I expect he will send for you tomorrow and give his instructions.'

The canon nodded gravely. 'I will be the formal negotiator. You sniff around the sidelines and see what you can find.' He smiled. 'That is the role Simon often played, when we worked together.'

'Don't count on me being as good as him,' said Tiphaine. 'Apparently, I am merely his dependant.'

Calais, 20ᵗʰ of February, 1347

On the front lines the trebuchets crouched like one-armed monsters in the mud, each surrounded by its wattle enclosure. Beside them the cannon sat on their frames, their black snouts silent and reeking of brimstone. The archers who harassed the garrison had pulled back and stood leaning on their bows, their hose and faded tunics patched and splattered with mud. They looked exhausted. It struck Tiphaine how unreal life was in Villeneuve-la-Hardie, with its taverns and shops and marketplace. Down here among the trenches and ditches and hurdles of the siege lines the war was ever-present.

'Shall we go?' said Brother Geoffrey.

She nodded. She wore her boy's clothes again, plain cote and hose, with her hair piled under a hood. She was not sure if anyone had seen through her ruse on the previous visit; probably they had, but it didn't matter. Spies came in many guises. Brother Geoffrey wore a cloak over his black habit and carried a staff with a white flag of truce fluttering in the wind. Side by side they walked out across the marsh, following a rough timber road laid down earlier by the besiegers to drag engines and boats towards the walls. As they drew closer she saw how the walls were scarred and pocked, the battlements broken by stone shot. She saw too the broken scaling ladders and sunken half-burned boats still lying in the moat.

The ramparts over the Saint-Omer gate were blackened with fire. The gatehouse had been assaulted at least three times that she knew of. Bedingfield was right, she thought. The defences are as strong as ever, and the French army is gathering at Amiens. Why would the town surrender? She pulled her hood forward, concealing her face.

Crossbows swung to cover them as they approached the gate, but no bolts flew. Brother Geoffrey halted and hailed the men on the gatehouse. 'King Edward sends a message to the people of Calais. Will you admit us? We are alone and unarmed.'

No one answered, but after a moment chains began to rattle and the drawbridge came down, settling into place with a thump. A postern in the main gate opened and a man-at-arms motioned them to enter. Inside were more men with weapons levelled. 'Who are you?' demanded the man-at-arms.

'I am Brother Geoffrey of Maldon, canon of the Augustinian order. My companion is called Le Normand. We ask that you take us to the mayor and the *échevins*.'

'Messire de Vienne is the governor of the town. We will take you to him.'

'He is welcome to join us,' Brother Geoffrey said calmly. 'But my message is to the townspeople.'

'You do not give orders here, brother,' said the man-at-arms, and he drew his sword.

'What is this?' demanded another voice.

They turned to see another man, richly dressed in black with fur trim on his cloak and a round black cap over long, fiery red hair. Eustache de Saint-Pierre, the mayor of Calais, glanced once at Tiphaine and then stared at Brother Geoffrey. 'Why have you come here?'

'To convey a message from King Edward to the people of Calais,' Geoffrey said patiently.

The man-at-arms frowned. 'We should take them to Messire de Vienne. He commands here!'

'Take them to my house,' said Saint-Pierre. 'Inform Messire de Vienne and the *échevins*, and ask them to meet us there. Those are my orders.'

Reluctantly, the orders were obeyed. They were taken to Saint-Pierre's big brick house, where servants ushered Brother Geoffrey into the hall, closing the door in Tiphaine's face before she could follow.

A valet motioned her into a parlour where she sat listening to the murmur of voices from the hall. She could not make out the words, but she could hear the tone of their voices. The deep commanding one, sounding angry at times, she guessed was Jean de Vienne, governor of the beleaguered garrison; another, sharp and resentful, she recognised as belonging to Maninghem. Brother Geoffrey's voice remained calm and measured, as always.

The door opened and Saint-Pierre entered, closing it behind him. He stood for a moment with his hands on his hips, looking down at her. His red hair shone like burnished copper in the pale light.

'I have only a few minutes. Why have you come back?'

'I carried your message to Bishop Hatfield as requested,' Tiphaine said.

'And why has he taken so long to answer?'

'Because the king was opposed to negotiation and forbade him to respond. Now, his Grace has reconsidered, but decided to conduct the negotiations himself. He sent Brother Geoffrey to open talks.'

'And why have *you* come, Le Normand? If that really is your name.'

'To see you, *messire*. Brother Geoffrey carries the formal message from the king, for of Messire de Vienne and his officers. I carry another, for your ears only.'

Saint-Pierre paused. 'What does he have to say to me that he would not say to Messire de Vienne?'

'The king knows your situation here. Once the English seal off the harbour, which they will do soon, your supplies of food and water will run out very quickly. You also suspect that someone in the town is spying for the English, and perhaps even willing to connive at undermining the defences. If the town should fall thanks to traitors within, it will be sacked and the population killed. You face a choice of a slow death by starvation or a quick one at the hands of the English soldiers.'

She saw Saint-Pierre's face change. *He does know there is a traitor*, she thought. *I wonder if he knows who it is.*

'The king holds all the advantages, you say. So why is he willing to talk now?'

'I could say that he is unwilling to let the townspeople suffer the horrors of famine or sack, but that would be a lie. The assaults on the walls have failed, and he is running out of patience.'

'And he knows the French army is mustering,' said Saint-Pierre.

'Of course, but he also has another problem. He does not trust Bishop Hatfield. So, you see, he wants to end the siege as quickly as possible. His terms are generous,' she added.

Saint-Pierre pointed in the direction of the hall. 'Are they? All Brother Geoffrey has offered so far is to allow the garrison to keep their arms and march out unmolested. He has said nothing about the town.'

'Because he doesn't want Vienne to know the real terms. I can tell you what those are, but first I need information.'

In the hall voices were raised, some men shouting, Vienne growling back at them. Saint-Pierre stared at her, trying to read her shadowy face. *He believes I am telling the truth*, she thought, *because he badly wants to believe. The future is dark for Calais, but I hold out a ray of hope. In his place, I would probably believe too.*

'What information?' Saint-Pierre asked finally. His voice was guarded.

'Nothing that need trouble your conscience, I assure you. What is your connection with Hatfield?'

The mayor blinked; it was not the question he was expecting. 'He came to Calais in 1328, and spent some weeks here. I got to know him, and we developed some business interests together. We maintained a correspondence until the start of the war.'

And probably after, Tiphaine thought. 'What brought him to Calais?'

'He was sent by the Earl of Lancaster, the one who died not long ago. There was much discussion about who would inherit the throne of France when King Charles IV died. Lancaster sent Hatfield and another man to hold clandestine talks with the French government about the possibility of King Edward being offered the crown. Those talks were held in Calais.'

'Who was this other man?'

'I don't think I ever knew his name. We spoke only once, and I gathered that his relations with Hatfield were not exactly cordial.'

Tiphaine nodded. 'Who represented the French side?'

'The French king's private secretary, and Étienne Aubert. He is the Cardinal-Bishop of Ostia now. Back then he was nobody, just a professor of law at the University of Toulouse. There was an observer from the Empire too, a clergyman.'

Quiet talks between low-ranking members of both courts, Tiphaine thought. Easy for both sides to deny the meeting had ever taken place. But Aubert, the man with designs on the papacy, was one of the conspirators.

The men in the hall were still shouting. 'I must return,' Saint-Pierre said. 'Tell me what the king is offering.'

'One more thing first. Jehan de Nortkerque, the man who deals in fish and whale meat. What can you tell me about him?'

'Nortkerque?' Again Saint-Pierre stared in surprise. 'Why are you interested in him?'

Tiphaine said nothing. Saint-Pierre glanced towards the door. 'He came from Poperinge a few years ago and settled here. He left not long before Christmas, to return to his home town. I was not sorry to see him go.'

'Why?'

'Nortkerque had connections with the Pilgrims, and I want nothing to do with them. They're dangerous, and loyal to no one but themselves.'

Tiphaine nodded. 'Once the town surrenders, the king will guarantee your lives and property. No English troops will enter the city. All you have to do, once the garrison has departed, is come out and swear fealty to him. Hostages will be given while you do so, to ensure your safety.'

She had no right to make this offer, but Saint-Pierre could not be certain. 'Vienne will never allow us to accept.'

'Then don't tell him. Order the townspeople to open the gates.'

Tiphaine saw doubt and anxiety and temptation all mingled in his face. He shook his head, abruptly. 'I must go.'

–

The negotiations did not last much longer. Tiphaine and Brother Geoffrey were escorted in silence back to the gate; the postern was opened once more, and they made their way back across the muddy wastes to the English siege lines. 'What did they say?' Tiphaine asked.

'Governor de Vienne was surprisingly civilised. He only threatened to hang me once. He has orders from King Philip to defend Calais to the last man, and is determined to do so. He threatened to expel or execute any of the burghers who opposed him.'

'Was Maninghem there?'

'A bald man with a beaked nose? Yes, he was there. He said very little, but I thought he seemed to be supporting Vienne. The rest were in favour of opening talks. However, I doubt if Vienne will agree. And you?'

Tiphaine told him about the conversation with Saint-Pierre. 'I wonder who this other man is. The one who came to Calais with Hatfield.'

Brother Geoffrey nodded. 'I must report to the king. Then, you and I need to talk.'

—

She waited at the house, alone. Mauro and Warin had gone with Simon to Bruges, but that was not why the little cabin seemed empty. Damn the queen, she thought furiously. Why did she have to interfere?

Geoffrey returned an hour later. 'What did you tell him?' Tiphaine asked.

'Only that the negotiations have failed, for the moment. The king has agreed to let the matter lie. I am ordered to depart for Trier as soon as possible.'

'I am worried, Geoffrey. I feel like the ground is melting beneath our feet.'

'Go on,' he said after a moment.

'There is weakness everywhere. Rebellion in Flanders, chaos in France, currencies debased, trade interrupted, the Knights of Saint John practically at war with themselves, the pope ill and weak, the Holy Roman Empire divided. These men are creating chaos, and we are doing little to stop them. The king and queen have pinned their hopes on this Flemish marriage. I tell you, I would not bet a farthing on it ever coming to pass, or on the King of the Romans coming to our aid. Our enemies will kill the count, and the king, and hell will erupt.'

There was silence for a while. 'You may be right,' Geoffrey said. 'I wonder, what are they waiting for? Why not strike now?'

'I don't know,' Tiphaine said. 'But we cannot wait much longer to find out. Simon and his friends in Bruges are trying to trace the money, but that may take too long. I want to know two things. Why did Jehan Nortkerque come from Poperinge to Calais? And why did he go back?'

Brother Geoffrey looked briefly puzzled. 'Why do the actions of a trader in whale meat matter?'

'I don't know,' said Tiphaine. 'But they do, if he is connected to Nicodemus. I must go, Geoffrey.'

He watched her, concern in his eyes. 'Go where, *demoiselle*?'

'Anywhere but here. I need to get away from the queen.'

'The queen? What has she done?'

'Offered me a post in her household,' Tiphaine said. 'She has asked me to become one of her damsels.'

The concern deepened. 'Why? Is she trying to separate you from Simon?'

'No. It has nothing to do with Simon.' That was not true, but it was an easy lie to tell. 'I cannot do it, Geoffrey. I cannot become a lady of the court, dancing attendance on the queen, while the war drags on and the Pilgrims murder people in the shadows. Simon will pursue the conspirators to the end. I cannot let him do it alone.'

'He is not alone,' said Geoffrey. Leaning forward, he kissed her on the forehead like a benediction, and rose to his feet. 'So long as you and I draw breath, dear sister in Christ, he will never be alone. Go and do what you must. I shall pray that God watches over you.'

After he had gone she waited for a while in the empty house, staring at the wall and thinking. Then she rose, still dressed in her boy's tunic and hood and hose, and went outside. In the marketplace she found some Flemish traders, women from Gravelines and Dunkirk selling eggs and fish and beer. There was no meat or cheese, for it was now Lent. She stopped in front of them.

'Can anyone tell me the way to Poperinge?' she asked.

17

The cannon boomed, ten guns firing one after another, sending clouds of smoke drifting across the marshes. The arms of trebuchets wind-milled across the sky, sending more stone shot to smash against the walls of Calais. From the ramparts, a French gun barked a defiant reply. Standing on the dunes north of the town, Merrivale watched companies of men edge cautiously towards the walls, Maurice de Berkeley's men from Gloucestershire shooting clouds of arrows at the ramparts. Iron Henry's mercenaries moving up close behind them, with Llewellyn's spearmen out on the flanks. Some of the Lancashire and Cheshire men-at-arms were there too, men from Lord Rowton's retinue. These cohorts were the last reliable men in the army. Many of the rest were too tired and sick to fight.

The attack, Merrivale knew, was a feint; King Edward was not going to throw any more men against the unyielding walls of Calais. Ignoring the archers and the cannon, the king stood with Hatfield, Warwick the marshal and the knights of his bodyguard, watching a flotilla of ships run down the wind towards the harbour entrance. 'Here they come,' he said with satisfaction. 'Now, by God, we'll show those bastards who has the whip hand. We may not be able to storm Calais, but we can damned well starve them out.'

There were five ships, each with a single mast and faded red sail. Weather-beaten, old and slow, they were about to be sacrificed. The king had finally approved Lord Rowton's plan to sink ships in the shallow water off the Rysbank and block the harbour entrance. Rowton was in command, on the leading ship; this venture was his idea, he said, and he would run the same risks as the sailors.

A brisk wind blew from the west, and waves crashed in white foam on the beach below the dunes. Standing beside the king, Thomas

Hatfield shook his head. 'This is madness. Lord Rowton is jeopardising the lives of the seamen, and costing us ships we can ill afford to lose.'

'On the contrary, the ships are expendable,' said Warwick. 'And the sailors are being well paid for the risk.'

'Paid with what? There is barely a piece of genuine money in the camp.'

The king glared at him. 'If you have a better plan, my lord bishop, kindly state it. If not, then I pray you remain silent.'

Hatfield stood silent, his cheeks burning. Warwick cleared his throat. 'If this attempt fails, sire, there is always the other idea. Occupying the Rysbank itself, and fortifying it to block the harbour.'

'Too risky,' the king said. 'I trust Eustace's judgement. This venture will succeed, I am convinced of it.'

The men around him said nothing. The king watched eagerly as the ships came on, rolling heavily in the waves. All were ballasted with stones to make certain they sank quickly, but the dead weight made them hard to handle in such strong seas. One was already drifting away from the others, its sail flapping as the crew tried to drag her around. Warwick shook his head.

'We've lost that one. She's heading straight onto the Rysbank.'

More cannon boomed. Far from being deceived by Berkeley's feint, the French had mounted guns on the city walls to cover the harbour, and these now opened fire on the oncoming ships. Stone shot splashed into the water beside the leading ship, another knocked splinters out of the vessel behind it. Rowton's ships could make no reply. Another shot hit the mast of the second ship, snapping it off cleanly and dragging the yard and sail down over the side. The watching men groaned as the ship sloughed around, drifting helplessly.

'Shit,' the king said under his breath.

The drifting ships grounded in the shallow water off the Rysbank at about the same time. The one with the broken mast rolled over onto her side; the men watching from the dunes could see the tiny figures of her crew struggling to reach shore before they were swept away by the pounding waves. The other stuck hard in the sand, the sea piling over her stern and scouring her deck clean.

'Come on, come on,' the king muttered.

The remaining three ships reached the harbour entrance. French cannon pounded them and crossbow bolts flew in black streaks from the town walls, but the ships lowered their sails and dropped anchor.

For a moment, nothing seemed to happen, and then all three ships began to settle rapidly. Within a minute only their masts were visible above the water. Their crews scrambled into small boats and rowed away, pulling hard against the tide. A stone shot smashed one boat, spilling men into the water; a second boat pulled alongside and her crew began dragging men aboard. Somehow the remaining boats managed to row out of the harbour and ride the heavy seas. Their crews landed on the beach not far from the king's position.

Lord Rowton strode up onto the dunes, his hair and clothes streaming with seawater; he had been in the boat that sank. 'Eustace,' the king said sharply. 'Are you hurt?'

'No, sire, by the grace of God. But I lost some good men.'

'Did you succeed in your aim?'

Rowton looked down at the ground for a moment, then back up at the king. 'No, sire,' he said flatly. 'We needed to sink all five ships in the channel. We have made it more difficult for the French, but their ships can still get through.'

'Then you failed,' Hatfield said angrily. 'This has all been for nothing! The garrison will be laughing at us.'

'Probably,' Rowton said. He stood in the cold wind, his clothes dripping as he gazed at Hatfield. 'Yes, my lord bishop, I failed. You too will fail one day, and when you do, I hope you have the good grace to admit it and take the consequences.'

Normally the king would have rebuked his quarrelling advisors, but now he simply stood staring at the masts of the sunken ships, too bitter and disappointed to notice. It was the Earl of Warwick who finally said, 'Peace, gentlemen. We have had a setback; we must shrug it off now, and plan for the future.'

'What future?' Hatfield said angrily, and he turned and walked away.

Another man came striding up from the direction of the siege lines, a man-at-arms with a yellow and red surcoat blazened with a white star; Hugh de Vere, one of Berkeley's men-at-arms. His gauntlets were stained with blood. He bowed to the king. 'I bring bad news, sire,' he said abruptly.

'What is it?'

'Sir Maurice de Berkeley is dead. He was killed by a stone shot from the French cannon just as we withdrew. We are bringing his body back to camp now.'

Back at the camp the king walked straight into his house without saying a word to anyone. Rowton, freezing in his wet clothes, watched him go for a moment and glanced at Merrivale. 'Join me, herald, if you will.'

Rowton's lodging was not a grand building like the King's House; indeed, it was very little larger than Merrivale's own. The hall did have a brick fireplace at one end and some wall hangings to keep out the draughts, but otherwise was bare. His lordship lived here in spartan simplicity, with just a few servants; Merrivale could not recall ever hearing of a romantic interest in his life. *How little I know about him.*

Rowton stood by the fire, pulling off his sodden coat and hose as a servant brought towels and fresh clothes. Merrivale stood for a few moments, waiting. 'Hatfield was right,' Rowton said finally. 'It was a dangerous and foolish venture. It cost us five ships and at least twenty men, including one of our best captains. I should never have persuaded his Grace.'

'Why did you, my lord?'

'Honestly? Because I wanted to show the king that I was right.' He paused. 'And I also wanted to prove Hatfield wrong.'

'Why was that important?'

Rowton ran a towel over his hair. 'You saw him today. He loves nothing better than pointing out other people's faults. It has always been thus with him, right from the beginning.'

The beginning of what? Merrivale wondered, but he kept the thought to himself. Rowton dropped the towel and reached for a dry shirt. 'However, I didn't call you in to talk about Hatfield. Have you learned anything more about this conspiracy against the king?'

'A little,' Merrivale said after a moment. 'For one thing, I think it is more widespread and has been in place much longer than we imagined. I believe it dates back to the events around the old king's death.'

Rowton looked up sharply. 'Why do you think that?'

'Because the same names keep coming up over and over again.'

'Have you told the king of your suspicions?'

'Yes, last summer. He was not interested.'

'No, of course not,' Rowton said. 'His Grace regards his father's death as a tragedy to be left behind. Many of those involved have been pardoned and accepted back into service. Even his mother has largely been forgiven. The past is past, he says.'

'With respect, his Grace is wrong,' Merrivale said. 'The past has its claws embedded in our souls. We can never escape it.' He watched Rowton carefully. 'If you were me, my lord, what would you do?'

'Keep what I know to myself,' said Rowton, pulling on a black woollen coat and buttoning it. The cloth was of fine quality, but was plain with no embroidery. 'At least, until I had absolute proof. And even then, be careful. You're playing with fire here. But you already know that, of course.'

'Thank you for the advice, my lord. Is that why you asked me here?'

'No. I wanted your opinion about the Count of Flanders. Will he commit to the marriage?'

'I believe so. I called on him again before I left Bruges, and found him eager to please.'

'Good. His Grace informs me that he will join the queen and Princess Isabella in Bruges before Easter. The intention is to sign the betrothal contracts and celebrate the marriage as soon as possible. The king wants to make absolutely certain of this alliance. As his friend and advisor, *I* want to be sure nothing happens to disrupt it.'

'Why do you think it might fail?' asked the herald.

Rowton stared at him for a moment. 'You know damned well that the French will stop at nothing to prevent this marriage going ahead. If it does, then farewell to their ambitions in Flanders.'

'Yes,' Merrivale said. 'But the French are not the only ones who will stop at nothing.'

'You think your conspirators are involved as well?'

'I know they are. They want to extinguish the entire Plantagenet line. Preventing Princess Isabella from marrying and producing heirs is a part of their work.'

'How do you know this?'

'The same way that I know the death of the old king is significant. These things are all part of the design, my lord. They all fit like pieces in a mosaic.'

Rowton looked irritated. 'Did you ever talk to Maurice de Berkeley, as I suggested?'

'I did. He was not as forthcoming as I might have wished. And now, of course, he never will be. If Berkeley had secrets, he has taken them to his grave.'

Lent, the season of shadows and gloom. The days were longer, but rain still swept in off the Narrow Sea and white surf foamed on the beaches below the dunes. Still the French supply ships crept into the harbour; still the rumours persisted of a French army mustering at Amiens, ninety miles away. Still the reinforcements from England failed to arrive.

The herald sat in his house, eating yet another Lenten meal of salt fish and bread while he listened to the rain pound on the roof. Tiphaine's letter lay on the table before him. The contents were simple and emotionless, a summary of what she had learned from Saint-Pierre. She did not say where she was going, or when she would be back.

He already knew that Hatfield had been sent to conduct secret negotiations with the French in the late 1320s. But who was the other man who had gone to Calais? He wondered about Northburgh, whom he had barely thought about for the past few weeks. Northburgh did not like Hatfield, and had never made much secret of it; but then, neither did Rowton.

Michael is a friend, and I do not want to think ill of him. But I must look more closely at him, and perhaps at his uncle too.

Tomorrow he would go to see Northburgh. The secretary would tease him about 'his *demoiselle*,' as he always did, but strangely, Merrivale thought, I shall not mind.

Where are you, Tiphaine? Where did you go? And why?

Calais, 25th of February, 1347

In the morning a letter arrived, brought by courier from Bruges. It was not, as he hoped, from Tiphaine. Breaking the seal, he saw the writing belonged to Sister Adela.

> *With the help of Meester Adornes, we have discovered the location of the Gistels family. They are living in poverty in Sluis. None of them has any knowledge of William Blyth and most had never heard of him. You were right, and the rumours directing you to Sint Anna were part of an elaborate*

trap. Meester Adornes denies all knowledge of this, and I believe him. I think the purpose of the trap was to discourage us, the Order of Saint John, from working with you.

Meester Adornes also informs me of the arrival in Bruges of Donato di Pacino de' Peruzzi from the banking house of Peruzzi in Florence. He has taken over the operations of the bank in Bruges, or what remains of them, and is seeking reparation for loans made to the previous Count of Flanders who was killed at Crécy. He is said to be demanding that the young count repay the loan.

The music school has begun in Bruges, and I have discovered that my young French friend can play the citole. I purchased an instrument for him and sent him out to join the school to learn more about your three musicians, Tomaset, Garnier and Marcelis. None has yet come to the music school, but some expect they will return to Bruges before Easter. I have not informed the authorities; I think it more useful to see if they do return, and follow them ourselves and see where they lead us.

Merrivale sat for a few minutes, holding the letter in his hand. *Donato de' Peruzzi*, he thought. *There is a name I have not thought about for years. Of all the extensive Peruzzi family, why is Donato the one who has come to Bruges, and why now? Is it coincidence? Possibly. But I don't like coincidences.*

His mind turned to Bessancourt. Unless the clerk was a very good player indeed, he would not be able to maintain the façade of a professional musician for very long. If spies were to be planted in the music school, they needed to be the real thing.

He found the two musicians, Nikolas and Havel, sitting at their usual tavern with tankards of beer and plates of what turned out to be smoked whale meat. 'This is delicious,' said Havel the Fiddler, chewing. 'We never see food like this in Bohemia.'

'There might be a reason for that,' Merrivale said. 'Have you had any further contact with Zajíc?'

'Not yet, sir,' said Nikolas. 'If another message arrives, we will inform you.'

'Mmm,' said the herald, thinking of Brother Geoffrey's mission. 'You told me that Zajíc ordered you to assist me if needed.'

The Bohemians looked at each other. 'Yes, sir,' said Havel. 'We are yours to command.'

'Tell me about the music school in Bruges.'

'It takes place every year during Lent,' Nikolas said. 'It's not really a school, not like a studium or a cathedral school. Music-making in public is banned until after Easter, of course, so we use this time to get together with our fellows. We practice our skills, learn new repertoire, gossip about clients, that sort of thing. People come from all over, France, Germany, Bohemia, even Italy and Spain.'

'You have both attended this school?'

Havel nodded. 'Several times.'

'Good. I want you to go again. I'll arrange it and see you are given money for your passage. While you are there, I want you to keep watch for three men. Their names are Marcelis, Tomaset and Garnier.'

Merrivale described them. Havel rubbed his chin. 'I think I may have met Garnier. There was a tenor singing at a fair in the Rhineland last year, called Garnier of Liège. It might be the same man.'

Nikolas nodded. 'There was a fiddler called Tomaset at the French court last year. I think he came from Liège too. I don't know any Marcelis.'

'Is Liège well known for its musicians?' asked the herald.

'It used to be, back in Bishop Adolph's day. These days, it is mostly known for despair. The revolt by the commune two years ago has turned the whole city on its head.'

Sister Adela had mentioned the revolt along with a connection to the Pilgrims. 'If any of the three arrive in Bruges, send word to me at once,' he said.

—

'Good afternoon, Michael. Is it possible to see his Grace?'

'He is closeted with the marshal and Bishop Hatfield,' Michael Northburgh said.

'Not Rowton?'

'His lordship contracted a rheum during his dip in the sea, and the physician has confined him to bed. Have a seat, the king should be free in a few minutes. How is your *demoiselle*?'

Merrivale smiled, sitting down on a bench and resting his stick beside him. 'She is well,' he said firmly. 'You look busy as ever, Michael.'

'Preparing for the king and queen to go to Bruges at Easter, to celebrate this wretched wedding. The king is determined that this should be a triumph.'

'Has he taken my advice about guarding the count?'

'Yes. Paon de Roet has gone with a company of men-at-arms and archers to ten Berghe, to reinforce the Bruges militia. The king and queen will also have a strong bodyguard, to make sure there is no repeat of last autumn's events. Hugh de Vere will lead this.'

'Who will command the siege while the king is away?'

'The Prince of Wales. Don't worry, he'll have Lord Rowton and others to hold his hand. Hatfield is going with the king, of course, as am I.'

Merrivale nodded. 'You are the fount of all knowledge about administrative matters, Michael. How long was the Peruzzi bank established in England?'

Northburgh raised his eyebrows. 'Thirty years at least, probably longer. They were important lenders to the old king and to his friends, the Despensers.'

'Towards the end of the old king's reign, when things were falling apart, did they also lend money to Mortimer and the queen?'

'So rumour had it, yes. You know bankers, they like to cover both sides of a bet. That way they always win, no matter what else happens.'

'The Peruzzi haven't won, though,' Merrivale said. 'They're bankrupt, or as good as, and are calling in all their loans in an effort to hold off their creditors. One of them is in Bruges right now, trying to gather in loans made to the late Count of Flanders. My suspicious mind wonders if he is trying to interfere with the betrothal.'

Northburgh smiled. 'Is there any part of your mind that is *not* suspicious?'

'Probably not. Your uncle the Bishop of Coventry used to be Lord Treasurer. He would know more about Peruzzi involvement in royal finances.'

'That is entirely possible. Would you like me to write to him?'

'If you would be so kind.' It would be interesting to see what, if anything, came out of this. 'Were you in London in the late '20s, when everything was falling apart?'

Northburgh's eyebrows rose again, but his voice was as friendly as ever. 'I was at Oxford, and I then served on my uncle's staff for a time. I went with him to Paris on his embassy there, did I mention that?'

'No, you didn't. What embassy was that?'

'The old king of France, Charles IV, had died. Uncle Roger was sent to press our king's claim to the French throne. Hopeless, of course, the French nobles had already decided to pick the Valois candidate.'

'Did you know the Earl of Lancaster had already sent an envoy to discuss that very subject?'

'Oh, yes, Hatfield's little excursion to Calais. We knew all about that. Lancaster had no authority to send anyone, of course. That was a bit of free-lancing on his part, trying to win advantage over Mortimer. Noblemen like to back both sides of a bet as well, it seems.' Northburgh hesitated. 'These are curious questions, Simon.'

'They are,' Merrivale acknowledged. 'And the answers are even more curious. I am groping around in the dark, Michael. And I have to say, I am starting to get damned tired of it.'

–

Hatfield and Warwick departed twenty minutes later, and one of the royal pages ushered Merrivale in to see the king. Edward was standing by the fire, his hands clasped behind his back. He looked up sharply as Merrivale entered. 'What is it, herald?'

Merrivale waited until the page had bowed and withdrawn. 'I need to borrow two of your musicians, sire.' He related the conversation he'd had with Nikolas and Havel, leaving out all mention of the Bohemia herald. 'If we can track down those men, we might be able to learn more about the Pilgrims.'

As usual, the king came straight to the point. 'You think the man from the north is controlling the Pilgrims.'

'Yes, sire.' Another thought came: *unless it is the other way around, and the Pilgrims are controlling him.*

'Very well, see Andrew Clarenceux and ask him to release them into your authority. Are you any closer to finding out who this man is?'

Merrivale remembered what Rowton had said. 'I am narrowing down the list of suspects, sire.'

'Narrowing it down. God damn it, Merrivale, you promised me last autumn that this plot had been broken up. All that was left was *a few tendrils*, you said. What is going on?'

'I don't entirely know, sire,' the herald said. 'I have suspicions only, nothing more.'

The king shook his head. 'Everything is going wrong,' he said bleakly. 'Those obdurate bastards in Calais won't surrender, and we can't break them. Rowton's plan went wrong. Warwick has some mad idea of seizing and fortifying the Rysbank, and that will probably also go wrong. Half our money is rotten, and half our army is rotten too, with disease and cold. The adversary is mustering a new army, while most of my captains sit on their arses in England. And now we have these men plotting behind our back. Where does it end, Merrivale?'

'It ends with the fall of Calais,' Merrivale said. 'It ends when Lancaster arrives with reinforcements and we blockade the city and starve it into submission, when the Count of Flanders marries Princess Isabella, and when I bring you the head of the man from the north. By these signs, you shall conquer.'

'Blasphemous as well as insubordinate. You never change, do you? Very well. Do whatever you have to do. But do not fail me. This time, too much is at stake.'

—

'Master Northburgh met with the bishop this afternoon, sir,' Warin said. 'They walked down to the siege lines and stood near the artillery, talking for a long time.'

'Yes,' Merrivale said after a while. 'I suppose that shouldn't surprise me.'

'What do you mean, sir?'

'I have assumed all along that one of our three is the man we are looking for. It was always possible that they might all be working together.'

Warin nodded. 'All flies on the same dungheap.'

'Only one can be the man from the north, *señor*,' objected Mauro.

'Agreed. But the other two could be working with him.'

'What are your orders, sir?' asked Warin.

'Keep watching them. But be careful. If they discover you following them, you could be in danger.'

'Yes, *señor*,' said Mauro. 'If the *demoiselle* was here, she would say that it is not right that only you should face danger.'

'But she is not here,' the herald said quietly.

The two servants withdrew. Merrivale stood, staring out over the barricades and salt marshes towards the battlements of Calais. Clouds swept in low over the flat lands around the town. His tabard was a brilliant splash of colour against the mud and rain that surrounded him.

The weather was as bleak as his mood. His leg pained him, and he realised that it probably always would. *I wonder what it is like to have peace*, he thought. *I wonder what it is like to have a home.*

III

18

Poperinge, 1ˢᵗ of March, 1347

The ruins began not far from the town, roofless barns and houses, fire-blackened walls overgrown with ivy and brambles. In the falling dusk Tiphaine saw a pair of bright eyes staring at her in the shadows of an empty byre. She froze for a moment; then the shadows moved and a dog fox ran out of the byre and fled across the fields.

A sound reached her, the creak of wagons and clink of harness; it was this that had startled the fox. A convoy of wagons came rumbling down the road. It passed on towards the horizon, and silence descended once more. Away in the distance a wolf howled, long and lonely, the voice of a lost soul in the falling night.

The towers of Poperinge were black against the darkening sky. Lanterns glowed in the belfry of a big church. The town gates were still open, guarded by detachments of men in rough coats and jerkins armed with spears and crossbows. They stared at her with hostile eyes as she approached.

'That's far enough,' one man said. He grounded the butt of his spear. 'Who are you, and what do you want here?'

Tiphaine stopped, hands clenched at her sides. 'I am a poor pilgrim, travelling in a perilous land,' she said, keeping her voice calm. 'In God's name I am weary, and I seek shelter.'

The men continued to stare at her, their faces giving nothing away. Finally the man with the spear nodded. 'Welcome among us, sister,' he said, and Tiphaine felt a surge of relief. 'Rest now, and give praise to God.'

He turned to the others. 'Take her to Fier Meike.'

Six men escorted her through the gates and into the town, led by a huge ox of a man carrying a double-bladed axe in one hand. Torches fluttered in the streets. By their light she could see some houses boarded up and deserted; others lacked roofs and showed the familiar marks of fire. But there was life here too; from behind the battered walls she heard the defiant clack of looms and the thump of fulling mills, industry carrying on even in the midst of war and chaos.

They came to the Grote Markt. More people waited in a pool of torchlight outside a house on the far side of the square. At their head was a woman, tall and strongly built with jet-black hair, wearing a cured leather breastplate with spaulders and vambraces over a rough wool tunic. She cradled a heavy wooden club in her arms. Torchlight winked off a huge metal spike protruding from its head.

The woman barely looked at Tiphaine. 'Who is this, Topaas?' she asked the big man.

'Don't know,' grunted Topaas. 'She came to the gate just now, and asked for shelter.'

'Did she, by God.' The woman made a sharp gesture with her hand. Before Tiphaine could move, two men threw her hard onto her back on the cobbles. She lay for a moment, winded and gasping, and the woman raised the club above her head, the spike pointed straight at Tiphaine's face.

'This is a *goedendaag*,' the woman said. 'One blow will smash your head like an egg. Now, who are you, and where are you from?'

The truth might open doors, or it might get her killed. Or both. Still struggling for air, Tiphaine found her voice. 'I am the *demoiselle* Tiphaine de Tesson. I come from the camp at Calais.'

'English, are you?'

'I am Norman, not English.' Though increasingly, she was no longer sure.

'So. You thought you could just stroll in and say *poor pilgrim*, and we would clasp you to our bosom and treat you as one of our own?'

'That was my hope, yes.'

'Kill her,' said one of the others.

'No!' Tiphaine said sharply. 'I need to find Jehan Nortkerque.'

'Nortkerque is in Calais,' said another man.

'No. He has returned. He is here in the town.'

The woman held the *goedendaag* unwavering above her head. 'Why do you want to see him?'

'To find out who he is working for. Nortkerque is a spy. He pretends to be a Pilgrim, but he receives instructions from someone else.'

They stared down at her, their faces unmoving. She tried again. 'Nortkerque and his masters are plotting to overthrow the thrones of France and England. We think they may try to kill the Count of Flanders as well.'

'Good,' said the woman. 'Death to all tyrants. But this is none of our business. We know nothing of these men.'

'But you are already working for them,' said Tiphaine. 'Don't you know? They control the Pilgrims.'

She watched the other woman's face and knew her life was once more hanging by a thread. 'They will betray you, in the end,' she said. 'John of Hainault, Guy of Béthune; these men have built their lives on betrayal. They will grind you into the dust, and never think twice about it.'

Something invisible had passed through the air around them. After a moment, the woman lowered the *goedendaag*. 'Let her up.'

Topaas reached down and took her hand, hauling her to her feet. 'We will talk inside,' the woman said. 'Topaas, come with us.' She made a gesture of dismissal towards the others. 'I'm certain you all have things to do.'

—

A fire burned in the hall of house. It was, it transpired, the home of the provost of Poperinge. There was no sign of the provost, or any of his household.

There was half a loaf of bread on the table, along with a wooden platter of sausages and a pot of mustard. Tiphaine stared at these longingly; she had not eaten since the previous day. Topaas remained by the door, leaning on his axe. The woman strode over to the fire and stood beside it, grounding the point of her *goedendaag* and chipping pieces out of the provost's floor tiles. 'That is a fearsome weapon,' Tiphaine said, trying not to think about sausages.

The woman rested one hand on the butt of the weapon. There was no mistaking the power in her arms and shoulders, even when half-concealed by leather armour. 'I inherited it from my mother,' she said.

Tiphaine blinked. 'Your mother?'

'She was a fuller, like me, and this is a fuller's weapon. *Moedertje* carried it at the Battle of the Golden Spurs, forty-five years ago. She took four pairs of spurs from the French knights she killed that day, and hung them up in the church at Kortrijk along with the others. What makes you think Jehan Nortkerque is a spy?'

'Does the name Nicodemus mean anything to you?'

'The good Pharisee?'

'This one is a murderer, among other things. He went to Nortkerque's house in Calais, where he identified himself as a Pilgrim and was admitted. Nicodemus has now disappeared, so I decided to find Nortkerque instead. That was when I discovered he had left Calais.'

Topaas shrugged. 'This means nothing. Nortkerque's meeting with that man could have been perfectly innocent.'

'No one who associates with this man is innocent. I think Nortkerque was deliberately destroying food stocks in Calais and damaging wells to put pressure on the town to surrender. Once his work was done, Nicodemus brought him fresh instructions and told him to return here. But I don't know why.'

The woman stroked her chin. 'You said these conspirators control the Pilgrims. Explain.'

'Your men outside,' Tiphaine said. 'Who pays them? The people of Poperinge?'

'No. We give our services freely to the oppressed, wherever we find them.'

'And who pays you? Come along, you have bread, meat, weapons. The money for them must come from somewhere.'

'What has this to do with anything?' demanded Topaas.

'Answer the question, and I will explain,' said Tiphaine.

The woman stroked her chin again. 'The money comes from our people at Liège.'

'Is any of the coin counterfeit?'

For the first time, the woman looked surprised by the question. 'No, it is all good coin. Silver pennies and groats from Flanders.'

'The conspirators are stealing from France and England, and probably Flanders as well,' Tiphaine said. 'They are producing false coins, and using the real silver to pay the Pilgrims. Last year, the Pilgrims tried to kill Queen Philippa of England in Bruges and King Philippe in Paris. They also murdered a clerk from the Chambre des Comptes in Paris.'

'There is proof of this?' asked Topaas.

'I was there with Queen Philippa, and there is a witness to the clerk's murder.'

'You are telling us a great deal,' said the woman.

'Yes,' Tiphaine said steadily. 'In hopes that you will trust me.'

The woman nodded. 'Topaas, go and fetch Nortkerque. His house is in Sint-Bertinusstraat. Let us hear what he has to say.'

–

After Topaas departed the two women stood in silence. Tiphaine's stomach began to rumble. 'May I be permitted some food?' she asked.

The woman gestured towards the table. Gratefully, Tiphaine cut a slab of bread, dipped a piece of sausage into the mustard and began to eat. 'Will you tell me your name?' she asked.

'I am called Fier Meike.' Tiphaine continued eating. 'You say you are Norman,' the woman said, watching her. 'How did you become involved in this matter?'

'An English herald, Merrivale, is trying to break this conspiracy. I am helping him.'

'A herald? That seems unusual.'

'He is an unusual man,' Tiphaine said.

'I do not greatly care what happens to England or France. But you said these conspirators have designs on Flanders.'

Tiphaine nodded. 'Merrivale thinks they intend to kill the young Count of Flanders and put someone in his place. Hainault, probably. Then, once the kings of England and France have been killed, they will take advantage of the chaos to stamp out the rebels and seize control of the cities.'

Fier Meike shook her head. 'Not Hainault. Béthune. He is the one who covets Flanders.'

'Oh?'

'Last September, after the old count died at Crécy, his brother Béthune tried to kill the heir young Louis, and seize control. Some Pilgrims stepped in, captured Louis and handed him over to Bruges. Béthune was foiled, but only for the moment. He still intends to seize power here if he can.'

'And will the Pilgrims allow him to do so?'

Fier Meike looked impatient. 'You speak of the Pilgrims as if we were one body, one mind. There is no king among us, no lord, no leader. There is only the voice of the wise sisters in Liège, reminding us of our purpose. Otherwise, we do as we will.'

'And what is your purpose?' Tiphaine asked, reaching for more sausage.

'The protection of the people against tyrants. That is why we were founded, that is why we exist.'

'So, I take it you don't want to see Béthune in control of Flanders?'

'No,' said Fier Meike. 'I want to see Guy of Béthune's head on a stake.'

'That makes two of us. Why?'

'After he failed to take his nephew, Béthune sent raiding parties into the heart of Flanders. They burned villages and monasteries and towns, and laid the land waste wherever they went. Béthune hoped to terrorise the League of Three into handing over the count. He failed, of course. But the blood of hundreds of innocents is on his hands.'

'And not only their blood,' said Tiphaine, thinking of last autumn in Scotland. 'I saw the ruins around the town. Is that Béthune's work?'

'No. That was done by the men of Ypres, six years ago, when they attacked the town.'

Tiphaine blinked. 'I know I keep asking this. But why?'

'Ypres claims sole right to manufacture cloth in this district. When the guilds of Poperinge refused to give up their trade, the Ypres militia stormed the town, killed anyone who resisted, broke all the looms and burned the houses of the guild leaders. After that, Poperinge called on the Pilgrims for aid.'

Tiphaine stared at her. 'Is everyone in Flanders at war with someone?'

'Of course. Fighting is like the air we breathe. French against Flemish, towns against country, nobles against commoners, fullers against weavers, Ypres against Poperinge. It has been thus for fifty years. I see little sign that it will change.'

What had Iron Henry said? *Fighting is a natural state of affairs, demoiselle. We have to learn how to dance and make music, but we are born with the ability to fight.* So it would seem, she thought.

The door opened and Topaas walked in, brushing rain off his cloak. 'Nortkerque is not here. The house is empty, with only one old servant guarding the door. He says his master is still in Calais.'

Tiphaine felt a sudden chill. 'No. He left Calais to return to Poperinge. I *know* he did.'

'Put a watch on his house,' Fier Meike said. 'If he returns, bring him here at once.' She turned to Tiphaine. 'Until we find Nortkerque, you will not leave this house.'

'I understand,' Tiphaine said.

'Now, I wish to be alone. Go upstairs and find a bed. You will be summoned when Nortkerque returns.'

–

Relieved to still be alive, Tiphaine slept the night through and woke late the next morning. Descending to the hall she found more bread, some cheese and a jug of fresh-brewed small beer. Fier Meike walked in just as she finished eating. 'Any news?' Tiphaine asked.

'No one in Sint-Bertinusstraat has seen Nortkerque, nor has he contacted the guild masters. But something is wrong.'

'Why do you say that?'

Meike laid the heavy *goedendaag* on the table and cut herself a slab of bread. 'You said the conspirators are dealing in false coinage.'

'Yes. In very large quantities.'

'Nortkerque comes originally from Bruges. Years ago, there was a coining scandal in city, and he was implicated. Several people were executed, and Nortkerque was exiled from the city. There were more rumours after he came to Poperinge. When you mentioned counter-feiting last night, I began to wonder.'

Tiphaine's scalp had begun to tingle. 'Are those rumours the reason why he moved to Calais?'

'I don't know. He went there some years ago, and I only arrived last year. But it bothers me that he left his house in Poperinge standing empty. Why not rent it or sell it? Why abandon a valuable property?'

'Perhaps it is not empty,' Tiphaine said.

Fier Meike picked up her *goedendaag* and walked to the door. 'Topaas!' she shouted into the courtyard.

'I am here,' the big man said.

'We are going to Sint-Bertinusstraat. Bring me a file of men and a battering ram.'

–

Nortkerque's house was a foursquare building of red brick with a tile roof. All the windows were shuttered on the inside; the windows themselves were dirty and full of cobwebs. Fier Meike knocked on the oak door with the butt of her *goedendaag* and waited for a moment. There was no sound of life within. The loudest sound was water trickling in the gutter behind them.

Meike stepped back from the door. 'Break it down,' she said.

Two men lifted the heavy wooden ram and swung it against the door. On the third blow the wood splintered and the door crashed open. 'Search the place,' Meike said. 'If you find anyone, bring them to me.'

'And look for any books or boxes,' Tiphaine said. 'Anything where he might keep records.'

Swiftly, with a precision born of experience, the Pilgrims fanned out to search the building. Tiphaine followed Meike into the hall, hearing more sounds of splintering wood as doors were forced and chests and aumbries pried open. A man shouted in alarm; a woman screamed, sharply, the sound quickly cut off. The hall was dark, unlit by lamps or candles, and more cobwebs hung from the ceiling. Something bubbled in a corner of the room, a tall wooden box with metal wheels and a dial on its face. Tiphaine realised it was a water clock; the bubbling came from a water reservoir hidden inside the box.

The bell of the water clock chimed the quarter hour, a single mellow note that hung in the air for a moment before fading. The searchers returned, herding four people in front of them; an elderly man, a middle-aged woman with hair coming down from under her wimple, a man in a shirt and drawers who looked like he had been dragged out of bed, and a girl, small, frightened, with hollow cheeks and deep shadows under her eyes.

Topaas pointed at the others. 'This is the doorkeeper. The others are house servants.'

'Did you find any papers?' Tiphaine asked.

Topaas shook his head. 'Not so much as a scrap of parchment.'

Either Nortkerque had destroyed his correspondence and business records, or he kept them elsewhere. 'No money, either,' said another man.

'I know where the money is,' the girl said.

The older woman turned on her, striking her viciously across the face. 'Keep silent!'

'What money?' Fier Meike demanded.

The man in the shirt looked down at his bare feet. The old man stared off into space, his eyes unfocused; Tiphaine wondered if he was blind. She looked at the girl, fingering the red mark on her cheek, and held out her hand. 'Come,' she said softly.

The girl did not move. Tiphaine knelt in front of her and took her hand, which was freezing cold, though the room itself was warm. Rising, Tiphaine led her away from the other servants. The older woman and the man in the shirt started to follow, but Topaas shook his head and they fell back into place again.

'What is your name?' Tiphaine asked.

'Sus,' the girl said after a moment.

'Has someone hurt you? Did the master hurt you?'

The girl said nothing, but her hands began to tremble. 'You are safe now,' Tiphaine said. 'Do you understand? You are safe, and no one will hurt you again.'

The trembling continued. How old was she? Tiphaine wondered. She looked like she was barely more than a child, but had the eyes of someone who had known little but fear and horror.

And I know how that feels…

'You said you know where the money is,' Tiphaine said.

The woman screamed in a voice full of venom and fear. 'Say nothing! Say nothing, you little bitch!'

Fier Meike hit the woman a back-handed blow across the face that knocked her backwards against the wall. Dazed, she dabbed at the blood running from a split lip down her chin. The younger man stared at his feet again; the old doorkeeper continued to gaze into emptiness.

'There is a well,' the girl said. 'The money is in a chest at the bottom of the well. In the courtyard. It is not deep.'

Topaas hurried out of the hall. The woman began to weep. Fier Meike turned on her again. 'Where is your master?'

'I don't know! If he finds that we have betrayed him he will kill us all!'

Meike pointed to the water clock. 'You have until that bell rings the quarter hour once more. Then, unless you tell the truth, *I* will kill you. Choose.'

The woman sank to her knees, sobbing and covering her face with her bloody hands. 'We don't know where he went,' said the old doorkeeper. 'He didn't tell us anything. He just said we were to stay here and not let anyone in until he returned to collect the money. We would be paid well for our silence.'

Tiphaine watched the girl's eyes. 'You know where he is,' she said softly. 'Don't you, *meisje?*'

There was a long silence, broken only by the bubbling of the clock. 'Tell me,' Tiphaine whispered.

'He has gone to Liège,' the girl said.

'*Liège!*' Fier Meike wheeled around. 'Why?'

'He was summoned there by a messenger.'

'Did you see this messenger?' asked Tiphaine.

'Only for a moment. He was tall and thin. He spoke Flemish, but strangely. He had a bow, and a quiver of arrows.'

'Nicodemus,' Tiphaine said to Meike. She looked back at the girl. 'How do you know about Liège?'

'I heard them speaking. The messenger brought orders for the master, and said they would travel together.'

'Where did the orders come from?'

'Béthune,' the girl said.

The silence that followed was like the aftermath of a cannon shot, deep and reverberating. Tiphaine felt her heart beating very quickly. 'From the Count of Béthune? Count Guy?'

'No,' said the girl. 'I heard them say her name. Yolande, she is called.'

–

Tiphaine rose slowly to her feet, breathing deeply. Topaas came in carrying a heavy wooden chest, banded with iron and dripping with water. 'Open it,' Fier Meike said.

The chest was locked but a couple of blows from Topaas's axe broke the bands and smashed it open. Silver coins danced and spun across the tile floor, gleaming in the pale light. There were hundreds of them, possibly thousands. The others stared. 'My God!' one man said. 'That is a fortune!'

One of the coins rolled next to Tiphaine's feet and stopped. She picked it up. On the face it looked shiny and new, bearing the image of a Paschal lamb with the legend LVD CO : F, for Louis, Count of Flanders, and underneath AGn' : DEI, the Lamb of God. She turned it over and saw the mint mark, VIL Ā DIFELIN. The silver foil covering the lead disk was already beginning to split.

'These are forgeries,' she said. 'Just like the ones I told you about. We knew they were forging French and English coin, but we didn't know they were making false Flemish coins as well.'

'Why?' Fier Meike demanded.

'Because when people lose faith in their money, they lose their trust in everything. The Flemings will turn even more against each other, and Hainault and Béthune and their friends will profit by the chaos. These coins were hidden here until the time is right. Doubtless there are other hidden caches elsewhere.'

'What do you mean, when the time is right? What are they waiting for?'

'Some great event that will shake the entire country. The assassination of Count Louis of Flanders by his uncle, Guy of Béthune, perhaps.' Tiphaine looked at Fier Meike. 'This girl needs to be kept safe. If Nortkerque returns, he will kill her, or the other servants will. And we may need her later as a witness.'

'We will protect her,' said Meike.

'I need to go to Liège. I must find Nortkerque and Nicodemus.'

'Topaas and I will come with you,' Meike said. 'We depart tomorrow.'

Tiphaine nodded. Liège was many days' journey away, she knew, and God knew what they would find when or if they got there. She stood still, her heart feeling like it was about to crack open; not for the girl beside her, but for Simon.

She was Iseult and Morgana and Blanchefleur, all rolled into one, he had said of Yolande. *She was the lily, and the rose.* Despite everything that had happened, despite even the events in Béthune, he still believed in her. In an age of treason, this was the greatest betrayal of all.

19

Pfalzel, 5th of March, 1347

'Why are you here, brother?' asked Zajíc the Bohemian herald.

Brother Geoffrey smiled. 'I am an ambassador,' he said. 'Just like you, my friend.'

'Friend. Are we friends, Geoffrey?'

The canon paused for a moment. 'An excellent question. For a moment, back at Lens and Béthune, I thought perhaps we were. Has something changed?'

Zajíc said nothing. They were in the larger room of Brother Geoffrey's lodgings, the canon seated before a blazing fire, trying to get rid of the cold that had settled into his bones. It had been a long journey from Calais across the wastelands of eastern Artois, along the valley of the Meuse and up over the wolf-haunted hills of the Ardennes before finally reaching the palace of Pfalzel, a heavily fortified enclave across the river Moselle from the city of Trier. Charles, King of the Romans was in residence here. Among his courtiers, Geoffrey knew, were the poet Guillaume Machaut, the king's secretary; Guy, Count of Béthune, his brother-in-law; and Guy's wife, the beautiful Yolande of Bohemia, the king's half-sister.

'To answer your first question, after our conversations at Lens and Béthune, I spoke to King Edward,' Brother Geoffrey said. 'He would like to discuss further the offer you made to Simon Merrivale at Calais.'

'Why did he not send Merrivale?'

'He is still not as well as we would like. Will King Charles see me?'

Zajíc watched him for a moment. 'Possibly. It is not down to me. You will have to speak to Poděbrady.'

'But you have influence with the king. It was the king, was it not, who instructed you to send the two musicians, Nikolas and Havel, to the English court?'

'Ah, so you have discovered them,' Zajíc said after a moment.

'It was not difficult to work out. It was a little surprising, though, to find that they were instructed to deliver messages to Thomas Hatfield rather than King Edward. And it was even more surprising that they were told to offer their services to Merrivale, should he need them. Was that the king's order as well?'

Zajíc did not answer. 'Poděbrady is the king's chamberlain. If you wish to speak to his Grace, you must see him.'

Geoffrey gazed at the herald for a moment. Zajíc looked steadily back at him. 'Whose side are you on, Vilém? Or is your mind made up yet?'

'Do you really think it is that simple, Geoffrey? Has it *ever* been that simple?'

'Tell me about Béthune. Is he in high favour?'

'Yes, but thanks only to his wife. Her influence is growing strong.'

'She is popular?'

'All of the nobles and courtiers are enraptured by her. They hold tournaments in her honour, and write poems about her beauty and nail them to the palace gates.'

Geoffrey smiled a little. 'Some things never change. Are the poems any good?'

'They are terrible. But Yolande is invaluable to the king. Many German nobles are indifferent to him, and some openly prefer Emperor Louis, but they are in thrall to Countess Yolande. They are becoming more loyal to her than the king.'

'I see. So long as she remains loyal to her brother, all is well. But if she is working with her husband and the man from the north, then there is danger.'

'Yes,' Zajíc said. 'However relations between Béthune and his wife are strained. They quarrel frequently. He is jealous, and has accused her of taking lovers.'

'Has she?'

'I don't know.'

'I suspect you do. What about her brother, the king? Does he trust Béthune?'

'He is a member of the king's council, and is present at official sessions. But there are other meetings where he is not invited. Poděbrady arranges them, often at the archbishop's palace in the city.'

'Does Béthune know what is said at these meetings?'

'Of course. Machaut, the king's secretary, is spying for him.'

'Yes, we know that. Do *you* know what goes on at these meetings? Are you present?'

'Yes.'

'So,' Brother Geoffrey said, 'Béthune is plotting against King Charles, and the king is formulating a counter-plot. Thank you, Vilém, this is all very useful. Why are you telling me this?'

'So that you understand the situation,' Zajíc said bluntly. 'Every moment you are here, you are in danger.'

'Don't be ridiculous, Vilém. I am an official ambassador travelling under a flag of truce, no one will touch me.'

The Bohemian herald snorted. 'Have you taken leave of your senses? Do you not realise what kind of people you are dealing with?'

'Then I must trust in you to keep me safe. If you think your masters pose a danger to me, restrain them.'

'It will not be easy,' Zajíc said. 'I meant what I said, Geoffrey. I am not your friend.'

'I know.' Brother Geoffrey smiled again. 'But with enemies like you, my dear Vilém, who needs friends?'

Pfalzel, 6ᵗʰ of March, 1347

It took Brother Geoffrey a couple of days to recover from his journey, and it was not until after dinner on Monday that he felt well enough to ask a servant to direct him to the Lord of Poděbrady. King Charles's chamberlain received him in a solar high up in one of the towers next to the river. Windows looked out over turbulent waters pockmarked with rain. On the far side, forested slopes climbed steeply until they were lost in cloud. A fire smoked on the hearth, a mixture of wood and coal. The chimney was new and badly designed, and the room was full of smoke.

Poděbrady waved the smoke aside. He wore a sober dark coat with no adornment. 'Sit down, brother. Zajíc told me of your arrival. I trust you are fully restored to health?'

Geoffrey smiled. 'For the most part, although my bones are still creaking. To my annoyance, I have discovered that I am no longer a young man.'

'It is the weather.' Poděbrady gestured towards the window. 'Every time it rains, I feel my joints swell up. Have some wine. It swells the joints too, but after a flagon or two you no longer care.'

A servant brought a jug of hot sweet Rheingau wine and two silver cups. 'You wish to see the king,' Poděbrady said when they were alone.

'If he will receive me, yes.'

Poděbrady ran a hand through his luxuriant beard. 'Have you anything new to say?'

Geoffrey pursed his lips. 'Not really. But we were hoping you might.'

The chamberlain looked doubtful. 'King Philippe is assembling an army at Amiens, and he has reinforced his garrisons on the Flemish frontier. More French convoys are preparing to resupply Calais. And your army still squats in the mud outside the town, growing weaker by the day. I'd say momentum is with the French.'

'English reinforcements are on the way.'

'They have been on the way for months, brother. And how will you pay them? According to rumours, your currency has been debased to the point where no one will accept it.'

'Rumours are not always true. And the same could be said of the French coinage.' Geoffrey set down his wine cup. 'As a matter of fact, I do have one new thing to say.'

He told Poděbrady about the mint at Abbeville. 'The French priory of the Knights of Saint John are clearly behind this. The entire operation is directed by Reynaud de Nanteuil.'

'What about these mint marks from Dublin?'

'We don't understand those, not yet. Merrivale has written to a contact in Ireland who may be able to help, but a reply will take time.'

Poděbrady nodded. 'Very well. How does this change the situation?' He was clearly rather more shrewd than he first appeared.

'It means the conspiracy is in motion. The assassination attempts last year were preliminary moves, designed to sow confusion; perhaps they were never meant to succeed. Now the real game has begun.'

'And recognising this, King Edward has chosen to open negotiations again.'

'Yes,' Geoffrey said. 'I admit our position is weak, my lord, but so is yours. The conspirators intend to control King Charles. If they cannot, they will kill him and replace him with someone more malleable.'

'They may try,' Poděbrady said. His beard bristled with outrage. 'They will not succeed.'

'No? From what I hear, they control the German nobles, through the king's sister. Charles is already unpopular with many of them. If someone gives them the lead, they will turn against him.'

'The Bohemians are loyal to the king. We will fight to defend him.'

'But there are not enough of you, my lord. Too many died at Crécy. *The conspiracy is a demon on the king's back*, Archbishop Balduin said. The only power that can help you now, that can get that demon off your back, is England.'

A few moments passed. 'What is your offer?' asked Poděbrady.

'We will support King Charles's bid to be crowned Holy Roman Emperor. In return, we want you to inform the French court about Nanteuil and his false mint.'

'Why not tell them yourself? You have channels.'

'They would not believe us. But they will believe you, their friends and allies. For all our sakes, we need the French to suppress the mint and stop the counterfeiting. It will not halt the conspiracy, but it will buy us time.'

Poděbrady stroked his beard again. 'Very well,' he said finally. 'Come to court tonight. The king must decide.'

—

The great hall glowed with light. Dozens of lamps and candles shone off walls hung with woven cloths depicting scenes from the life of Charlemagne. Fires crackled and sparked and smoked, keeping out the chill. Stepping into the big room, Brother Geoffrey saw fifty or sixty people talking quietly and drinking wine, all dressed in sombre colours without jewels.

Music murmured in the air, the hum of a viol, the sweet notes of a lute, a clear tenor voice joining in. Geoffrey stood in the doorway for a moment. Public performances of music were forbidden during Lent, but that was not what gave him pause. He knew that voice, and those instruments; he had heard them before, in the house of the burgemeester of Bruges.

For he who walks without light
Is led by a blind guide

But for he who has a true leader
Every hour is light
You who lead us now
Confound those who would lead us astray
And lead us down the paths of light
So that we may find true peace

The three musicians were in a gallery overlooking the hall. Geoffrey glanced at them once and looked away again. King Charles sat in a gilded chair near one of the fires, hunched over a little. Poděbrady and Zajíc stood behind him; their eyes met Geoffrey's, but neither made any move. Turning his head, Geoffrey saw another man, dark-haired, dressed all in black, staring back at him; Guy, Count of Béthune.

Béthune's face was immobile, but his eyes were alive with anger. Geoffrey tensed a little, waiting for the other man to make a move. After a long moment, Béthune bowed and turned away. Geoffrey let out his breath a little. The music continued to play.

He heard a sudden movement behind him, and turned. Yolande stood smiling, dressed all in white, her fair hair bound up under a plain wimple. The prohibition on jewels clearly did not apply to scent; she smelled of roses and vervain. Unlike her husband, her eyes were warm and kind.

'Brother Geoffrey! How good it is to see you again.'

'You too, my lady. You are as beautiful as ever.'

'I am not, but you are courteous to say so. I am sorry I was not able to welcome you when you came to Béthune.'

That could be read in two ways, Geoffrey thought. He bowed.

'What news of Simon? Is he well?'

'Simon is indestructible,' he said. He was aware of Béthune, watching them from the far side of the room.

'So I recall. Have you come to see the king?'

'Yes. But I have not yet been summoned.'

She laid a hand on his arm. 'We are terribly informal here at Pfalzel. Come, I will take you to him now.'

Yolande smiled graciously at the people around her as they passed across the room, greeting one or two by name as they bowed. Ten years ago in Savoy she had been a callow, impressionable girl, Geoffrey thought. Now she is a princess, full of power and grace. No wonder people are ready to follow her.

The musicians had struck up another tune.

Blessed Virgin, mother of Christ
What joy you bring to a sad world.

Geoffrey looked at Yolande and raised his eyebrows. 'Music during Lent?'

'The king has a dispensation to hear music each day. It eases his pain.'

Geoffrey smiled. 'Especially if the music is composed by Master Machaut. Did he recruit the musicians too?'

'I believe so, yes. They are very good, aren't they?'

'I have seldom heard finer,' said Geoffrey.

They bowed to the king. 'Your Grace,' Yolande said. 'I bring you Brother Geoffrey of Maldon, the envoy from England.'

Slowly, the king raised his head. Charles, King of the Romans was thirty years old, but looked older. *Pain ages a man*, Geoffrey thought. In the confused, chaotic fighting the morning after the battle at Crécy, Charles had been shot twice in the leg; according to rumour, one arrowhead was still embedded in the bone.

'An envoy, you say,' the king said finally. His voice was low and strained. 'Are you certain he is not a spy?'

'Your grace is perceptive,' Geoffrey said. 'All too often there is no difference.'

'Brother Geoffrey is a man of God, sire,' Yolande reproved.

'A cassock can hide a multitude of sins,' said the king. 'Leave us for a moment, sister. I wish to speak to this man alone.'

She bowed and stepped away, moving in the opposite direction from her husband. The king waved a hand and Poděbrady and Zajíc stepped back too, leaving King Charles and Brother Geoffrey alone amid the crowd.

'The Lord of Poděbrady has told me about the false money,' the king said quietly. 'I shall write personally to King Philippe and tell him what we have learned.'

'Thank you, sire. This is a generous act, and my sovereign lord will be grateful.'

'I am sure he will. But I want something in return.'

'Name your desire, your Grace.'

'Come closer,' the king said. 'No, closer still.'

Geoffrey moved up until he was standing no more than a foot from the king, his body shielding the latter from the gaze of the crowd. Charles spoke, his voice no more than a murmur. 'I want you to rid me of Guy of Béthune,' he said.

'How?' said Brother Geoffrey after a moment.

'I leave that to you. I know your reputation.' The king nodded. 'That is all.'

The musicians watched Brother Geoffrey as he bowed and walked out of the hall.

Ask your Son, oh compassionate Lady
To drive away the evils and torments we suffer.
Oh Light of Light, we are dragged down
From the highest heaven to the lowest hell.

20

Pfalzel, 7ᵗʰ of March, 1347

In the morning Geoffrey sent a message to Poděbrady, asking to see him again. There was no answer. Not that he had expected one, of course; Poděbrady was one of the king's closest confidantes, and undoubtedly knew what the king had asked him to do. He was distancing himself.

He dined alone in his lodgings, pondering his next move. Later in the afternoon Zajíc came to see him. 'Archbishop Balduin bids you call on him at the Aula Palatina.'

'Why did he not write directly to me?'

'Security. Béthune will intercept any messages you receive or send.'

'And the message itself? Is it genuine, or an attempt to lure me into an ambush?'

'An excellent question,' Zajíc admitted. He stirred a little, the white lion with two tails shimmering on his tabard in the pale light. 'I think I shall come with you.'

Geoffrey shook his head. 'Vilém, I was fighting my way out of ambushes when you were still in swaddling clothes. Besides, for all I know, you are the one who will stick the knife in my back.'

'Heralds are forbidden to carry weapons, you know that.'

'That has not always stopped them.'

Zajíc shook his head in irritation. 'We are on different sides in this war. But I am no threat to you, Geoffrey, and I never have been.'

Geoffrey raised his eyebrows. 'Oh? Have you now made up your mind as to which side you are on?'

Zajíc said nothing. Geoffrey relented a little. 'The offer of an escort was kindly meant, I am sure. But I am used to risking my neck. I will go alone.'

'I hate these wars in the shadows,' Zajíc said. 'Things were different when the old king was alive. You knew where you stood with him.'

'Yes,' said Geoffrey. 'Usually, up to your neck in shit. But I agree King Jean had a direct and uncomplicated view of the world.' He stood up and reached for his cloak. 'If I am not back by nightfall, Vilém, you are welcome to come and rescue me.'

Trier, 7th of March, 1347

No ambush waited on the road along the north bank of the Moselle, or the long bridge across the river. The gates were open and the guards admitted him without question. Thoughtfully, Brother Geoffrey walked into the city.

Trier claimed to be older than Rome, and perhaps it was. Ancient glory lingered in its streets; doorways were adorned with plundered floral capitals, and here and there the faces of long-forgotten gods peered out of the masonry. The churches and cathedral and the castle of Saint Barbara that crouched on the ruins of an old bath complex were reminders of a time, a millennium ago, when Trier was the capital of an empire spanning Europe.

The archbishop's palace was the Aula Palatina, the old basilica that had somehow survived through plunder and wreck. A gatehouse had been added, along with defensive turrets and parapets on the high walls; the town had been peaceful for thirty years, but Archbishop Balduin owed his survival to his habit of not taking chances. Inside the basilica the air was blessedly warm and dry; the floor mosaics were chipped and broken, but the encaustic heating beneath them still worked as well as when it was first built, a thousand years ago.

A young grey-robed Franciscan with a heavily tonsured head showed him into the archbishop's private chambers in the apse. Balduin looked more sour and discontented than ever; his face reminded Geoffrey of an apple left to wither on a shelf. 'Any trouble?' he asked.

'None. Zajíc warned me your message might be a trap.'

'There is hippocras in the pot. Help yourself. Zajíc sees traps every-where,' the archbishop said as Geoffrey filled a cup and took a seat. 'That's because he doesn't know where his own loyalty lies. His duty is to his new master, but he is still in thrall to his old allies.'

'Are you, my lord?'

A book with heavy wooden covers lay on a side table. Balduin picked it up and handed it to Geoffrey. 'This is my gift to you.'

Geoffrey opened the book. It was a treatise by Jean Buridan, *Duae quaestiones de universali*. 'Thank you, my lord. May I ask what I have done to deserve this?'

'I enjoyed your hospitality at Lens. The grilled rabbit in particular was exceptional.'

Geoffrey smiled. 'Poděbrady says you don't really trust us,' the archbishop went on. 'This is an attempt at reassurance. We have some damned strange habits here in Germany, but by and large we don't tend to give people books before we kill them. At least, not unless we can get the book back without bloodstains.'

'So, you have made your choice, my lord.'

Balduin took a sip of hippocras. 'God forbid I should speak ill of the dead, especially when they are my own kin, but Jean of Bohemia was a bitter bastard who wanted an empire and didn't care whose bodies he walked over in order to get one. When he failed, he led the best men of his generation into that slaughterhouse at Crécy to die with him. His son is not perfect, but given time he could develop into a decent and reasonably honest ruler.'

'And Zajíc? Is there hope for him?'

'He listens to me; I'm part of the old order too, after all. It is still possible that we might save his soul.'

A sudden thought struck Brother Geoffrey. 'Was it you who sent the two musicians? And instructed them to put themselves at Merrivale's disposal if needed?'

'Poděbrady gave the orders, but it was my idea. I wanted a channel into the English court. I wanted also to offer assistance to you and Merrivale. Nikolas and Havel are capable men.'

'Why then instruct them to make contact with Hatfield, rather than directly with the king?'

'I know Hatfield,' the archbishop said. 'I met him during the negotiations at Calais years ago to discuss putting your King Edward on the throne of France. I was impressed by him. He struck me as trustworthy.'

Geoffrey blinked a little. 'If I may be so bold, my lord, why was a German archbishop present at negotiations over the crown of France?'

'I lived much of my life in France; I studied in Paris, if you recall. I knew old King Charles of France well, and most of the rest of the family too. My role was to remind the French negotiators what the nobility would accept, and what they would not.'

Brother Geoffrey nodded. 'One of the other negotiators was Étienne Aubert,' he said quietly. 'Professor of philosophy at Toulouse and now Cardinal-Bishop of Ostia. He is also a member of the conspiracy.'

The wrinkled face gazed back at him. 'Are you saying Hatfield is also a conspirator?'

'We are not certain yet. But it is entirely possible.'

'Then I have bet on the wrong horse,' Balduin said. He sounded annoyed.

Geoffrey watched him. 'And meanwhile, Guy of Béthune is plotting to kill King Charles and, with his wife's help, seize the throne himself. What are you doing about it?'

'Nothing as yet,' the archbishop said slowly. 'Charles has the German clergy behind him, and the Bohemians, but Guy can control the nobility through Yolande. He has the advantage.'

Geoffrey nodded. 'So why did you summon me here, my lord?'

'To ask a favour,' Balduin said. 'I want you to help my nephew.'

I want Guy of Béthune dead. Poděbrady knew; so did the archbishop. *For God's sake*, Geoffrey thought irritably, *I'm an Augustinian canon, not the Old Man of the Mountain*. He rose to his feet, picking up the copy of Buridan.

'I shall do what I can,' he said.

—

Darkness had fallen by the time Geoffrey left the Aula Palatina. The young Franciscan offered a lantern to light his way, but he refused; if trouble was waiting, he wanted to see it before it saw him. Walking back past Saint Barbara's castle he crossed the bridge and turned towards the lights of Pfalzel twinkling in the middle distance. Clouds still hung over the mountains, blocking even the faintest glimmer of moonlight or starlight. Geoffrey walked slowly, planting his feet carefully in the darkness, all his senses alert.

Up ahead, the shadows moved. He halted, holding his breath. Sound came to his ears, grunting and straining, bodies struggling against each other in the mud; then came a convulsive choking and gagging that he recognised all too well, the sound of a dying man, struggling to breathe. He thought about hurrying back to the city and calling for the watch, but by the time help arrived it would be too late; and if he moved now the killers would spot him and he was not sure he could outrun them. Sick at heart, all he could do was stand and pray for the soul of the man who was being murdered.

The choking noise ceased. Silently, the moving shadows vanished into the greater darkness. Brother Geoffrey walked forward, feeling his way carefully until he came to a cloaked shape lying on the ground. He felt for the man's neck, seeking for a pulse. There was none. Instead, his fingers found a mass of blood welling from a narrow but deep gash in the throat where a ligature had been wrapped around the neck.

He ran his hands down the body. The man was carrying no weapon. Under his sodden, muddy cloak he wore a stiffly ornamented tabard. Geoffrey followed the lines of embroidery with his fingers, picking out the shape of a lion with two tails.

If I am not back by nightfall, you are welcome to come and rescue me. Vilém Zajíc had chosen his side.

-

They brought Zajíc's body into the palace an hour later. Poděbrady was waiting, red face alarmed and beard bristling with shock. 'What in Christ's name happened?'

'He was attacked on the road,' Geoffrey said. 'I don't know if the ambush was meant for him, or for me.'

Poděbrady looked at the bloody wound around the neck. 'Who did this?'

'That wound was probably caused by a catgut string, pulled tight around his neck until he strangled. Something like a string from a lute, or a viol.'

The chamberlain looked at him. 'The musicians.'

Yes, Geoffrey thought, *he really is much sharper than he looks. Unless he knew already...* 'Machaut engaged the musicians to play for the king.'

'Mother of God. If Machaut brought hired killers into court, I will skin him alive.'

'No,' Brother Geoffrey said grimly. 'Leave this to me. Keep everything quiet for the moment, and let the court think his death was accidental. And now, if you will forgive me, my lord, I have work to do.'

Machaut's office was in a cabinet near the entrance to the king's private quarters. He looked up as Geoffrey entered the room. 'His Grace is not giving audiences today.'

'I am not here to see his Grace. I am here to see you.'

Without waiting for an invitation, Brother Geoffrey sat down. He studied the man opposite him. Guillaume Machaut was in his mid-forties, a little thicker through the waist than Geoffrey remembered; a little more weather-beaten too, but that tended to happen to men in Jean of Bohemia's service. Two decades of riding across Europe through Italian suns and Prussian snows took its toll, even on secretaries.

'I assume you have heard about Zajíc,' Geoffrey said.

'Yes.' Machaut's lips were tight. He knew what was coming.

'It was a wicked act. Zajíc was a herald, he did not bear arms. What happened last night was murder, plain and simple.'

Machaut said nothing. 'Vilém Zajíc tried to serve two masters,' Geoffrey continued. 'Much as you are trying to do… It couldn't go on forever, of course. I wonder what is passing through your mind this morning, Guillaume? Are you wondering if you will be next? Tonight, tomorrow night, next week, will you too be found dead on the road?'

'I don't know what you are talking about.'

'The three musicians, Garnier, Tomaset and Marcelis. Did you hire them?'

'Yes. I heard them play at the music school in Bruges last year. When I learned they were in Trier, I engaged them to play for the king.'

Slowly, Brother Geoffrey shook his head. 'Guillaume, my son. The protection given to heralds is a sacred oath. What happened to Zajíc was a crime in the eyes of God, and every lie you tell puts your immortal soul in jeopardy. *Oh Light of Light, we are dragged down, from the highest heaven to the lowest hell.*'

Machaut said nothing. 'Let me tell you what I know,' Geoffrey said. 'The three musicians are Pilgrims, and assassins for hire. And the men who control the Pilgrims are also the men who employ you to spy on the king. Guy of Béthune is one of them.'

Machaut sat frozen in his chair. 'One thing I don't know is whether Zajíc was killed deliberately or by accident,' Geoffrey went on. 'It is possible that the three musicians were waiting for me, and Zajíc stumbled into their ambush. Equally, it is possible that Guy of Béthune suspected him of playing a double game. Either way, it doesn't really matter. The consequences will be the same.'

'What do you mean?'

'King Charles will not allow the murderers of his herald to escape unpunished. He will order an inquisition. And if that inquisition discovers that you, the man who brought the musicians to court, are also spying on the king, suspicion will fall directly on you. Yes,' he said, watching Machaut's face. 'I know you are working for Béthune. Don't insult my intelligence, or your own, by pretending otherwise.'

Once again, Machaut lapsed into silence. 'You have a great gift for music,' Geoffrey said. 'You are one of the finest poets of our age, and executing you would be like breaking a nightingale on the wheel. But unless you help me, I will not hesitate to condemn you.'

'I swear to God,' Machaut said, 'I had nothing to do with Zajíc's death.'

'I accept that, for the moment, at least. I shall also take for granted that you know Béthune, with his wife's help, is planning to overthrow the king. Here is the puzzle I need to solve. Yolande and her husband are not on good terms, and there is a rumour that she has lovers. Has she?'

Machaut shook his head, relieved that the questions had turned away from him. 'No. You're right, he is jealous of her, but it was he who brought her to court in the first place and encouraged her to use her charms. And Yolande would never dare to be unfaithful to him. He controls her absolutely.'

'How?'

'He has their son,' Machaut said. 'And he has made it clear that if she disobeys him, he will harm the boy.'

There was a short silence. 'Just when you thought you had seen all the evil in the world, more rears its head,' Geoffrey said. 'Do you know where this boy is?'

'He is a page in the household of one Guy's knights, at a place called Vaudricourt, not far from Béthune.'

'A page, and also a hostage. How do you know this?'

'The countess told me herself.' Machaut looked down at his hands for a moment. 'I think she was hoping I could help her.'

'Really? Did she also know you are Béthune's spy.'

'...I think so. Yes.'

'I see.' Geoffrey stood up. 'Thank you, Guillaume. You have been most helpful.'

Alarm shot through Machaut's face. 'What are you going to do?'

'About you? Nothing. You have chosen to confess your sins to me, and I will not violate the sanctity of the confessional. I shall leave you to consult your conscience, and devise your own penance. The rest is in God's hands now.'

Pfalzel, 9th of March, 1347

The chapel bells rang sext. One of the bells needed recasting, Brother Geoffrey thought. He waited, watching the glow of candles reflecting off painted walls and winking against the gemlike brightness of stained glass. Slowly, the echo of the bells faded away.

The chapel door opened. A woman, dressed all in white, walked slowly forward to the high altar and stood, her head bent. Brother Geoffrey let the silence linger for a time, and then cleared his throat.

'Good day, my lady.'

She turned and stared at him. 'Geoffrey. Why are you here?'

'Waiting for you. I was told you often come here at midday.'

'Yes. I offer prayers for the soul of my late father.'

'Prayers which he undoubtedly needs. And also, I think, you pray for the safety of your son.'

He saw a moment of anger in her eyes. 'Did Simon send you?'

Geoffrey shook his head. 'Simon has enough problems. He needs to stay away from you, my lady.'

The anger faded. 'Earlier, you said he was well. Is he?'

'He nearly died. He is well enough now, though he walks with a stick and probably always will. That is the physical harm, of course. I cannot begin to tell you what damage has been done to his soul.'

Her hands twisted in front of her. 'I never sought to harm him.'

'My lady, the path of history is lined with the graves of people no one ever sought to harm. Intention is never enough. You must have learned that lesson by now.'

'How many times,' she said, 'and how bitterly.'

'I know where your son is,' Geoffrey said.

She considered this in silence. 'Explain,' she said finally.

'I control the rebels of eastern Artois. Their nearest post is only a few miles from Vaudricourt. At a word from me, they will find your son and bring him to you.' He paused. 'Does Guy know the boy is Simon's son?'

The skin of Yolande's face was white, stretched taut as vellum over the fine framework of bones beneath. 'Yes.'

Geoffrey nodded. 'I will bring him to you safely. That is my sacred promise.'

'And what must I do in return?'

'You know where the musicians are,' Geoffrey said. 'Garnier, Tomaset and Marcelis. Give them the order.'

'What makes you think they will obey me?'

'Killing Zajíc was a mistake. This is their one chance for atonement.'

She frowned a little. 'Bring me my son, and I will consider it.'

Geoffrey shook his head. 'No, my lady. When it is done, and only when it is done, will your son be safe.'

Trier, 9th of March, 1347

We are hunted, the message from Garnier of Liège had said, *and we need your help. Come alone to the Castle of Saint Barbara after nightfall. You know what will happen if we are taken.*

Cursing, Guy of Béthune cut the small scrap of parchment into shreds and threw them down the garderobe chute. Those damned musicians were supposed to go into hiding as soon as they had finished Zajíc. Instead, they must have loitered too long, and been spotted. The threat in the letter was real; he had no doubt they would tell everything to save their own skins.

In the palace courtyard he called for his horse. Dusk was already falling; it would be full night by the time he reached the city. At least they had chosen a sensible place to meet; there was plenty of open ground around Saint Barbara, a wasteland full of ancient ruins where men could meet without being observed. Riding through the gates, he spurred his horse and galloped down the road towards the distant lights of Trier.

He reached the river and slowed, turning his horse to cross the bridge. A man lunged out of the shadows and seized the bridle. Béthune raised his riding whip but more hands pulled him from behind, dragging him out of the saddle. His head hit the ground hard and he lay for a moment, half-stunned. His sword and dagger were torn from their scabbards and sent spinning into darkness. Struggling for air he looked up to see three dark figures bending over him. 'You bastards,' he gasped. 'You have betrayed me.'

'You betrayed yourself, my lord,' said Garnier, and they dragged his head up and slipped the catgut noose around his neck, and pulled.

Somehow, Béthune managed to get his fingers under the noose before it tightened. He felt the ligature bite through his gloves and into his hand, but his free hand lashed out, punching and jabbing at the men clustered around him. Garnier cursed, and someone else cried out in pain as Béthune's fist hit him in the mouth. He shook them off and struggled to his feet. He felt a sudden stabbing pain in his back, followed by another, but he ignored the blows and ran across the bridge towards the city, clawing at the noose. If he could reach the city gate, he would be safe.

They caught him halfway across the bridge. Béthune turned and lashed out once more, landing several hard blows with his fists, but his strength was fading. Despairing, he tried to haul himself up onto the stone balustrade, hoping to walk or at least crawl towards safety. Another knife ripped into his belly. Twisting in agony, he rolled over the balustrade and felt the void open beneath him. His final thought was, *I won't give you the satisfaction, you bitch*, and then his body hit the water.

Up on the bridge the three men peered into the river, breathing hard. 'I can't see him,' said Tomaset, wiping blood from his lips.

'It has been raining for days,' said Marcelis. 'The river is in spate. He'll be far away downstream by now.'

'What if he manages to get ashore?'

'He won't.' Garnier held up a bloody knife. 'He'll bleed to death before he can swim to shore.'

Marcelis nodded. 'All right. Let's go collect the money, and then moving.'

'Where are we going?'

'New orders. We are leaving for Bruges, as soon as possible.'

Pfalzel, 10th of March, 1347

'They found his horse and weapons this morning,' Yolande said quietly. 'There is no sign of a body.'

'Never mind,' said Brother Geoffrey. 'There are plenty of weirs and mill races downstream. I'm sure the corpse will fetch up in one of them, sooner or later.'

She fretted. 'It would be better if there was a body.'

'Then let the Lord provide one. Find the body of some unfortunate, put it in a closed coffin and bury it with all due ceremony. When the real body turns up, dispose of it quietly. That should not be beyond your abilities.'

'And you? Will you keep your word?'

'A messenger is already on his way to Artois.'

She nodded. 'Thank you,' she said, although she did not sound particularly grateful. 'What will you do now?'

It had all been rather easy, Geoffrey thought. *Too easy, perhaps?* Aloud he said, 'My work is done. And you, my lady, are free.'

'Am I?' she asked. 'Are any of us truly free, Geoffrey?'

'You need a metaphysician for that,' he said. 'Buridan, perhaps, could answer your question.'

'You think you have struck a blow. You think you have disrupted the great conspiracy. But you are wrong.'

Sudden suspicion formed in his mind. 'What do you mean?'

'Guy's death means nothing, Geoffrey. What is about to happen, will happen. And there is nothing you, or I, or anyone else can do to stop it.'

21

Wanze, 12th of March, 1347

Storms of sleet raked down the valley of the Meuse, driving even the hardiest travellers off the road. As evening fell, Fier Meike led them to an abandoned barn on the outskirts of a village. Across the river, the castle of Huy frowned from its steep bluff. Topaas and the five Pilgrims who accompanied them remained on the floor of the barn, while Meike and Tiphaine climbed up into the loft. The barn had been stripped bare and there was nothing with which to make a fire, but at least they were out of the weather.

'Why did you insist on coming with me?' Tiphaine asked.

Meike began wringing water out of her black hair. 'The roads are not safe for lone travellers. Also, if you want to find Nortkerque, you need to speak to the sisters. If he is in Liège, they will know about it.'

'You mentioned them back in Poperinge. The wise sisters, you called them. Are they your leaders?'

'I told you, we have no leaders. They are women, known to everyone for their goodness and piety. That is all.'

Piety was not a concept Tiphaine had ever associated with Fier Meike. 'You claim there are no leaders in the Pilgrims, but aren't you a leader? When you speak, Topaas and the others obey you.'

'That is their choice,' Meike said. 'I make no claim on them, and I have no dominion over them. They are free to choose their own destiny. It is the same for us all.'

'Who are the Pilgrims? What do you believe in?'

A fresh shower of sleet rattled against the roof of the barn. 'We believe in peace and justice,' Fier Meike said. 'And it may surprise you, but we also believe in love.'

Tiphaine blinked. 'Love?'

'The Reverend Mother Hadewijch said it well, a century ago. *Be on your guard, and let nothing disturb your peace. Do good at all times, without thinking of profit or blessedness, damnation or salvation or martyrdom, for all that you do should be in the name of love.'*

Tiphaine pointed to the *goedendaag* lying on the floor. 'I do not see that as an instrument of love. Or peace, come to that.'

'No,' said Meike. 'But it knows how to dispense justice.'

'Why did you join the Pilgrims?'

'Do you always ask so many questions?'

'Yes.'

Meike tucked her hair back inside her hood. 'I was once a fuller in Ghent, a master with my own shop, the only woman in the city in my position. Two years ago, I threw it all away to lead a revolt by the fullers against the tyranny of the weavers.'

'What happened?'

'We lost,' Meike said. She spoke with a quiet dignity. 'Have you not heard of the revolt in Ghent?'

'No. Two years ago, I was a prisoner in Normandy.'

'Why were you imprisoned?'

'Because I was my father's daughter,' Tiphaine said.

Meike nodded, understanding. 'The weavers controlled the city's wealth, and so they were the ones with the power. After they defeated us I lost my workshop and all my property. I was driven out of the city with nothing but my *goedendaag* and the clothes on my back. The weavers ruled Ghent once more, as they still do. I resolved that henceforth I would fight tyrants wherever I found them. The Pilgrims offered me a place among them.'

'And so you went to Poperinge.'

'The people of Poperinge are no better, or nobler, or more worthy of salvation than any other. But Ypres is one of the League of Three, a power in the land, and the burgemeester and the guilds use their power to oppress the towns around them. I believe Poperinge deserves justice, and peace.'

'And love?'

'This is Flanders,' Fier Meike said. 'Let us not reach for the impossible.'

–

Later, as darkness was falling and they made ready to sleep, Meike stirred a little. 'This herald, Merrivale, the one you are helping. He must mean something to you, if you are prepared to lay your life on the line for him.'

'He saved my life,' Tiphaine said. 'Twice, in fact.'

'Mm. Are you fucking him?'

'Oh, for God's sake!' Tiphaine said crossly. 'First Queen Philippa, now you. Yes, occasionally, when it suits us both. So what?'

'You are angry with the world because you have suffered,' Meike said. 'But think about others. That girl back in Poperinge, for example. Imagine what she has suffered, and her life has been shorter than yours. You are not the only one who endures pain.'

'I never said I was.'

'Then stop raging for what you have lost, and start being thankful for what you have.' Fier Meike lay down, pillowing her head on her rolled up cloak. 'Get some sleep. Tomorrow, we shall arrive in Liège.'

–

In the morning as they prepared to set off, Topaas laid a hand on Tiphaine's arm. 'Forgive me,' he said quietly. 'But I overheard a little of your conversation last night.'

The others were out of earshot. 'What of it?'

'There is something you should know about Meike. She lived and worked in Ghent for many years, but she was born in a village near Kortrijk. That's where her family lived.'

Tiphaine knew was coming. 'What happened to them?'

'When the Count of Béthune's raiders swept through Flanders last year, they burned much of the country around Kortrijk and killed everyone they found. All of Meike's family were slaughtered, even her children. She is the only one left alive. She spends much of her time wondering why.'

'Dear God,' Tiphaine said softly. 'No wonder she wants Béthune dead.'

'Dead? Death is too good for a maggot like Béthune. I would put him in the fire, and keep him there for a long, long time so I could watch him suffer.'

'No,' said Tiphaine. 'I've done that. It brings no relief.'

Liège was a bleak grey city falling down the hillside towards the banks of the Meuse. The skulls of dead bishops dangled like windchimes over the arch of Saint Walburga's gate, bumping and swaying in the breeze. You could tell they were bishops because someone had taken the trouble to make mitres out of painted copper and nail them to the heads. A single banner, a black lion, flew overhead.

The watch on the gate were Pilgrims, bearing the usual motley collection of weapons and armour. They knew Fier Meike, and she and her party were admitted without question. They walked down cobbled streets towards the river, seeing the half-built towers of the cathedral wrapped in scaffolding and cattle grazing in the meadows beyond. Another church stood to the right, roofless and burned out with its tower standing drunkenly askew and ivy crawling up its walls. The streets were nearly empty; every second house was shuttered or boarded up. The few people they met hurried past with downcast eyes. In the marketplace a man stood stripped to the waist with his hands lashed to a wooden pole while another man in a dark cassock flogged him with a scourge. Two armed Pilgrims stood watching. None of the men made a sound.

'What is his crime?' Tiphaine asked.

'Gambling, probably,' said Topaas. 'Or fornication. They're very strict on morals here in Liège.'

The gates of the bishop's palace had been smashed down, and the palace itself was dark and lifeless. The cathedral, on the other hand, was full of light and bustle, a sharp contrast to the silent streets outside. People hurried to and fro carrying rolls of parchment, or stood in little groups talking in low voices. Most were men in clerical robes with tonsures, but there were quite a few women too. A table near the door was stacked high with loaves of bread and people came in and helped themselves, apparently without paying. At another table two more women in black robes sat with stacks of silver coins in front of them, disbursing money to a queue of people. Candles blazed in the chapels before the altars of saints, Anne, Gudula, Christina Mirabilis, Elizabeth of Hungary. The air smelled of wax and incense.

'Would someone care to tell me what is going on?' Tiphaine asked.

Meike turned her head, the candlelight glinting off her hair. 'This is the beating heart of Liège,' she said. 'The guilds have their own halls and regulate their own affairs, but this is the centre of the commune. People come here for aid and comfort, and for justice.'

'And food?'

'No one goes hungry here. What is available is shared freely by all. That is the way of the Pilgrims.'

Along with assassination in the dark? Tiphaine thought, but she kept silent. A woman in black barred their way. She had grey hair falling in strands from under her wimple, framing a face that might have been chiselled out of stone. 'What is your business?' she demanded.

Meike bowed her head. 'We are here to see the sisters.'

The woman stared at them. She might have been a Beguine, but in Tiphaine's experience Beguines did not act with such authority. 'Why?' she demanded.

'We seek a man, Jehan Nortkerque of Poperinge and Calais. He came with another, an Englishman named Nicodemus. We need to find them.'

'Why?' the woman repeated.

'I would rather explain to the sisters,' Fier Meike said.

The woman frowned. 'Only Sister Juliana is here, and she is at prayer. If you intend to waste her time with some trivial matter, there will be consequences.'

'This is important,' Meike said quietly. 'Please take us to Sister Juliana.'

—

The Beguine led the way to a chapel in the apse of the cathedral, behind the high altar. In the ambulatory many of the ornamented tombs had been prized open and emptied; fragments of smashed stone still littered the floor. A woman in black knelt in prayer before the altar, head bowed, lips moving without sound. She held up a hand for silence and continued her prayers, the other hand clutching a small wooden cross. When she had finished she continued to kneel for a moment, staring at the altar with unfocused eyes, before rising slowly and turning to face them.

'Meike,' she said. Her voice was low and musical. 'Welcome among us. What is the news from Poperinge?'

'All is quiet. Most of the Ypres militia are away fighting the French. Sister Juliana, we seek news of Jehan Nortkerque. Has he come to Liège?'

The woman ignored the question, gazing instead at Tiphaine. She was young, Tiphaine saw, not much more than thirty; her eyes were an intense deep blue, almost black. 'Who is this? She is not one of us, I think.'

'She is a friend,' Meike said.

'Is she? I smell sin on her.'

Tiphaine stared back at her. 'You cannot smell sin.'

'That is because you are surrounded by it. If you were truly pure, you would know its reek.' Sister Juliana pointed at the painted altarpiece, where a woman in red with a halo and angelic wings contemplated an image of the crucified Christ. 'Saint Christina Mirabilis was woken from her grave by the stench of sin, and floated up to the ceiling where she could breathe pure air. I often wish I could follow her example.'

'Or you could just fetch a ladder,' said Tiphaine.

The older Beguine drew in her breath with an angry hiss. Sister Juliana stared at Tiphaine for a long time, eyes boring into her face. 'There is much darkness within you,' she said.

'You have no idea,' said Tiphaine. 'It might, of course, be the company I keep. For example, Jehan Nortkerque, who is a receiver of counterfeit coin and also beats and rapes young girls. Or his friend Nicodemus, a traitor and murderer who once sold children into slavery. Are you harbouring them in Liège?'

Sister Juliana's eyes flickered. 'This is a place of light,' she said calmly. 'God's holy love has filled it with radiance.'

'That does not answer my question.'

'It does, but the darkness prevents you from listening. *I am God, says Love, for Love is God and God is Love.* So said the blessed Marguerite Porete, shortly before they fed her to the flames in Paris. We remember her words, and the words of all those who came before and after, and suffered in the name of truth. We walk the path of Love in the sure and certain knowledge that we are doing God's work. We would never receive men such as you describe, and we have no knowledge of them. Now, go in peace.'

'Do not fob me off with cheap philosophy,' Tiphaine said. 'We know they came here, we have a witness who overheard them speaking. I think they are here, and I also think you know where they are.'

'I will not quarrel with you in God's house,' said Sister Juliana. 'Meike, I am sorry you have had a wasted journey, but as you have heard, the men you seek are not here. You may lodge where you will for the night. Tomorrow, I think you should return to Poperinge. The people there have need of you.'

Meike bowed and turned away, followed by Topaas and the other men. Tiphaine turned on her heel and walked after them. Outside in the marketplace the man in the cassock was flogging someone else, a woman this time. She sobbed as the whip bit into her back. It had begun to rain.

—

They found shelter in an empty house up the hill, not far from the ruined church. There was bread and beer and pottage but no meat, for it was still Lent. From the house next door they could hear a child crying. 'What in God's name is going on?' demanded Tiphaine. 'What is this place?'

'Liège is a free commune, ruled by its people,' said Fier Meike. 'They have driven out the nobles and all the religious orders except the Beguines. They have no masters other than themselves. For Pilgrims, this is a place of inspiration.'

'You find public floggings inspirational?'

'Freedom does not mean chaos,' Topaas said. 'Order must be maintained.'

'You must understand what happened here,' Meike said. 'The commune has been at war for nearly forty years. When the nobles attempted to suppress it, the people fought them in the streets and won. When the surviving nobles hid in the church of Saint-Martin, the people set fire to the church and burned them all.'

Thank you for another nightmare to add to my list, Tiphaine thought. 'And the clergy?'

'Things were peaceful under old Bishop Adolph, but when his nephew became bishop in turn, he tried to dismantle the commune and impose his own rule. He also accused the Beguines of heresy.'

'For preaching about love? Yes, I can see why that would annoy a bishop. What happened?'

'The commune turned to the Pilgrims for aid. We defeated the bishop's army and sent him into exile.'

'And then, I presume, the people opened the tombs of former bishops, dragged out the bones and hung the skulls over the gate,' Tiphaine said. 'How very brave to take revenge on the dead. Do you think Sister Juliana was telling the truth?'

There was silence for a moment. The child next door continued to wail. 'I see no reason to doubt her word,' Meike said finally. She looked at Tiphaine. 'Even if she is wrong, I am sure there is a good explanation. There was no need to antagonise her as you did.'

'There was no need for her to insult me. She knows who Nortkerque is. She recognised the name at once, it showed in her face. And again, where does all the money come from? As well as the free bread there must have been twenty marks of silver on that table, and they were handing it out like Maundy money. Who pays for this, and who feeds and arms the Pilgrims?'

'We don't know,' one of the other men said. 'We have never felt it necessary to ask. God is love.'

'Suffering Christ,' said Tiphaine. 'These people are working for *Béthune*! If not directly for him, then for his friends! Will you let them get away scot-free?'

She saw the look on Meike's face, and regretted her words at once. She drew breath. 'Very well. What are we going to do?'

'You heard Sister Juliana,' Topaas said. 'We return to Poperinge.'

'But she is not your leader,' Tiphaine insisted. 'As everyone keeps telling me, you have no leaders. She gave you no orders.'

'No orders were given,' Topaas agreed. 'But they will be obeyed nevertheless.' He looked at Fier Meike, who sat staring at her *goedendaag*. 'All the same, we have had a hard journey, and I suggest we rest before starting back. A day will make no difference.'

'No,' Meike said, brooding. 'You are right, Topaas, we should rest. We need our strength.'

'Well, that at least is true,' Tiphaine said bitterly.

Liège, 14th of March, 1347

In the morning the rain had stopped and the air was clear. When Tiphaine stepped out into the street she heard the soft music of wild birds, flying north in long skeins across the sky.

Topaas followed her outside. 'Where are you going?'

'To follow an instinct. I won't be long.'

Wrapping her cloak around herself to ward off the keen east wind, she walked down the hill towards the cathedral. The streets were empty, and she saw again the silent shuttered houses. It was Lent, of course, but that did not entirely explain the sense of desolation she could feel in the air. No one starved in Liège; thanks to the Pilgrims, there was plenty of food and money to go around, but somewhere along the way the joy of living had been snuffed out.

And perhaps that was deliberate, she thought. Perhaps that was part of the new vision of the future being created by the man from the north and his allies.

The punishment post in the marketplace was empty, which was a blessing. Instead there was a column of wagons guarded by armed men on horseback, horses and vehicles alike all splashed with mud from hard travelling. Goods were being unloaded and carried into the cathedral, barrels of flour and stockfish and salted eels. Tiphaine had travelled with an army long enough to recognise a foraging party.

No one goes hungry in Liège, she thought. *Of course not; they are robbing and pillaging the countryside to feed their own. Damn them all for hypocrites.* She pulled the hood of her cloak forward to hide her face, and waited.

She had hoped Nortkerque might come to the cathedral. Instead, Sister Juliana came out and stood for a moment under the carved and painted arches of the west door. She watched the foragers unload before pulling up her own hood and walking across the marketplace. To Tiphaine's surprise, she went straight to the ruined gates of the bishop's palace and passed into the courtyard. Tiphaine waited for a few moments, and followed.

The courtyard was silent and empty. She walked across the cobbles to the kitchen door. This too had been smashed down and the empty doorway was full of cobwebs. Pushing her way through these, she crossed the lifeless kitchen and tiptoed into the screens passage beyond. She heard a woman speaking quietly, her voice echoing a little in the cavernous space of the hall. She held her breath, straining her ears to hear.

'All is arranged,' said Sister Juliana. 'They will meet us here to receive their final instruction. Is everything ready in Bruges?'

'The pieces are in position,' said a man's voice.

Tiphaine went rigid with shock. She knew that voice, very well; she had been a guest in the man's house for several weeks last year. It was William Blyth, the fugitive banker from Newcastle.

233

Blyth was still speaking. 'The money has been delivered, and the musicians will be on their way to Bruges by now. All we need is Nortkerque and his men.'

'They are ready,' said Sister Juliana. 'Nortkerque is on his way here now. Oh, my brother! How long we have waited for this moment!'

The door from the screens passage into the hall was slightly ajar. Crouching down, Tiphaine looked through the narrow crack. Blyth and Juliana were embracing tightly; when they finally stepped back, she could see a gleam of tears on the woman's face. 'It has been a long time,' she said. 'So many years of planning and scheming, hoping and dreaming. If only our mother were alive to see this day!'

'We shall avenge her well,' Blyth said. 'The men who killed her will suffer, along with all the others.'

'We shall tear the world to pieces,' said Sister Juliana. 'And we shall remake it as it should have been made. No sovereigns and princes, no bishops and popes. Only the true love of God shall prevail.'

'Amen,' Blyth said quietly. He turned his head. 'Ah. Our friends have arrived.'

Two more men had entered the hall. One was the lean, angular figure of Nicodemus, longbow and quiver slung across his back. The other was stocky and square-faced with a sword belt around his waist. He bowed to Sister Juliana and Blyth. 'We are yours to command,' he said. 'Tell us what you need.'

Nicodemus stiffened, holding up one hand. 'Wait. Someone is here.'

Shit, thought Tiphaine, *how did he know?* She rose and backed away from the door, but it was too late; Nicodemus was already running towards her, unslinging his bow and nocking an arrow, and Nicodemus, she knew, was a deadly shot. She fled through the kitchen into the courtyard, but Blyth and the other man were already outside, swords in hand, cutting her off from the gate. Sister Juliana followed them, her face a mask of stone. 'It is the woman who came with Fier Meike,' she said. 'Kill her.'

Nicodemus raised his bow. Blyth held up a hand. 'No,' he said. 'Not yet. She belongs to Merrivale. She could be useful.'

Tiphaine spat at him. 'I belong to no one.'

'Indeed? Then why are you here? Merrivale sent you, of course. You are his creature. How much does Merrivale know?'

'Ask him yourself,' said Tiphaine.

'Perhaps I shall, when next he comes to Bruges.' Blyth turned to Sister Juliana. 'Can you keep her secure?'

'If you wish it, yes,' she said reluctantly. 'There is a prison cell at Saint Walburga's gate. But I still think you should kill her.'

'Your brother is right,' said Nicodemus. 'She is more use to us alive than dead. Hold her until we send for her.'

Blyth took an oilcloth packet out of his cloak and handed it to the stocky man. 'Here are your orders, Nortkerque. There are also final instructions for Donato de' Peruzzi, telling him where and how to make the payment.'

Nortkerque nodded. 'To whom do I report when I arrive?'

'No one. The Count of Flanders is your responsibility. Arrange matters however you wish—'

Everyone froze. From the marketplace came the sound of running footsteps, coming closer. Fier Meike ran into the courtyard, followed by Topaas and the rest of the men. Nicodemus raised his bow again, fingers tight on the string; it would take only a second to draw and release. 'Come no closer,' he said. 'One more step and I will shoot.'

The Pilgrims halted. 'You can kill one of us,' said Meike. 'Perhaps two, but no more.'

The arrow point never wavered. 'Then choose which two of you will die with me. Or does someone wish to make the sacrifice?'

Blyth looked at Nortkerque. 'Is there another entrance to the palace?'

The other man nodded. 'There is a gate onto the river. A boat is already waiting.'

'Good. Nicodemus, make certain they don't follow us.'

Blyth and Nortkerque ran back into the palace. Topaas took a step after them. 'No!' Tiphaine screamed.

Nicodemus smiled. He swung the bow slowly, covering Topaas, Meike and their men one by one, and then finally herself. Tiphaine went rigid. 'You said I was to be kept safe,' she said.

'I have my orders,' said Nicodemus.

Tiphaine closed her eyes. She heard the hard twang of the bowstring and felt the wind from the arrow brush her face like the wings of death. Behind her someone gagged with sudden pain and she heard the rustle and thud of a body sliding to the cobbles. Disbelieving, she opened her eyes and turned. Sister Juliana was lying on her back, hands clutching feebly at the arrow embedded in her chest. Within a few seconds the hands relaxed and she went still. By the time she was dead, Nicodemus had already gone.

22

Bruges, 23rd of March, 1347

'Counterfeit money has begun to appear in the markets,' said Sister Adela. 'Not just French and English coins, but Flemish too. The people have begun to blame the burgemeester.'

There were buds on the trees outside; spring was coming at last. 'And how has the burgemeester responded?' Merrivale asked.

'He has imposed stiff penalties for anyone passing counterfeit money, even if they do so without realising the coins are false. Needless to say, this has made people even more discontented.'

'Which is, of course, exactly what the conspirators want,' Merrivale said.

He was tired and his leg was giving him pain. He had arrived in Bruges early, ostensibly to smooth the path for the royal party before their arrival, but in reality to look for any signs of trouble. They were expected at Sluis in three or four days, and would lodge at the castle of Maele east of the city; Merrivale had already taken up residence there.

'And the stolen money?' he asked. 'The Knights' gold?'

Sister Adela nodded to Bessancourt. 'We think we have worked it out,' the young Frenchman said. 'As we suspected, the Knights at Maldegem used some of the silver to buy gold ducats from other priories at a favourable rate. I couldn't work out why at first. Financially, this made no sense. It is like your English phrase, stripping Peter to clothe Paul. The only advantage, as we discussed earlier, is that gold is less bulky and easier to transport. Then, just as I was considering this, the entire operation shut down. The Knights at Maldegem stopped buying gold.'

He seemed different, Merrivale thought; more confident, more assertive. Sister Adela was a good teacher. 'Why?'

'We don't know for certain,' said Adela, 'but our guess is that they had enough for their purpose. They bought exactly one thousand ducats and stopped.'

'Thirty thousand marks, give or take,' said Bessancourt. 'Depending on purity, the prevailing exchange rate and so forth.'

'Thirty thousand marks,' said the herald. 'Just like thirty pieces of silver. In any case, a great deal of money.'

Bessancourt shook his head. 'Compared with what they must have stolen from the French treasury, it is a drop in the ocean. And then there is the money Blyth brought with him from England. They're sitting on a dragon's horde. But here is the important thing. The money is no longer at Maldegem. None of it, not the silver or the gold.'

'Where is it?'

'Heer Adornes and his agents have been very cooperative. The silver was sent by secret convoy up the River Meuse to Liège.'

'If it was a secret convoy, how did Adornes come to know about it?'

'Because the Knights made an error,' Adela said. 'They took out a sea-risk insurance policy, a common enough thing, but they should have gone to Ghent or Antwerp. Instead they came to Bruges, and Maartin Adornes was part of the syndicate that bought the policy.'

There was silence for a moment. 'It doesn't really matter,' Merrivale said finally. 'The money is in Liège, in the hands of the Pilgrims. All our efforts have been in vain.'

'Not entirely,' said Bessancourt. 'The gold didn't go to Liège. It was sent to Bruges, where it was received by the Italian banker, Donato di Pacino de' Peruzzi. The guild of bankers knows all about the transaction, even though Peruzzi is officially a foreign merchant and not part of the guild. He claims he is recovering money from loans made to the old Count of Flanders.'

'Has Peruzzi had any contact with the young count?'

'Yes, he visited him at ten Berghe about a week ago, to discuss the repayments. The burgemeester gave his permission.'

'Of course he did,' Merrivale said. 'The burgemeester wouldn't recognise a plot if it bit him on the arse. So, Peruzzi now knows the defences of ten Berghe and how many men we have there. By now, the man from the north must know as well.'

'Are they planning to assassinate the count?' asked Adela.

'That makes sense. The count dies, the betrothal never takes place, the alliance is broken, the war continues. Meanwhile, the markets are flooded with false coin, order breaks down, the League of Three begins to crack and the Pilgrims are waiting for their moment. I think they will try to kill him, very soon, before the betrothal.'

'How do we stop them?' asked Adela.

The herald sat for a moment, thinking. Sunlight glittered off his tabard. 'Peruzzi offers us an opportunity, perhaps. I can't go near him; he knows me from the old days in Florence, and knows who I used to be. He will be suspicious at once.'

'But he doesn't know me,' Bessancourt said. 'He has never seen me.'

'It will be dangerous,' Merrivale said.

'Not half so dangerous as life will be if the Count of Flanders is assassinated and those Pilgrim bastards take over. What do you want me to do?'

Kasteel Maele, 24th of March, 1347

'Master Nikolas and Master Havel are here, sir,' said Warin.

Merrivale looked up from his writing desk. 'Show them in.'

Nikolas of Prague and Havel the Fiddler entered the room a few moments later, bowing and removing their hats. 'Were you followed from the city?' Merrivale asked.

'No, sir herald,' said Havel. 'Definitely not. We have some skill in these matters,' he added.

'I'm certain you do. What news do you bring me?'

'Garnier and his friends are in Bruges, sir. I recognised him straight away. The other two are Tomaset and Marcelis, just as you said. The French lad has been helping us observe their movements.'

The herald frowned. 'I thought I told Bessancourt to stay out of this. I have other purposes for him.'

'He's eager to help, sir, and he fits in well. No one suspects him, or us.'

Havel nodded. 'So far, there's not much to report. They're doing the same as the rest of us, meeting old friends, sharing songs and so on. They have some *minnesang* tunes from the Rhineland that I haven't heard before. Marcelis bought some new strings for his lute. That's about all.'

'Have they met anyone other than fellow musicians?'

'Not that we know of, sir.'

The plot was becoming visible now. Garnier, Tomaset and Marcelis were the assassins who would kill Louis of Flanders, and Peruzzi must be their paymaster. How in God's name did Donato de' Peruzzi get mixed up in a scheme like this? Merrivale wondered. In one respect the answer was simple; the Peruzzi were bankrupt, and desperate for money. Even so – Donato had always been a ruthless bastard, but this?

He could inform the burgemeester and ask for the musicians to be arrested, but then Peruzzi would disappear along with the gold. There were many other killers for hire waiting in the shadows; Nicodemus, for instance.

'I want to know if any of them try to contact Peruzzi. If they do, send word to me at once.'

Havel looked doubtful. 'There's three of them, sir, and only two of us. And they know us. We'll need the French lad's help again.'

'I can help, sir,' Warin volunteered. 'They haven't seen me. Mauro can look after things here.'

Merrivale thought for a moment. Warin was more than just a groom; he had proved his toughness and resourcefulness many times over, from the mountains of Spain to the moors of northern England. He knew how to look after himself, far better than Bessancourt.

'Very well,' he said. 'Make it so. Thank you, all of you.'

Warin and the two Bohemians departed. Merrivale sat for a moment, staring down at the parchment on the table before him. *I am missing something*, he thought. *But what?*

Bruges, 25th of March, 1347

Peruzzi is greedy, the herald had said to Bessancourt, giving him his instructions. *Money is his Achilles heel, and always has been. Offer him enough money, and you will tempt him.*

It was Palm Sunday. Green boughs hung everywhere, imitating the palm leaves that had decked the roads when Jesus entered Jerusalem. Crowds of people lined the streets, talking and laughing, for this was a day of celebration as well as solemnity; and besides, in a few days Lent would be over and everyone could have a decent meal again. Standing on the Meesterstraat, wearing a heavy black Benedictine robe with a hood shading his face, Bessancourt listened to a pig grunting in its sty and wondered if the animal knew its time was running out.

The air had a bittersweet tang, a mixture of incense and ammonia from the dyers' workshops that lined the street. Armed men from the town watch mingled with the crowds of people; this was a holy day, but there had been trouble in the Grote Markt yesterday over false coins, and Metteneye the watch commander was taking no chances. The procession was on its way from the Kruisport, long lines of clergy in black and white and grey bearing a painted red-robed figure of Christ before them. Mendicants moved through the crowd, chanting hymns and holding out begging bowls. Bessancourt walked casually along the street like a man in search of a better view, finally stopping beside a man in a dark brown coat with a sable ruff. He had a long, dour face and an aquiline nose. '*Goeden dag*,' Bessancourt said amiably in Flemish.

The man ignored him. Bessancourt switched to Latin. 'It is a pleasure to make your acquaintance, *Dominus* Peruzzi.'

The man did not turn his head. 'Whatever you are selling, I am not interested.'

'I am not selling,' Bessancourt said. 'I am buying. You can perform a service for my master, and he is prepared to pay a good price for it.'

There was a pause. Two of the town watch were standing only a few feet away. 'Wait,' Peruzzi said.

The procession passed by in a fog of incense and chanting. Most of the crowd followed it. Peruzzi motioned with his hand and they walked to the Meebruck, a slender stone bridge over the Groenerei. Peruzzi stopped in the middle of the span. 'Who are you? French, I think, by your accent.'

'I was born in France,' Bessancourt said. 'Now, I have no country.' That was likely to be true, he thought. 'I am in the employ of a very powerful man who needs a service performed. He sent me to find you.'

'Since you know who I am, you must know full well that my family are no longer engaged in moneylending. We have no money to lend.'

Bessancourt nodded. 'My commiserations on your family's misfortunes. But, as I said, I am buying, not selling.'

'And what is this service your master wants?'

Bessancourt looked around carefully, checking to make sure there was no one within earshot. 'An assassination.'

The expression in Peruzzi's face did not change. 'Who?'

'That does not concern you. I am not asking you to kill anyone yourself. Find men prepared to do this deed, introduce them to me, and I will pay you a commission.'

'You have come to the wrong person,' Peruzzi said shortly. 'I have no idea what you are talking about.'

'Of course, no Florentine banker ever ordered the assassination of anyone. You are all as pure as snow. Do you want the money, or not?'

'How much?' Peruzzi demanded.

'Ten thousand florins,' said Bessancourt.

'I am sorry. I cannot help you.'

'Twenty thousand.'

Peruzzi looked him in the eye. 'This is so important to you?'

'You cannot even begin to guess how important,' Bessancourt said. 'No one will ever connect you to the killing. Bring the men to me, and I will give you the money and you can leave the city. You will be over the horizon before they begin looking for you.'

'Suppose I can find such men,' Peruzzi said finally. 'What then?'

'Meet me outside the Chapel of the Holy Blood at vespers in two days' time. I will tell you what to do next. Now, turn and walk away. Do not look back.'

The banker turned and walked across the bridge. Bessancourt waited until he was out of sight and then hurried through the empty streets to the Hospital of Saint John. Sister Adela was waiting in the cloister.

'I think he took the bait,' Bessancourt said. 'He as good as admitted that he knew where to find assassins. If it is the three musicians, we can trap them. Do we inform Captain Metteneye?'

Adela shook her head. 'Not yet.'

'But—'

'No. We can't be sure where Metteneye stands, or where his loyalties lie. Be patient, young man. We will know when the moment is right.'

Juliana Gistel has been murdered in Liège, the letter said. That was all; there was no signature, no identifying mark, the seal was a shapeless blob of wax. Sister Adela fetched her cloak and went out, walking south through the city in the falling dusk until she came to the Begijnhof, a low brick building surrounded by a wall. The porter at the gate admitted her without question, and Adela walked across the courtyard and down a short passage to the cloister. A white-haired woman in the black robes of the Beguines looked up as she entered. 'Adela. What brings you here, sister?'

Adela handed her the letter. The other woman read it, then laid it quietly aside. 'What do you want to know?'

'Was she one of you? A Beguine?'

'Yes. I brought her into our order. After her mother's execution, her father and brother fled to England, leaving her abandoned. We gave her a home.'

'How long have you known she was in Liège?'

'Since the beginning. She came to see me before she went away.'

'Did you know she was a Pilgrim?'

'Yes.'

'Are you?'

The white-haired woman frowned. 'I am true to my faith, sister. We do God's work here, and have no interest in secular affairs.'

'But you know what goes on in the world. I think you know why Juliana went to Liège. And I think you also know why she was killed.'

'If you want answers, why not ask the person who wrote this letter? Do you know who it is?'

'The Knights of Saint John have a hospital in Liège. It is much reduced since the Pilgrims took over, but a few of our nursing-brothers cling on. Word must have reached them that I was searching for Juliana, and one of them wrote to me. If they had known more, they would have told me.' Adela stared at the older woman. 'Well? Do you know what happened, reverend mother?'

'I do not meddle. And I advise you to keep out of this as well. You are putting yourself in danger.'

'It is too late for that. What is coming, reverend mother?'

'The end,' the other woman said. 'The end of tyranny, the over-throw of the godless, and the dawn of a new age of hope. Thrones will topple and crowns will be shattered, and the angels shall stand on the four corners of the earth.'

'Babylon is fallen,' said Adela. 'And so, the age of God begins with a woman's murder? Is that the future you desire?'

'Juliana's soul is safe,' the other woman said. 'Is yours?'

Adela did not answer. She turned and walked out of the Begijnhof, hurrying back up the long streets to the hospital. She needed to get Brother Frido to alert the Knights, and she had to get word to Merrivale so he could warn his own people. She wondered too about the Beguines. They knew about the plot; were they also part of it? How many other Beguines were also Pilgrims? Their beliefs, bordering on the heretical, were not unalike.

The streets were very dark now, lit only by the lights from a few unshuttered windows. The lamps on the bridge over the Dijver had been extinguished too, and at once her mind moved from calculation to high alert. Danger swirled out of the darkness. She opened her mouth to shout for help, but a hand from behind clamped over her mouth. A hard fist hit her in the stomach, knocking the air out of her lungs. Something cold and thin dropped around her neck, and she felt the catgut noose begin to tighten.

-

Be patient, Adela had said, but Bessancourt was young and patience was not one of his strengths. He had done all he could for the moment with Peruzzi; he wanted to get back to the music school, where the others were. In the evening he put on his disguise – ragged tunic, red hose that had seen better days, scuffed boots and a moth-eaten hood – and slung the battered old citole across his back.

The music school was meeting that evening at the White Bear tavern, a rambling building on the north side of the Grote Markt. The rooms were full of people talking, playing, listening to music. The air was full of coal smoke and hot wine fumes and sweat. People nodded to Bessancourt as he passed through the crowd, wine cup in his hand. He was a familiar sight now, Hugolin the citole player who dropped in occasionally to listen to the masters and learn from them.

In one of the smaller rooms a grey-haired German *meistersinger* was playing a gittern and singing an old song while his audience watched his fingers dancing across the frets.

Love is sweeter than honey
Love is more bitter than gall
Love is cold and hot and lukewarm
Love is faithful and treacherous
Love is blind and faithless
Love is all-seeing and kind

'You were told to stay away,' Havel the Fiddler murmured in his ear.

'I can't,' whispered Bessancourt. 'You need my help. Are they here?'

'Marcelis is over there, at the table by the wall. We haven't seen the other two all day. Nikolas is out looking for them now.'

'Go and help him. I'll keep watch here.'

Havel hesitated. 'All right, but stay out of trouble. If you need help, Warin is in the next room.'

'I can look after myself. Go.'

The song ended. The watchers applauded respectfully, and Havel rose and departed. A Spanish man, who was a luthier as well as a player, asked a question about frets and how the gittern compared to the Moorish *guitarra*. Still sitting by the wall, Marcelis listened intently, nodding. 'I am intrigued by the construction of this instrument, master. The ribs are different, much lighter, I think. I have not seen this design before. May I ask where this was made?'

'The Frauenlob workshop in Mainz,' said the other man. 'I am told Frauenlob himself built this one with his own hands.'

'Then it is a rare and remarkable instrument, master. It must be a real honour to play it.'

They talked for a while longer before Marcelis bowed and went out. Bessancourt made himself wait for a few moments, finishing his wine. The Spaniard offered to teach the group some *cantigas* written in honour of Our Lady; everyone was listening to him, and no one noticed Bessancourt pick up his citole and depart.

The next room was larger, busy and bustling. Servants were handing around wine jugs and platters of hot pies while two men played an organistrum, one turning the crank while the other worked the keys. A deep musical drone filled the air. Warin stood by the wall licking gravy off a piece of pie crust, a battered lute lying on a table beside him. Bessancourt glanced at the instrument. 'Can you actually play that thing?'

'Better than you, I imagine.' Warin grinned. *He is enjoying the play-acting*, Bessancourt thought. Well, it had to be better than looking after horses all day.

'Did Marcelis come through here?'

Warin nodded. 'He's sitting just over there by the fire, talking to someone.'

Bessancourt glanced towards the fire and looked quickly away again. Marcelis and the man beside him had bowed their heads and were not looking at each other, but he could see the other man's lips moving. He had a long bony chin and a prominent, beaked nose. 'Christ,' he said. 'It's Peruzzi.'

'The banker?'

'Yes.' He sat down quickly, his back to the two men, pretending to concentrate on the strings of his citole. His heart was racing. Merrivale had been right; Peruzzi had taken the bait. 'Can you see them? Are they still talking?'

'Yes, and yes,' said Warin. 'No... wait. Peruzzi is getting to his feet. He is leaving.'

'He might be going to find the other two. Perhaps Marcelis gave him directions. I'll follow him.'

Warin frowned a little. 'Is that wise?'

'We have to stop these people. That means taking risks.' Bessancourt stood up, slinging the citole across his back. 'Keep an eye on Marcelis.'

'That's what I'm already doing,' Warin said, and he took another bite of his pie.

Outside the night was cold, the marketplace largely empty at this hour. Bessancourt spotted the tall figure of Donato de' Peruzzi striding towards the market hall and belfry. My God, he thought, if they could arrest the three musicians and put them to the question, they might be able to unravel the entire plot. Half-excited, half-terrified, he followed the banker.

He had gone perhaps fifty yards when chaos erupted in the White Bear behind him. He heard men yelling, a woman's voice screaming in fear, the sound of smashing wood, and then a man ran out into the square, cupping his hands around his mouth and shouting at the top of his lungs. 'Send for the town watch! Quickly! A man has been murdered here!'

Bessancourt forgot about Peruzzi. He turned and ran back into the tavern, shouldering his way through the crowd. One of the musicians had blood on his face, another was holding the remains of a shattered lute. A crowd had gathered around something on the floor. Pushing them out of the way, Bessancourt looked down.

He had half expected to see Marcelis. Instead, it was Warin who lay on his back on the floor, blood still flowing from the knife wound in his chest, staring up at the ceiling beams with sightless eyes.

23

Bruges, 27th of March, 1347

The bodies were laid out in the mortuary of the Hospital of Saint John, wrapped in winding sheets of white linen. 'Sister Adela will be laid to rest in the vault of our Order,' Brother Frido said gently. 'We will do the same for your man, if you wish.'

'That is kind of you,' said Merrivale. His mind was full of sorrow and bitter anger, and he was having some trouble speaking. Behind him, Bessancourt was weeping openly. Mauro stood with his hands clenched, his face like stone.

'I would like masses to be said for their souls,' the herald said. 'I will leave money.'

'Our priests will pray for them. There is no question of money.'

'All the same, I would like to pay.'

Brother Frido nodded. 'I understand... I am sorry we could not send word until this morning. Metteneye ordered the gates closed so the watch could search the city for the killers. No one was allowed in or out until this morning, not even our own men.'

'The killers, or course, are the three musicians. I assume they have not been found.'

'Metteneye and the watch are still searching. My own men are with them.'

'There are fifty thousand people in Bruges, and God knows how many sympathise with the Pilgrims,' the herald said. He almost spat the words out. 'They are searching for a needle in a meadow. Do you know why Sister Adela went out?'

'She called on the reverend mother of the Beguines, and was on her way back to the hospital when she was attacked. I have been to the Begijnhof this morning. They were horrified by the news, but know nothing about the attack.' Brother Frido hesitated. 'Some of the Beguines are also sympathetic to the Pilgrims. But I doubt if they would condone murder.'

'If they support those villains, they are capable of anything,' Bessancourt said angrily. 'We should put them to the question.'

'We cannot arrest women of God,' said the herald. 'The Beguines are popular with the people, and there is enough unrest in the city already. What happened in the tavern?'

'Someone started a fight,' Bessancourt said. 'The usual thing, punches, some broken furniture, nothing serious. Then someone noticed Warin...' He stopped, biting his lip.

'Did anyone see Marcelis leave?' Merrivale asked.

'No.'

'Where are Nikolas and Havel?'

'Helping the searchers. They know the taverns where Marcelis and the others used to play. They have been out all night. I am sorry, sir herald, so sorry. I shouldn't have followed Peruzzi. I should have stayed with him.'

'In which case you would be dead too, and we would know even less about what happened,' Merrivale said. His anger was clear to see. 'The responsibility is mine. I put both Sister Adela and Warin in danger's path.'

'They offered their services, *señor*,' said Mauro.

'That makes no difference.'

Bessancourt wiped his eyes. 'What about Peruzzi? Do we go after him?'

'Peruzzi had left the White Bear before Warin was killed, and he was nowhere near the scene of Sister Adela's murder. He will claim he had no idea who Marcelis is. You were unable to hear their conversation. We have no evidence to bring charges against him.'

'I wasn't thinking of bringing charges,' Bessancourt said. 'I was thinking of ambushing him in the street and killing him.'

Brother Frido stirred, the crusader's cross on his red cloak glowing a little in the light. 'I have considered this too,' he said. 'But if we start assassinating people in the street, what is the difference between us and them? Murder will not bring our friends back to life.'

Merrivale nodded. 'Peruzzi is a symptom, not the sickness. We can only truly avenge them by killing this disease at the root. All the same, we will watch Peruzzi like a hawk. Brother Frido, when your men return from the search, ask some to disguise themselves and set a vigil on him. Note all visitors he receives, and if he leaves the house, follow him.'

Brother Frido nodded. 'It shall be done.' He raised one hand, making the sign of the cross over the bodies, and departed. After a moment, Bessancourt followed him. Silence fell in the cold room. After a minute or so, Merrivale turned to Mauro.

'It is permitted to weep,' he said quietly.

'I cannot, *señor*. The pain is so great that my soul is empty, even of tears.'

Merrivale put à gentle hand on his shoulder. 'That will pass.'

'Perhaps, *señor*. When I was enslaved, I lost all my family. I never saw them again and to this day I do not know where they are or if they are still alive. Warin was all I had in the world. He was my brother.'

'I know. I also lost my family when I was young. Over the years, Warin has become part of my family also. We have both lost one of our own.'

'Then let us avenge him,' said Mauro.

Kasteel Maele, 27ᵗʰ of March, 1347

The royal party arrived from Sluis without fanfare, having come by water from Calais. The king, Merrivale thought, seemed irritated and worried; the queen looked exhausted. Princess Isabella by contrast was almost revoltingly cheerful, skipping around the courtyard and chattering with her ladies. Thomas Hatfield, the Bishop of Durham, and Michael Northburgh, the king's secretary, did not look at or speak to each other.

Alice Bedingfield tapped Merrivale on the arm. 'You're to go in directly. Their Graces want to see you in the solar.'

'Thank you. What is wrong with Hatfield and Northburgh?'

'They had a falling out on the voyage. They have been arguing about the terms of the betrothal contract, it seems.' Bedingfield nodded. 'There is the king's page, coming to fetch you.'

The king was standing by the solar window, holding a cup of wine. The queen leaned back in a chair, her feet up and hands resting on her belly; Elizabeth Chandos stood watchfully behind her. 'Where is your *demoiselle*?' the queen demanded.

'I don't know, your Grace.'

'When she returns, send her directly to me. I want to speak to her.'

Merrivale bowed. The king looked even more irritated than before. 'What is the situation, herald?'

'We believe the conspirators intend to kill the Count of Flanders before the betrothal can take place,' Merrivale said. 'They have already spied out ten Berghe. I have informed Sir Paon de Roet, and his men are alert.'

'What other measures have you taken?'

'We think the assassins are the same three men who were present during the attempt on her Grace last year. We were watching them, but unfortunately they became aware of our surveillance, and last night they killed one of my servants and a lay sister of the Knights of Saint John. The town watch are searching for them, so far without success.'

The king stroked his chin. 'Is someone protecting them?'

'Yes, but we don't know who. The Pilgrims almost certainly have friends in some of the guilds, possibly even the city government. There is also the banking house of Peruzzi. Your Grace will remember them, of course.'

His Grace looked like he would rather forget. 'We should move the betrothal ceremony forward,' said Queen Philippa. 'Arrange it for the day after tomorrow; that will give Hatfield time to produce a final version of the contract. Once that is signed, there is no going back.'

The king nodded. 'Her Grace is right. We will sign the contracts the day after tomorrow. Following that, we will attend the Good Friday procession in Bruges.'

Merrivale raised his eyebrows. 'Is that wise, sire?'

'It is a gesture of goodwill towards the people of Bruges. But I take your point, we should not expose the count to danger. He will remain at ten Berghe until the wedding. That will take place the day after Easter, and the Count and Countess of Flanders will take ship for England along with her Grace the queen. They will remain at court with her, where they will be well protected.'

'Yes, sire.'

'Meanwhile, track down those musicians. I want them found and stopped, do you understand?'

Merrivale bowed. 'Yes, sire.'

'And find the *demoiselle*,' the queen instructed. 'It was very careless of you to lose her, Merrivale. She is to return to court before I depart for England. That is my order.'

'Guy of Béthune is dead,' said Brother Geoffrey.

Merrivale stared at him. 'What did you say?'

'He is dead. Yolande had him killed.'

'*Yolande?*'

'She ordered the three musicians to kill him and they did so, the same day.'

Slowly, Merrivale sat down. 'Tell me.'

Brother Geoffrey told him about the deaths of Zajíc and Béthune. The herald sat silent and motionless, listening. 'Are you all right?' Geoffrey asked at the end.

'I am reflecting on the fact that losing someone you hate is nearly as great a shock as losing someone you love. Something important goes out of your life... And Yolande,' Merrivale repeated. 'Why did she do it?'

Geoffrey watched him with eyes full of sympathy. 'She hated him, of course. But... I'm sorry, old friend. But it seems clear she is deep in the conspiracy herself.'

Merrivale said nothing for a long time. 'Why was Zajíc killed?' he asked finally.

'At a guess, Béthune thought Zajíc was about to betray the whole plot to King Charles, and decided to silence him.'

'I never trusted Zajíc; I never liked him, if I am brutally honest. But I am sorry he is dead.'

'He did not make friends easily,' the canon agreed. 'But no, he did not deserve that fate. And, of course, it rebounded on Béthune and cost him his life. John of Hainault, we can agree, would have handled the matter with more finesse.'

'So would the man from the north,' said Merrivale. 'Is it possible, Geoffrey, that Yolande had already received her own orders? She had already instructed the musicians to kill Guy before you intervened?'

'The thought has occurred to me. Yolande's final words were, *whatever is about to happen, will happen*. What did she mean, do you think?'

'They are plotting to kill Count Louis. Garnier, Tomaset and Marcelis are already in Bruges, preparing to strike. They know we are looking for them. Two days ago they murdered Sister Adela.' Even now, the words came with difficulty. 'They also killed Warin,' he said.

'Oh, God.' Geoffrey folded his hands for a moment in silent prayer. 'Adela,' he said softly. 'That is a blow. We shall miss her talents very much, I think. And Warin... My dear old friend, I can only imagine the grief this is causing you.'

'He was always there to protect me,' Merrivale said. 'Sometimes, indeed, from myself.' He looked at Geoffrey. 'There was no need to kill him. He was a watcher, nothing more. They could have shaken him off, or knocked him on the head and tied him up. But they killed him deliberately, to send a message to me.'

'And to punish you,' Geoffrey said quietly. 'This has become a personal feud now.'

'Then let the bastards confront me directly. Let them stand up and fight, rather than killing my friends. I miss Warin dreadfully, Geoffrey, I have no words to say how much.'

Merrivale stared for a moment at the table in front of him. Without warning, he gripped the edge of the table and sent it flying across the room to crash into the wall. Both men sat in silence, watching as wine from a broken cup dripped slowly down the wall.

Bruges, 28th of March, 1347

'Is Peruzzi still in his house?' the herald asked.

'Yes,' said Bessancourt. He looked like he had not had much sleep. 'He has been inside since... since that night. I waited for him outside the Chapel of the Holy Blood, but he did not come.'

'He must know he is under suspicion,' said Brother Geoffrey. 'Why is he still in the city? Why not get away while he can?'

'He is waiting for something,' said Merrivale. 'Or someone. If he is the paymaster, as I suspect, then he will be waiting to give the musicians their fee once the count is dead.'

He looked around the room, the same plain vaulted chamber in the Hospital of Saint John where he had first met Adela and Commander DuSart. He reflected for a moment that both were now dead, two more names on the growing list of people he had lost. Nikolas and Havel stood by the wall; Brother Frido waited by the door. 'The king has brought forward the signing of the betrothal contract,' the herald said. 'The ceremony will take place tomorrow at ten Berghe. We must assume the man from the north knows this already, and has issued new orders.'

253

'Then we have very little time,' said Brother Geoffrey. 'Master Bess-ancourt and I will keep watch on Peruzzi. He could be a messenger as well as paymaster. The new orders might come through him.'

'Yes,' said Merrivale. 'Havel, Nikolas, we need you to trace Garnier and the others, as quickly as possible. I think they are hiding in Bruges, and someone at the music school may know where. Mauro has offered to help you.'

Havel looked at Mauro. 'Thanks, brother. We could use a hand.'

Mauro nodded. He too had slept very little, but his face was calm. 'It will be my pleasure, señores.'

'What about you, sir?' Nikolas asked.

'I am going to ten Berghe. If anything happens, send word to me there.' Merrivale looked at Brother Frido. 'I am concerned that the Pilgrims may attempt some sort of diversion, an attack on some other public figure perhaps, to draw our attention away from the count.'

Brother Frido inclined his head. '*Deus hoc vult*. I shall call my men together.'

Kasteel ten Berghe, 28ᵗʰ of March, 1347

Paon de Roet saluted as Merrivale dismounted. 'All is quiet, sir herald.'

Merrivale looked around the courtyard of the big brick castle. 'Has the count received any messages in the last few days?'

'No, nor has he tried to contact anyone. He seems very content, and is looking forward to the big day tomorrow. Three days ago he asked if he could go out hawking, which he isn't really supposed to do during Lent, but he said he needed to exercise his horses. I saw no harm in it.'

'You gave him an escort?'

'Of course. I spoke to the captain afterwards, and nothing untoward happened.'

Merrivale nodded. 'Take me to him, if you please.'

Spring sunlight flooded the solar, glowing off tapestries and painted walls. The young count rose to his feet as Merrivale entered. 'Welcome, sir herald. What news do you bring me?'

'All is ready, my lord. The contracts have been prepared, and the king and queen are coming tomorrow to witness the ceremony. And you will meet your bride for the first time.'

The count smiled. 'I cannot wait. I am so glad I listened to you, sir herald.' His smile faded a little. 'I also remember my own behaviour with some shame. Permit me to make my apologies.'

Noblemen rarely apologised to heralds. *He is still young*, Merrivale thought; *he will get over it*. 'There is no need, my lord. You were being pushed and pulled by strong forces trying to control you. Now you are about to regain your freedom.' He paused. 'However, as Sir Paon will have informed you, there is still danger, and I must ask you not to leave the castle again, at least until the contracts have been signed.'

'Of course. Will you remain here until the ceremony?'

'Yes, my lord. I will do everything in my power to protect you.'

The count smiled again. 'Good,' he said. 'I feel safer already.'

Kasteel ten Berghe, 29th of March, 1347

Trumpeters on the castle walls, clad in brilliant red and gold, played an ear-splitting fanfare as the queen's carriage rolled into the courtyard and came to a halt. The king and his attendants followed on horseback, flanked by columns of armoured men-at-arms led by Sir Hugh de Vere. A company of mounted archers brought up the rear, and these jumped down from their horses and ran up onto the battlements to take station beside Paon de Roet's men and the Flemings.

The queen's ladies helped her down from the carriage as the king and the rest dismounted. Princess Isabella stepped out behind her, and Count Louis bowed to the royal party. 'Your Graces, welcome to my humble home. I have prepared no flowery speeches, I am afraid, for I am not an eloquent man. But I am proud to receive you, and I am grateful beyond measure that you have chosen to welcome me into your family.'

'Your words do you great credit,' the king said, smiling. The queen smiled too. 'My lord, we present our daughter and your future wife, Princess Isabella of Woodstock.'

Blushing like a peach, Isabella stepped forward and did a curtsey. The count bowed low and reverently. 'I had been told you were beautiful,' he said. 'No one said that you were like the sun glowing in a summer sky. Your radiance, Highness, is all the warmth I shall ever desire. I shall spend the rest of my days humbly striving to be worthy of being your consort.'

Isabella's face shone with happiness. 'And you, my lord, are as hand-some as they said you would be, and more.' Rapturous, she reached out and took his hands in hers. 'You are the only man in the world for me.'

Some looked horrified by this breach of protocol; others clearly found it charming. Alice Bedingfield looked like she was fighting back giggles. De Vere was scanning the courtyard, watchful, hand on the hilt of his sword. The count bowed, ushering his royal guests inside. Michael Northburgh, his face a study in worry, hurried up alongside the king. 'Sire,' he said, his voice low and urgent. 'I beg you one more time. Please reconsider.'

The king shook his head angrily. 'Not *now*, Michael.'

The trumpets sounded once more as they processed into the hall. Two clerks laid out papers on the high table, directed by Bishop Hatfield. The king and queen waited, chatting to the young count and smiling while Princess Isabella gazed at him with adoring eyes. Northburgh stood to one side, still frowning. De Vere stood by the door, directing his men into position around the hall and up into the gallery.

Leaning on his stick, Merrivale walked over to him. 'Something has happened,' he said.

De Vere looked around to see if anyone was listening. 'Yes. North-burgh spotted a mistake in the betrothal contract.'

'What sort of mistake?'

'Come with me.' De Vere led the way out of the hall into the vestibule at the top of the stair, where they were alone. De Vere was Maurice de Berkeley's brother-in-law, and he had taken Berkeley's retinue into his own service after the latter was killed at Calais, and was winning his own reputation for quiet confidence; it was for this reason that he had been chosen to command the royal bodyguard. 'There is a clause relating to inheritance should the marriage fail to produce an heir,' he said quietly. 'The prince requested that in this case, the County of Flanders should pass to the next male heir in the family, his uncle, Guy of Béthune.'

It took Merrivale a moment to control his voice. 'And Hatfield saw nothing wrong with this?'

'Apparently not. That is how the laws of inheritance work, he says, and we have no legal right to challenge them. So if the count or the princess dies without producing an heir, we lose Flanders.'

'Suffering Christ. If Louis dies, the county should be entailed to Isabella. That was the whole point! What was Hatfield thinking?'

'God knows,' de Vere said bleakly. 'Northburgh pointed this out to the king, several times. The king said it is too late to turn back. They will sign the contract now and negotiate a retrospective change later. He is desperate to commit Flanders to the English alliance.'

'But the contract means nothing,' Merrivale said. 'The young count – and now, Princess Isabella – are in mortal danger.'

De Vere stared at him. 'What are you talking about?'

'We have uncovered a plot to kill the count. The same group who organised the attack on Queen Philippa last year are behind this attempt as well. Guy of Béthune was one of them.'

He did not tell de Vere that Béthune was dead. 'Christ,' de Vere said softly. 'Who else is involved? Do you know?'

'John of Hainault, among others. We think this has something to do with the old king's death.'

De Vere stood for a moment, thinking hard. Merrivale watched his face. 'What is it, Sir Hugh? What do you know?'

'Did you ask my brother-in-law about this?'

'Yes, but he was not forthcoming. Why do you ask?'

After a long time, de Vere nodded. 'I wasn't sure what to do about this,' he said. 'Maurice told me he thought you suspected something, but wouldn't say what. After his death, I went through his effects before sending them back to my sister. I found a letter, with instructions that it should only be opened after his death.'

'What was in the letter?'

'Past history, mostly. Especially the events around the old king's death. At times it felt like a confession. It is clear he knew more about what happened than he let on.'

'I guessed as much,' said the herald. 'Did he say anything about Mortimer's messengers, the ones who came to Berkeley castle?'

'Yes. There were three, I recall. Hainault, Holland and Rowton.'

'Rowton? Which one?'

'The old lord, Gerard Rowton. Eustace's father. That's all he said.'

'Where is this letter now?'

'I kept it back. It is in my baggage at Calais. You may have it when we return.'

They heard footsteps, and one of the men-at-arms hurried into the vestibule. 'Sir Hugh? The king commands your presence. You too, sir herald.'

Good Friday; Sorrowful Friday, they called it here, the anniversary of Christ's death. For once the rattle of loom weights and thump of fulling mills had ceased. No work would be done, no masses would be said in church, and the altars would remain dark and unlit. Today was a day of mourning, a day of silence. The clip-clop of hooves on cobbles echoed in the empty streets and out over the quiet canals.

Dismounting at the Hospital of Saint John, the herald handed over his horse and went into the hall. He had hoped to find Brother Geoffrey, but to his astonishment he found Tiphaine waiting for him. She looked thinner, and even more ragged. Her dark red hair, dirty from travelling, spilled out of her hood and down over her shoulders.

With her was a strongly built woman in a battered leather cuirass carrying a barbaric wooden club with a steel spike in its head. 'This is Fier Meike,' Tiphaine said.

The woman looked at her. 'Really? This is the one?'

'Usually, he looks happier than this,' Tiphaine said.

'Where in God's name have you been?' Merrivale demanded.

'Poperinge. And then Liège. Sit down. We have news for you.'

Merrivale sat, hands resting on the pommel of his stick, listening while she told him everything that had happened. 'Why did they kill Sister Juliana?' he asked at the end.

'My guess is that she had served her purpose,' Tiphaine said. 'She had funnelled the money from Blyth into the Pilgrims' coffers and in return the Pilgrims had done her bidding. Or at least, some of them had.'

'Too many,' Fier Meike said bleakly. 'Even now, the scales have not fallen from their eyes.'

'What about you?' the herald asked.

'I thought I had found a home among the Pilgrims,' said Meike. 'I thought their beliefs were my beliefs. I see now how mistaken I was.'

They could hear voices in the chapel, uplifted in prayer; the Knights, followers of the cross, would be at their own devotions today. Tiphaine put a hand on the other woman's arm. 'Peace, love and justice are noble ideals,' she said. 'It is the Pilgrims who have strayed from the true path, not you.'

Meike's hand tightened on the butt of her *goedendaag*. 'It amounts to the same thing,' she said.

'Will others follow you?' asked the herald.

'Some have already done so. Perhaps more will, given time.'

'Nortkerque, Blyth and Nicodemus escaped together?'

'The first two, yes,' said Tiphaine. 'They got away by boat down the Meuse, or the Maas, as the Flemings call it. Where Nicodemus went, we don't know. But Nortkerque and Blyth were definitely coming to Bruges.'

'All of this sounds like something rather more than a simple assassination,' said Merrivale.

Tiphaine nodded, 'They talked about revenge for the death of their mother, Katelijne Gistel. *We shall tear the world to pieces*, Juliana said. *We shall remake it the way it should have been made. No sovereigns and princes, no bishops and popes. Only the true love of God shall prevail.*'

The herald pondered for a moment. 'Perhaps this is a diversion,' he said finally. 'The musicians have been ordered to kill the Count of Flanders. Nortkerque is arranging something else, a distraction to draw our attention away while Garnier and his friends do their work.'

'What sort of diversion?' asked Fier Meike.

'I am not sure yet.' He had an idea, but it would need to be tested. 'The Pilgrims have many sympathisers in Bruges. Can you contact them, Meike, and ask if anyone knows about the movements of Blyth and Nortkerque?'

'I can try.' Meike hefted the *goedendaag* over her shoulder and went out. Tiphaine remained, staring at Merrivale. 'Something has happened,' she said. 'I see it in your face.'

'I lost Warin,' Merrivale said bleakly.

'Tell me.' Her voice was soft. He told her about Warin's death, and Adela's, and watched her hands curl into fists as she fought down her own emotion. Warin had been kind to her, too; he and Mauro had fed her and clothed her last summer after Merrivale found her in the burning streets of Carentan, and made her feel at home. She too had lost a friend.

'There is more,' Merrivale said, and he told her about the killing of Béthune and Yolande's part in it. She nodded again, her face full of sympathy. 'In Poperinge, I learned that Yolande was giving orders to some of the plotters,' she said. 'I was worried about how to tell you.'

'There is no need to worry,' he said heavily. 'I have suspected for some time. I feel a fool for denying what I knew in my heart to be true.

I let the emotions of the past colour my thinking. That is a mistake I won't make again.'

'What now?' she asked finally.

'Mauro and the others are hunting for the musicians... I am worried, Tiphaine. We have lost control, and I cannot see where the next move will be made.'

'I know. These people frighten me, Simon. Blyth's sister loved him and believed in him, and yet he sacrificed her without a qualm.'

'Nicodemus killed her after Blyth left the scene,' Merrivale said. 'Perhaps Blyth did not give that order.'

'Perhaps.'

'There is something else,' Merrivale said finally. 'The queen wants to see you as soon as you return.'

'Oh, God,' Tiphaine said quietly. 'I suppose I cannot put this off any longer.'

'Put what off?'

'The queen has offered me a position in her household, as one of her damsels. I suspect she wants me to accompany her back to England.'

'She does... Will you accept?'

'I don't know. There is a condition attached to the offer.'

'What is it?'

'I have to marry you first,' she said.

'I see,' Merrivale said finally. 'I suppose I shouldn't be surprised. She and the king like their retainers to be married to each other. In theory, it makes them more loyal... But why me?'

'She seems to think we are a suitable match,' Tiphaine said.

'I can't imagine why.'

'Can't you? Why not?'

'I... Let's start with the differences in age. How old are you?'

'I am twenty-one,' she said calmly.

'Twenty-one? For God's sake, I have boots older than that.'

'How fortunate that I am not susceptible to flattery. How old are you?'

'Thirty-six.'

'Fifteen years. It's not exactly May and December, is it?'

Merrivale stared at her in blank astonishment. 'Tiphaine. Are you saying you *want* to marry me?'

'Not when you behave like this. I must answer the queen by Easter. That is two days from now.'

'Two days… Tiphaine, we have no time for this, not now. The world is about to erupt in our faces. Tell the queen we need more time.'

'You tell her,' said Tiphaine, and she turned and walked out of the hall. Merrivale stood for a moment, staring into the empty space where she had been and thinking of the words he should have said.

Do not go. I need you. I cannot imagine doing this without you.

24

Bruges, 30ᵗʰ of March, 1347

All day the herald waited at the Hospital of Saint John, leaning on his stick, his bright tabard catching the rays of sunlight coming through the windows of the hall, as the messages came in.

A runner came from Paon de Roet at ten Berghe. The garrison was still on alert, the count was keeping to his own quarters, nothing was stirring on the roads or canals. All was quiet.

A boy arrived bearing a small wooden box and demanding a penny for his services. Merrivale paid him and opened the box. Inside was a wax tablet incised with Brother Geoffrey's terse script. *Bands of men are arriving in the city through the Gentpoort and the Kruispoort. They are unarmed, but there are very many of them. The watch are making no attempt to stop them.*

A big man who bore the unlikely name of Topaas reported in. 'Fier Meike and the Norman girl sent me. We have not found Blyth or Nortkerque, but the Pilgrims are gathering at houses in the Magdalena quarter and all along the Langestraat.'

'What are they doing?' the herald asked.

'Praying,' Topaas said. 'It is Sorrowful Friday, the day of prayer and remembrance.'

'Do they have weapons?'

'Not that we have seen. To all appearances, these are peaceful gatherings.'

Tension droned in the air. In the afternoon, Mauro returned to the hospital. 'When did you last sleep?' Merrivale asked him.

'I cannot sleep, *señor*. When I close my eyes, all I can see is my friend's face, lying on that table in the mortuary.'

'I know,' Merrivale said quietly. 'It is the same with me. Is there any news of the musicians?'

'Havel and Nikolas are watching a house on Blind Donkey Street. According to the neighbours, three men are living there, but they have not been seen for several days. Should we go in after them?'

Merrivale hesitated. In his mind a new possibility was forming; that the musicians were the diversion and Nortkerque and his Pilgrims were the real threat, the opposite of what he had assumed. 'Not yet,' he said finally. 'Inform Brother Frido, and ask him to send men to help you. Make sure no one enters or leaves the house.'

'Yes, *señor*.'

'Is it known who owns the house?'

'Señor Bessancourt believes it belongs to Señor Peruzzi.'

The herald reached for his stick. 'It's time I talked to Peruzzi.'

—

Cloaked figures lurked in the street outside the Italian banker's house, Frido's men waiting and watching. Bessancourt was there too, looking tense. 'I've just come from the town hall where I checked the records. He took title of the house in exchange for part of the debt from the Count of Flanders. That is the story, at least, but I'm not sure I believe it.'

'Come with me.'

The hall of Peruzzi's house was full of wooden boxes and chests bound with iron. Many had complicated locks on the front. Peruzzi himself stood over them, his nose more beak-like than ever. 'Greetings, *signor*,' the herald said. 'Surely you are not thinking of travelling on Good Friday.'

'I am merely making my final preparations,' Peruzzi said. 'I depart in the morning for Sluis, where a ship will take me back to Italy.' He glanced at Bessancourt, standing at the herald's shoulder. 'Have you had any luck procuring your assassin?'

'You knew who I was all along,' Bessancourt said.

'Your story was good and you played your part well. But I had already anticipated your master's next move.'

'If you knew we were trying to trap you, why did you meet Marcelis at the White Bear?'

'To ask if he and his companions were free to travel to Italy. I could use his services there.'

'I don't believe you,' Bessancourt said angrily. 'If that is the case, why are he and the other two hiding in a house you own?'

Peruzzi's eyebrows rose in two perfect arches. 'Are they? I gave them no permission. Perhaps you should inform the watch that they are trespassing.'

Silence fell. 'I congratulate you, Donato,' the herald said quietly. 'You have played the game very well. But then, you have been playing it far longer than I have.'

'Of course,' Peruzzi said. 'And, as was amply proven when we met in Florence, I am also your superior in wit and intelligence. On this occasion, you have come close to the truth, but sadly for you, not quite close enough. And now, it is too late.'

The herald glanced at the boxes and chests. 'You think you have won.'

'I know I have. And please, Simon, do not think of doing anything so crude as asking the watch to arrest me or forbid me to leave the city. My family may have fallen from their high pinnacle, but they still possess enough power to ensure that if I suffer, Bruges suffers. No more Italian loans for Bruges merchants, no more orders for Flemish woollens, no more pepper in Bruges markets; you understand, I am sure. The burgemeester and the guilds certainly will.'

Slowly the herald raised his stick, resting the ferrule on Peruzzi's chest. 'Go in peace, Donato,' he said. 'But the chaos that will erupt in Flanders when the count dies will rebound on your head. Bruges needs your money and spices, but you need Flemish markets too. You have won, but your victory will come back to haunt you.'

'When the count dies?' Peruzzi said. 'How very amusing. And now, I think this conversation has lasted long enough. Be so good as to take your leave, Simon, and save me the trouble of asking my servants to throw you out.'

In the street outside, Merrivale drew a long breath. 'Is there nothing we can do?' asked Bessancourt.

'Not this time,' said the herald.

-

One of Hugh de Vere's esquires was waiting at the Hospital of Saint John. 'Greetings, sir herald. Sir Hugh bids me tell you the king, queen and Princess Isabella have left Maele by water, on their way into the city. The barges will moor on the Dijver and the party will walk to the Burg, the main square.'

'The Good Friday procession,' Merrivale said. So much was pressing on his mind, the Pilgrims, the three musicians, Tiphaine, that he had almost forgotten. 'From where will they observe it?'

'A pavilion has been erected outside Sint-Donaaskirk, the church on the Burg. The burgemeester and aldermen will receive their Graces there.'

'How will they be protected?'

'Captain Metteneye has provided two hundred men from the town watch. Half of the royal bodyguard will go ahead to scout the route. The rest under Sir Hugh will accompany the royal party.'

'Very well. Tell Sir Hugh I will join him there.' In the back of his mind a tocsin rang steadily, sounding the alarm. He wondered whether to suggest the king return to Maele – after all, the threat now was as much to Princess Isabella as to the count, for her death would annul the contract – but he knew the answer he would receive.

'I'll come with you,' Bessancourt said.

'No. Go back to Blind Donkey Street and help the others.'

'But—'

'You're not a fighting man, Hugolin,' the herald said gently. 'Leave this to those who are.'

The light was fading. The streets were full of people now, some wearing sackcloth robes over their coats. The herald moved silently through the crowds, making his way to the Burg. Several thousand had already gathered there, silently, holding lamps or candles that flickered in the night breeze. From a distance it looked like the big square was full of stars. The first of De Vere's men-at-arms and archers had arrived and were deployed around the pavilion and rows of raised benches where the royal party would view the procession. The burgemeester and aldermen were there, some looking nervous. Merrivale wondered what rumours had been circulating.

'Sir herald,' said Coudebrouc. He was one of the ones who looked nervous. 'Are we expecting trouble?'

'Yes,' said the herald. 'May I ask you a question, *meneer*? Do you recall a case some years ago when several people were arrested for forging and distributing false coinage? One of them was a woman named Katelijne Gistel.'

Coudebrouc looked startled. 'Yes, I do recall. It was some time back, as you say, but… Yes, I remember the Gistel woman's execution.'

'Who was the examining magistrate in the case?'

'I was.'

From inside the darkened church came the sound of prayers softly sung. *We shall tear the world to pieces*, Katelijne Gistel's daughter had said. *No sovereigns and princes. Only the true love of God shall prevail.* The alarm bell in his mind kept ringing, over and over, its note like the beat of a drum.

'Why do you ask?' said Coudebrouc.

'Idle curiosity,' said the herald.

A movement in the twilight caught his eye. He turned to see Tiphaine coming swiftly through the crowd. The big man, Topaas, was behind her. 'What is it?'

'The Pilgrims are arming. They must have had weapons stored inside their meeting houses. Two companies are moving up Langestraat towards the Burg, and four more are preparing to follow them. Brother Geoffrey reckons there are least a thousand men.'

He knew what to expect now. 'Topaas, go to the Knights. Tell Brother Frido to arm every man he can find and bring them here.'

Topaas sped away across the square. Merrivale turned to the nearest English man-at-arms. 'Find Sir Hugh. Tell him this is a trap, and he must return the royal party to Maele. Tell him also to send word to ten Berghe and order Sir Paon de Roet to bring his men to the city. We need every man we can muster.'

'It's too late, sir herald. Look, they are here.'

De Vere and the rest of the bodyguard were coming into the square. Merrivale could see the royal red robes of the king and queen and Princess Isabella, surrounded by their attendants. Hatfield was there, richly dressed in episcopal robes; Northburgh was beside him, plain in corvid black. The people in the square bowed, candle flames flickering.

Coudebrouc bowed too. 'Your Graces, welcome once again. It is an honour to receive you—'

'I beg your pardon, burgemeester,' Merrivale said sharply. 'Sire, we are about to come under attack. We need to get you to a place of safety. You too, burgemeester, and your aldermen.'

Coudebrouc gaped at him. 'Attack from whom?'

'The Pilgrims,' Merrivale said. 'Six groups are marching on the Burg as we speak.'

'But surely the watch will stop them.'

'For God's sake, burgemeester! By now, half the watch have probably joined them. Sire, I suggest you take refuge in the Chapel of the Holy Blood. It is easily defensible, and there is a door from the vestry onto the Dijver. We can get you away by boat.'

De Vere nodded. 'I will send a small escort with you, sire, and remain here myself with the rest. We will draw the enemy's attack while you make your escape.'

'No,' said the king. 'I want you with us, and you too, Merrivale. My wife and daughter must be protected.'

In the distance they could hear chanting, the beating of drums, the first clashes of metal and screams of men; the first of the Pilgrims brushing aside the town watch. More cries and screams went up in the Burg as people began to flee. The queen's ladies were already hurrying towards the chapel on the far side of the square, Bedingfield and Chandos supporting the queen. Tiphaine ran to join them.

The king pulled his cloak aside to reveal a sword girdled at his wait. 'Go with them, burgemeester,' he said. 'You too, Hatfield, Northburgh. I will join the rearguard with Sir Hugh.' He turned to the rest of the bodyguard. 'Hold them off as long as you can. If they threaten to overwhelm you, get inside the church and bar the door.'

'Yes, sire.'

The king turned to Merrivale. 'Are we expecting reinforcements?' he asked.

'Yes, sire. But I don't know how long they will be.'

'Do your best,' the king said to his men. 'I can ask no more than that.'

The Chapel of the Holy Blood was built on top of the larger and older chapel of Saint Basil. The only access from the square was up a steep stone stair. De Vere was already giving orders. 'Kyriel, get out through the vestry entrance onto the canal. Try to signal the boats and bring them along. The rest of you, find anything you can to wedge this door. I don't care if you have to use the altar furniture, just do it.'

The drumbeats were closer. Merrivale turned to the king who stood, sword in hand, staring out into the shadowy square. 'Sire, I urge you to go upstairs and join the ladies.'

The king looked at him, smiling a little. 'Your care for my safety is touching, herald. But I am a fighting soldier, and I will not leave my men.'

'You are unarmoured, sire.'

'So are you. And don't give me that nonsense about your herald's tabard being your armour.'

'Here they come!' De Vere said sharply.

Drums boomed and roared off stone and brick walls. A flood of orange torchlight filled the square. Looking out, Merrivale saw the enemy pouring down every street into the Burg. Some wore mail or bits of plate armour, others were in hardened leather, heads protected by helms and bascinets and iron caps. They carried spears and axes and clubs; a few had crossbows. Apart from the drums they did not make a sound; there were no shouts, no war cries, just a silent grim purpose. On the far side of the square the bodyguard stood drawn up, men-at-arms with swords and spears ready, archers with arrows at the nock, but the oncoming men ignored them, halting in the centre of the square and waiting.

Most of the people gathered to watch the procession had fled, but a handful remained. As Merrivale watched, some of these called out to the Pilgrims and pointed at the Chapel of the Holy Blood. 'God's death!' De Vere said. 'They had watchers in the square.'

'Yes,' Merrivale said grimly. 'Now let's see how well this door holds.' Even as he spoke, the drums rolled and thundered again and the packed body of men in the square turned and charged straight towards them.

By the time they arrived, de Vere's men had slammed and wedged the door. Clubs and hammers pounded on the door outside, but the solid oak held. Almost at once the noise ceased and they heard footsteps retreating. Some of the men looked at each other, puzzled. 'Have they given up?' one asked.

The king shook his head. 'They'll bring up a ram.'

Something bumped against the door. Faint but distinct came the smell of brimstone. Merrivale and de Vere looked at each other, the latter's eyes wide behind the visor of his bascinet. 'Gunpowder,' Merrivale said.

'Get away from the door!' de Vere screamed and they ran towards the stair, but they were too late. The door blew apart with a flash of light and a cloud of stinking smoke and splinters. Half of de Vere's men went down in the blast, knocked off their feet by flying debris.

Something hit the king on the head and he stumbled and dropped his sword, falling to his knees. Merrivale seized his robe and dragged him up just as the first Pilgrims stormed through the door, stabbing and hacking at de Vere's stunned men before they could move. A spear clattered off de Vere's breastplate and he stabbed back viciously, his sword blade coming away coated in blood. 'Save the king!' he screamed at Merrivale. 'I will protect you. Go!'

Ears ringing from the blast, Merrivale pulled the still dazed king up the stairs, de Vere close behind them. At the stop of the stairs an English archer was shooting quickly, arrows hissing in the air, but down below a crossbow clacked in reply and the archer went down with a black bolt in his chest. Men raced up the stair, and de Vere turned to fight them off. Merrivale and the king reached the top and hurried into the chapel. Northburgh was there, face pale in the reflected torchlight.

'Sire! You are injured!'

'Never mind that,' gasped the king. Blood was pouring down his face. 'Save de Vere. Get him out of there, herald.'

Merrivale ran back to the head of the stair. De Vere was still halfway up, fighting single-handedly against a tide of men. Bodies were already piling up on the stair, his assailants clambering over them to attack him. Another crossbow bolt glanced off his breastplate, leaving a dent the size of a fist, but de Vere barely noticed it. A swinging hammer crashed into his bascinet and this time he wavered, momentarily stunned, just long enough for a fresh wave of men to hit him and knock him off his feet. The Pilgrims lifted their weapons, ready for the kill.

Running down the stair, Merrivale slammed into them and drove them bodily backwards. Two, knocked off balance, slipped and fell down the stair. A third raised his sword but Merrivale smashed his stick into the man's face and the swordsman dropped his weapon and clapped his hand to his mouth, spitting out teeth. A fourth man turned on him, and the herald drove a booted foot into his groin and kicked him backwards down the stair on top of the others. There was a second or two of breathing space, just enough for de Vere to clamber to his feet again.

'Thank you,' he said to the herald.

'My pleasure.'

The Pilgrims regrouped and came up the stair again. Merrivale stepped behind de Vere, protecting his back, but de Vere was watchful and deadly intent. Time and again the Pilgrims attacked, and time and again they staggered back bleeding or slumped down dead on the stair. The stone steps became slippery with blood. Hurt and bleeding himself, gasping with pain, the captain of the bodyguard never wavered.

Another archer crouched at the top of the stair, looking for a shot; Kyriel, the man sent to find the boats. 'Have they arrived?' Merrivale asked.

'Yes, sir herald.'

'Get everyone into the boats, now. Sir Hugh and I will follow.' A fresh wave of attackers hurled themselves up the stair and sagged back bleeding and dying. A crossbow bolt narrowly missed Merrivale's head, ricocheting off the stone behind him. He rapped hard on de Vere's armguard. 'Time to go,' he said.

They ran up the stairs, slamming the upper door just as another bolt thudded into the wood. The door was thinner and older than the lower one. 'It won't hold them for long,' de Vere gasped.

'Long enough. Let's go.' They ran through the empty chapel, past the high altar where the golden casket holding the relic of the holy blood glinted faintly in reflected torchlight. Just as they reached the vestry entrance the door smashed open and a man ran into the chapel. De Vere turned, bloody sword in hand, but before he could take a step a longbow arrow came out of the shadows like a thunderbolt and hit him in the throat. He dropped his sword, clutching at the arrow with one hand, then sank to his knees and fell forward onto his face.

Merrivale looked up. Nicodemus stood ten yards away, a fresh arrow on the nock. Behind him, more Pilgrims were coming through the shattered door.

Outside in the Burg a single voice began to chant, over and over. *Deus hoc vult! Deus hoc vult! Deus hoc vult!*' Others joined in, followed by the clash of sword hilts on shield and then a single indistinct hammering of violence as the Knights of Saint John charged home.

The men in the doorway hesitated, looked at each other for a moment, and fled. Nicodemus lingered, his eyes on Merrivale's face. 'This is not finished, herald,' he said.

–

'They were concentrating so much on you that they never saw us coming,' Brother Frido said. 'As soon as we started to chant, they broke and ran. Your men at Sint-Donaaskirk saw their moment and attacked too, completing the rout. What news of the king and queen?'

'They got away safely,' Merrivale said. 'They landed Coudebrouc and the aldermen and collected the rest of the bodyguard before returning to Maele. Has anyone seen Nortkerque?'

'No. Where are you going, sir herald?'

'To execute justice,' the herald said. 'You might want to come along, brother.'

Moonlight reflected off roof tiles and chimneys in Blind Donkey Street and the sparkling waters of the Dijver beyond. Havel, Nikolas, Bessancourt and Mauro were waiting outside one of the smaller houses. 'Are they still in there?' the herald asked.

'No one has come in or out,' said Havel.

The herald rapped on the door with his stick. 'Garnier of Liège,' he said. 'Tomaset and Marcelin. I know you are in there.'

Silence. 'The Pilgrims have been defeated,' Merrivale called. 'The king and queen, the princess, the burgemeester and aldermen are all alive and safe. You have failed.'

'Go down to hell where you belong, herald,' said a voice from inside.

'You can still save your lives. Tell me the names of the men you work for, and I will set you free.'

'You lie. You'll torture us and then execute us. We prefer to die on our feet.'

'We are ready to face God!' another man shouted. 'Pain will only make us stronger, herald!'

'Break down the door and drag them out,' Bessancourt said.

Brother Frido shook his head. 'These men are zealots. They are ready to die and also, I venture, they will know little of consequence. Their masters will have concealed the full truth from them.'

Silence fell in the street. 'Then it is time to make an end,' the herald said.

'Let me do this,' said Mauro. 'For Warin.'

Bessancourt looked at him as if he was mad. 'You are only one man. All you have is a knife.'

'It is all he needs,' Merrivale said.

Mauro kicked the door hard. On the second blow it broke, and he tore the splintered wreckage off its hinges and walked inside. Out in the street they heard the sounds of struggle, the grate of metal on bone, a single choked-off scream, and then all was quiet. Slowly, like a falling veil, peace descended on Bruges.

Kasteel ten Berghe, 31st of March, 1347

The morning was bright and clear. All was quiet; Paon de Roet and his English troops were still in the city, helping to search for Pilgrims, and only the Flemish militia remained at their posts. Count Louis of Flanders strolled out into the courtyard and approached their captain. 'My horse needs exercise, and so do I. I'm going out for a ride.'

'I'll send an escort with you,' said the captain.

The count raised his eyebrows. 'Surely there's no need for that. Not now.'

'I'm sorry, my lord, but I have my orders.'

'Of course you do. But just make it a couple of men, will you? I'd like to enjoy the peace of the morning, without an entire troop of horse thundering after me.'

The captain, who had hopes of promotion and perhaps a place at the young count's court after the wedding, smiled. 'As you wish, my lord.'

Out in the open fields east of ten Berghe the count spurred his horse to a canter. It was indeed a beautiful morning, and he longed for some really wide open fields where he could put the horse through its paces. Here the land was constantly cut by drains, hemming him in. *Thank God I'll be out of this place soon.*

The church spires of the town of Damme came into sight ahead. He spurred the horse again, scanning the landscape. The two militiamen, not natural riders, laboured behind him. 'My lord!' one of them called, 'we cannot keep pace with you!'

'Wait here, then,' the count called over his shoulder. 'I'll ride up to the next drain and then come back and join you.'

'Very good, my lord.'

Damme was close now, only about half a mile away. Obediently, the two militiamen pulled up and waited. The count rode on towards the line of the next drain, enjoying the wind in his hair and savouring the freedom that would soon be his. As he drew closer to the drain the count slowed his horse to a walk, finally halting right on the edge of the ditch and looking down at the men concealed inside it. He smiled.

'I am a poor pilgrim, travelling in a perilous land,' he said. 'In God's name I am weary, and I seek shelter.'

Jehan Nortkerque removed his hat and bowed deeply. He too was smiling. 'Welcome among us, brother,' he said. 'Rest now, and give thanks to God.'

IV

25

Guînes, 21st of April, 1347

'A leper house. How charming,' said Raimon Vidal. 'Is that what we have become now? Outcasts, shunned by our fellow man?'

They stood next to a high stone wall, surrounding an enclosure on the edge of the marsh. The belfry of the little chapel of Saint-Quentin could just be seen; the rest of the leper house was invisible behind the wall, shut off from the rest of the world. A quarter of a mile away the powerful castle of Guînes frowned out over the marshes. French banners flapped from its towers. William Blyth motioned towards the castle. 'Will the garrison give us trouble?'

'They have been ordered to stay away from us,' said John of Hainault. 'They tend to stay clear of the lazarette in any case, for obvious reasons. Also, they are distracted by the English troops passing by.' He looked at the man from the north. 'They were defeated, heavily. Did you have a hand in this?'

Two days earlier, the Earl of Warwick and Count of Holstein with three hundred men had joined forces with Flemish troops to attack the French citadel at Saint-Omer. There they had been ambushed by a smaller French force and thrown back in disorder; the Flemings, it was said, had taken heavy losses. Warwick and Iron Henry were now retreating to Calais; their little army could just be seen in the middle distance, picking its way across the misty marshes.

'I warned the garrison in Saint-Omer that they were coming, yes,' said the man from the north. 'In the same way that I warned the Flemish captain at Cassel that the French were preparing a surprise attack on the town. It is a matter of checks and balances. We must prevent either side from gaining the upper hand.'

He looked around the circle, five men and one woman in a long black cloak. 'Where is Machaut?'

'He has declared his loyalty to King Charles,' Vidal said. 'I suspect Brother Geoffrey discovered his role as our agent and blackmailed him. Geoffrey does that sort of thing very well. What a pity he isn't on our side.'

Jehan Nortkerque stared at him. 'You would admire an enemy?'

'Why not?' said the cardinal's secretary. 'Our enemies are often admirable people. More so, in some cases, than our friends.'

Nortkerque flushed a little. 'What do you mean by that?'

'I mean that Geoffrey is a wise and intelligent man, well-educated and well-read, and a deep philosophical thinker. You, on the other hand, are a dealer in whale meat. I know whose company I prefer.'

Nortkerque's hand went to his dagger. 'Enough!' snapped the man from the north.

Sullenly, Nortkerque lowered his hand. Vidal smiled a little. The man from the north turned back to Hainault. 'What news do you have for us?'

'Some good, some bad. The good news is that Odo of Burgundy has agreed to accept the crown of France if we can dispose of Philippe and his son. Burgundy is from the old nobility. The others will accept him.'

'And the bad news?'

'Reynaud de Nanteuil and all the senior Knights of Saint John from the French priory have been arrested in Paris. The Grand Master sent his deputy, the Grand Prior of Saint-Gilles, to oversee the matter personally. They will be on trial for crimes against the Order. The prior of Germany has been active too, suppressing the house at Maldegem and arresting some of our supporters.'

'Too late,' said the man from the north. 'The Knights were there to provide us with money, and we now have all the money we need. The Count of Flanders has the subsidy in gold he asked for, and we have armed and equipped the Pilgrims and turned them into a force that will do our bidding. Are they ready?'

His cheeks still burning, Nortkerque nodded. 'Our losses in Bruges were slight, only a few dozen. At the moment, most of us are serving with the Flemish army at Cassel, scattered in secret among the various militia companies. We await your orders.'

'Good. For the moment, do nothing. We wait until the time is right.'

'And when will the time be right?' asked Vidal.

'When Calais is ready to fall. The entire plan depends on Calais, as it has ever since Crécy. But Calais cannot fall until England and France have built up their full strength. The English must think Calais is about to fall into their hands; the French must believe they have a good chance of breaking the siege.'

Nortkerque looked puzzled. 'We do nothing while our enemies grow stronger?'

'Exactly. We play King Log.'

'What about Merrivale?' asked Nicodemus the archer. 'What do we do about him?'

'Nothing. I said I would manipulate Merrivale, and I have. First we let him think we intended to kill the Count of Flanders. When he discovered the Pilgrim attack in Bruges, he pulled Paon de Roet's men out of the garrison at ten Berghe and enabled the count to escape. He has served his purpose admirably.'

Vidal stirred. 'You won this round. But I warn you, do not under-estimate this man. If you make one mistake, he will kill you.'

'I think not. We have another weapon to use against him, remember?' The man from the north turned to the woman, who had so far not spoken a word. 'Well, my lady? Are you ready to play your part?'

'I have always been ready,' Yolande of Bohemia said calmly. 'Like you, I have waited a long time for this moment. I am yours to command.'

—

One by one they mounted and rode away, disappearing into the mist. The man from the north held up a hand as Blyth prepared to mount. 'I need to speak with you. Wait until the others have gone.'

Blyth waited. 'How may I be of service?' he asked.

'I instructed Nicodemus to kill your sister. Does that concern you?'

Blyth raised his eyebrows. 'No. Should it?'

'According to reports, she was overjoyed to be reunited with her brother after such a long separation. Did you not feel the same?'

'Of course not. I hadn't seen her or even thought about her for twenty years, at least. Finding her in Liège was a stroke of serendipity which played nicely into our hands, but it didn't awaken any feelings of brotherly love. Once she had performed the service required, she was just a loose end needing to be tied up.'

'Indeed,' said the man from the north. 'And what about yourself, Blyth? You too have performed a valuable service. You liquidated your own fortune and that of Gilbert de Tracey, and you handled the money that came to us from the Knights. What reward do you wish in return?'

'We have already spoken of this,' Blyth said. 'A second fortune, of course, far larger than the first. Land, a title, a wife to replace the one I left behind in England, perhaps a few mistresses here and there to provide variety. You can arrange all of this, I am sure.'

'Of course,' said the man from the north. 'And you are quite correct, we did discuss all this and more. But now, your work is done. You too are a loose end that needs tying up.'

The man from the north drew his sword, and before Blyth could move, stabbed him hard in the belly, withdrew the blade and stabbed him again. Blyth opened his mouth to speak, but no words came. His knees gave way and he fell face down in the mud where he lay twitching and clawing at the ground. The man from the north watched him for a while; then, satisfied that the other man would soon bleed to death, he mounted his horse and rode away.

Calais, 10th of May, 1347

To my esteemed friend the heraldus Simon Merrivale, greeting. You will forgive me for the length of time it has taken me to answer your letter. The events in question happened some years ago and no official records remain. It has taken time, money and a large amount of wine to prize open the memories of those involved.

There is currently no mint in Dublin, or Difelin, but a mint was established there in 1340. Its purpose, insofar as I can ascertain, was highly dubious. Rather than coining legitimate money, the mint masters struck false coins, pennies and half-pennies mostly, with a view to releasing them into markets in the Irish towns. This would cause a loss of faith in the currency and undermine the position of the Irish lords, which would in turn strengthen the hands of the English. There was also a plan to strike false coins in other currencies, French and Flemish at least, for the same purpose.

The following year, 1341, the lord chancellor in London discovered the existence of this mint and ordered its closure,

*deeming its purpose to be both illegal and dishonourable. The
dies were to have been destroyed, but there is a rumour that
they were stolen by, or possibly sold to, the man who ordered
the mint's establishment in the first place. I am still trying to
discover who this man was, and will communicate further news as
it becomes available. Kindly send my regards to your demoiselle,
your obedient friend and servant, Nicholas Courcy of Kingsale,
miles.*

Bessancourt handed the letter back to the herald. 'The dies from the
Dublin mint must be the masters of the ones I saw in Abbeville. But
my God! How long have they been planning this?'

'Twenty years,' said Merrivale. 'Perhaps more.'

'You can't just go around setting up mints wherever you like. This
man must have had royal authority.'

'Or pretended to. Courcy could find no records in Ireland, but
copies of the documents may have been sent to London. I shall see if
my friend Lady Mary can help us.'

Silence fell. Merrivale looked at Bessancourt. 'I have been most
grateful for your help and your company over the last months. But
surely you need to take up the reins of your own life once more.'

Bessancourt shook his head. 'Not until we've seen this through. I
owe something for Adela and Warin, at least... When Adela rescued
me, she wrenched me out of my old life, and I am not sure where to
find a new one. Besides, where would I go?'

'You could go back to Paris. You must have friends there, family.'

'And if anyone discovers I have spent several months working with
the English, I will be denounced as a traitor. People have been hanged
for far less.'

'I understand. You are welcome to stay with me as long as you
wish.'

'I've been thinking about that. I can't keep living on your charity,
I must find work. And you need a groom.'

Merrivale smiled a little. 'Yes. I understand you have been looking
after the horses already.'

Bessancourt nodded. 'My father was a farrier in the royal stables. I
can turn my hand to most things.'

'Have you discussed this with Mauro?'

'I have. He has given me to understand that, while I will never replace Warin, he would not find my presence in the household intolerable.'

The herald smiled again. 'In that case, your offer is accepted. Thank you.'

'It is I who should thank you, sir herald. And I shall try not to disappoint your horses.'

Tiphaine came into the room after Bessancourt had gone. 'I assume you overheard us,' the herald said.

'Yes. You made a wise decision, and a humane one. You will not regret it.'

'And you? No regrets about not accompanying the queen back to England? The opportunity might not come again.'

'It will. The queen has given us more time. Bedingfield had a word with her, I think.'

Merrivale smiled. 'You have forgiven Bedingfield for flirting with me?'

'It is not my place to forgive, or even to pass judgement. Elizabeth Chandos told me a little of her history.'

'A long time ago, when I was crushed and broken on the floor, she picked me up and put me on my feet again,' Merrivale said. 'I owe her for that.'

Tiphaine smiled back at him. 'So do I... Here comes one of the king's pages. I think he is looking for you.'

—

'The adversary is on the move,' Warwick said. 'In response to our attacks on Saint-Omer and Béthune, he has moved his main field army up to Arras. We do not yet know what strength he has, but this move is a grave threat to us.'

The marshal pointed to the map. 'The French have two choices. First, they can attack the Flemish at Cassel. If they dislodge them, they can move north to take Dunkirk and Gravelines. As you know, most of our supplies and reinforcements from England come through those ports. If they fall, we will be cut off from Flanders and home.'

'And the second choice?' asked the king.

'They can move up past Béthune and Saint-Omer to attack our positions here directly, and try to lift the siege.'

'If the adversary is advancing towards us, he must be confident of his strength,' said Lord Rowton. 'Either that, or he has forgotten the punishment we inflicted at Crécy.'

'What is our present strength, Thomas?' asked the king.

'We have had some reinforcements, sire,' said Warwick. 'But we continue to be afflicted by sickness. Warm weather has brought a return of the flux. We could muster perhaps eight thousand men, half of them archers.'

'Are more expected?'

'Huntingdon and Oxford are on the way, but we don't know when they will arrive. Lancaster and Sir Walter Mauny are still collecting men.'

'Send word to England and tell them to hurry up,' the king snapped. 'I shall instruct the bishops and clergy to offer prayers for us. I'd rather not have to rely on divine intervention, but it may come to that.'

'I will prepare the letters, sire,' said Michael Northburgh.

The king was irritable, Merrivale thought. He was concerned about the queen, of course; she had finally departed for England a few weeks previously, not accompanied by the *demoiselle* de Tesson. He was also angry, as they all were, at the continued delay in procuring enough ships and men to prosecute the siege effectively.

'French supply ships are still getting into the town,' Rowton said. He too looked tired and irritated. 'According to my spy, they ran in two more convoys last month. We *must* find some way to block the harbour.'

'We have tried everything,' Hatfield said. Despite his error with the contract, he was still in favour; once the king's anger faded, he tended to be quick to forgive.

'Not quite everything,' Warwick said. 'If we can take and hold the Rysbank, we can place artillery there to block the channel.'

'Not this again.' Hatfield shook his head. 'How do you expect men to hold the Rysbank? At high tide it is underwater!'

'The spit connecting it to the mainland is,' Rowton said. 'The island itself is not. You have mentioned this before, Thomas, and I am afraid I was sceptical, but I am beginning to think we have no choice. Do you really think it can be done?'

'Wait until Huntingdon and Oxford arrive,' Warwick said. 'Their men will be fresh and ready for a fight. The French will try to stop us, of course, and it is likely to be a hard struggle. But if we can place cannon on the Rysbank, Calais is ours.'

'Good,' said the king. 'Start planning the attack now. Eustace, give Thomas whatever assistance he needs, send some scouts to watch the French army. If the adversary moves past Arras, we will advance and block his path. We'll leave a screening force here at Calais to stop the enemy from sallying out, but apart from that I want every man we have ready to face the enemy. Even the sick.'

He paused for a moment. 'Very well, gentlemen. You have your orders.'

The captains and officials bowed and departed. The king pointed at Merrivale. 'Remain a moment, herald.'

Merrivale waited. The king studied the map for a moment, frowning and fingering his moustache. 'Someone has lit a fire under Philip's backside,' he said. 'He has spent all winter doing absolutely nothing to lift the siege apart from sending supplies, and now suddenly he is advancing full tilt towards us. Why?'

'France has had severe problems raising money,' Merrivale said. 'Now that Nanteuil has been arrested, perhaps someone honest and competent is in charge of the royal finances. The adversary has never lacked for men, only the money to pay them.'

'So have we all,' the king said with feeling. 'I'm worried about the Flemings, Merrivale. Will they remain loyal, do you think?'

'They need the wool trade, of course, and they need our army to bolster their militia. But if we should suffer a significant defeat, the League of Three might decide to negotiate with France, and with Count Louis.'

'You're right, of course. Rowton says the same. Damn that young bastard Louis! Not only did he insult me and my family and reduce my poor daughter to tears, but he has jeopardised our whole position in Flanders. I swear to God, if ever I lay hands on him, I will hang him without trial.'

Princess Isabella had, understandably, taken the count's escape as a personal rejection. During a scene full of tears and screaming which the entire court overheard, she had denounced the entire male portion of humanity and announced her intention to enter a convent as soon as she returned home. The queen had promptly forbidden this, which led to more tears and screams. By the time they left for England, mother and daughter were still not speaking to each other.

'The escape was carefully planned and organised,' Merrivale said. 'The conspirators were willing to pay the count more than we were. Peruzzi gave him a thousand ducats in gold, probably when he visited the count at ten Berghe.'

'You are certain this is all part of the same plot. Another of your *tendrils*.'

'I'm afraid so, sire,' Merrivale said. 'And I fear also that what we are seeing is the culmination of events that began around the time of your father's death, if not before.'

He waited for the king's anger. It did not come. When he spoke, Edward's voice was quiet. 'Why do you say that, herald?'

'I have suspected this for quite some time. I said as much last summer, if you recall. But it was information received from Sir Maurice de Berkeley that turned my suspicions into certainty. Through him, I learned the name of the final conspirator in the plot to kill your father. It was Gerard, Lord Rowton, the late father of Eustace Rowton.'

There was a long silence. 'You do realise what you are saying,' the king said. 'Eustace Rowton is one of my oldest friends.'

'Yes, sire.'

'You think he has some sort of grudge against me because of his father. But Gerard was reconciled to me before he died. Eustace helped to arrange it. I forgave Gerard his crimes, for the sake of my friend. All was well between us during Gerard's final years.'

Merrivale nodded. 'Yes, sire. But some old resentments and angers persisted.'

'What are you telling me? That the same men who conspired against my father are plotting against us now? Surely no one harbours resentment for that long.'

'I fear that some men do, sire. Brother Geoffrey and I came across part of this plot in Savoy, although I have only just realised this. There are tendrils of this plot not just in England but in nearly every kingdom and duchy and free city in Europe, and it is still very much alive.'

'Why are they doing this? Have we any idea?'

'I think they want to show how powerful they are. There is always profit in chaos, of course, and I have no doubt that these people intend to enrich themselves. But there is a kind of mania that comes with power, a collective madness that drives men to extremes, for no other reason than to demonstrate their prowess to the world.'

'Yes. I can understand that,' the king said reflectively. 'How do we stop them?'

'The same as with any monster,' said the herald. 'Cut off the head.'

26

At dawn the storming parties assembled behind the grass-covered dunes. The Earl of Warwick called his captains together. 'This is our last chance,' he said. 'The French army is approaching. We must seize and hold the Rysbank, if we are to take the city before they arrive. Do not fail, gentlemen.'

'You can count on us,' said the Earl of Oxford. He was a handsome, eternally cheerful man in his late thirties. 'I shall enjoy this,' he said. 'Good to see some proper fighting again, after a damned dull winter.'

'If it was that damned dull, you should have joined us earlier,' Warwick said. 'What kept you, anyway?'

'I had some very important business in London to attend to. I'll introduce you to her, when this is over.' Oxford grinned. 'Are we ready?'

Warwick looked at the tide, glistening as it receded over the mudflats around the Rysbank. 'Ready.'

There was no fanfare or trumpet call; Oxford simply ran forward across the flats towards the Rysbank, holding his sword aloft, and his men-at-arms and archers followed that gleaming blade. Shouts came from the ramparts of Calais on the far side of the harbour, and a cannon barked, stone shot kicking up a fountain of mud. Oxford and his men ran through it, reaching the Rysbank after just a few minutes. Following them came the king's carpenters and workmen, dragging heavy wooden beams behind them. The French guns continued to pound them with shot, but the foundations were quickly in place. More cannon thundered from the walls, smoke belching out over the harbour and forming a thick screen. The carpenters hoisted another beam into place and a cannon shot smashed it almost at once.

'Here comes the counter move,' said Warwick.

Out of the smoke came boats full of crossbowmen, crawling over the water. Black bolts streaked through the air, and on the Rysbank men fell, rolling over in the mud or falling into the shallow water. The English archers shot back, picking off the crossbowmen one by one, but more boats came, some full of men-at-arms and spearmen. The crossbow bolts were fire-tipped now, and in places the wooden beams began to burn.

The English archers continue to shoot, but they were outnumbered and the volleys of crossbow bolts were taking their toll. The leading French boats grounded on the mud and the men-at-arms stepped out and floundered forward, swords and spears in hand. Arrows slashed through their ranks, knocking men down, but the French came steadily on.

'Now,' Warwick said.

Another fresh company, Huntingdon's men, launched itself along the spit towards the Rysbank followed by the best of the rest, Llewellyn's Welsh spearmen and Rowton's archers. The crossbowmen in the boats raked them, but they never slackened their pace and they crashed into the French flank just as the latter reached the fortification and began attacking the carpenters. Some of the enemy were knocked off their feet by the impetus of the charge. The English and Welsh ran on, slashing and stabbing and shooting; the French fought back desperately, but were slowly driven down to the water's edge. Some managed to regain the boats; the others were cut down one by one.

With the arrival of Rowton's men there were more than two hundred archers on the Rysbank and arrows flew thick as hail across the waters of the harbour. The crossbowmen were driven back into the hanging smoke. The French cannon continued to boom, but now the English guns were being dragged forward by teams of men, straining and splashing in the mud. The fires on the wooden fortification had gone out. Warwick clapped his hands. 'By Christ, we've done it!'

Merrivale smiled. 'Congratulations, my lord. I shall inform the king.'

By midday the French cannon emplaced on the walls of Calais to cover the harbour had been put out of action. A battery of English guns covered the harbour, and as the smoke began to clear two English ships sailed into the entrance and dropped anchor. Their crews smashed open their hulls with hammers and abandoned ship, and both vessels began to settle into the water. This time they made no mistake. The entrance to the harbour was now completely blocked.

'Calais is cut off,' Warwick reported. 'There will be no more relief convoys, no more runs by Marant and his friends from Boulogne. When the granaries are empty, they will have to surrender or starve.'

'Let's reinforce the point,' the king said. He was all bustle and energy again, his good humour restored. 'Tell Master Coloyne to prepare a banquet. We'll eat in the open air, in plain view of the walls. It will give the garrison something to think about, while they wonder where their own next meal is coming from.'

'May I suggest we also send a message to the garrison, sire?' Merrivale said. 'Invite them to surrender now, rather than face hardship and hunger.'

'Excellent idea, Merrivale. Clarenceux, carry the message yourself tomorrow, under a flag of truce.'

Andrew Clarenceux bowed. 'With respect, sire, this was Master Merrivale's idea. He should be the one to go.'

'Very well,' said the king. 'Make it so.'

—

The previous day a raiding party had brought back a small herd of live sheep. These were now slaughtered and set to roast in firepits along with a variety of geese, chickens, pigeons and capons. By chance, an easterly wind blew the smoke of cooking into the city. Trestle tables were laid out on the highest piece of ground and the king and Prince of Wales, robed in brilliant scarlet, sat down at the high table, with their nobles and knights and men-at-arms around them. Extra rations were handed out to the common soldiers and they too ate and drank well, everyone lifting their cups from time to time in mocking toast to the garrison watching from the walls.

Iron Henry watched it all with disapproval. 'I think this shows bad manners,' he said. 'I would never permit my own men to behave in such a way.'

'You would not mock your enemies?' Brother Geoffrey asked.

'I am a mercenary, brother. We always behave well towards our enemies. Next week, they might be our friends.'

'Very prudent,' said Tiphaine.

Iron Henry smiled at her. 'I met a most intriguing woman last week, while my men were scouting the enemy positions around Arras. A Fleming, and most unusually she was captain of a company of militia.'

'That is not so unusual as you might think,' said Merrivale. 'More than one woman serves in the Flemish militia.'

'Well, this one was certainly unusual. I admired her.' He took a bite of his mutton and smacked his lips with pleasure. 'These sauces are excellent. Your cooks have excelled themselves. I think I might have to hire one for my own men.'

There were two sauces with the mutton, one fresh with green herbs, one red and sharp with wild garlic. Tiphaine laid down her knife. 'If you steal the king's cooks, he will tear up your indenture,' she said. 'By chance, was this woman called Fier Meike?'

'Why yes, she was! So you do know her. She claimed your acquaintance, *demoiselle*, but I did not know whether to believe her.'

'Yes,' said Tiphaine. 'I know her.'

'Ah. Well then, you might want to hear the message she asked me to give you. It concerns someone called Jehan. She said to tell you Jehan was waiting for something. That was all.'

'Jehan is always waiting for something,' Tiphaine said lightly. 'He is one of those people who only exists to obey orders. Is there any other news?'

Iron Henry shook his head. 'The French and Flemings are fighting steadily, raid and counter-raid almost every week, but both sides are at a standstill. The Flemings are still concentrated around Cassel, and the French forward posts at Saint-Omer and Béthune are battered but continue to hold firm.'

He paused. 'It is said that the Countess of Béthune has returned to her husband's castle, with her son, and has taken command of the defence. Yet another woman soldier! Times are certainly changing, and I would say they are changing for the better.'

Tiphaine glanced at Merrivale, who said nothing. 'Why is that, count?'

'As I have said, fighting is natural. It is good that women should fight if they wish. In Germany we already allow women to fight duels with swords. We should let them join the ranks along with the male soldiers, and follow their natural tendencies.'

'And Fier Meike certainly follows her natural tendencies,' Tiphaine said. 'Do you really admire her?'

'Of course! She is big, she is strong, she speaks her mind, and that club she carries could stun an ox. What a woman!'

Calais, 24th of May, 1347

He had intended to go into Calais alone, but Tiphaine and Brother Geoffrey overruled him. 'You have never been inside the town,' Geoffrey said. 'We have.'

'And I know Saint-Pierre, the mayor,' Tiphaine added. 'You don't.'

The revelry after the banquet had gone on late into the evening. In the morning, the three of them walked through a silent camp and down through the field fortifications past batteries of cannon and silent rows of trebuchets and picked their way across the muddy fields towards the city. 'What did Fier Meike's message mean?' Merrivale asked.

'*Jehan* refers to Jehan Nortkerque,' Tiphaine said. 'The Pilgrims have secretly joined the Flemish militias, but I think Nortkerque still controls them. He is waiting for orders.'

'Orders for what?' asked Geoffrey.

'Start a mutiny perhaps, turn and attack their fellow Flemings. Or the French, or us. It all depends on what we think the man from the north is trying to achieve.' She looked at Merrivale. 'How many people know what Hugh de Vere told you?'

'The two of you, Mauro, Hugolin Bessancourt, and the king. No one else.'

'But someone told Nicodemus to kill de Vere,' Geoffrey said.

'To stop him talking to me?'

'To stop him talking to anyone. Whoever it is, they must have also spoken to De Vere and realised what he knew. Simon, my friend; what do you want to do about Yolande?'

'Nothing,' said Merrivale.

Crossbowmen on the walls covered them as they approached. A postern gate opened to admit them. Men with levelled spears confronted them as they stepped through. 'I am Simon Merrivale, herald to King Edward of England,' Merrivale said. 'I have a message for your governor.'

'Wait here.'

They waited in the warm morning sun. The town was even more battered than before, roofs punctured and chimney stacks broken, bricks and stone shot littering the street. Something shook the air with thunder; a cannon firing from the Rysbank.

Five men walked up the street towards them. Three were men-at-arms; their leader bore the red eagle device of Jean de Vienne, governor of the garrison. Two were in the black robes of burgesses; one, red-haired, wore the mayor's chain of office around his neck.

Vienne stopped in front of Merrivale. 'What do you want?' he asked without ceremony.

'May we talk privately, my lord?'

Vienne waved the guards away. 'My message is from King Edward,' the herald said. 'He invites you to avoid further suffering, and surrender the town now.'

'Whose suffering would I be avoiding? Yours, or ours?'

'Both,' said Brother Geoffrey. 'The lives of all men are equally precious in the eyes of God.'

'Geoffrey of Maldon. I know your reputation, brother. There is not much about human life that is precious to you, is there?'

'Perhaps so,' said Geoffrey. 'But then, I am not God. Calais is encircled now, and more men are arriving in the English camp every day. The Flemish rebels are strengthening their forces as well. You have no hope, my lord.'

'The French army is on the way. Any day now, they will march to relieve the siege.'

'What is stopping them, my lord? Why have they not marched already?'

Vienne said nothing. 'King Philippe is not as strong as you would like to believe he is,' Merrivale said. 'If he does march on Calais, he will face the English to his front and the Flemings on his right flank. He would need a powerful army indeed to confront both. So, he waits, building up his strength, while you run out of food and begin to starve.' He paused for a moment. 'The end cannot be escaped, my lord. Surrender now, and you and all your men can walk out of the city and go free.'

'My orders are to hold this city until the end,' Vienne said. 'With respect, I think this conversation is over.'

Merrivale waited until Vienne and his men-at-arms had gone, and turned to the two burgesses.

'This is Eustache de Saint-Pierre, mayor of the city,' Tiphaine said. 'His colleague is Andrieu de Maninghem.'

Merrivale nodded. 'Do you agree with the governor?' he asked.

'If you guaranteed our lives and property, we would surrender today,' Saint-Pierre said bluntly. He indicated Tiphaine. 'I have already told your spy this. The war is ruining our businesses and our lives. We want to make an end.'

'King Edward is not in a mood to bargain,' the herald said. 'He has expended much treasure and many lives on this siege. He is tempted to hand over the city to his men and let them do their worst. You will have heard of the sack of Caen.'

Saint-Pierre went pale, but the bald man, Maninghem, smiled a little. 'You say he is not in a mood to bargain,' he said, 'but I smell a bargain in the air nonetheless. You would not be here otherwise.'

Tiphaine looked at the two burgesses. 'Do you trust me, gentlemen?'

'No,' said Maninghem.

Saint-Pierre waved a hand, irritably. 'What have you to offer?'

'You have been in secret contact with Bishop Hatfield, through me,' Tiphaine said. 'Meneer Maninghem has likewise been in correspondence with his cousin Lord Rowton. Do not continue to deny it, please. Lord Rowton himself makes no secret of this.'

Maninghem fell silent. 'One of the two is a traitor,' said the herald. 'One of the two, Hatfield or Rowton, is conspiring against both France and England. And one of you knows who it is.'

The two men looked at each other. 'We both do,' Saint-Pierre said.

There was silence in the street. The guards waited, still out of earshot, wondering what was going on. 'We formed an alliance early on,' the mayor said. 'We shared our secrets because we had to. We owe these men no loyalty, we are acting entirely out of self-interest. Our first priority is to save the town. Our second, if that is not possible, is to save ourselves.'

'Go on,' said Merrivale.

'Guarantee our lives and property will be spared. When the town falls, get us out safely. As soon as we are free, we will tell you the name of your traitor. But we need to be assured of our safety before we speak. Is that clear?'

'Yes,' said Merrivale. 'When will the town fall?'

'There is enough food in the granaries to last until autumn.'

Brother Geoffrey shook his head. 'Too late. The longer we delay, the more time Philippe has to build up his forces and advance to your rescue. We will give you two months. Then the town must surrender.'

'Last winter, someone was spoiling food and water to weaken the garrison,' Tiphaine said. 'Was it Nortkerque?'

'Yes,' Maninghem said reluctantly. 'He fled when Vienne's men discovered what he was doing.'

'Then you must do the same,' she said. 'Slowly, carefully, so you are not caught. When the city falls, we will be waiting to save you. Do we have a bargain?'

There was a long silence, broken by the echoing roar of another cannon. 'Yes,' said Saint-Pierre.

Calais, 1ˢᵗ of June, 1347

To my friend the heraldus Simon Merrivale, greeting. In response to your request, I have invaded both the Chancery and Treasury, compelling the clerks to search for any documents relating to the former mint in Dublin. According to them, no such documents exist. This is surprising to me, because there is nothing our clerks love better than keeping records. They hoard parchment like magpies gathering tinsel. I am therefore drawn to conclude that either the clerks are deceiving me, which I doubt, as I am not easy to deceive, or the records have been deliberately destroyed. Either way, I feel this bodes no good.

I have taken the liberty of informing my father and we will continue to make inquiries, but I fear we can make no promises.

We hear news that King Philip had gathered a vast army and will advance shortly against your position at Calais. Our thoughts and prayers are with all of you. With respect and friendship, Lady Mary.

The morning was chilly but the air was bright and clear. In the golden light of sunrise the sea seemed carpeted with sails, a hundred ships or more coming in slowly from the west. Banners flew from their masts, bright specks of colour above the red sails. Horsemen raced down the causeway into the camp and in a moment the news was running like fire. *Lancaster is coming. He has two thousand men, at least. They will land at Gravelines and march to join us.*

'Splendid news!' said the Prince of Wales, slapping his thigh with delight. 'Now old Henry is here, we really shall see some action. What do you think, herald?'

Henry of Grosmont, Earl of Lancaster, was thirty-seven years old, enough to make him appear ancient in the prince's eyes. 'Don't raise your hopes too greatly, Highness,' the herald said. 'His Grace is determined to starve the enemy out, rather than lose more men in an assault on the walls.'

'What about the French army? They'll advance against us soon.'

'They have made no move so far,' Merrivale said. 'They are waiting until they feel strong enough to attack us.'

'Well, I wish they would hurry up. This siege feels like it has gone on forever. When are you coming back into my service, herald?'

'When the king gives me leave, Highness.'

'I wish he'd hurry up too. I miss having you at my court. You always sound like you are talking good sense, even when you are rebuking me.'

Merrivale smiled. 'Especially when I am rebuking you, Highness.'

The prince chortled, slapped him on the shoulder, and went off to play hazard with his friends. Merrivale stood, leaning on his stick and watching the ships.

Always a good soldier, Lancaster oversaw the disembarkation of his men and ensured they were encamped and fed before riding down from Gravelines in the evening. The king met him outside the King's House, watched by thousands of men, and embraced him as he dismounted. 'It is good to see you at last, cousin.'

'I am sorry I am so late,' Lancaster said. Tall and fair like the king, he was a little quieter, more grave in manner. 'My men will follow tomorrow.'

'Good, good. What news of the queen?'

'She is resting at Windsor, surrounded by her ladies. I carry letters from her.'

'Come inside and I will tell you more about our situation.'

Lancaster was another friend from the king's youth, trusted, respected, honoured. He and the king talked privately for several hours, and it was late before the earl finally departed. Merrivale was waiting for him outside the King's House. 'Greetings, my lord. I wonder if you would honour me with a word in private?'

Lancaster smiled at his former herald. 'Of course. Come with me.'

The earl's lodgings were another wooden hut of the same type as Merrivale's own, though larger and more spacious. Lancaster waited until the candles were lit and dismissed the servants, pouring two cups of wine with his own hand and adding water. 'It is good to see you again, Simon.'

'You too, my lord. The king has missed you.'

'I know. I am three months later than I should have been. Despite the king's explicit instructions to raise a new army, there has been nothing but confusion, obstruction and delay. Letters and reports have gone missing, summonses and writs have not been delivered, orders have been given but not carried out. I have never seen such a state of chaos. The chancellor and Archbishop Stratford are as mystified as I am.'

'Do you think someone was deliberately trying to impede you, my lord?'

'The thought occurred to me, more than once. The king told me about his conversation with you. Can all these things be connected?'

'I believe so, though I am not certain how. My lord, I need to ask you some questions about the events of twenty years ago.'

Lancaster sat down. 'I will answer if I can, but I'm not certain how much I can tell you. I was in my father's service, but I had only just turned seventeen when the old king... met his end.'

'It is your father I wanted to talk about. He was regent of England during King Edward's minority. I believe the regent's council employed Michael Northburgh as clerk. Did you know him well?'

Lancaster hesitated for a moment. 'I saw him at council meetings. He appeared to be a good and faithful servant, very diligent in performing his duties.'

That is damning with faint praise, the herald thought. 'Thomas Hatfield was also employed by the council, but not just as a clerk, of course. Did you know about the secret meeting in Calais?'

'I knew of it, though I had nothing to do with it. A rather misguided move of my father's, I fear. His sight was beginning to fail by this point, and I fear he did not always make good decisions.'

'Will you tell me what happened, my lord?'

'My father always believed Mortimer was a threat to the kingdom, he and John of Hainault and their allies. When the old king of France died, he saw an opportunity to press King Edward's claim to the French crown. If the French had agreed, it would have been a feather in my father's cap and increased his power at the expense of Mortimer.'

'The French sent a strong delegation. A royal secretary, a professor of theology, an archbishop. We sent a young and unknown cleric. Why?'

'An excellent question,' Lancaster said dryly. 'My father wanted to go himself, but his blindness prevented him. He trusted Geoffrey of Maldon to go in his place, but Mortimer prevented him. Mortimer sent Hatfield and Eustace Rowton instead.'

'*Mortimer* sent Rowton?'

'Yes. Rowton's father, Gerard, had fallen out with Mortimer over the king's abdication. But Eustace was deemed a safe pair of hands, even though he too was still quite young. His loyalty to the king was well known.'

'Was any record of this meeting kept?'

'None.' Lancaster smiled a little. 'So far as the world is concerned, the meeting never happened. Both sides wanted it that way.'

'The meeting failed in its purpose. A year later, Mortimer was dead and the king was in full control. That was the end of negotiations with France.'

'Not quite,' Lancaster said. 'There was another meeting a year later, in 1331. This time I attended, along with the king. Rowton was there again, and so was Michael Northburgh. John of Hainault brokered the meeting.'

–

'I was sceptical from the beginning,' Lancaster said. 'I was surprised when the king agreed to go, and absolutely astonished when King Philip – I beg your pardon, when our adversary agreed to meet him. But Hainault insisted he had been approached by people in Paris who said the French were willing to bargain.'

'So it was all Hainault's idea.'

'Yes. He insisted the whole thing be kept secret. We crossed over to France in disguise, myself and the king as merchants, Rowton and Northburgh as our servants.'

'Not Hatfield?'

'No. He was engaged somewhere else, I don't remember where. We met at Pont-Saint-Maxence, not far from Beauvais. I advised the king to be conciliatory, but he wouldn't have it. He insisted on laying down demands.'

'What did he want?'

'France must drop its claim to sovereignty over Aquitaine and allow the English crown to hold the duchy in its own right. In return, King Edward would consider dropping his claim to the French throne.'

'I imagine that went well,' the herald said dryly.

'About as well as you might expect. The French turned us down and walked out of the meeting. Edward was furious, and blamed Hainault for making him look like a fool. He didn't even wait until we returned home, he sent Rowton ahead on a fast horse to get back to England as soon as possible, and instruct the council to order Hainault's dismissal and exile.' Lancaster chuckled. 'I remember the queen was delighted. Hainault may be her uncle, but she cannot stand the sight of him.'

'Was that the end of the matter, my lord?'

'Not quite. We were ambushed on the way home, not far from Dieppe. On the surface it seemed like an everyday event, bandits attacking a couple of merchants. But I think those men knew exactly where to find us. I believe we were betrayed.'

'By whom, my lord?'

'It is a hard thing to say, herald. He has given many years of good service to the crown, with never another hint of anything suspicious. But in my heart, I have always believed it was Michael Northburgh who told those bandits where to find us.'

–

Quietly, Merrivale let himself into his lodgings. The others were waiting for him; Brother Geoffrey, Tiphaine, Mauro and Bessancourt, eyes bright in the candlelight. 'Well?' asked Tiphaine. 'What did you learn?'

'That what we suspected is true,' Merrivale said quietly. 'It is him. It can only be him.'

'Can we prove it?'

'No, not yet. Not to a level that would satisfy the king. Now, we must be patient. When Calais is ready to fall, then he will show his hand.'

27

Calais, 6th of July, 1347

To know who the traitor was, to see him almost every day, was painful. But they were still running blind. They knew who he was, but had no idea what he intended to do. The timing had to be as precise as a water clock; strike too early and there was a risk the traitor's co-conspirators would carry on without him. Strike too late and they would be... well. Too late.

In London, the obstacles Lancaster had spoken of suddenly disappeared. Troops and ships poured across the Narrow Sea. In the camp at Calais, the English army's numbers grew almost daily. By the middle of June fifty ships lay hove to off Calais; by the end of the month it was a hundred. Thirty miles away at Cassel the Flemings were also building up their strength.

'A messenger came out of Calais this morning,' Warwick reported. 'We captured him trying to make his way through our lines. He was carrying a letter from Governor de Vienne to our adversary. Food supplies in the town are almost exhausted. Vienne reckons he can hold on for another month at most.'

Hatfield looked surprised. 'They received at least a dozen shiploads of supplies before Easter. They can't have gone through several hundred tons of food already.'

'According to my agent, they are having the same problem as last winter,' Lord Rowton said. 'Barrels of salt beef and stockfish have gone rotten, and the flour is mouldy and full of maggots. And the wells are starting to run dry.'

'Ironic, given the amount of water around us,' the king commented. Exceptionally high tides had flooded the marshes around Calais again, driving the besiegers back onto higher ground; from a distance, the town and the English camp looked like islands in a turgid sea. Cases of flux were still on the rise.

'What did you do with the messenger?' the king asked.

Warwick grinned. 'Gave him back his message and sent him on his way. There is no harm in the adversary knowing the garrison is on the point of collapse. It might tempt him into making a move at last.'

'We still have no idea of their strength,' Hatfield pointed out.

'Whatever it is, we will deal with it,' Rowton said. 'Better to have a confrontation and get it over with. If we sit here much longer, our fresh troops will rot away. We need action, now.'

'I agree,' said the king. 'The adversary will have to respond to that letter, or else sacrifice Calais. Either way, he is playing into our hands.'

Calais, 13ᵗʰ of July, 1347

> *To that most esteemed and honourable of men, Simon Merrivale, heraldus, I give greeting. There is a matter I wish to discuss with you which, if you are agreeable, may be of great profit to you. I invite you to call on me at Béthune as soon as possible, so that we may discuss it in greater detail.*

There was no signature, but the seal on the letter bore the imprint of a lion rampant with two tails. That, and the scent of roses and vervain clinging to the parchment, was enough to identify the sender.

'The time has come,' said the herald. 'They are making their move.'

Tiphaine put down the letter. 'Are you going?'

'Of course.'

'Alone?'

'No. I shall take Geoffrey with me.'

'Oh, that's all right then. You'll be as safe as the Tower of London. You do remember what happened last time you rode to Béthune?'

'Every time my leg pains me, I remember. I am sorry, Tiphaine, but this is how it must be.'

She waited until the herald and Geoffrey rode away, and then turned to Bessancourt. 'Find me a horse, Hugolin. If anyone calls, tell them I have gone away for a few days.'

'I know where you are going,' Bessancourt said. He nodded at Mauro. 'We're coming with you.'

'No, you're not.'

'Yes, we damned well are.'

'You are a groom,' Tiphaine snapped. 'Do as you are told.'

'Piss off.'

'Hugo,' Mauro said in tones of reproof. 'Respect the lady's rank.'

'All right. Piss off, *demoiselle*. We've come down a long road together, and risked our lives together, too many times. We are coming with you.'

Béthune, 15ᵗʰ of July, 1347

'Simon!' said Yolande of Bohemia, Countess of Béthune, and her lips curved into a warm smile. 'It is good to see you again.'

Merrivale bowed, one hand resting lightly on his stick. 'I came as soon as I received your letter.'

Dust motes, trapped in the sunlight, circled slowly in the warm air of the hall. 'I am grateful that you came at all,' Yolande said. 'After... After what happened last autumn, I would not have blamed you if you refused.'

'Things are different now,' said the herald. 'Guy is dead.'

'I thank God for it, every day. I am safe now, and so is Jean.'

Merrivale looked around. 'Is he here?'

'He is having lessons with his tutor. I will send for him later, so you can meet him.'

'I would like that... Does he resemble me in any way?'

'If anyone, he resembles my mother,' she said, laughing. 'His colouring is pure Sicilian. But I would say he has your temperament.'

'Gloomy, miserable and hard to get along with?'

She laughed again. 'You were never gloomy, or miserable.' Her smile faded a little. 'Except when I made you that way.'

'It wasn't you that wanted to kill me,' Merrivale said. 'It was your father and his friends. I am sorry to speak ill of the dead, but I feel much safer knowing they are out of the way. However, I am sure you did not invite me here to discuss the past.'

'No,' she said, and the warm smile was back. 'It is the present that concerns us now, and the future. Your future, and mine.'

'Together?' asked Merrivale.

'That remains to be seen,' said another voice. 'You see, Simon, a great deal depends on you.'

Merrivale turned. Ramon Vidal stepped into the hall. He wore his usual brown Franciscan habit girdled with rope, its aura of simplicity and honesty wholly at odds with his personality. His face was round and a little flabby, but his eyes were dark and sharp. 'We have an offer for you,' he said.

'Who is *we*?' the herald asked.

'Princess Yolande and myself, of course. Who did you think?'

'What about Cardinal Aubert, your master? Where does he fit in?'

'I am acting in my master's interests, although he doesn't know it. May I be completely honest with you?'

'I doubt it,' said Merrivale. 'But it will be interesting to hear you try.'

Vidal smiled. 'Very amusing. Did you come alone?'

'Yes.' Strictly speaking it was true; he and Brother Geoffrey had parted company five miles from Béthune.

'Good,' said Vidal. 'We can talk without fear of interruption. Shall we get down to business?'

-

They sat down at the high table, keeping a distance between them. 'My master, as the world knows, has only one ambition,' Vidal said. 'He wants to become pope. The men he has been… associating with for the past few years have promised to help him realise this ambition. However, the cardinal has decided that they cannot necessarily be trusted.'

'And what has led to this sea-change?'

'He has had his doubts for some time. However, the tipping point was a rumour that the group may have another candidate they wish to promote for the papacy. In other words, they are going behind his back.'

'Would that candidate be Thomas Hatfield, Bishop of Durham?'

'Ah.' Vidal's eyes sharpened for a moment. 'Intriguing… To come to the point, the cardinal is looking for another sponsor. That is where you come in.'

'You will need to explain,' Merrivale said.

Vidal nodded. 'Her ladyship will do so.' Merrivale looked at Yolande, raising his eyebrows.

'I know where the Count of Flanders is,' she said.

There was a long pause. Merrivale nodded slowly. 'I see. After Count Louis, Jean is the next in line to inherit Flanders. We eliminate the count, I marry you and we rule Flanders together through the boy.'

'Don't tell me you hadn't already thought of this,' Yolande said, watching his face.

'You know me well. Of course, we would have to keep his true parentage secret. He could hardly claim to inherit Flanders if it was known he was my son.'

'That is easily done,' said Yolande. 'And there is more. The counties of Hainault, Holland and Zeeland are currently held by Empress Margaret, the wife of Emperor Louis. When my brother dethrones Louis and takes the crown for himself, he will hand all three counties over to me as thanks for my support. All the wealth of the Low Countries will be at our command.'

'That will make you one of the wealthiest people in Europe,' Merrivale said. 'Why do you need me?'

'You are a favourite of King Edward. You can sign a treaty with England, guaranteeing protection against France and the continuation of the wool trade. England will have the strong bulwark in Flanders it desires, and we will have peace and security.'

'Interesting,' said Merrivale. 'Can we get back to Cardinal Aubert?'

Vidal nodded. 'There is only one way to be elected pope,' he said. 'One must persuade the College of Cardinals that God has chosen you as the instrument of His will.'

'You mean, one must bribe the cardinals.'

'Exactly. You and Princess Yolande will be Cardinal Aubert's new sponsors, and will lend him the money he needs to demonstrate the true grace of God to his colleagues. And in gratitude, Cardinal Aubert will also support the English cause against France.' Vidal smiled. 'There. Do you find the offer sufficiently tempting?'

'France would not tolerate the election of a pope who favours England.'

'France will have her own problems to deal with. You tried to set up an English pope once, remember? Now is your chance to make good.'

'There will be obstacles,' Merrivale said.

Yolande smiled. 'You and I, working together, will overcome them. This is our moment, Simon. This is what we have been waiting for.'

'Mm. You assassinated your last husband. What is to say you won't do the same to me, if it pleases you?'

Yolande flinched as if she had been struck. She looked down at the floor for a moment, swallowing hard, and when she looked back up again he saw tears in the corners of her eyes. 'If only you knew how hard the last ten years have been,' she said quietly. 'If only you knew how much I suffered at that man's hands, the pain and humiliation, the fear I endured when he took my son away; *our son!* I dreamed of killing him, Simon. I prayed to God for his death, and when the opportunity finally came, I seized it with both hands! You would have done the same.'

'Probably,' said the herald, watching her.

'I swear by the blood of God, Simon, I would never willingly do anything to hurt you. I would sooner kill myself that harm a hair of your head.'

'Willingly,' the herald said. 'That is the essential word, isn't it?' He looked back at Vidal. 'Why should I trust you?'

'You don't have to,' Vidal said. 'You can reject the offer, ride away now and nothing more will happen. Cardinal Aubert will look elsewhere. But I am surprised at your reticence, Simon. I thought this offer would appeal to you. A man of your talents should not be a mere herald.'

Merrivale said nothing. 'Or is there another reason?' Vidal asked. 'The Norman girl, perhaps. If she is an impediment, it would be easy to remove her.'

'So there it is,' Merrivale said. 'I kill my mistress and the Count of Flanders, and in return I will have power, riches and a life with the woman I love. But you have forgotten one thing. The Pilgrims. Your erstwhile friends control them, Raimon, and if we try to steal Flanders from under their noses, they will turn the Pilgrims against us.'

Silence. Yolande looked at Vidal, wiping her eyes. The cardinal's secretary nodded slowly.

'You know what I want, Raimon,' the herald said. 'If you are going to betray the conspiracy, you must betray it absolutely. It is the only way I will ever be able to trust you. Tell me the name of the man from the north.'

'Join us,' Vidal said. 'Kill the girl and the count, marry the princess. Then we will tell you.'

Merrivale turned on Yolande. 'When did your bed become a bargaining table?'

She wiped her eyes again. 'When was it ever anything else? You used me in Savoy, and you are using me again now. Back then, I loved you so much that I didn't care, but I care now. I love you still, Simon, but I will not be manipulated by any man. Join me, commit yourself, and you will learn what you want to know. That is my position, and I will not move from it.'

There was a long silence. 'I need time,' Merrivale said.

'Events are moving at speed,' Vidal warned. 'We haven't much time to spare.'

'I know.' Gently, Merrivale took Yolande's hand in his. When he raised her fingers to his lips, they were ice cold. 'I will not keep you waiting for long,' he said quietly. 'You will hear from me again, very soon.'

—

At a crossroads five miles from Béthune the herald halted his horse and waited. Perhaps half an hour passed before another horseman came riding up hard from the south. Brother Geoffrey pulled up alongside him, wiping perspiration from his face.

'You were right,' he said. 'The French are coming, straight towards Calais. The main body are keeping to the high ground, but they have scouting parties all across the country.'

'What numbers?'

'I couldn't get close enough to see clearly, but this looks like the entire royal army. I did get glimpses of the baggage train. It must be five miles long.'

They kicked their horses into motion. 'In Vidal's words, events are moving at speed,' Merrivale said.

'Vidal was there?'

'Yes. The offer was the one we expected, with a few embellishments. They want me to kill Tiphaine.'

Geoffrey raised his eyebrows. 'Yolande is jealous of her?'

'Possibly. I expect they also want proof of my commitment to the cause. They did offer to betray the other conspirators, but only if I do their bidding.'

'It was always a faint hope,' Geoffrey said.

'But it was a hope nonetheless. I thought if I could detach Yolande, get her on her own, I could persuade her to tell me. I wasn't prepared for Vidal's presence. Now, we have just two options. We can wait and hope that Nicholas Courcy finds the information we need in Dublin. Or we can extract Saint-Pierre and Maninghem from Calais.'

'Our enemies may have other agents in the town,' Geoffrey warned. 'Once it is known we are trying to get them out, they will be killed.'

'I know. But I have a plan.'

Cassel, 17th of July 1347

Overnight the weather had turned and rain came sweeping across the plains of Flanders. The hill of Cassel was shrouded in mist. The camp at its base was full of bustle and activity, horses being harnessed, wagons hitched to their teams, bread ovens and barrels of flour and stockfish loaded aboard. 'What are you doing here?' asked Fier Meike.

Topaas was with her, and a company of men including some of the Pilgrims from Poperinge. So much for the Pilgrims not having leaders, Tiphaine thought.

'Looking for you,' she said. 'What is happening?'

'We are preparing to march. The French are approaching Saint-Omer, and we are moving up to the line of the River Aa to block their passage if they turn north.'

'Are you supporting the English?' Bessancourt asked.

'Not necessarily.' Fier Meike looked Tiphaine. 'Who is the boy? Did you trade the herald for him?'

'He is my groom.'

'Good choice. Keep your friends close and your grooms closer. Are you joining us?' She looked at Bessancourt and Mauro. 'I can find you some crossbows.'

There were several other women in the ranks around her, Tiphaine noticed. One was carrying a standard with the black lion of Flanders. 'You said Nortkerque was waiting for something. What is it?'

'This.' Meike gestured around her. 'He has been going through the army all morning, talking to the Pilgrims.'

'What is he saying to them?'

'Three words. *Babylon has fallen.*'

'What in Christ's name does that mean?'

'We don't know. I'm not sure Nortkerque knows, yet.'

'Wait a moment,' said Bessancourt. 'Do the authorities know Nortkerque is with the army? Why haven't they arrested him?'

Topaas looked at him, pityingly. 'For the same reason they haven't arrested any of the Pilgrims. There would be another popular revolt in Flanders if they even tried. Also, they need men, and the Pilgrims are hard fighters.'

'It turns out Nortkerque fought in the Peasants' War twenty years ago,' Meike said. 'Then he served as a mercenary with a company from Holstein, and made enough money to buy his house in Poperinge and set up a business. When he offered his services, the League of Three bit his hand off. Metteneye is in command here, and Nortkerque is one of his senior captains.'

Mauro looked puzzled. 'But he led the Good Friday attack in Bruges.'

'He wasn't in the city when the fighting happened, and there is no evidence to suggest he was involved at all,' Meike said. 'The only people who know are keeping quiet. And we must do so too, if we want to live.'

She looked at Tiphaine. 'Well? Are you coming with us?'

'For the moment,' said Tiphaine. 'I want to see what happens.'

Calais, 27th of July, 1347

The first French scouts appeared on the heights of Sangatte in the morning, and by midday the entire French army was arrayed, companies of crossbowmen and spearmen, rank upon rank of armoured men-at-arms on restive horses. Their shields and banners were splashes of brilliant colour, glowing like jewels.

The English army was drawn up outside the camp, its own solid lines of men-at-arms flanked by wedges of archers. 'Do we know their numbers?' the king asked.

'Not for certain,' said Warwick. 'Enough to cause us trouble.'

'What are they waiting for? Why don't they advance?'

'My guess is they are waiting for word from the town,' Lord Rowton said. 'We know the defenders are just about starved out. People are eating rats, even leaves and grass.'

cloud covered the sky. Hatfield squinted into the milky is this? A flag of truce?'

Two horsemen were coming down from the heights, a white banner fluttering overhead. 'Go and see what they want, Clarenceux,' the king said to his senior herald. 'Merrivale, go with him.'

Near the foot of the heights lay the village of Nielles, deserted and burned out like every other village and hamlet around. The two Frenchmen waited for them here; Montjoie, the king of France's herald and, undistinguished in brown, Raimon Vidal. Courteous as ever, Montjoie greeted them. 'Well met again, Andrew. I am glad to see the rigours of the siege have not born too heavily on you.'

'I confess there were times last winter when I began to feel my years,' Clarenceux said. 'I am pleased to see you well. How is your wife?'

Clarenceux and Montjoie exchanged gossip for a few moments. Merrivale looked at Vidal. The two men dismounted and walked behind the wall of a ruined house. 'Have you thought any more about our proposal?' Vidal asked.

'I have thought of little else. What does Montjoie want?'

'To propose negotiations that will save Calais and bring the war to an end. Representatives from each side will meet here, between the two armies. A neutral party, Cardinal Aubert will chair the discussions.'

'Neutral?'

'Do not get too involved with words, Simon. This gives the cardinal a chance to discreetly sound out the English about the possibility of his switching sides. He is also interested in this notion that Hatfield may be seeking the papacy. He wants to meet him, and has requested that Hatfield be part of your negotiating party.'

'He will jump at the chance' Merrivale said dryly. 'He likes to be at the centre of things. Very well. I will create an opportunity to speak to Aubert.'

'He doesn't want you. He wants to speak to King Edward personally. In private, without the French knowing about it, of course.'

Merrivale stared at him. 'How? We can't smuggle the cardinal into our camp, the French would be bound to hear of it.'

'No. You must bring the king here, to the negotiations.'

'There is no possibility of Edward attending unless King Philippe is also here.'

'Good,' said Vidal. 'Because Philippe has already agreed. His son, the Duke of Normandy, will accompany him. They are serious, Simon. The loss of life at Crécy last year and the strain on the finances have brought France to her knees. Your country is in little better condition; we know the king has pawned his crowns once more to pay for the siege of Calais. It is time to make an end.'

28

The argument about whether the king should attend the negotiations lasted long into the night. Lord Rowton had been passionately against it. 'Why bother to meet them at all? They won't act in good faith, they never have. They'll keep us talking while our strength withers away, and Calais slips through our fingers.'

'Delay will weaken the French as well,' Hatfield pointed out. 'Eustace, you said yourself that Calais is about to fall. They cannot delay the inevitable much longer.'

The king looked at Warwick. 'Thomas? What do you think?'

Warwick frowned. 'The choice is talk, or fight,' he said. 'We would win a fight, I think. Their numbers are not as great as we have been led to believe, and we have the Flemings protecting our flank. But unlike at Crécy, the French have the advantage of high ground. We would win a victory, but it might be a Pyrrhic one.'

'Very well,' the king said finally. 'We talk. Tell the French to pull back their forward positions so there is a wide separation between the armies. We'll spend tomorrow making the arrangements and preparing our negotiating tactics. Eustace, I want you to concentrate on Calais. No one gets in or out of the town to carry messages. Brother Geoffrey will advise you, as he knows the routes.'

'I will attend to it, sire,' Rowton said sourly. 'I would far rather this duty than sit and listen to whatever pointless proposals the French offer.'

The king grinned at him. 'Clarenceux, tell the cardinal we will meet him and the adversary day after tomorrow. Tell his highness the prince to attend on me also. Very well, gentlemen, make it so.'

Calais, 29th of July, 1347

A pavilion had been erected near the ruins of Nielles. A handful of bodyguard troops from both sides stood around it, staring at each other suspiciously. The king dismounted and strode into the pavilion, followed by the Prince of Wales and their attendants, Bishop Hatfield, the Earl of Warwick, Clarenceux and Merrivale, Northburgh and a few clerks. Cardinal Aubert, in full episcopal regalia, bowed deeply. 'It is an honour to receive you, your Grace. I recall your gracious hospitality last year at Lisieux.'

The French party arrived a few minutes later. Nearly twenty years older than his English rival, Philippe VI of France was already growing grey. He stood for a moment as if not knowing what to say. 'Greetings, cousin,' he said a little stiffly. 'I trust you are well.'

'Very well,' King Edward said heartily. 'And I hope *you*, cousin, are fully recovered from the wounds you received last August?'

Philippe flushed and sat down heavily. His son Jean, Duke of Normandy, glanced once at the Prince of Wales and then the two younger men ignored each other. Another man entered the tent and King Edward looked up sharply. 'For God's sake! What is *he* doing here?'

'Greetings, sire,' said Count Louis of Flanders smoothly. 'I trust all is well with you, and your lady wife? Is there any word of her accouchement?'

'Of her... You lying, treacherous piece of shit. I swore I would hang you if I ever saw you again, and by Christ I will!'

'Sit down, cousin,' said the king of France, in the voice of a man weary of arguing. 'No one is going to hang anyone. I invited Count Louis here, as it is quite possible that the future of Flanders will come into the discussions. He is under my protection.'

'I will not breathe the same air as this man,' Edward said shortly, and he turned towards the door.

Cardinal Aubert barred his way. 'Sire, may I remind you of our purpose here? There are more important issues to discuss than the actions, appropriate or otherwise, of the Count of Flanders.'

The cardinal didn't wink, Merrivale thought, but he came close to it. Edward stood for a moment, remembering the real reason he had agreed to come here. 'Very well,' he said shortly. 'But keep that little prick as far from me as possible.'

They took their positions, the English on one side of the long table, the French on the other, the clerks at smaller tables to one side. At the head of the table, Cardinal Aubert cleared his throat. 'Let us turn to the first item on the agenda,' he intoned. 'We shall now proceed to discuss the sovereignty of Aquitaine...'

—

In the cool blue dusk Tiphaine slipped back into the camp, wearing a shapeless leather coat with her hair tucked up under a steel cap. Merrivale regarded her. 'Do I need to know where you have been, and why you have stolen my servants?'

'I have been with the Pilgrims,' she said. 'There is something in the wind, but I don't know what. Even Fier Meike is prevaricating. Do the words *Babylon has fallen* mean anything to you, apart from the obvious?'

'*Babylon the great is fallen, is fallen, and has become a dwelling place of demons...* Hedge preachers foretelling the end of the world sometimes speak of this, but it doesn't sound like the man from the north and his friends. If anyone is Babylon, it is them.'

'But they could be using the Pilgrims' beliefs to control them, or at least some of them. And the Pilgrims have wormed their way into the heart of the Flemish army. According to Fier Meike, there are members in every militia company.'

'Are you going back?'

'Yes, at once. Mauro and Hugolin are waiting for me. I came to see if there was any news. How are the negotiations?'

'Agonising. Cardinal Aubert loves God, but he loves the sound of his own voice even more.'

Tiphaine looked at him for a moment. 'What else has happened?'

Merrivale handed her a sheet of parchment. 'This arrived today from Ireland while I was in the negotiations. It is the news we have been waiting for.'

'Trust Nicholas Courcy to wait until the last minute,' she said, glancing at the seal. She read the parchment and stood for a moment, very still. 'It is what we suspected. But this is the worst possible result, isn't it?'

'Yes. Of all the three, why in God's name does it have to be him?'

'Is this enough to accuse him?'

'Not quite. Courcy says he has witnesses, but they are in Ireland. Yolande and Vidal will not speak. We must have those men in Calais. Only they can give personal testimony.'

Calais, 30ᵗʰ of July, 1347

'We're shifting position. Prepare to move.'

The order came from Nortkerque, riding down the Flemish line. He had acquired a mail coat, Tiphaine saw, and an open-faced helmet with a plume of black feathers that made him instantly visible. Mauro and Bessancourt had been watching him all day, and reported that he seemed popular with the Flemish troops. He spent most of his time riding around giving orders, which he claimed were on behalf of Captain Metteneye, but Tiphaine wondered whether this was always true. He had yet to spot herself, hidden in the ranks of Fier Meike's company. Quietly, she touched the crossbow strapped across her back.

'Come on, shift yourselves.' That was Fier Meike, snapping at her company.

'Where are we going?' someone asked.

Nortkerque had overheard. 'This marsh will flood when the tide comes in. We're moving south onto dryer ground.'

South meant closer to the French. Tiphaine looked up at the heights and saw the distant ranks of men-at-arms, little sparkling glints of steel in the light. They splashed forward through the mud, other companies moving around them. A column of light armoured horsemen trotted past, churning up the shallow water as they rode. Jan Metteneye, formerly watch commander in Bruges and now commanding the Flemish militia, rode up alongside Nortkerque. 'What are you doing? Where are you taking these men?'

'We need to move positions, sir. The tide is coming in.'

Metteneye looked at Nortkerque for a long moment, then turned his horse and rode away without a word. *Why didn't he assert his authority?* Tiphaine wondered. *What is he afraid of?*

The French were moving too; as they reached firmer ground, a column of heavily armoured men-at-arms came down the slope and rode towards them. Nortkerque held up a hand to halt the Flemings. The French came steadily on, finally stopping a few yards away. 'What the devil are you doing?' their leader demanded. He was a big arrogant man in full armour with a red lion device on blue and gold bars. 'You are in breach of the truce! We're within our rights to attack you, you know.'

Nortkerque waited for a while before replying. The wind off the sea hissed through the long grass around them.

'I am a poor pilgrim, travelling in a perilous land,' the Fleming said finally. 'In God's name I am weary, and I seek shelter.'

The other man stiffened. After a long moment he raised his hand. 'Welcome among us, brother,' he said. 'Rest now, and give praise to God.' He turned to his men. 'There is nothing for us here. Let us return to our own lines.'

—

They waited. The ground was indeed more solid, and their boots began to dry out. The white pavilion where the two kings were meeting lay next to a ruined village about half a mile away. Something drifted through Tiphaine's mind, nagging her, and she suddenly realised what it was.

She turned to Fier Meike. 'Did you say Nortkerque served as a mercenary in the Count of Holstein's company?'

'Yes, so he claims. That was before the count took service with England.'

'I need to see someone,' Tiphaine said.

She splashed her way back across the marsh towards the English lines. Some of the archers were still watching the Flemish companies, puzzled by their sudden advance. Iron Henry's men were deployed along the Saint-Omer causeway, ready to move forward and reinforce the archers if needed. The truce was in force and the men were in relaxed mood; they sat on the grass with their helmets off, some talking or playing dice. Iron Henry waved a hand in salute as Tiphaine approached. 'Demoiselle de Tesson! Or should I say, Diana the huntress? That crossbow is a bit large for you, I think.'

'It was the smallest they had,' Tiphaine said. 'May I ask you a question, my lord? Do you often take men from other lands into your troop?'

'Of course. We call ourselves Holsteiners, but we have men from other parts of Germany, Spain, France, the Swiss cantons, Bohemia. We even have a couple of Moors. So long as a man can fight, he is welcome among us.'

'Do you recall a Fleming who served in our company a few years ago, before the present war started? His name is Jehan Nortkerque. He did very well with you, apparently. He earned enough to return home, buy a big house and start a business.'

Iron Henry's face went red. He stared at her, eyes dark with anger. 'Nortkerque! He told you this?'

'No. Someone else did.'

'Nortkerque is a thief and a liar. Yes, he served under my command when I led a company in the service of King Magnus of Sweden. We were paid our fee in gold, but Nortkerque stole the money and fled. I swore that if I ever found him, I would skin him alive.' Iron Henry paused. 'Do you know where he is?'

'Yes. First, let us work out what he is trying to do. Then I will lead you to him.'

–

'At first I thought Nortkerque was trying to provoke the French and break the truce,' she said to Merrivale later that day. 'That would put an end to the negotiations, which I assume is what they want. But that French captain knew the Pilgrim identification and response. They must have friends in the French army.'

'And probably in our own as well,' Merrivale said.

'I don't think we should wait any longer, Simon. We should arrest him.'

'The king would never countenance it. And if he escapes, he will go into hiding and become even more dangerous than before. We must bide our time, Tiphaine. It is the only way.'

Calais, 31ˢᵗ of July, 1347

Babylon is fallen. The whisper ran through the ranks of waiting Flemings. Some raised their weapons, faces full of grim determination. Others looked around, perplexed, trying to see what the rest were doing, looking for some sort of guidance. Fier Meike's company waited in silence, watchful.

Babylon is fallen. Nortkerque rose to his feet, holding up his sword. The woman with the black lion standard stood beside him. Another man, in battered armour with a dog-faced bascinet, visor covering his face, moved up behind them. 'Now is the time,' Nortkerque said.

Babylon is fallen. Babylon is fallen. The whisper rose to a low-voiced chant. The Pilgrims broke ranks and began to walk, slowly at first, towards the burned-out village and the white pavilion beside it. Others followed them, puzzled still, drawn by curiosity as much as anything. The English army was a mile away on one side, the French an equal distance up on the heights. There was only empty space between the Flemings and the pavilions.

Babylon is fallen. 'What are you doing?' Tiphaine screamed at Fier Meike. 'Go after them! Stop them!'

'Stop them from killing tyrants? Why should I? If the men in that pavilion die, I will not grieve.'

'Peace and justice and love,' Tiphaine said viciously. 'You're a damned hypocrite, just like the rest.' Turning, she ran through the Flemish lines, crossbow bumping on her back. Those who had failed to follow the Pilgrims were milling about in confusion. Metteneye rode up and dismounted, shouting at them, trying to restore order. Tiphaine ran up beside the captain's horse, jumped into the saddle and kicked the animal hard. Metteneye lunged for the bridle but it was too late; she was away, racing across the marshes towards the Holsteiners' position.

Iron Henry looked up in astonishment as she arrived. 'I know what Nortkerque is doing,' she gasped. 'Come and help me kill him.'

–

'We now come to the suzerainty of Flanders,' Cardinal Aubert said. 'Here, I fear, we have a somewhat thorny issue with which to grapple.'

'On the contrary,' King Philippe of France said sharply. 'Flanders is a vassal state of France, and always has been.'

'I fear I must contradict your Grace,' said the Bishop of Durham. 'France's claim dates only to 1305. The count of Flanders surrendered his rights under duress following the French conquest. Your suzerainty has never been recognised by other states, including England.'

The Duke of Normandy sneered at him. 'You said it yourself. We hold Flanders by right of conquest. There is an end to the matter.'

'Right of conquest,' the Prince of Wales said under his breath. 'You couldn't conquer a boil on your arse.'

'I heard that!'

'You were meant to, idiot.'

Cardinal Aubert held up a weary hand, but before he could speak the pavilion door opened and one of the French royal bodyguards ran in. 'I beg pardon, your Graces, but there is a large body of armed men moving directly towards us.'

There was a moment of stunned silence. Philippe of France shot to his feet, stabbing one finger accusingly at Edward of England. 'Treason! By God, you won't get away with this!'

'They're not *my* men, for Christ's sake!' Edward shouted. 'You cowardly bastard! You won't face me on the battlefield again, so you try a trick like this instead!'

'You damned fool, Edward! I'm the one who suggested the negotiations in the first place!'

'Yes, so you could lull us and catch us off our guard. These talks are finished, *cousin*! From now on my sword will be my voice!'

'You desire battle, Edward? Come on, then! Choose the day, choose the place! I will be waiting for you!'

Others were shouting all around them. Merrivale's voice cut through the din. 'Do these men have any device, any banner?'

'A black lion, sir herald. The device of Flanders.'

'They aren't my men,' said the Count of Flanders in a shocked voice.

'No, my lord. They are Pilgrims, and they are coming to kill all of you! Get their Graces away and back to their own lines, *now!*'

Men of the royal bodyguards came running, hustling the kings and princes away. Hatfield stood with a look of pure terror on his face before Northburgh pulled him after the rest of the English. Cardinal Aubert had already disappeared. Vidal seized Merrivale's arm. 'Is this your doing?' he demanded.

'No,' said the herald.

'I don't believe you. Those men are coming to kill the cardinal too, you know. And you claimed not to know who the man from the north is.' Vidal shook his head. 'How much did they pay you to betray us?'

'I don't know what you are talking about, Raimon.'

'Or did Yolande betray us? Yes, perhaps that is it. Forget the offer I made you, Simon. I will never have dealings with you again. Whatever you and that scheming bitch decide to do now is up to you. I will have no part in it.'

Vidal turned and walked out of the pavilion. From somewhere quite close at hand men's voices were chanting, *Babylon is fallen, Babylon is fallen*, and then the screaming began.

–

Her hands shaking, Tiphaine unslung the crossbow, fitted a bolt in the channel and, gritting her teeth with effort, drew back the string and cocked it. Beside the Holstein mercenaries waited in readiness, a solid rank of powerful, heavily armed men. Raising the bow, she pointed it straight at Nortkerque as he rode towards her. He saw the weapon and reined in his horse, and the men marching behind him halted too.

'Turn around and ride away,' Tiphaine said.

'The girl from Liège. I told Nicodemus he should have killed you instead of the Beguine.'

'You were right. He should have. And now I am going to shoot you unless you ride away.'

Nortkerque shook his head. 'My soul is with God. These men will carry out my orders, whether I live or die.'

'Don't you dare speak the name of God, you foresworn bastard!' Iron Henry bellowed. 'There is a place in hell ready for you, Nortkerque, and now we are going to send you there!'

'Still holding a grudge over the money, Heinrich? Put it behind you. The love of money is the root of all evil, you know.'

Men were coming forward through the ranks of the Pilgrims, raising crossbows of their own. *Shit*, Tiphaine said to herself, *I should have thought of that*. She Her arms and ached with strain as she sighted on Nortkerque's head. 'I will give you one more chance,' she said.

Nortkerque spat at her. 'Babylon is fallen!' he shouted, raising his arms, and his followers joined in, chanting. '*Babylon is fallen! Babylon is fallen! Babylon is fallen!*'

Tiphaine pulled the trigger. The bolt streaked out and hit Nortkerque in the face, burying itself up to the flights. He jerked once and fell out of the saddle. The men around him shouted, raising their weapons. Iron Henry rode ahead of Tiphaine, interposing himself between her and the oncoming men. He was just in time; two crossbow bolts, meant for her, thumped into his shield. More would follow.

'Put up your weapons! Put them up, now!' Fier Meike ran through the mob, shouting orders. Her company followed, ripping swords and bows out of the hands of those who were still advancing. One man raised a sword against Meike and she clubbed him down with the *goedendaag* like she was swatting a fly. The rest of the men hesitated. Reaching the front, Meike turned to face them and pointed at Nortkerque's body.

'Why did you follow him?' she raged. 'This vermin killed Sister Juliana! He stole from the sisters in Liège, and now he is working with the Count of Flanders! He has conspired against us all! *Why did you follow this carrion?*'

The power of her voice stunned them into silence. The woman with the banner looked down at the corpse. 'How do you know these things, Meike?'

'I witnessed the killing,' Meike said. She pointed to Tiphaine. 'So did this woman. The murderers escaped before we could stop them, but Nortkerque was there. He was one of them!'

'Lies!' someone shouted. 'Nortkerque is a martyr! Let us avenge him in blood!'

Meike pointed with her *goedendaag*. 'Step forward, you! If you want blood, I'll give it to you!'

Silence again. Tiphaine sat motionless in the saddle, listening to her own heartbeat. 'We have our orders,' said another man.

'Orders? We are Pilgrims! We take orders from no one! Ask yourselves, brothers and sisters, do you wish to die for a man like this?'

'You came to kill the kings,' said Tiphaine. 'But they have been warned, and they have gone and are already safe. If you fight now, you will die for nothing.'

The Flemings looked at the steel lines of the Holstein men. The mercenaries looked grimly back at them, weapons in their hands. It would take only a word from Iron Henry to send them charging into the oncoming mob. Tiphaine held her breath, waiting to see what would happen.

Finally the woman with the banner stirred a little. 'If this man killed a Beguine, he should burn for eternity,' she said. She turned and walked back towards the Flemish lines. A man hoisted his crossbow over his shoulder and followed her. A kind of collective sigh went up and one by one the entire body turned away.

Tiphaine dropped her own crossbow and leaned over the neck of her horse, drawing deep ragged breaths. 'What changed your mind?' she asked Meike.

'I hate kings. But, and God alone knows why, I have decided I like you. I came to stop you and your friend from being killed.'

'And we are very grateful to you,' said Iron Henry. He pointed at the *goedendaag*. 'That is the most splendid weapon I have ever seen. May I take a closer look?'

'Iron Henry, I believe you already know Fier Meike,' Tiphaine said. 'I will leave you both to become better acquainted.'

29

Calais, 2ⁿᵈ of August, 1347

The day after the negotiations failed, King Philippe sent Montjoie herald to repeat his offer; let the English march out and give battle, at a time and place of their choosing. But Edward's blood had cooled, and he declined the offer. He would wait where he stood; if the French wanted to relieve Calais, they would have to come through the English army. Metteneye had regained control of the Flemings now, and moved them up to reinforce the English positions. So, if the French thought they were strong enough to fight their way across the marsh under cannon fire and a hail of arrows; well, let them come.

They did not. A day later, the French army burned its camp on the heights of Sangatte and marched away south. The following day, three hundred and forty-three days after the siege of Calais began, the banners on its pock-marked towers and battered ramparts came down.

Andrew Clarenceux and Merrivale met Governor de Vienne and Saint-Pierre at the gates. 'We ask for terms,' said Vienne. 'Let the garrison march out with their arms. We will pledge not to take up arms against England for a year and a day.'

Clarenceux shook his head. He looked unhappy; a gentle, scholarly man, he did not like being the bearer of bad news. 'I am afraid our king is not a generous mood. The siege has been long and expensive. His first impulse was to order the destruction of the town and everyone in it.'

Saint-Pierre went pale with shock, staring at Merrivale. 'This is barbaric!' Vienne protested. 'There are still women and children in the town! My God, and your king dares call himself an honourable man?'

Clarenceux held up a hand. 'Fortunately, he has reconsidered. He demands that six of the leading burgesses surrender themselves into his hands. They will be publicly hanged, as an example of what happens to those who defy his authority. They must deliver themselves to the camp by midday tomorrow. If not, the town will be sacked.'

'What about the garrison? What happens to my soldiers?'

'I have separate terms for them. Come, let us discuss them.'

Clarenceux and Vienne walked away, talking. Saint-Pierre was still staring at Merrivale. 'We had an arrangement,' he said.

'We still do. You and Maninghem must be two of the six. Pick four others who know nothing about any of this. If the conspirators think you are about to be hanged, they will not bother with you.'

'And how do we know you *won't* hang us?'

'Listen to me,' Merrivale said quietly. 'This is a piece of mummery, staged for your benefit. You must act the part like your lives depend on it, because they do. As mayor, you will nobly volunteer to be one of the six. How you pick the others is up to you; draw lots, call for volunteers, whatever it takes, but make sure Maninghem also comes forward.'

'Then what?'

'Do what you would expect to do on the last night of your life. Pray, confess your sins, make your peace with God. In the morning, tie ropes around your necks, signifying your readiness to be hanged, and walk out to the English camp. You will be taken under guard and brought before the king, who will condemn your lives. Then, unexpectedly, he will pardon you, and you will be held under a strong guard until the time comes.'

Saint-Pierre let out a long breath. 'Is this the only way?'

'Yes,' said Merrivale. 'Dispel your doubts, *meneer*. We will keep our word, and you and your wealth will be safe.'

He paused. 'There is one more thing. The carpenters are building gallows as we speak, setting the scene for the play. If you fail us, the mummery becomes real, and you will hang on those gallows before tomorrow's sunset.'

'Can we trust them?' Brother Geoffrey asked when Merrivale returned to the English camp.

'I think so. I hope so. This is the last throw of the dice, Geoffrey. If this fails, I don't know where we turn.'

In the tower of Notre-Dame a single bell tolled, over and over, its tone bleak with mourning. The gate opened and six men stepped out. They were dressed as penitents, barefoot in sackcloth robes with ashes sprinkled on their heads and ropes around their necks as requested. Slowly they made their way across the open ground between the town and the English army.

Men from Llewellyn's company moved quickly to surround them. Merrivale had taken the Welsh captain partly into his confidence the night before. 'Only men you can trust, Llewellyn, men whom you have known for years.'

'They will be my own flesh and blood,' Llewellyn had said. 'Mind you, most of my company are related, in one way or another. We mountain dwellers don't get out much.'

Merrivale watched the men around the king. Warwick was smiling with satisfaction; eleven months of hard labour were finally receiving their reward. Lancaster watched with slightly puzzled eyes, stroking his chin. Michael Northburgh looked unhappy. So far as everyone knew, the six were to be executed. Northburgh, a humane man, had argued against this. 'Mercy is one of the attributes of kingship, sire. Show clemency now, and the army and people will applaud you as a wise and just sovereign. Such an act will add lustre to your name.'

'No, Michael,' the king had said. 'This is how it must be.'

Hatfield had recognised Saint-Pierre. The blood drained from his face and he started forward, but Merrivale put a hand on his arm. 'No, my lord,' the herald said quietly. 'It is too late.'

'This is unconscionable,' the bishop whispered. 'This man has served us! We cannot let this happen!'

'Wait,' Merrivale said.

Lord Rowton stood beside the king, hands behind his back. There was no expression on his face. Merrivale glanced at Maninghem, but the alderman was staring at the ground as he plodded forward, refusing to look at anyone.

The six men knelt before the king, bowing their heads to the ground. The king said nothing. The men around them waited in silence, listening to the wind ripple the bright banners overhead.

Finally the king spoke. 'I have expended much time and blood and treasure on this siege,' he said. 'Had you been reasonable men and obeyed my summons to surrender last September, all of this could have been avoided. But you did not, and so you have brought your fate upon yourselves. You will now be hanged, and let your deaths be an example to the world. This is the fate of those who defy me.'

Still kneeling, Saint-Pierre spoke. 'We accept your judgement, sire. But we beg you to be merciful, and spare our lives.'

'Why should I?' demanded the king.

For God's sake, Merrivale thought, *don't drag it out too long...* 'Think of our wives, our children, our families,' Saint-Pierre implored. 'Think of your own lady, the good and gracious Queen Philippa, back at home giving birth to your own child. For their sakes, sire, spare us.'

'You invoke the name of my queen,' King Edward said. He steepled his hands. 'What would she say if she were here, I wonder?'

Merrivale cleared his throat. 'Your queen is a tender and merciful woman, sire. She would advise you to pardon these men and set them free.'

As expert an actor as he was a soldier, the king paused for a few moments. Then he nodded. 'I agree. And to honour my lady wife, I shall do as she would wish. I pardon you for your offences against me. You may rise.'

Slowly, the six men stood. All looked a little dazed, even Saint-Pierre and Maninghem. Right until the last minute, they could not have been sure if the English would keep their word. 'Llewellyn, keep them under close watch,' the king said, and he rose and swept away, followed by most of his attendants. Lancaster and Warwick followed. Rowton remained, looking at the row of empty gallows and frowning.

'A curious turn of events, my lord,' Merrivale said.

'What?' Rowton turned and looked at him. 'Oh, that. It's typical of him. Pretend to be hard and arrogant, and then show his soft side. Northburgh was right. People will love him for this.'

They followed the others back towards the King's House. 'And so it is done,' Merrivale said. 'Calais is ours at last. You must be pleased, my lord.'

'No one is more pleased than the king, I should think. The prize he desires is finally in his hands.'

'But credit must go to you for suggesting the taking of Calais in the first place. It would have been far simpler to lease Gravelines or Dunkirk from the Flemings, which would have given us the same result; a port on the continent, a bridge over the Narrow Sea from which our troops could enter France. But Calais is a bigger prize, is it not?'

'It's a better harbour, if that's what you mean. Gravelines is silting up, and Dunkirk lacks protection from northerly winds.'

'Indeed,' said Merrivale. 'Changing the subject, my lord, did you know that your cousin, the man who was spying for you in the city, was one of the six the king saved just now?'

Rowton's voice was sharp. 'I recognised him, of course. How did *you* know?'

'When I was in the town yesterday, I asked that he be included in the six. When you thought the king intended to hang him, were you not tempted to plead on his behalf? Ask the king to spare his life?'

Rowton halted. 'Why did you ask for him? What are you playing at, herald?'

They were outside the King's House. 'We need to find somewhere private, my lord,' Merrivale said. 'I think we need to talk about Bishop Hatfield.'

—

The ground-floor parlour was a spacious room with windows looking out towards Calais. The wall hangings, installed last year, were now a little grimy with smoke and damp. 'You are not on good terms with Hatfield,' the herald said.

'It is no secret that we disagree on matters of policy.'

'He has made some remarkable blunders, too. The betrothal contract was not the first or only mistake he has made. Think of his insistence that the town was on the edge of surrender and he could deliver it to us. That was remarkably arrogant of him, don't you think?'

'He presumably had some plan in mind.'

'Or he was trying to delay us, and prevent Lord Warwick from prosecuting the siege more strongly. Let me be frank, my lord. We know that one of the king's inner circle is a traitor, but there are only a limited number of possibilities as to who it can be. For a long time, I suspected Michael Northburgh.'

Rowton's face was still devoid of emotion, but his eyes were watchful. 'And?'

'As the king's secretary, Northburgh was ideally placed to commit treason. And he has fallen under suspicion before. Some say it was

Northburgh who helped arrange the attempt to ambush the king in France, back in 1331.'

'You have been talking to Lancaster.'

'But it wasn't Northburgh, of course. He would hardly walk into an ambush in which he himself might be killed. He also lacks the subtlety to plan and organise a scheme which has been running for twenty years. And finally, he lacks the contacts outside the kingdom. I hardly think he has had time to forge a relationship with John of Hainault, for example.'

'So, clearly you think it is Hatfield.'

The herald frowned. 'There is a case to be made against Hatfield, of course. The patronage of Queen Isabella gave him the opportunity to build alliances with men such as Hainault and Aubert. He is trusted by the king, and like Northburgh, this offers opportunities to a man bent on treason. And he had an agent in Calais during the siege, just like you, my lord.'

Rowton said nothing for a long time. 'Have you laid this information before the king?' he said finally.

'No, my lord. Do you think I should?'

'Why ask me? You have been in his service many years.'

'But you have been longer still, and are closer to him. You know his mind better than most. How will he react to the news that one of his favourites is a traitor?'

'Badly,' said Rowton. 'But if he *is* a traitor, then we must act.'

'Indeed,' said the herald. 'And does that mean, my lord, that you are willing to explain your own activities over the past twenty years?'

'What? I thought you were making an accusation against Hatfield.'

'No, my lord,' said Merrivale. 'I am making an accusation against you.'

–

The door opened and the king strode in, followed by the Prince of Wales and Lancaster. Brother Geoffrey followed them and behind him came Tiphaine and Bessancourt.

'No ceremony,' the king said abruptly as Merrivale and Rowton bowed. 'Very well, herald. Let's hear it.'

'I must beg your Grace's pardon for awakening painful memories. Three men rode to Berkeley Castle the night your father died. The names of two, Sir John Holland and John of Hainault, were well known. Only recently did I learn the identity of the third. According to Sir Maurice de Berkeley, it was Gerard, Lord Rowton.'

Rowton looked at the king. His voice was confident, his manner calm and assured. 'Surely I cannot be blamed for the sins of my father, sire.'

'No,' said Merrivale. 'But it turned out Sir Maurice was mistaken.' He turned to Lancaster. 'My lord, can you kindly confirm what you told me? That Gerard Rowton had already broken with Mortimer by the time his Grace's father died?'

'Yes,' Lancaster said. 'I remember my father telling me. Mortimer wanted to compel the king's abdication. Gerard disagreed. They quarrelled, and never spoke again.'

'Thus it is very unlikely that Mortimer would ask him to help kill the king,' Merrivale said. 'It was not Gerard who went to Berkeley that night. It was his son, Eustace Rowton.'

Rowton shook his head. 'For God's sake, herald. I was one of the king's closest companions. I helped him plan the overthrow of Mortimer. Why in God's name would I want to kill my friend's father?'

'Because you and John of Hainault had more ambitious plans,' Merrivale said. 'I will gloss over the next few years, including your visit to Calais where you met your cousin Andrieu Maninghem and Aubert, the future cardinal. Hainault arranged that meeting. Then in 1331 you and he spotted another opportunity. You led the king into an ambush in France where he was nearly killed.'

Rowton looked at the king. His voice was full of sorrow rather than anger. 'Sire, I don't know what disorder of the mind the herald is suffering from, but I should not have to listen to this, and neither should you. May we remove him from your presence?'

'Let him continue,' the king said.

'You and Hainault first met in Flanders,' Merrivale said. 'It was then that you first came into contact with the Pilgrims. Later, you saw how you might control them. Blyth, the banker, helped with this. Unfortunately we cannot summon Blyth as a witness. His body was found, badly decomposed, near a leper house outside Guînes.

'But you needed more money than Blyth could provide, and so you devised the scheme for false coinage. This had the benefit of both sowing chaos and filling your own coffers. Master Bessancourt has ample evidence to confirm this.'

Bessancourt nodded. For the first time, Rowton exploded with anger. 'This man is a servant! I will not stand accused by him!'

'He was formerly a clerk in the Chambre des Comptes,' Merrivale continued. 'Your assassins made a grave error when they failed to kill him. We know how you channelled money to the Pilgrims, and also used some of it to bribe the Count of Flanders to escape.'

'I had nothing to do with that, your Grace!'

Merrivale handed a silver penny to the king. 'This is one of the forged coins. The mint marks suggest it was made in Dublin, but Master Bessancourt can confirm it was actually made at Abbeville. Someone bought the dies from the Dublin mint when it was closed, kept them secretly and handed them over to the mint masters at Abbeville.'

He gave the king a small piece of parchment. 'This is a letter from your subject Sir Nicholas Courcy of Kingsale. He has witnesses who will swear that the man who established the mint in 1340 was Eustace, Lord Rowton. Further, following the closure of the mint in 1341, it was Lord Rowton who bought the dies and took them away.'

Rowton's face changed. At long last he realised he had failed; his schemes had collapsed and there was no way of rebuilding them. He glanced around the room, but there was only one door and Lancaster and the prince were standing in front of it. The king dropped the letter on the floor. 'I think Lord Rowton has something to answer for,' he said. 'But I am not yet fully persuaded. Bring in your witnesses, Merrivale, and let them have their say.'

Lancaster opened the door. Llewellyn entered, followed by Saint-Pierre and Maninghem. The two burgesses had been allowed to wash the ashes and mud away and given clean robes. They bowed low to the king. 'We thank you once again for your clemency, sire,' Saint-Pierre said.

The king was holding himself together with an effort. Merrivale could only guess at the torrent of emotions flowing through his mind. Rowton stared at the king, as though willing him not to believe what he was about to hear. Edward stared back, his face rigid with anger, but his eyes when Merrivale glanced at them were full of sadness.

'I will not detain you for long,' the herald said to the burgesses. 'Meneer Maninghem, you are Lord Rowton's cousin, several times removed. Did he ask you to spy for him inside Calais?'

'He did.'

'What else did he ask you to do?'

'To instruct Jehan Nortkerque to destroy food stocks and wells in the town according to a prepared schedule. Everything had to be carefully timed. If the garrison was too well provided, Vienne would feel he could hold out and would not send to King Philippe for help. If they ran out of supplies too early, the town would capitulate before the French army could arrive. For some reason, he wanted to make certain the French came to Calais at a particular time and place.'

'You can confirm all of this?' Merrivale asked Saint-Pierre.

'I can. Andrieu came to me, asking what he should do. I was in favour of anything that would compel the early surrender of the town, so I advised him to carry on.'

'Why was the timing important?' asked Lancaster.

'The Pilgrims needed time to prepare and organise,' Merrivale said. 'Once they were ready, acting on Lord Rowton's instructions, Cardinal Aubert proposed bringing the two kings together to negotiate. His Grace, acting on a rumour that the cardinal might be willing to change sides, was induced to take part. This meant that both kings, their heirs and the Count of Flanders – and, incidentally, Cardinal Aubert – would be isolated from their armies and in easy striking range of the Pilgrims.'

There was a long silence. The king walked slowly forward and stood in front of Eustace Rowton. 'Why?' he asked. 'You were my friend. I trusted you. Why betray me?'

A look of disgust crossed Rowton's face. 'Your *friend*? What favour did you ever show me? You gave plenty to your other friends, Salisbury, Northampton, Arundel; Huntingdon, even, for God's sake! They got rewards, lands, titles, power. I received nothing. You made Warwick marshal of your army; for Christ's sake, you even gave a command to Hatfield, but when have you ever allowed me to lead men in the field? I'm not your friend, I'm a lapdog you keep close by, to stroke or to slap, depending on your mood. I'm sick of you, sick to death, and have been since the beginning. But you were never more than a means to an end.'

He paused, drawing breath. The others stared him in fascination. 'You never knew me,' said Rowton. 'You never knew, or wanted to know, that I have intelligence and skills far greater than any of those sycophants you keep around you. You were so pleased with yourself when you brought the men who worked against your father into your court and befriended them. How does it feel now to know that one of those *friends* has been making a fool out of you for the last twenty years?'

'It was you who planned the old king's death,' Merrivale said. 'Wasn't it?'

'Of course it was me. Who was going to miss the useless old bastard? I planned his death, I put the idea into Mortimer's head, and I took the orders to Berkeley Castle.' He sneered at the king. 'And you never even guessed.' He spat at the king's feet. 'That is how much I think of you, and all your family.'

Without a word, the king held out his hand. The Prince of Wales drew his sword and presented it. The king looked down at the blade and, in a single smooth motion, rammed it through Rowton's body.

'Damn you,' Rowton gasped. 'I enjoyed making you look a fool. But my God, it was so easy...'

The king pulled out the sword and stabbed him again. This time the sword point crunched on bone and pierced Rowton's heart. He fell to the floor, blood pooling quickly around him. The king threw the sword down and walked blindly out of the room. From the hall next door they heard the sound of convulsive, heartbroken sobbing as he wept for the loss of the man he had called his friend.

–

'Was that really why he did it?' Tiphaine asked that evening. 'He wanted an earldom, and was angry that the king overlooked him?'

Merrivale shook his head. 'He was disappointed and jealous of the favour shown to others, and doubtless that festered over time. It may have bolstered his resolve. But I think the chaos of the 1320s, at home and in Flanders, showed him an opportunity. He wanted to bring down kingdoms, partly to profit himself, but partly to prove to the world that he could.'

'I used to believe that there was a seed of good in everyone,' Brother Geoffrey said quietly. 'And, for the most part, I still do. But some people are born with corrupted souls. I think Eustace Rowton may have been one of them.'

'What happens now?' asked Tiphaine.

'I once said Rowton was the kingpost. Take him away, and everything else collapses. I think that for once in his life, Vidal was being genuine when he said Cardinal Aubert wishes to abandon the conspiracy. King Charles of the Romans has already done so. That leaves only Hainault, and I doubt if he will carry on alone. He is drawing on in years, and out of favour in both England and France. I think he will opt now for a discreet retirement.'

He paused. 'There are the Pilgrims, of course.'

'People are deserting them already,' Tiphaine said. 'Given time and lack of money, they will wither away. Their beliefs will be preserved in other places and other ways. By the Beguines, perhaps.'

'They will fade away, but their spirit will never die,' said Brother Geoffrey. 'Whether that is good or bad is a matter of opinion. There is one more person you have not mentioned, Simon. What about Yolande?'

'I had not forgotten,' Merrivale said. 'Tomorrow, I shall ride to Béthune.'

'You could write her a letter,' Tiphaine said, pointedly.

'No. I need to see her.'

30

Calais, 4th of August, 1347

Tiphaine woke to the sound of someone pounding on the door of the hut. She lay in bed for a moment, realising she was alone. She heard Bessancourt open the door. 'Who is it— Oh. It's you.'

'Learn some manners, groom,' said Fier Meike. 'I must speak to the *demoiselle*.'

'I am here.' Wrapping the blanket around herself, Tiphaine hurried into the hall. 'What is it?'

'Where is your herald?'

'On his way to Béthune. He left without waking me. What is wrong, Meike?'

Fier Meike hefted the *goedendaag*. 'You told me Guy of Béthune was dead. So why did I see him this morning, alive and well?'

Bessancourt stared at her. 'Mother of Christ,' Tiphaine said. 'Where?'

'Riding down the Saint-Omer road. Do you remember the man with the dog-faced bascinet? I couldn't see his face before, but this time he had his visor up.'

Brother Geoffrey came out of his room. 'Was he alone?'

'Yes. But why is he still alive?'

'We can answer that question later,' Geoffrey said. 'He must know where Simon is going. We need to find him and stop him.'

Tiphaine raised her voice. 'Hugolin! We need horses, right now!' Diving back into the chamber she shared with Merrivale, she dressed in her old tattered coat and hose. Back in the hall she picked up a piece of bread from the table and stuffed it into her mouth. Outside, Bessancourt and Mauro were saddling horses, Topaas helping them. 'I had to borrow a couple of horses from Lord Warwick's stables,' Bessancourt said. 'I'll inform him when we get back.'

'You're not coming. Neither is Mauro.'

'Oh, Christ,' said the groom. 'Not this again. Mauro?'

'We are coming with you, *señorita*. There must be no argument about this.'

'When we get back to England, I am hiring new servants.' Tiphaine climbed into the saddle, the others following her. 'Lead the way, Meike.'

Around them the camp lay silent, everyone exhausted from the rigours of last night's celebrations. A few sleepy sentries watched them cross the causeway towards Saint-Omer and disappear into the morning haze. They rode all day through the summer heat, but they saw no sign of Béthune or the herald.

—

Merrivale had saddled his own horse and departed at first light, leaving the rest of his household sleeping. He rode cautiously, checking the country around him as he did so. There was one other person they had forgotten to include in their discussion last night; Nicodemus the archer, Rowton's hired killer. Even if Nicodemus knew Rowton was dead, he might still regard Merrivale as unfinished business.

By the time the herald reached Saint-Omer, blackened and battered by recent Flemish raids, his instincts told him someone was following him. Pulling his horse off the road and into a stand of trees, he dismounted and waited, watching the road and listening. No murmur of sound came to his ears, no dust plume stirred on the horizon. Mounting again, he rode on, but the instinct persisted.

He had hoped to push all the way to Béthune, taking advantage of the long summer days, but caution took over once more. Reaching the burned and overgrown remains of the little town of Aire, he halted and listened again. There it was, right on the edge of hearing, the distant tap of hoofbeats, fading, reappearing, fading again. Dismounting, he crossed to a sapling tree springing up in the old marketplace and rested his hands on the slender bole. Now he could feel distinctly the tremor in the ground; a single horse, far away but drawing gradually closer. *Had there been other traffic on the roads*, he thought, *I would never have noticed*. Now, this deserted land was so silent that every movement could be felt and heard.

Quietly, he led his horse into the ruined church and took off its bridle so the bits would make no sound. Tethering the animal, he stood by the door and listened again. The other horse continued to draw closer, but just before it reached the town it halted. After a pause of several minutes the hoofbeats started again, echoing off stone as the rider crossed the bridge over the river Lys and then beginning to fade into the distance.

Merrivale stepped quietly out of the church, eyes following the direction of the sound. A lone horseman was making his way across the marshes to the north-east. He wore plate armour but no surcoat, and there was no sign of a longbow. It was not Nicodemus.

But it could have been a Pilgrim scout, Merrivale thought. He looked up at the sun, sinking red in the west. If he rode on now, he would not reach Béthune until nightfall, and after dark spotting any pursuers would be more difficult. The ruined church was as good a place of concealment as any. Opening his saddlebag, he gave the horse a measure of hay, then took out a half-loaf of bread and a small flask of wine and settled down for the night.

Marais de l'Aa, 5ᵗʰ of August, 1347

'Where in God's name are they?' demanded Tiphaine.

They had spent the night in a damp field not far from the river Aa, well north of Saint-Omer, and woke to find the air thick with fog.

'The *señor* will have a long start,' said Mauro. 'If he left at dawn yesterday, he could be four or five hours ahead of us.'

'Béthune left much later,' said Fier Meike. 'I would swear it was no more than half an hour before we departed.'

'But a single rider will always go more quickly than a group,' said Brother Geoffrey. 'And in this murk, we could be within a few furlongs of him, and never know.'

'We need to mount a full search,' Meike said. 'Which means we need more men.'

'There is the garrison at Cassel,' Topaas suggested.

Not all of the Flemings at Cassel had marched away to Calais; Metteneye had been careful to leave a sizeable garrison to ward off any French surprise attacks. 'Find as many men as you can,' Meike said. 'We will carry on. Meet us at the fishermen's huts near Béthune town.'

Topaas rode away, the sound of his horse quickly swallowed up in the fog. 'What do the rest of us do?' asked Bessancourt.

'I suggest we divide our forces,' Brother Geoffrey said. 'I suspect we haven't seen Guy of Béthune because he is close to his home now, and worried that anyone he meets might recognise him. He is following the byways and tracks instead of the high roads. *Demoiselle*, Meike, I suggest you do the same and see if you can find his trail. I shall ride directly to Béthune and either intercept Simon on the way, or if he arrives before me, warn him and Yolande.'

'What if you meet Béthune?' Tiphaine asked.

Brother Geoffrey smiled. 'I am not quite so decrepit as I look, *demoiselle*. I still know a few tricks.'

Béthune, 5th of August, 1347

The tap of rain on the windows of the solar awoke Yolande. She had been sitting in her favourite chair dreaming about the past, remembering the sunlight and warmth of her youth; a child of the south, she had never grown accustomed to the fogs and rains of Flanders. She sat for a moment, watching raindrops travel in ragged rivulets down the thick glass.

A noise came from the hall below, the thud of a door closed carelessly. She frowned. The servants needed to make less noise, lest they wake Jean. The boy had been ill for several days now, running a fever, and he needed his rest. Still half-dreaming, she wondered what path in life the boy might follow. He had his father's stubbornness and dogged determination, that was true, but he was also quiet and studious. His tutor had hinted that he might do well in the church. She wondered what Simon would think of that…

The door thudded again. Perhaps someone had left it open and the wind was blowing it to and fro. Rousing, she gathered her skirts and went down the long stair to the hall. The afternoon light was dim, and someone had lit tapers and a couple of candles and set them on the high table.

A man was sitting in the high seat at the table's head, the place Guy had always occupied when he was home. She looked at the man, wondering for a moment who this stranger was; haggard, thin, wearing battered armour of a rather antique style spotted with rain, bearded face framed by straggling wet dark hair. He reminded her of Guy, and then she screamed in sudden shock.

It *was* Guy. Either that or his ghost, come back to torment her.

A cup of wine and a sword lay on the table in front of him. The blade of the sword glistened with blood. He raised the cup in mocking salute. 'Aren't you going to welcome me home?' he said.

Shivering, she managed to find breath to speak. 'Where did you come from? How did you get here?'

'You mean, why am I not dead? I very nearly was. Fortunately, cold river water cools the body and stops the blood from flowing quite so freely. Even so, I damned nearly drowned before I managed to crawl ashore. A hospital of nuns in Mülheim took me and nursed me back to health. Once I was well enough to ride, I came looking for those who had betrayed me.'

'Guy, I—'

'Don't speak. I went looking for Rowton first, because I reckoned it was him that told you to kill me. I joined the Flemish army disguised as a Pilgrim, but I was too late. The peasant Merrivale finally managed to follow the trail to its end. Rowton is dead. So, I thought, why not return to my ancestral home and be restored to the arms of my loving wife?'

The first shock was wearing off. 'The world believes you are dead,' she said. 'I buried you myself. All I have to do is summon the guards and denounce you as an impostor.'

'Yes, you *could* do that,' Béthune agreed. 'Unfortunately for you, I told the guards they were needed to quell a disturbance at the town gate and sent them all there. I also sent all the servants away too, including that sickly little Dominican. Is that the best tutor you could find for our son? Oh – I beg your pardon. I forgot for a moment who he really is. The point is, there are no guards or servants, and if you call for help there is absolutely no one to hear you.'

She was growing angry now. 'Get out of here and never return,' she said with venom in her voice. 'This is my home now, mine and my son's.'

'Don't worry, darling. I shall go, very soon. I know when I'm not wanted. Were you intending to replace me with Merrivale? He is on his way to see you, right now. Or at least, he was.'

Fear began to mingle with the anger. 'What do you mean?'

'Don't you want to know whose blood is on my sword?'

She said nothing. 'I met him on the road this morning,' Béthune said. 'The air was full of fog, and he didn't even see me until he was practically on top of me. The poor peasant had no sword, of course, only that ridiculous tabard. So, I finished the work I began last autumn. What's the matter, beloved? Don't you believe me?'

Yolande walked towards him, her hands clenched, her knuckles white. 'No, I don't. What a pathetic story. I cannot count the number of times you've tried to kill Simon, and always you failed. Simon could kill you if he wanted to, without thinking twice.'

'Simon.' Béthune took a drink of wine. 'Simon,' he repeated, rolling the name around in his mouth. 'Very well, my sweet. The blood on this sword is not *Simon's*. Have another guess. Whose do you think it might be?'

'Didn't you hear me earlier? Get out!'

'He has been unwell, hasn't he?'

'Who?'

'The boy.'

Yolande froze in sudden horror. 'The tutor told me, before I threw him out,' Béthune continued. 'He said the boy must not be disturbed. So, I was quiet when I went up to his chamber, and I opened the door *very* slowly. I didn't wake him; trust me, I really didn't. He just lay there sleeping, looking so peaceful… He was a handsome little fellow, I will give you that. What a pity he will never grow up to know who his father is. So, my adored, angelic one. Do you believe me this time?'

The blood on the steel blade glowed garnet-red in the candlelight. Yolande screamed, a long tearing shriek of rage and grief and loss, and ran straight at Béthune with her hands upraised like claws, tearing at his eyes. Her nails raked the skin of his face; he dodged her, cursing her, and drew the dagger at his belt and stabbed her once, twice, thrice in as many seconds until she doubled up retching with agony on the floor. He stood over her, breathing hard, blood dripping from his face and from the blade in his hand.

'I should have done this a long time ago,' he said softly. 'You and the brat both. Now, I shall go and find your lover and kill him too. You can all roast together in hell.'

Yolande could say nothing. She lay sobbing softly, drowning in a well of pain and feeling her strength ebb slowly away as she watched Béthune walk out of the hall. His boots echoed on the stair down to the courtyard, and he was gone.

The guards at the gate were arguing with each other. The men from the castle claimed they had been sent to help with some sort of disturbance, but the watch on the town gate insisted all was quiet. The castle guards commented that the gate watch might be going blind, or possibly addled in their wits, and the gate watch suggested that the men from the castle needed to answer some hard questions about their own parentage. Eventually they noticed the black-robed canon waiting patiently on horseback in the rain.

'How can we help you, brother?' said one of the men from the castle.

'I have business with the countess,' Geoffrey said pleasantly. 'Is she at home?'

'She is, brother. Another visitor came in about half an hour ago. He's the one who told us about the trouble down here. Shall I show you the way?'

'No need,' Geoffrey said. 'I have been here before.'

He rode through the quiet town, crossing the marketplace past the belfry and coming to the castle. The gates stood open, and he rode into the courtyard and dismounted.

A voice in his mind screamed a warning, but too late. He heard the hard *thwack* of the bowstring in the same moment that the arrow hit him. Pain tore through his body like a jet of fire. Looking down, he saw the arrow embedded in his body almost up to the fletchings, and realised the arrowhead must be sticking out of his back. He slumped down onto the cobbles and lay still, closing his eyes. Raindrops tapped softly on his face.

Controlling the pain took an effort, but it was possible. He heard footsteps approaching, and smelled the other man's sweat mingling with the reek of his own blood. 'It's the carrion crow,' said Nicodemus, standing over him. 'Pity it wasn't that fucking herald, but you can't have everything. Meanwhile, brother, I think I'd better cut your throat, just to make sure.'

A hard hand gripped the collar of Geoffrey's robe and pulled his head up off the cobbles. Geoffrey opened his eyes in time to see the knife blade flashing towards his neck. He seized the other man's wrist with both hands and twisted. Nicodemus swore but kept hold of the knife. Ignoring the fresh pain ripping through his belly, Geoffrey

339

dragged hard on his arm, pulling him off balance, and bit him savagely on the fleshy part of his hand. Nicodemus yelped, this time dropping the knife onto the cobbles. Seizing the knife, Geoffrey stabbed the other man in the leg. The archer stumbled backwards, giving Geoffrey enough time to clamber to his feet. The arrow still protruding from his body, he advanced on the archer.

'Yes,' he said, half to himself. 'I still know a few tricks.'

Nicodemus lunged for his knife arm. Geoffrey let his momentum carry him past, then seized him from behind and dragged his head back. One swift stroke of the knife and it was done. The archer fell to the cobbles, his blood turning pink as it mingled with the rainwater.

Geoffrey stood, breathing hard. He knew he had little time left. The thought did not bother him; the philosopher in his soul recognised that all things must come to an end. But he had brought this on Yolande, and on Merrivale, and he had to do what he could for them. Staggering, feeling his punctured organs rip and tear with every movement, he crossed the courtyard to the foot of the stair leading up to the great hall. As he reached the bottom of the stair he heard a woman up above screaming like demons were tearing out her soul, and he halted, knowing he was too late.

Béthune came down the stair, bloody sword in hand. More blood dripped from the long furrows on his face. 'Geoffrey of Maldon,' he said. 'You come at an opportune time, brother. I owe you a death too. Where is Merrivale?'

So he is not yet arrived. Thank God. 'On his way. He knows you are alive. He will get the better of you. He always has... Run, run while you can.'

'Tell me where he is.'

Another wave of pain shot through Geoffrey's body. 'He is coming,' he whispered. 'He is coming for you.'

Béthune killed him with a single blow of his sword and stepped over the body, walking across the courtyard. Ignoring the corpse of Nicodemus, he led his already saddled horse out of the stable and mounted. In a moment, he was gone.

–

The guards were still arguing when Merrivale arrived at the gate. His herald's tabard, like Geoffrey's canonical robes, were his passport; they

340

allowed him through at once. Nerves tingling with premonitions of disaster, he rode to the castle.

The corpse of Nicodemus still lay in the middle of the courtyard. He ignored it, hurrying instead to the black-robed bundle lying at the foot of the stair. He turned it over. Geoffrey of Maldon's face looked up at him, rain falling into his sightless eyes.

His first instinct was disbelief. Brother Geoffrey was indestructible; no matter how dangerous or desperate the mission, he always returned. Even when he had been dragged away to the Bishop of Bayeux's prison last year, Merrivale knew he would find a way to survive. Now, suddenly and terribly, he was gone.

Despite the rain, the body was still warm. His soul had not long passed over to the other side. Merrivale knelt beside his friend, sick with shock.

A sound from above came faintly to his ears. Gripping his stick, Merrivale rose and went up the stairs. Treading carefully, making as little noise as possible, he stepped into the great hall.

Yolande was trying to crawl towards the door. A trail of blood marked her passage across the rush mats. Dropping his stick, Merrivale knelt beside her, touching her face with his hand. Her skin was waxy with impending death, but when she opened her eyes she recognised him.

'Simon.' Her voice fluttered like a caged bird. 'I was coming to find you.'

'And now you have,' Merrivale said, his voice soft and gentle.

'Guy. He is searching for you.'

'Guy did this.' It was a statement, not a question.

'Yes. Simon… He killed our boy. Our little boy… You never had a chance to meet him.'

He took her hand in his, squeezing it gently. 'I know. Hush, now. Lie still. Help will come soon.'

'No. It will be too late, too late… He was beautiful, Simon. So like you.'

Pain flooded through his chest, constricting his throat. Speaking took a great deal of effort. 'And very much like you, I'm sure. You did say he was beautiful.'

'Simon, I am so sorry.'

'There is no need for sorrow,' he said quietly, caressing her hand. 'There is no need for regret. What is done, is done.'

Her eyes were dark now, the light beginning to fail. 'I wish it had all been different, Simon. I truly do.'

'God chooses our path,' he said. 'All we can do is obey His will.'

'Yes… Simon… Did you truly love me?'

He paused, almost choking on his grief, but he kept his voice calm. 'You were the fire and the flame,' he said. 'You were the lily, and the rose.'

She sighed, a slow soft exhale of air, and lay still. When he felt her neck for a pulse, there was nothing.

—

Softly, with a lover's touch, he closed her eyelids and bent and planted a single kiss on her forehead. Outside, he heard a horse clatter into the courtyard.

He picked up his stick and walked to the door. He saw a saddled horse steaming in the rain, and someone in a ragged cloak kneeling over Geoffrey's body. Tiphaine looked up and stopped, staring at him, her lips parted. She had no need to ask what had happened. His face told the story.

'We have Guy of Béthune,' she said. 'Fier Meike's men are holding him.'

'Take me to him.'

Fier Meike, Topaas and their men were waiting near the fishermen's huts where he had once bid farewell to Warin. Bessancourt and Mauro were there too. Guy of Béthune knelt in the mud, his face half-covered in sticky blood. His armour had been stripped off, and his hands were clasped on top of his head. One of the Flemings stood behind him, a sword blade resting against his neck. 'He rode out of town and down the road, straight into our arms,' Topaas said.

'I wanted to kill him,' Fier Meike said. She hefted her *goedendaag*. 'But your people say you have a prior claim. What do you want to do with him?'

'Let him stand up,' said the herald. 'Give him back his sword.'

Tiphaine stared at him. 'Simon! What are you doing?'

Merrivale shrugged off his tabard and dropped it on the ground. 'Give him his sword,' he repeated. 'Give me one, too.'

'*Señor*,' Mauro said sharply. 'It has been many years since you handled a sword!'

342

'I know,' said the herald.

One of the Flemings handed him a sword. He looked at the curved cross guards and the long blade tapering to a wicked point and hefted it in his hand. Béthune was on his feet, his own sword in hand. 'Are you offering me trial by combat, Merrivale? If I win, I can go free?'

'You won't win.'

'How fascinating,' said Béthune. 'The peasant intends to fight like a gentleman. I warn you, my methods in killing you will be anything but gentle.'

'Stop talking,' said the herald.

-

A moment of silence in the rain, and Béthune lunged, sword point aiming for the herald's face...

...and suddenly the years rolled back and the sword hilt was resting feather-light in his hand, blade moving like an extension of his arm, guided by his will. He could no longer feel the stiffness in his leg; he felt light as a dancer, moving in soft extensions, heel and toe, shoulders turned, arm forward, and the steel blade sang in the rain.

He parried Béthune's first blow and drove the count backwards through the mud, attacking from every angle, blocking every attempted thrust and riposte. Once Béthune came in low under his blade, attempting to grab his sword arm, but Merrivale read the move even before it began and kicked Béthune hard, catching him off balance and knocking him onto his back in the mud. At once Merrivale lowered his sword.

'Get up,' he said.

Béthune stumbled to his feet. Merrivale advanced again, attacking high and low, opening a gash on the other man's cheek, cutting his left arm open to the bone. Furious, the count tried to counter-attack but Merrivale's blade was like a steel wall with no opening. After five desperate minutes Béthune was at the water's edge, his back to the marshes with nowhere to go. Both men stood looking at each other, breathing hard.

'Finish him!' shouted Fier Meike.

The words, meant as encouragement, nearly cost Merrivale his life. Distracted, he almost didn't see the sword blade coming. He parried it away from his body but the point stabbed into his leg instead. There was no pain; that would come later, but he felt the blood running down his leg and knew he was losing both strength and mobility. He would have to end this soon. He stepped back, saving his energy, concentrating on defending himself, and Béthune gave a half-strangled grunt of triumph and launched himself at the herald. Steel blades clashed and grated and shrieked, the count pressing hard, trying to use his weight to drive Merrivale physically backwards and knock him off balance.

Gritting his teeth, Merrivale riposted and hit the injured left arm again, but Béthune ignored the blow and charged at him before he could withdraw the sword, barging hard into him. Reversing the sword in his hand he hit Merrivale on the side of the head with the pommel. Lights flashed before the herald's eyes. He could hear Tiphaine screaming at him, and he drew a deep breath and smashed his head forward into Béthune's face, hearing the other man grunt as the blow went home.

Once again they stopped for a moment, throats rasping as they sucked in air. Béthune's face was covered in fresh blood. 'Now I shall kill you, peasant,' he gasped.

Merrivale raised his sword, gripping the pommel in both hands and bringing it down like a thunderbolt towards Béthune's head. The count saw the blow coming and parried it, ducking under the swinging blade, but before he could release his own weapon Merrivale disengaged and stabbed. The first lunge ripped across Béthune's ribs; the second tore through the flesh of his neck; the third caught him across the side of the head, a killing blow, and threw him sideways into the mud. One hand clawed briefly, groping for his fallen sword, and then Béthune lay still.

Now Merrivale's leg was beginning to hurt, shooting pains running along its length. He handed the sword back to its owner. 'Thank you,' he said.

The others stood staring at him. Tiphaine's face was chalk white in the rain.

'I must go back,' he said. 'I hope you understand.'

'Yes,' she said.

Merrivale turned away towards his horse. He had taken two slow steps when Bessancourt shouted. '*Look out!*'

Ignoring the pain, Merrivale wheeled around. Béthune was on his feet, sword gripped in his muddy hand, face now completely covered in blood. He let out a roar of incoherent pain and rage and, with the last of his strength, rushed towards Merrivale, raising his sword.

Fier Meike threw the *goedendaag*. The iron spike, travelling with terrible force, hit Béthune in the side of the head and split his skull open. He crashed forward onto his face, the sword falling from his hand again and landing at Merrivale's feet.

For a few moments, no one moved. The herald looked at Meike. 'I am glad,' he said. 'I was wrong to take this on myself. It should have been you that killed him, all along.'

Fier Meike walked forward and picked up the *goedendaag*, carefully wiping the spike clean. 'What matters is that he is dead. Go in peace, herald.'

'Babylon will fall, one day,' Merrivale said.

'I know. When it does, I will be waiting.'

Fier Meike turned away, followed by Topaas and the other men. Tiphaine stood facing Merrivale. Bessancourt and Mauro waited to one side, watching.

'You have lost every precious thing in your world,' Tiphaine said. 'Go alone, if that is what you wish. When you return, I will be waiting. If that too is what you wish.'

Merrivale closed his eyes for a moment. Rain washed like tears down his face. He opened his eyes again and looked at Tiphaine. 'I have misjudged my own strength,' he said. 'I do not think I can face them again. Not alone.'

Tiphaine took his arm. 'Lean on me,' she said, and supporting Merrivale's weight with her own body, she walked him slowly to his horse and helped him mount. Mauro picked up the tabard and began to wipe the mud off it. Bessancourt led the other horses out of the huts. In silence, the four of them rode away and back down the road towards Béthune.

Acknowledgements

Twenty years ago when we sat down to write *The Road to Crécy*, our history of the 1346 campaign, we little dreamed that we would go on to write three novels on the same period. It has been a fascinating journey, made possible by so many people over the years: historians, archaeologists, guides, fellow authors, agents, publishers and friends. To everyone who enabled these books to come to life, we offer heartfelt thanks. Special thanks are due to the archive and document delivery staff of The National Archives in Kew who made finding and working with 14th century parchment so straightforward and enjoyable, even under Covid-19 restrictions. They helped to negotiate the intricacies of some unfamiliar documents for which we are hugely grateful. The original documents always bring people and places to life and we were fortunate to be able to include research from these in *The Fallen Sword*.

Covid-19 prevented us from travelling to the areas of France and Belgium that we wanted to while writing this book, so sadly no wonderful lunches with friends were possible. We were at least able to hold a launch party for the previous book, *A Clash of Lions*, and many thanks to Kate at Dogberry & Finch, Okehampton's wonderful independent bookshop, for hosting the event and for all her support over the years.

Our agents, Jon Wood at RCW and Heather Adams and Mike Bryan at HMA, have been a constant supporting presence. The Canelo team have been brilliant as ever. Kit Nevile's enthusiasm for this series has been a real boost, helping us to get through when the pressures of work were overwhelming and we wondered if we would ever get finished, and it has been an absolute pleasure to work with him. Copy-editor Elodie Olson-Coons has done her usual excellent job ('Nooooooo!' was one of our favourite comments), and thanks to Nick Venables for a fittingly dark and bleak cover. We only ever seem to call on Gary Beaumont at the last minute for maps, but he always comes up with the goods.

And so, the series comes to an end. It seems fitting that we should now turn a new page in the life of Simon Merrivale, and go back to the beginning.